EDWARD CHIP
NOW LEAVING SUGARCANE

EDWARD CHIP:
NOW LEAVING
SUGARCANE

Kaiden Traister
Quinn Ellis

Copyright © 2022 by Kaiden A. Traister and Quinn H. Ellis

First edition 2022

Cover Illustrations by Robert G. Schiebel
Inner illustrations by Kaiden A. Traister

ISBN: 979-8-9860569-2-0

Published through IngramSpark

Dedication

Caitlin Barrett: For being the reason we wrote this book. Had it not been for your encouragement and support when getting this whole idea started in 2016, this book would not exist.

Our families: Your unwavering support in the making of this book and your hours of putting up with our shenanigans has not gone unnoticed.

Table of C🍪ntents

Pr🍪logue:

Edward Chip is a living cookie. Yes, you read that correctly. A real-life, walking, talking, cookie. In fact, every single character in this story is living. I mention this because every character is some sort of dessert or food. Why, you ask? Well, dear reader, it's because in this universe, everything is made out of food.

Take Edward's home planet, it's named "The Dessert" and no, I did not mean desert. On "The Dessert" there is a small town that goes by the name of Sugarcane, where Edward and his comrades live. Walls are not made out of bricks or stone in this universe, but out of chocolate bars. Floors are no longer made of tile, they are made of graham crackers. Dirt consists of crushed up Oreos and chocolate chips. And chairs— well, you get the point.

Now, at the beginning of time, there were only four planets: "Veggie," "Fruity," "The Diner," and "The Dessert." "Veggie" and "Fruity" were too far away from the other two planets that "The Diner" and "The Dessert" didn't know about them until centuries later. From each planet came a race of beings. From "Veggie", Vegetables; from "Fruity", came fruit; from "The Diner", came foods such as meatloaf and tacos. And from "The Dessert", came desserts.

Desserts and foods were kind to each other and helped each other out. Until one day… when King Ice of Cream Sr, who was the ruler of "The Dessert" at the time, became greedy. He became so power hungry that being the ruler of one planet wasn't enough and he tried to steal "The Diner" ruler's throne. This spiraled out of control immediately and turned into an all out intergalactic food fight. It was a terrible time. The dark ages of the foodiverse. So many desserts and foods died that a truce was finally called after five years. Yet, tensions were still high and the truce wasn't always obeyed. Foods, dessert and other, all have been slowly disappearing ever since, and no one knows why, but they do know that they need to figure out why before the entire foodiverse is covered in "Missing Food" signs. Separation of the food groups still existed. They were not warm-hearted towards each other. So, we start our story 200 years after the great war…

Part 1: Edward Chip

One dry and dreary day as the sun beat down on the sidewalk of the town of Sugarcane, Edward Chip, (the living cookie) sauntered slowly to Dessert Middle School, ignoring all the "Missing Food" signs that plagued the walls of shops. Out of the corner of his eye, he noticed a dark, cloaked character looming over the school for two seconds before vanishing into thin air like Haupia Houdini. The only sign that it was ever there was a small trickle of orange string cheese. Edward thought if he owned a cookie blaster he could have used the net function to shoot out a net to capture the dark character.

Ah, the cookie blaster; a sleek and fat weapon with over twenty different types of projectile options to use against your enemies. It was lightweight, and best of all, it was made of cookies. Need to defend yourself? Use a cookie blaster! Need to heat up your dinner? Your cookie blaster could do that. Hungry? Yup, that's correct, just take a bite out of your cookie blaster! Each food, of course had their own version of a cookie blaster; cakes had cake blasters; chocolate bars had chocolate blasters and so on. This weapon had to be implemented after a particularly nasty attack from The Diner in which an entire city of desserts had disappeared. It was rumored that there had been a large white glow and claws came from the sky, snatching their victims away. The dinner foods were blamed for this despite no one actually seeing them as they were all blinded by the light.

Edward thought this occurrence of the dark figure to be very strange and wanted to tell his friends: Derek Donut and Cassie Cake.

"Did you get a glimpse of the strange little man on the roof?" Edward asked his friends when he found them.

"No, but, come on!" Cassie told Edward, "You're just a little nervous about school, it's probably just your nervous eyes seeing strange things."

"Yeah!" Derek teased, the glaze on his body glinting in the sun, "Or your eyes are turning into my grandma's!"

"Stop teasing, Derek!" Cassie shot back. Her icing was especially immaculate today. On top of her normally white frosting, there was a wavy line of red icing that encircled her entire body. Arches had been carved under the wavy line and she had decorated the top of her head with a plethora of rainbow sprinkles.

"Just having fun," Derek pouted.

"Ugghh!"

"Guys, come on, I'm *not* going crazy or anything!" Edward retorted. "I swear I saw a little man disappear into cheese."

"Fine, we give up," Derek said while sneaking a look of concern to Cassie.

"I'll see you at lunch." Edward stormed off, feeling as though his friends were being supremely idiotic in that moment. However, he had known them since 1st grade, and he didn't feel particularly like making new friends. It was so much work nowadays. This was due to the fact that you couldn't just make friends like a kindergartener and walk up to a random dessert and be like, "Do you wanna be friends?" Instead you had to get to know them first, then ask for their phone number, maybe work on a project or have the same class with them. It was too much hassle. Edward decided to not let his friends' shenanigans get to him.

Edward couldn't wait for his first class to end. Everything about his school was boring. The tasteless gummy bricks, the dull and colorless (dessert) desks, and the worst of all: the teachers. They all wore plain suits and spoke in monotone voices. His social studies teacher kept on talking about Dessert heritage and its history and was boring half the class to sleep. Well, everyone except for Simone Sponge Cake (with no sprinkles or icing, nothing), aka, the nerd who nobody likes. Simone looked completely entranced in the lesson, her hand always shot up when a question was asked. She also made sure to correct someone whenever possible. Edward was pretty sure she was one of the most annoying deserts in the world.

She was saying, "We come from a great ancestor where we have…"

But all Edward heard was, "Blah, blah blah ARGGGGGG!!!" The shouts of the teacher and children jolted him out of his daze. He glanced around but didn't spot any problem until an extremely soggy taco dropped to the ground and exploded. Goodbye history room! Edward ran as he investigated who dropped the taco. Out of the corner of his eye, he glimpsed the cloaked figure, who was on top of the school, right before he smashed into a pile of string cheese that appeared out of nowhere. There hadn't been a disaster like this since Jelly Jim went missing in first grade. It was reported that a giant sausage claw piloted by evil dinner foods had taken him away and Jim was never to be seen again.

Principal Pudding's obnoxious voice came from the loudspeaker and bounced off the walls, "Everyone please report to the chocolate track field while we take care of a minor problem, I repeat everyone to the chocolate track NOW!!!!!."

Really? This is minor? Edward thought. It was clear from the wavering in his voice, the principal had no idea what to do in this situation. Edward ran into the hallway where other frantic students were pushing their way out the school doors. Edward changed his course to the track field when another disgusting taco dropped to the ground in front of him. Edward took off like a bullet in the other direction but he was too slow and the taco exploded, black walls filled his vision and he passed out much to his own protest. . .

When Edward woke up, the school building was a ghost town. He slowly raised himself to his feet and found out part of the building had been reduced to rubble. He ran around the building, or what was left of

Part I: Edward Chip

it. Fires had exploded, sending intense heat everywhere, melting the chocolate chips off Edward. Holes covered almost every inch of the halls and all the lockers had been burned down with the Cookieology Room.

Edward felt furious that the notorious person dared to burn down his favorite room. Many memorable moments happened in that room. The great times laughing with friends and devouring delicious delicacies. . . Edward dragged himself out of his thoughts and decided he needed to find the cloaked figure and put a stop to the madness. Then he might go to bed afterward.

After all, Principal Pudding was too cowardly to step up. After turning through the maze-like school (seriously, who designed schools to have so many hallways!?) and finally reaching an exit, Edward spotted the mysterious taco dropper camping outside the building admiring his work. The cloaked figure sprinted to the Hot Cocoa Springs when he saw Edward. Edward chased after the Cloaked Figure until his thighs hurt. The ground beneath his feet was soft and malleable; his feet left large dents in the damp oreo soil. As he chased the mysterious man to the springs, the ground became increasingly slippery as puddles of brown liquid began to appear beside him. The cloaked figure turned sharply to the left and Edward tried to follow. He ended up slipping and completely landing face first into a mini lake of hot chocolate. Licking the tasty liquid off of his lips as he stood up, he realized that the cloaked figure had vanished once again. Edward kicked at the ground in frustration. If only he'd been faster. If only that stupid puddle of liquid chocolate (which by the was tasted fantastic— not that it would help his prediciment) hadn't been there. He felt himself completely give up and flopped down on the ground, his dough now soggy with hot chocolate.

From his new vantage point however, he noticed divots in the mushy ground leading away from him. The food responsible for the exploding tacos might be able to disappear from the regular dessert's eye, but luckily he (she?) had left a path for Edward to follow. Edward scooched to his feet and followed the tracks for several miles, barely looking up at his surroundings. His eyes were fixated on the dirt and the tracks smushed into it. The attacker's feet appeared to be much like Edward's: oval shaped with the inner part of the foot slightly longer than the outer part. Then, the tracks stopped. The ground was still wet in this area of The Dessert but there were no more footprints up ahead. Instead, there just lay a small pile of string cheese. Edward sighed and finally looked around at where he was. Giant sticks of french toast sprouted from the ground all around him and the warm lakes of hot chocolate were nowhere to be seen. It was at this moment Edward lamented that he was hopelessly lost in French Toast Forest. He wandered for hours until night but still wasn't anywhere close to Dessert Middle School. Edward finally lay down from fatigue, wondering what kind of sleep he would achieve.

Part I: Edward Chip

Edward awoke with a start and rolled over into a deep brown hole three times his size. S'more spiders along with rainbow-colored gummy worms were frantically trying to bury themselves back into the brownie dirt. *"The man must have tried to break me but missed,"* Edward thought, *"I could have used a cookie blaster then."*

"Look, he's awake!" A strange voice told another. Edward climbed out of the hole and spotted Derek Donut and Cassie Cake each holding a bow with pastry arrows.

"Where... Why?... How" Edward's questions swarmed around his head just like banana split bees.

"We ran straight here after we realized where you traveled off to," Cassie explained to him.

"What?" Edward asked.

"Okay, Edward let me explain," Cassie told Edward. Then, she explained how they realized that Edward never made it to the chocolate track field and how they looked through the sherbert security system.

"...and so we followed your footprints and found you sleeping peacefully with the ETM over you." Cassie filled Edward in.

"Then he shot a taco at you but missed, when the ETM saw us he fled the scene, thank goodness we bought these." Derek bragged, showing a pastry arrow, "and Cassie told me that it was an impulse buy that I would never use again."

"Hold up," Edward said, feeling confused, "ETM?"

"Oh, that stands for Evil Taco Man" Cassie informed.

"And how do you know that is his name?" Edward asked, still confused.

"I found this in one of the trees," Derek still boosted holding up a cloak, "it possesses the magical power of turning the wearer invisible on command."

"It also has his name written on the sleeve," Cassie said, showing the name.

"We need to follow that ATM," Edward exclaimed. Cassie opened her mouth to correct him, but he interrupted her, "we must follow him before most of the forest is destroyed!" Suddenly a loud ear-splitting BOOM echoed through French Toast Forest, making the ground shake and french toast crash to the ground.

"We must run now!" Cassie instructed while throwing on the ETM's cloak, "and Edward it's ETM, not ATM!"

"What now about the ATM!" Edward yelled back over the noise of toast crashing to the ground.

"Later!" Cassie screamed back because the rumbling was louder than ever. Yellow toast fell to the ground in sheets and brown dirt crumbled into the hole Edward was sitting in seconds ago. As the trio sprinted through the woods dodging falling items until the ground stopped shaking and the toast quit crumbling. Edward had crashed into something and now a lump the size of the moon started forming on his head.

Part 1: Edward Chip

11

Part I: Edward Chip

The trio collapsed into a sweaty heap. Cassie and
Derek lost their bow and arrows in the chaos and when
Derek realized it, he grumbled about how they cost him
$10. Cassie laughed and called him a sucker. They had
come to the edge of the forest and were now staring out
to the open plains made of popsicle sticks. They peered
into the distance and saw a lone figure. As Edward
stared, he noticed it was a taco.

"That's the ETM..." Derek muttered.

"Wait," Edward whispered, "he doesn't appear
to give out money, that ATM."

"ETM stands for Evil Taco Man," Derek said back.

"I thought it was called the ATM—" Edward tilted
his head, confused.

"ETM! GET IT RIGHT!" Derek yelled.

"Keep it down boys," Cassie yell-whispered "or
the ETM might hear us!"

Just then Edward heard the ETM say, "Were you
talking about me, *amigo*?"

Edward turned around and found that the ETM
had teleported behind them and was standing
menacingly, hands on his hips. The ETM laughed at their
shocked faces and threw two more explosive tacos
towards Edward and his friends.

"DUCK!" Cassie screamed.

"Ooh, where?" Derek asked.

"NO, DUCK YOUR HEAD!"

"Well, you should have told me that!"

"I'm sorry *amigo,* but that won't be enough," Evil
Taco Man laughed, taking out a bottle of hot sauce and

pouring it over his explosives, "I hope you like the kick to this one!"

"RUN!" Cassie ordered at the top of her lungs.

"I thought you wanted me to duck!" Derek yelled back.

"Yeah, change of plans!" Suddenly a plan formed in Edward's mind. He knew what he had to do. Edward charged at the flying hot sauce soaked tacos as Cassie and Derek yelled at him to stop. But he was on a roll and there was no turning back now. He jumped, Cassie screamed, the ETM (or was it ATM?) laughed evilly, and Edward caught the tacos in his hands. Edward yelled and threw his body over the tacos as they exploded and for the second time that day Edward blacked out. But not really.

Edward had never lived in two places at once before and decided he hated it. He saw the ETM in his face and heard Cassie and Derek yelling at him to back off while something spoke in his mind.

"Hello Edward," a faded image showed in his eyes so he could still see what Cassie and Derek attempted to do.

"You are about to enter your mind's world," a fortune cookie said in a sweet and soothing voice. She was dressed in a white tunic and held a shining silver lyre that sang in sweet voices. Her skin was deeply tanned; her tunic sparkled like diamonds. She wore a raspberry pie scented perfume that smelled enchanting.

Part 1: Edward Chip

Meanwhile, in the real world, Derek picked up a stick and was trying whack the ETM upside the head while Cassie screamed something indistinct at Edward. The Taco Man whipped out a blaster shaped like a taco and started firing randomly at his friends. Edward was reminded once again how much he wanted and needed a cookie blaster.

"Come, I am Adrienne," the fortune cookie said, "you have many amazing abilities, you just need to unlock them."

"Huh. . ." Edward replied in a daze.

"Oh, don't bother replying, it will only distract your friends," Adrienne said. Sure enough, Cassie yelled something else indistinct and sprinted over to Edward just to have to fend off the ETM again.

"If you want a cookie blaster you'll have to be brave and fight the ETM."

"How did she know I wanted a cookie blaster?" Edward thought.

"Oh, I know lots of things."

"Did she just read my thoughts?" Edward thought.

"Oh, I can also read your mind," Adrienne said, "you can speak to me by thinking your words. You're obviously smarter than I thought!"

"Ok, so Cassie and Derek don't know I'm speaking to you?"

"I can make them forget a lot of unimportant facts and thoughts if you want!"

"NO! I mean please no."

Part I: Edward Chip

While Edward and Adrienne had been chatting Derek got smacked in the head with some non-explosive tacos and fell to the ground, passed out. Cassie ran next to him muttering something that sounded like,

"Stupid boys all passed out and the ETM ran away," Cassie stormed off back to the destroyed French Toast Forest.

"So you're the one who makes me forget my homework?"

"Homework is not important to live!" Adrienne complained, "All children waste all their time working on homework, FOR NO REASON!" Edward was about to express his agreement but was interrupted by Adrienne's rage. Adrienne struck the floor with the butt of her staff, making the ground shake vigorously. The sound hit Edward so hard it almost made him pass out in his brain. Then he wondered if that was possible.

"It's not, and you shouldn't try." was Adrienne's answer to his unspoken question, "Now we *must* get to business before you wake up fully, and no questions till the end." Adrienne led Edward down a narrow hallway lined with statues.

"Wait, so I'm not dead?"

"Nope, just extra crispy for now."

"What the— how?"

"Nevermind that. For now I am just going to take you to a treasure chest that possesses the strengths you must unlock," Adrienne said. Millions of years passed as they walked along the bare walls. Edward started to notice the hallway getting wider and soon they were standing at a white marble circle with a treasure chest in the middle. More statues lined the circle holding solid white scythes.

"Now you must unlock it, Edward, you must unlock it to defeat the ETM," Adrienne ordered, "Do it now!"

Edward took one small step towards his chest. Suddenly, he felt the chest pulling him towards it until his feet were sliding on the marble. The visions of Cassie and Derek had vanished.

Adrienne screamed, "Edward don't panic, control it, don't let it control you! If your feet slam into the treasure chest you will lose all of your abilities!"

Edward formed a plan inside his head. At the last second, he jumped over the chest and skidded to a stop. Something inside Edward said the scythes in the marble statues hand's were magical, so he followed his gut. Edward sprinted over to one of the marble statues and grabbed its scythe. He pointed the scythe at the chest and it burst open. The contents of the treasure chest flew into Edward's hands.

He grinned at Adrienne, *"Did I do it right?"*

Astounded all Adrienne could muster was, "Mghhee???!!!!!" Edward looked down and realized that the new abilities were dissolving. He must have looked freaked out because Adrienne told him that was supposed to happen.

"Edward, you must wake up now or your friends will be worried," she told him. With that, she snapped her fingers and Edward woke up.

Part I: Edward Chip

When Edward woke up he felt stronger and more refreshed, but he was starved and as Adrienne had promised earlier, extra crispy.

"Thank goodness!" cried Cassie, "I thought you were crumbled!"

"Yeah, I know!" Edward happily said, "How long was I asleep?"

"Three days," Derek said matter of factly.

"THREE DAYS!" Edward yelped, "Really?"

"No, it was only like five hours, but you must have been having a really bad dream because you kept screaming in your sleep," Cassie told Edward. Edward felt ashamed so he put on his mental list to make Derek and Cassie forget that moment. But for right now he felt elated until he realized the ETM must have escaped again!

"Where did—" Edward asked.

"Past the Pastry Plains," Cassie informed him. "We were waiting for you to wake up before we traveled to him."

"We should grab some food before we travel again, right?" Edward asked.

"Yes we should," Cassie said, "I could run back to my mom's house and grab some food."

"That's a bad idea," Derek complained, " I have to stay with Edward to make sure he stays out of trouble."

"I'm not that bad of a troublemaker." Edward protested.

"Yes, you are," Derek sarcastically stated.

"I am not!"

"Boys be quiet and stop fighting!" Cassie ordered, "Derek will go back to his house and get the food and I will stay with Edward. In the meantime, we will scout for the ETM."

"Yes!" Derek exclaimed. With that, he scampered off of the forest, or what was left of it.

"All right," Cassie turned to Edward, "Let's go follow that ETM."

Edward was astounded, "Number one, how do you know where the ETM is? And you're going to leave Derek behind!?"

"Well I shot the ETM with a tracking device from my cake blaster, and we will come back for Derek, we need the food."

"How do you own your blaster and I don't?" Edward complained.

Now it was Cassie's turn to be astounded, "You don't own a blaster!? Didn't your parents give you theirs?"

"No, they were not the heroic type." Edward admitted.

"Well, my mom received hers by saving a drowning child. She ended up loaning me hers because she didn't believe that I would ever do anything to earn my own." Cassie confessed.

"Seriously?"

"Yeah, lately — I don't know why — but it seems like I can't ever do or be enough to make my parents proud."

Part 1: Edward Chip

"That literally makes zero sense." Edward put a hand on her shoulder, "You are literally the coolest and smartest dessert I know. If they aren't proud of you, then that's their issue, not yours." Cassie sighed and thanked Edward, however Edward had the feeling he hadn't really helped ease her mind that much. Cassie pulled out her cake blaster. It smelled of frosting and sprinkles and looked just like a cake, shaped like a blaster. Which is to be expected, Edward guessed.

"Now all we have to do is follow this map," Cassie said, pointing to her blaster's screen.

"I have another question," Edward said, "Why didn't you capture the ETM with the net function?"

"Did I mention that this was my mom's?" Cassie said, gesturing to her blaster, "the old blasters were not as cool as the new ones are. Can we just get on with finding the ETM?"

"Fine, OK." Edward and Cassie traveled deeper into the forest in silence for quite some time.

"Edward?" Cassie said, finally breaking the silence.

"Yeah?"

"Have you ever thought about why you want a cookie blaster?"

Edward paused, "No I haven't. Why?"

"Well, ever since I've known you, you've only wanted one thing; a cookie blaster. And everyone else also wants their own blaster, rightfully so. But, you seem to be fixated on it. Like a lot."

"I guess, I've always felt restless with how my life was playing out. As a young child I'd see snippets of the news where dinner foods were accused of attacking Sugarcane and I remember thinking 'there's got to be a way to end this.' And I guess that's what I plan to do." Cassie probably would have said something else had they not noticed that they had arrived at their destination. It was a sloppily made hut formed by french toast, syrup dripped from all the walls and Edward could tell it wasn't meant for long term living. While Cassie gawked at the hut, Edward stood once more in uncomfortable silence.

"Ummm," Edward said, interrupting the silence, "How are we going to get back to meet Derek, because I have no idea where we are, like, at all."

Cassie groaned, "I have taken care of everything Edward; now in order to bust into the hut we must find or make more weapons, that's the problem at hand." As if on cue, Derek burst through the forest, arms full of delicacies, looking completely lost.

"I found—home—ran away from poisonous gooey beans with salt—" Derek gasped, "and—"

"Wait, " Edward said, "Slow down, and tell us what happened to you."

Derek had run to his house, grabbed as much food as he could, then asked his parents for their donut blasters. Turns out they hadn't even earned their own blasters yet. After he received everything that he needed, he sprinted back to French Toast Forest. But, disgusting beans had invaded a river. One young waffle fell in it so Derek grabbed a rope and pulled the child to safety. After that, the child ran away crying about how much it stung him. Then Derek told how he zapped the river clean with the new donut blaster that he earned.

"Great job Derek!" Cassie quietly congratulated, "This will help us capture the ETM!"

"Oh, by the way," Edward whispered, gesturing to the sloppy hut, "the ETM is inside that."

"I have a plan to capture the notorious ETM," Cassie explained, "Edward will run into the hut and scare the ETM, then Derek and I will capture him with our blasters, and after that, we turn him into the police."

"Great plan, but I'm hungry," Derek complained, "Let's eat first."

After the trio ate they went over their plan again.

"Wait a sec," Edward said, "how am I supposed to walk into the hut unnoticed?"

"I don't know," Cassie thought

"Wait, the cloak!" Derek realized, feeling proud he thought of a solution on his own, "it will turn you invisible!"

"Yes, great idea. I'll wear the cloak and scare the ETM out of here!" Edward exclaimed all in one breath. That's when they started their plan.

Edward tiptoed to the hut wearing the cloak. The door creaked loudly and he stumbled back.

"Go on!" Cassie whispered from a tree. Edward stepped into the hut and found the ETM calmly inside eating a sandwich. Edward walked as quietly as he could until he was right behind the ETM.

"RAA!" he screamed at the top of his lungs. The ETM jumped out of his chair and stumbled out of the

door of his hut. Cassie and Derek yelled as they jumped
out of the tree firing their blasters. Edward raced after
his friends and the ETM. He realized pretty quickly that
he was too far behind to do any help and urged himself
to run faster. Surprisingly, his feet responded to his
metal request and he sprinted forward faster than ever
before.

"The abilities." The cloak on his shoulders fell off
and landed in a tree. The cloak and the tree promptly
disappeared, never to be seen again because they were
both invisible now. Soon he had caught up with ETM
and grabbed him using a strength he never knew he
had. The word abilities flashed through his mind once
again. He snatched up the ETM by his neck, if tacos have
necks, and slammed him down into the ground. The
ETM growled and summoned an exploding taco which
Edward promptly ripped out of the taco's hands and
tossed it aside exploding several french toast sticks to
his left.

The ETM began to stand back up and Edward
tackled him screaming, "Oh no, you don't!" The two of
them began to roll down a hill, hands grabbing at each
other's hypothetical necks, crashing into various
shrubbery and knocking down a plethora of french toast
sticks along the way. At the bottom of the hill, they
splashed into a large maple syrup river, splashed being a
strong word. They merely rolled into it and began to sink
slowly down. Edward tried to climb onto the river bank
but realized that the ETM was still stuck to his front. The
two struggled to clamber out of the sticky river and the

Part I: Edward Chip

syrup gluing them together was already beginning to dry.

"Get off of me amigo!" the ETM demanded.

"You have to get off of me first!" Edward retorted, still thrashing around. Derek and Cassie stumbled through the wreckage of the French Toast Forest, out of breath and drenched in sweat.

"Cassie help!" Edward screamed.

"*Heeey,*" Derek said, "why didn't you ask me for help?" Cassie and Edward ignored Derek's question for the time being and Cassie fired her cake blaster at the pair of them. Edward and the ETM broke free of each other, the energy from the blast shooting them several feet in opposite directions.

"Wait a second," Derek said, "This is the river I was just telling you about! With the waffle kid and the beans. The police must still be around!" The donut ran off to find law enforcement.

"GO AWAY YOU PESKY KIDS," the ETM shouted as he threw another taco. "VAMOS!" Cassie tried to shoot it out of the air with her blaster but her aim was all over the place. As a last ditch effort to stop another explosion, she threw the blaster into the air and it collided with the taco, vaporizing the blaster and taco, but leaving herself and Edward unharmed. As both the ETM and Cassie watched the taco explode, Edward had been sneaking around to the back of the ETM. When the cake blaster exploded, Edward jumped on the taco and once again summoned his abilities. At this moment, Derek burst back into the clearing by the river, popsicle police in tow. Using his new found strength, Edward grabbed the ETM and threw him at the incoming law enforcement. The Evil Taco Man collided with Derek's face and skidded to a stop right at the foot of one of the popsicle police. The ETM was handcuffed with a pair of gummy lifesavers connected by a bit of twizzlers and another officer marched up to Edward and his friends.

"Thank you, sir, you have earned your own cookie blaster," the officer said, handing Edward a cookie blaster he conveniently had in his pocket. Edward beamed at the sight of the shiny weapon. However, two seconds later the ETM burst out of the police station, yelling, "It's not over *amigo,* I'll be back!" as he flew back to the sky where he came from. Edward and his friends looked at the place where the ETM had just left.

"Wow," Cassie said, "that's depressing." As the group cleaned themselves up, Edward noticed a pile of crushed technology on the ground. Further inception revealed it to be Derek's donut blaster. It appeared to have been crushed when the ETM collided with Derek.

"Aw come on! I WORKED SO HARD—" Derek raged in the background.

Two days later, Edward Chip sauntered to Sweets-R Us, their local shopping mall with his sisters, Sugar Cookie and Chipette. Sugar Cookie was his older sister, she was quite annoying and constantly on her phone. Doing what, Edward had no idea as Sugar Cookie barely told him anything. Her body was made of, as her name suggests, a sugar cookie, and today she had donned a light yellow icing with small blue sprinkles. Chipette, on the other hand, was lively and never seemed to stop talking. Like Edward, she was made of a chocolate chip cookie. On the left side of her head she wore a purple bow, baked out of a special colored marshmallow, which always flapped wildly when she spoke.

All was quiet despite the dramatic attack from the ETM. Sugar Cookie had dragged him and Chipette along to the mall so she could look at dresses for an average time of four to five hours. She chatted on her phone with Tammy Tart, her best friend at Brownie High: founded by IAm A. Brownie. Edward still attended Dessert Middle School (because it had been rebuilt with an even boreinger {is that a word?} history room. Dang it!), while Chipette went to Chocolate Lil'Sweets Elementary School. Chipette had run inside the store before Edward and Sugar Cookie and ran into a dessert shop and gotten a free cupcake. She ran out eating it delightfully, when a nearby grandpa cupcake yelled at her, "Cannibal!"

They finally were at the mall, when, before they even got inside the mall, they heard a loud BOOM! Several posters, depicting an apparently missing family of oreos, fell off the side of the building and his friend Sarah Smoothie burst out of the doors of Sweets-R Us, running and screaming. One of the displays behind Sarah had flooded with burrito beans.

Edward first thought of the ETM, but quickly remembered that the ETM was tacos not burritos.

Part I: Edward Chip

Beans were flooding out of what used to be the doorway, and a giant tortilla was floating above Sarah, who was still running toward him. The tortilla dropped on Sarah, curled into an impenetrable ball, embracing her, and took off at at least 90 miles per hour.

The ball flew towards a giant, floating burrito shaped ship hovering over the sugar planet, which opened a circular hatch in the bottom, allowing the tortilla ball containing Sarah to enter. The hatch closed, separating Sarah from the outside world. Another torpedo looking object dropped from the back of the Burrito Ship.

Edward pulled out his Cookie Blaster (which he just earned two days ago and recently saw some kid find out, the hard way, if you use it when there's no emergency, you get arrested for 2 years) and yelled out, "Pull your blasters out!"

The cookies pulled out their cookie blasters, the cupcakes pulled out their cupcake blasters, and so on. They all sprinted towards the dropping burrito torpedo and knelt down abruptly so they could try firing at it to stop it from landing on Mr. and Mrs. Madeira (some random old biscotti couple everyone knew for some reason). They were too late. The tortilla didn't even stop or get damaged a little bit, instead it descended on the two biscotti. Seconds later, a flying tortilla ball containing Mr. and Mrs. Madeira soared towards the Burrito Ship. The desserts wondered who would be next.

Part 1: Edward Chip

The next few days no torpedoes dropped down on Dessert Planet, but foods were still aware of sudden drops. The giant ship was still hovering in their atmosphere. Cassie, Edward's nerdy friend, walked over to him and started blabbering about a bunch of scientific stuff that he didn't even understand.

He was like, "What?"

And Cassie was like, "Whatever," and walked away towards the library.

"Typical," Edward said, not knowing he wouldn't see her for a long time.

The next day at school, they had an assembly about safety and to remain calm if a tortilla dropped down. Principal Pudding was very strict, and if a dessert started talking, he'd send them down to the office.

"We all learned from dat Evil Taco dude five days ago dat tacos are bad and are not good for you. I will be removing them from the lunch menu," he mumbled.

Edward thought, *Wow. He goes way off topic.*

There was a chorus of, "Come on!" and "Seriously?" Even the lunch lemon bars looked unhappy about this. Then a torpedo burst through the roof, and cheese, meat, and beans flooded the room to knee height.

Principal Pudding went into a screaming frenzy. He grabbed a terrified Derek Donut by the leg, holding him upside down for 5 seconds, and then throwing him like a frisbee, removing a third of his sprinkles, the tortilla catching him like a glove catching a baseball. The tortilla took off at light speed, the mothership, a fishing rod, the tortilla a fish, —pulling it in. Principal Pudding said looking down, "I didn't do that."

The next day Principal Pudding was arrested by the Pie Police (the popsicle police were put out of commission for letting the ETM escape prison after living there for 3 seconds). Their new principal was the best. Her name was Principal Peanut Butter Cookie. She passed out free donuts every day. The donuts thought the rest of the students were savages.

Principal PC (for short) received a postcard that she read on the loudspeaker and displayed on the TVs. There was a picture of former Prisoner Principal Pudding in a prison uniform looking extremely bored in his casual captivating cavernous customary cell, with, "Wish You Were Here" printed in a sad font in the corner of the peaceful perfect printed poster.

All of a sudden, someone stumbled in the main entrance— Sarah Smoothie. She stood there for a single second, then collapsed to the ground, her straw falling away from her head and her contents spilling everywhere.

Edward ran over to Sarah, who was lying down. He tried not to step in any of her blended berries but untumently still got a few drops on his toes. He shook her awake, and she screamed. "Sarah, it's me! Edward!"

"Edward, thank goodness!"

He carried Sarah into the new (New) History room (it's been destroyed twice. Maybe it's a sign?), and laid her down on the sofa. Sarah was gasping, her eyes bloodshot.

"Sarah, look around! You're safe!"

"I'm not feeling right, Edward! I feel sick— I have a sore throat— Edward, help— get me some honey water!"

What is going on? Edward thought.

"Edward! I'm sick! I'm sick!" Edward grasped her hand to stop her arms from flailing around. Edward cried out in pain as a burning sensation hit his hand. He pulled back and realized that there was a mark on Sarah's hand, the shape of a bean.

"Oh no," Sarah said sadly, "I've infected you, I'm so sorry..."

Edward spun around, his head foggy and vision jumbled. A feeling of a sore throat crawling into his mouth and his sinuses clogged up all in a matter of a seconds. Edward had to gasp for breath as his vision turned blurry and his arms went limp. All Edward saw was Sarah scream before he fainted.

Edward woke up in a giant room, like a tornado shelter, but except there were thousands of cookies, wheeling around carts with sick desserts. Edward murmured, "Wow." When he saw the sign on the wall— *SCL: Secret Cookie Laboratories, Established since Forever Ago.* His nurse at the foot of his bed pushed him back down, telling him, "You've got the Bean, like most of the patients here."

She told him about the Bean, a disease caused by a microscopic bean embedded in your body spread through physical contact with a first degree patient. (A first degree patient was a dessert that the burritos infected on purpose who then would go around and unintentionally infect other desserts). She told him he was recovering and would be well by tomorrow. Edward felt like he was going to pass out, and that's exactly what he did.

The next morning, Edward woke up, and there was a breakfast of pancakes with syrup and frosting on top with a side of gumdrops, which he devoured instantly. He looked at the screen at the foot of his bed, and the screen read:

CURED! :) You may go now.

He hopped out of his bed and went to his closet, at least that's what he thought it was. He opened it and saw it led to a large room, and there were hundreds of citizens of his town standing there chatting with each other. In the corner, he spotted a package a little bit taller than him and next to it a sign that said:

Part 1: Edward Chip

This package is for Edward Chip. If anyone takes it, I swear to all the gummy gods I will hunt you down and take it back. -Adrienne.

He ran over to the package, ripped it open, and inside was a suit of futuristic armor and his cookie blaster, which he must have lost when he got infected. He put the armor on, and everyone fell silent. He picked up the cookie blaster and slid it into the holder on the side of the belt. Then everyone started chanting, "Be our hero! Be our hero! Stop the burritos!"

They ushered him out the door and pointed him to a starfighter— twenty feet long and ten feet tall. When Edward saw the city, he stumbled backward in surprise. There was fudge fire everywhere. Cannoli cars were flipped over, and cookies had their cookie blasters out. They were firing at burritos, who deflected the incoming shots with their laser sticks. There were shuttles everywhere, burrito warriors spilling out with blasters and laser sticks. Edward sprinted over, jumped in the starfighter, and pressed a button. All of a sudden the ship was flying out of the atmosphere.

Edward finally got the hang of the controls, flying the ship towards the burrito ship. Edward considered flying through the hole where the tortillas entered, but then he saw a red button with an explosion icon on his ship's console. Edward craned his head over to get a good look at it, but then his seat belt snapped. Edward's entire body flung against the ceiling and his buttcheek hit the button.

Part 1: Edward Chip

The next thing Edward knew, a missile-like object flew out in front of him, then into the side of the ship, blowing a giant hole and sending four burritos flying out of the landing port entrance, flying into the wall, knocking them out. Edward's ship flew in the hole, about to crash into the wall on the other side.

Edward thought *I jump, or I die.* He leapt, grasping the edge with all his might, the starfighter coming in for a rough landing behind him. He pulled himself up, into the burrito ship, glimpsing a sign. **CONTAINMENT ROOM** ↘ it read. Edward sprinted down the staircase, and found himself in a large room full of cages, containing all sorts of foods, desserts, and even drinks.

He spotted a cage containing Mr. and Mrs. Madeira, Derek Donut, and even to his surprise, a knocked out Sugar Cookie. He wondered where she had been (not that he missed her or anything). She was holding her phone, no surprise. Then he felt a sharp pain in his back before he blacked out (for like the millionth time in the last week. This was getting old).

He woke up in chains, imprisoned in a cell with lasers instead of iron bars. He wished he could run free.

"Yes, your excellency," a voice was saying, "I know the ETM failed to infiltrate the SCL, but I won't... The child and his friends are being dealt with... Hang on sir, I think he's stirring."

Part I: Edward Chip

"It won't end like this," Edward whispered to no one.

"Or will it?" Edward finally opened his eyes to see a burrito in a red cape and a collar like a vampire.

"I am Captain Burrito. Your disintegration will begin in five seconds.

"Five… Four… Three.. Two… One…"

Edward pressed a button on his armor, ready to die.

He opened his eyes... He was alive!

He looked for Captain Burrito, but he was 10 times as tall as before. A giant pair of shackles fell, clattering to the ground before him. Edward realized what had happened; he had shrunk and was now 6.78 inches tall.

Not even a second later, the loud buzzing of the disintegration machine was heard along with a dough splitting zap. Edward heard a yelp and saw beans and cheese fly everywhere and a vampire cape slowly floated to the ground. Captain Burrito had disintegrated, or so he thought.

Edward ran out of his cell, in between the bars, and pressed the button again. He was back to normal size. His first thought was to run back to his spaceship and escape, but it wasn't where he had last parked it. Just his luck. In its place was a small handwritten note that read:

IOU one spaceship

Part I: Edward Chip

He didn't have time to linger, as more burrito guards were coming upon him and he slunk into a different room. There was a cell in the room containing a baby chocolate dragon (these are extremely rare). Its entire body was made of various types of chocolate bars and Hershey's kisses at the joints and M&M's for scales.

Edward shrunk down again, ran through its bars, and picked the locks on its shackles. He looked all around for a way out. He saw a machine requesting a password. He sat around for ages (20 minutes), trying different codes. He flopped his head on the screen, pressing random numbers. A door slid open. Edward was stunned. He couldn't believe it.

"We're gonna have to work together, okay?" He said to the dragon. The dragon nodded and accidentally incinerated the burrito guard walking down the tunnel. Thankfully Edward had his armor on. Edward climbed onto its back and embraced its neck tightly, and the dragon took off.

Edward could feel air pelting his face as the dragon flew through the ship, crashing through the wall into the containment room. Edward flew the dragon over to the cages, and the dragon hooked its claws around the tops of the cages, and lifted a burrito off the ground, holding him by the scruff. "Where's the ship's weak spot?" he demanded.

The burrito squeaked, "The power generator is in the center! Fly down the south hall and you'll find it!"

Part 1: Edward Chip

Edward was so frantic. He and his dragon dropped the cages which slid through the halls of the ship and fell out of the hole Edward had blown in the side of the ship.

"I'll come back for you!" Edward shouted, but he wasn't sure anyone heard him.

Then a unknown figure jumped onto the back of his dragon, pulling himself/herself up the tail. Edward turned around to face them and saw the face of his old mysterious friend— Adrienne.

"Now?" he asked.

"Yes, Edward. Now." She huffed.

"Why?

Suddenly, she leaped off the dragon, landing on a different dragon twice the size of the one he currently rode on. "This is Meliton, my gingersnap dragon. It's the male out of the last two."

Edward was dazzled. He thought gingersnap dragons were legends. He never imagined he'd get to see one in person.. Edward needed a name for his dragon. He decided to call it Lilith (It was a female).

They flew into a large room full of lasers. There was a large glass tank in the middle of the room full of electricity. Adrienne swerved in between the lasers like nobody's business. Edward, however, had a hard time. His head almost got blasted off 20 times, he counted.

Then approximately 20 burritos ran out screaming menacingly. Then when they saw the dragons, they froze, dropped their weapons, and turned around screaming and ran, but this time in terror. Adrienne leaped off her dragon and turned about 20 burritos into piles of beans and cheese with her silver scythe.

Edward's mouth fell open and he almost crashed Lilith into the wall, but turned in the nick of time, but came in for a rough landing. He grunted and tumbled off Lilith's back. Edward ran over to the generator, looking for a way to turn it off. He found a locked hatch that read, POWER. CAUTION. He tried fiddling with the lock using a bobby pin he found on the floor, but Adrienne walked over and blew it up with her scythe. He wondered if she could destroy the whole generator if she used enough strength.

"I wouldn't try," Adrienne said. "It's a bad idea. I learned it the hard way."

Edward had forgotten Adrienne could read minds. The entire burrito ship shuddered as the power was cut off, the lights started flickering and all the electricity powered cages promptly unlocked.

"Initiate backup power," a voice cracked over the loudspeakers, "engage hyperspeed and set destination for Capital Of The Diner. And to those desserts aboard our ship. Just know, we have identified you. That's right we know who you are, Edward Chip, and Adrienne the Assassin. And we know your sisters too Edward, Chipette Chip and Sugar Cookie Chip. If you stop this madness now, we might let everyone live." Edward didn't realize that Chipette was also here, it made sense though, because Sugar Cookie was here as well.

"Wait, you're an assassin?" Edward asked.

"No! Well. No, not anymore," Adrenne refused to look Edward in the eye. Edward tried to ask another question but Adrienne gave him a look that said not to push her.

So instead, Edward said, "We should go, I don't really feel like going to the capital of the foods."
Adrienne nodded and the two jumped on their dragons.

"Hyperspace takes off in six hours," the loudspeaker crackled, "we need to gain enough energy."

"Let's get some rest first," Adrienne told Edward, "I know you're tired."

"What!? How did you—? Oh right. The mind reading thing," Edward said. Edward then nodded to Adrienne and layed down on the back of his dragon and promptly fell asleep.

He woke up looking at Meliton's back. He was currently on Lilith, still behind Adrienne and her dragon. Edward strategically climbed over to Adrienne and sat behind her on the saddle.

Adrienne said blankly, "Good morning Edward, thank goodness you woke up, you've been asleep for 7.95 hours. Your breakfast is ready. It's next to Lilith." He turned to go eat his bread, but there was already someone eating it.

He saw a macaroon child, with big eyes that shone, adorably innocent. He was about two years old. He must've been hungry. He was stuffing his face, the crumbs of Edward's breakfast tumbling in his lap.

"Hey!" Edward shrieked. The kid ran over to him and hugged him.

Part I: Edward Chip

"What's your name?"

"Tiriaq. I fwom the nowth pole on The Dessert."

"Are you lost?" Edward looked around, possibly hoping to see a banner that said, "Over here Tiriaq!" No such banner.

"No, cweampuff pawents didn't wike me so I wan away and got captuwed bwut when all the cwages got unwocked I was twhe only one stwill captured. Everyone else ecwaped."

"Come meet Adrienne," Edward said.

"NWO NWO! NWO!" Edward tried to process, but he got distracted, something in the distance caught his eye. Was that... another fortune cookie? Edward blink and the vision was gone. Tiriaq threw himself to the ground, crying and kicking, an innocent-looking devil child. Edward rubbed his eyes and picked up the screaming Tiriaq and brought him to Adrienne.

"This is Tiria—"

"Tiriaq!" Adrienne screamed. She grabbed him from Edward and hugged him ever so tightly.

"Are you guys-?"

"He's— he's a long lost friend."

"Come on guys," Edward said, mounting his dragon, "let's fly out of this ship."

As Adrienne mounted her dragon, Edward could have sworn that he saw another fortune cookie in his peripheral vision. Then suddenly a streak of blond hair. He turned his head and it appeared his eyes were playing tricks on him. He blinked several times as Tiriaq climbed up behind Edward and they urged their dragons to take off.

The three had been flying around the ship for a while looking for an exit with no luck. Edward suggested that they make their own exit. The dragons tore a hole in the side of the ship using their long claws. Alarms blared all around them as soon as the damage to the show was done and Edward swore he saw the second fortune cookie again. This time it was running in the opposite direction.

"You were warned, now you will face the consequences. Ingredient Ascertainer active," the loudspeaker oversaid screamed. Edward panicked, he didn't know an Ingredient Ascertainer was, but it didn't sound good. He looked to Adrienne for guidance but she had been curiously quiet this whole time. Edward tried to talk to her mentally but had no such luck; it seemed as if something else was occupying her mind at that time.

Then just before they were going to exit, Adrienne turned to Edward and murmured, "Sorry, Edward." She took her scythe and swung it at Edward, but he ducked.

"Traitor!" he yelled.

"Edward! Duck!" Edward heard from behind him. He turned around to see Sugar Cookie and Chipette swooping up to them in a small homemade looking space pod. Sugar Cookie then proceeded to throw her phone from inside the ship.

Part 1: Edward Chip

The tool flew through the air, hitting Adrienne smack dab in the eye and bouncing right back into Sugar Cookie's hand, just like a boomerang. Apparently physics isn't a thing in space. Adrienne shrieked in pain, her arms flailing.

Just for a second, Edward thought he saw the mark of the Bean on Adrienne's palm. Just as quickly as he saw it however, it slowly faded off her skin.

"Must've been possessed," Adrienne gasped.

Chipette peaked her head out the window of the rickety spacecraft and jumped out. She flew heroically up to Adrienne and kicked her straight in the face. The bean mark on Adrienne disappeared even faster as the fortune cookie let out a cry of pain. Right as it happened, they exited the Burrito Ship, and Adrienne went flying into empty space. Meliton dove after her, accidentally knocking everyone off the platform— including Edward and his sisters–into the endless space.

Lilith was woken into movement by all the action. When the dragon saw Edward hurtling through the air, it shrieked and dove, and Edward landed smoothly on the dragon's back. Edward pulled the reins, steering Lilith into a steeper dive. Adrienne fell, screaming. Once he was side by side with her, he reached. So did Adrienne.

They grabbed hands and Edward pulled Adrienne behind him. The dragons tried to dive to catch Sugar Cookie and Chipette but the two had been thrown farther than Edward and soon fell out of sight before the dragons could reach them. Edward could only hope they would be ok.

Abruptly, a great thundering was heard and Edward glanced upwards; it appeared the Burrito Ship's engines had finally charged up and the ship exited The Dessert's atmosphere.

"Edward. I'm sorry. I was being possessed," a very distraught Adrienne gasped, bringing Edward's attention back to the current situation.

"Adrienne. I understand. Who possessed you?"

"I don't know."

"Or do you?" whispered someone behind him.

He turned to face another fortune cookie, with blonde hair.

"Hello. I am Parthenope. Adrienne's sister."

Edward and Adrienne (holding Tiriaq) crashed down onto a gingerbread cliff. Black sky surrounded them, with barely any stars in sight. Edward looked around and realized they were back on his planet, The Dessert. He also realized that the Sugar Cookie and Chipette were nowhere to be found.

Adrienne quickly told the dragons to flee to the safety of the Secret Cookie Labs as Parthenope would stop at nothing to eliminate the dragon race. At her command, the dragons took off immediately. Parthenope floated down safely using an umbrella she had stuffed inside her hollow shell.

As soon as her sister landed, Adrienne charged, scythe in hand. She swung, but Parthenope just ducked, turned her umbrella into a sword, kicked Adrienne square in the nose, and pointed the sword at her throat.

"If you wish to stay alive, I suggest you back down."

Parthenope grabbed Tiriaq and whispered to Edward.

"Move and he gets it."

"Whaaa—No—Wait!" Edward lunged at Parthenope and she proceeded to throw the macaroon child off the cliff into black emptiness, while flailing his arms and legs and screaming at the top of his lungs. Edward quickly tied himself to a bungee cord he found in his armor and he jumped after the child.

Parthenope whispered, "Master will be pleased. First I master the use of the Bean and now I take down the new rebels!"

"Who's your master, you evil witch?" Adrienne asked.

"You'll find out, won't you, little sis? Just as soon as I capture you."

Adrienne roared in rage and swung at Parthenope with the dull end of her scythe. Parthenope just laughed and waved her hand. The scythe passed through her as Adrienne swung it. Suddenly the scythe was flung from Adrienne's hands and onto the edge of the cliff.

"What sorcery is this?" Adrienne asked, horrified as she watched Parthenope kick her scythe into the blackness where Tiriaq and Edward continued to fall.

"It's called Vishnu, a magic that none other can beat because it is so powerful."

Part 1: Edward Chip

"But I also use Vishnu!" Adrienne gasped.

"I must just be stronger than you," her sister replied.

Meanwhile, Edward kept diving after Tiriaq, never letting the little cookie out of his sight. It felt like he had been falling for hours but it had only been a few minutes. Suddenly a rock fell off the cliff and hit a button on the back of his armor. In a flash, Edward's armor detached and he started to freefall. Darkness started to enclose Edward and he started to panic. Just at the last second before Edward, chasing Tiriaq, was swallowed in darkness, Edward grabbed Tiriaq and hugged him close. That moment, the little child stopped screaming but was still gasping very hard.

"H-howm much wonger till we land?" asked Tiriaq.

"I have no idea," Edward replied.

Edward had no idea how long he and Tiriaq had been free falling, for the landscape never changed, just pitch dark all the time. Tiriaq gripped Edward like a koala gripped a tree. They must have been a rare sight, two cookies stacked on top of each other, one large and one small. After what seemed like hours, a flash of light tumbled past Edward and he knew it might save him and the child he held.

"Tiriaq," Edward said, "Climb on my back and hold on tight!"

"Why Wdward?" Tiriaq asked

Part 1: Edward Chip

"No time to explain," Edward explained.

"Ok."

With that, the boy climbed onto Edward's back. Then, Edward tucked his head in and the speed of his fall doubled. Soon he caught up to the shiny object and realized it was Adrienne's scythe.

"Oooooh gimme shiny blade" Tiriaq yelled while climbing back around to Edward's waist. While the scythe took every bit of strength for Edward to lift, Tiriaq lifted it with ease.

"W-up!" The child yelled, and he stopped falling and hovered in midair while Edward still tumbled down.

"Cwatch Wdward!" and soon Edward was too hovering in midair. Tiriaq waved the scythe in a circle around his head and suddenly Edward and the child shot back up and landed on a ledge near the top of the cliff.

When they landed, Edward complained, "I'm hungry."

Tiriaq swung the scythe in the shape of a star to reveal a shell of crust and all sorts of fruits inside.

"Pie?" Tiriaq asked. Suddenly a "Pop!" sounded overhead followed by a scream so they flew back up to the top of the cliff as quickly as possible, leaving two slices of pie. Little did Edward know, one black shelled insect showed up and devoured the slices of pie and multiplied into over one hundred of the insects! Soon all the insects began making their way up the cliff side and were still multiplying.

To Edward's surprise, the battle was still raging between Adrienne and Parthenope. A burst of yellow light shot out of Adrienne's hand,

"You will never win, sister." Parthenope shot a jet of purple light at Adrienne who deflected it with her magic. The beams collided and they went flying to the edge of the cliff. Edward and Tiriaq peered anxiously over the cliff. The sisters shot power beams that collided. Smoke appeared where the power beams intersected.

When the smoke cleared, there lay Adrienne and Parthenope, both looking lifeless. Edward cried when he saw Adrienne's and Parthenope's bodies lying on the cliffside after the duel. "Adrienne sacrificed to save us," Edward groaned. Then he looked over to see Tiriaq sobbing very hard.

"NWO! " Just then out of the darkness, a giant mass of blackness loomed out, speaking,

"Defeat...Kill…Who...Awakens…"

The giant mass of blackness was a large cluster of fanged insects. They formed a hand shape and flew at Edward

"NWO!!!" Tiriaq cried and slid. He kicked Edward to the side and was lifted up by the large black hand. Edward grabbed the scythe, realizing even as he did that a mere week ago, before he fought the ETM, he'd have never been able to perform such a feat, and jumped. He landed on the hand, which was in a fist trapping Tiriaq inside. Edward chopped off what would be the fingers, but it was no use. The fingers would just reform within milliseconds. Edward dropped the scythe and fell into the fist with Tiriaq.

"Thank you for saving me back there," said Edward. "At least we'll die together."

Suddenly a silver glint appeared and slashing sounds filled the area around them. The insects appeared to be scared by the light and all scurried away, dropping Edward and Tiriaq back down onto the ground of the cliff. Edward and Tiriaq looked up to see the source of the light and were greeted by Adrienne, looking disheveled, filled with fatigue but triumphantly holding her scythe.

As glad Edward was to see Adrienne was alive again, Adrienne didn't seem happy to see Edward, "You had to mess with the Ayomide Nimat Amani Nour!?" Adrienne yelled, gesturing to the piles of dead insects.

"What? I didn't mean to set off the Ami Nimy Ami Noir or whatever they are called!" Edward retorted, sputtering out the confusing words, "Tiriaq and I just ate pie and then we heard fighting and flew up to see what was going on!" Edward was very mad. Then Adrienne looked scared,

"Wait, you had pie?" she asked, her lip quivering, "Are you sure you ate the pie?"

"Well nwo" Tiriaq piped up, "We flew wup to save you and fo-got abwout the pie!"

"OH NO!!!!" Adrienne exclaimed, "If we don't kill all the insects before the hour is over, they will have begun to eat and munch on the very surface of our planet"

"Is that a problem?" Edward asked

"*IS* that a *PROBLEM!?*" Adrienne was practically shouting now, "Do you know that the Ayomide Nimat Amani Nour will eat through literally the entire universe in less than one day! WE MUST STOP THEM BEFORE IT'S TOO LATE!!!!!"

"Oh…" Edward said, trying to process all the new information. This task was very difficult because someone kept crunching in his ear. When Edward turned his head he saw that Tiriaq was eating potato chips while shooting fireworks out of the scythe in his hand.

"Tiriaq, will you please be quiet? I'm trying to figure out a way to get off this graham cracker cliff!"

"Wumm… Edward? It tis wactually a ginger bwead cwiff." Tiriaq said, "and Adrienne and Edward cwan fwy."

"Oh... then I need to figure out a way so I can fly!"

"Really? Edward," Adrienne exclaimed, "the Abilities!"

"Yes! Thanks, Adrienne, I would have not thought of that!" Edward said while Adrienne sighed.

It took a half hour for Edward to figure out how to fly while Tiriaq took a nap and Adrienne paced back and forth muttering insults at Edward for taking too long

Part I: Edward Chip

in ancient cookienese. Finally, when Edward was hovering five feet in the air and Tiriaq with the scythe in hand was flying, Adrienne shouted to Edward "let's go!" and flew down the side of the cliff. Edward and Tiriaq followed her and hurdled to the ground.

Instead of floating down majestically like Adrienne, he tumbled head over heels and then crashed into the ground causing the side of the cliff to detach from the rest of the cliff and hurtle, like Edward, towards the ground. Tiriaq screamed and ran towards a bridge in the distance at full speed but before he crossed it, a chunk of gingersnap crushed the bridge and Tiriaq screamed and ran to Adrienne whose face was pale.

Adrienne shouted to Edward while gingersnap crashed down around them, "We have to save Parthenope!" Edward looked over his shoulder and saw Parthenope lying on the ground, but still breathing.

"Why!" Edward shouted back, "she a witch!"

"She is also my SISTER!!!" Adrienne screamed as she tore off to her sister, "no matter how bad they are, NEVER abandon your family!" Tiriaq, who realized what Adrienne was doing, screamed and ran to Edward. Edward was also running to help Adrienne get Parthenope, so Tiriaq screamed again and ran around in circles dodging hunks of gingerbread. Adrienne and Edward heaved up Parthenope and started running toward the broken bridge.

"Tiriaq!" Adrienne screamed, "You better do something helpful or I'm going to ground you!"

"Wh-At!" Tiriaq's voice cracked as he put on a pouty face

"ONE!"

"NO!"

"TWO!!"

"NO!"

"THR-"

"FINE!" Tiriaq pulled out his scythe and shouted, "Nwew BWIDGE AND NWO FALLWING ROCKS!!!!!!!!"

The world almost froze, everything had suddenly slowed down. Edward could see Adrienne running towards Parthenope. The bridge in the distance rebuilt itself. When Edward tried to run towards Adrienne, his feet wouldn't move fast, in fact, he himself was running in slow-motion.

"Come *ON* guys!" Tiriaq shouted, and Edward looked over to see Tiriaq running across the new bridge at normal speed.

"How are you doing that!" Edward asked although because he was talking and running in it sounded more like:

"HHHHOOOOOOOWWWWWWWSSSRRRRRRRRRSSS UUUUUUUUSSSSSSS DOOOOOOOONNNNNNNNNNN DDDDDDDAAAAAAAAAATTTSSSSSSSSSSS!!!!!!!"

Then Tiriaq's spell faded and the world returned to normal speed. Adrienne and Edward reached Parthenope's body at the same time and managed to drag her out of the way before getting crushed by the falling rocks. Together, Adrienne and Edward lifted Parthenope and headed for the bridge. They had barely made it half across the bridge, which was swinging violently over the chasm, before the Ayomide Nimat Amani Nour seemed to recover from Adrienne's earlier attack. They merged themselves into the shape of a singular giant bug and marched their way to the bridge. Adrienne and Edward placed Parthenope down and Tiriaq gave Adrienne back her scythe. Edward pulled out his cookie blaster and Adrienne shook her head.

"That won't do anything on them," she told him and proceeded to pull out a pair of glowing blue knives out of midair.

"Woah, these are really cool," Edward said. At the word "cool," the knives morphed themselves into freeze ray guns and Edward quickly shot out a wall of ice in front of the bridge blocking the path. The giant black bug howled in anger and began picking up boulders and chucking it at the ice wall. Within three hits, the wall's structural integrity was compromised and Edward knew they had to get off the bridge. As the fourth boulder hit the wall of ice, Adrienne waved her scythe to try and reenforce it with Vishnu but a falling rock knocked it out of her hand.

"OFF THE BWIDGE!" Triaq yelled.

They all dived forward off the bridge. But not Edward, he dived for the scythe. His fingertips barely grazed the handle when Edward felt a boulder land on him, crushing his legs. The last thing he saw was Adrienne's mystical weapon falling into the void before another boulder smashing into his body, crushing him into a million places. Then, he blacked out (again).

Part 1: Edward Chip

When he woke up, he was in a familiar place. Edward was in a giant room, like a tornado shelter, but except there were thousands of cookies, wheeling around carts with sick desserts.

Edward yelped, "Again!" When he saw the sign on the wall— *SCL: Secret Cookie Laboratories.* His nurse at the foot of his bed pushed him back down, telling him, "Yes hon, again, you see hon, when your dragons arrived we knew something was wrong so we sent a support squad! Too bad you and your other friends had been crushed into a million pieces! But then we just rebaked you!"

The cookie nurse looked at her cookie watch and exclaimed,"Oh no hon I have to go see ya!" with that the nurse bolted out of the room.

Edward had so many questions to ask the nurse lady, but she had left him before he could. Edward looked around the room he was in, he saw his cookie blaster and the freeze ray guns on a dessert decorated dresser across his room.

To his left, more rooms for sick patients, to his right, he saw a sign that said: **Evil Food Chamber!!!** → **DO NOT ENTER** → Many more signs were behind that sign and they said: **TURN BACK now!** ← and **Don't go one more step.**

Edward, ignoring the signs, grabbed his weapons and marched forward to the Evil Food Chamber. Much to Edward's surprise, all the cells in the Evil Food Chamber were empty, except three. One imprisoned Meliton, Adrienne's gingersnap dragon. Edward was shocked why Meliton was in the cells. He quickly looked in the other cells. Lilith, Edward's chocolate dragon, was locked in the second cell, and in the third cell lay Parthenope, Derek Donut, and his friend Cassie Cake.

Without thinking, Edward shot the locks on all the cells with his cookie blaster. Soon Meliton's, Lilith's, Parthenope and his friends' cells were opened. The two Dragons roared and stretched their wings, enjoying the freedom, when a voice shouted, "Stop it right there!" It was a cookie cop and he was holding up his cookie blaster. Edward looked behind him and shot the cop in the face with his freeze ray gun.

"Come on guys!" Edward urged his friends as they hurried past the frozen cop, "We need to find Adrienne and Tiriaq! I have reason to think this place is corrupted!"

"Yeah, no kidding" Cassie sarcastically commented

"And we saw the extraterrestrial eggs. They're running around giving the Bean to everyone!" Edward remembered when he had the Bean and shuddered at the thought. Then Edward asked, "What are extraterrestrial eggs?"

"Evil mind meddling little minions! If they get the chance, they will tear you apart!" Parthenope intervened.

"You know what? Nevermind, we have business to get to!" Edward said, "Let's get Adrienne!"

The four desserts dashed down the hall, only to be stopped by more cookie cops, "We do not have permission to let you escape!" a cop said in a dazed voice, "All hail Supreme Lord Mac-N-Cheese!" All the cookie cops who heard his cry dropped what they were doing and shouted in dazed voices, "ALL HAIL SUPREME LORD MAC N CHEESE!!!!!" and walked toward Edward and his friends.

"Ok... That's just a little weird." Cassie pointed out.

"No duh!" Derek retorted.

"The evil food must have found a formula for hypnotizing desserts!" Parthenope exclaimed.

Meanwhile, the dazed cookie cop zombie walked toward the group forming a circle while saying, "Must obey the rules! Eat the sugar cookie! All hail Supreme Lord Mac-N-Cheese! Must obey the rules! Eat the sugar cookie! All hail Supreme Lord Mac-N-Cheese!" over and over again. Edward tried to think of a way to bypass the hypnotized cookie cops without hurting them. Edward had no success thinking up a plan, luckily, Parthenope thought up a plan. Suddenly she shouted, "ÊsingÂÌorius" and a pink symbol floated in the air :

The effect was instantaneous, all the cookie cops dropped down and fell asleep. Edward looked at Parthenope in awe.

"What are you gawking at!" Parthenope demanded.

"Uhhh... nothing," Edward said in a small voice.

"Well then let's get started!"

Part 1: Edward Chip

They ran, but they were opposed by The Cheese Wizard, a can of Cheez Wiz with a bad attitude, who materialized out of thin air as soon as they turned the corner, showering shredded cheese everywhere.

"ALL *HAIL* SUPREME LORD MAC N CHEESE!!" the wizard yelled, raising his cheese block staff and the sleeping cookie cops woke up and replied, "All hail Supreme Lord Mac N Cheese!"

"You children will never win! FOR I HAVE THE POWER OF ONE THOUSAND DESSERTS!!!!! BWAU HA HA HA HA HA HA HA HA H-"

"Alteortis!" Derek shouted, interrupting the Cheese Wizard. A blue symbol etched itself in the air:

A pit of glowing fire consumed the wizard, melting the cheese and softening the cookie cops so they melted back into dough. The wizard emerged from the fire, threw a glowing lasso around Derek's neck, and started pulling him into the fire.

"NOOOOOO!!!" Edward shouted.

As Derek was engulfed by the flames, Edward pulled a random licorice hanging from the ceiling and a bucket of water dumped on the fire. Steam rose and there was Derek, in an obsidian sarcophagus locked in with the wizard. On the coffin, there were pictures engraved into the stone of Derek and the Cheese Wizard in an endless battle.

Part I: Edward Chip

"Well, at least Derek has a 12.34 percent chance of survival." Cassie pointed out hopefully.

"How do you know that?" Edward asked suspiciously, "Are you an imposter!?"

"NO no no no no no no no no, I can't do magic so Parnethlope taught me to be a Math Wizard!"

"Oooh yeah, she taught me the art of the Vishnu magic!" Derek happily added, his voice muffled by the coffin. Edward was very stunned but glad his friend was alive. First Parnethlope was fighting Adrienne, now she was helping his friends; Edward was confused.

"Anyway let's just find Adrienne!" Parnethlope said cheerfully.

"What about Derek!" Edward protested.

"Oh, he'll be *fine!!*" Parnethlope said, and marched forward as if the matter was settled.

"Come on Edward!" Cassie said a little too joyfully. Edward had no choice but to follow one friend, leave one behind, and walk Melton and Lilith toward Adrienne.

Hours later, they found Adrienne sleeping fitfully in a white bedchamber and Tiriaq sitting by her side, trying to wake her up. Nothing the little macaron did seemed to work until Parnethlope touched her sister, Adrienne gasped, sat up, and yelled, "GO TO THE ASYLUM! FREE LEMON DROP!!!!!!!!!!!!!"

"Calm down sister." Parnethlope said gently, "Now tell us."

Part I: Edward Chip

"There's Lemon Drop Dragon is locked up in the Athaliahus Asylum, it might be the key to stopping the Ayomide Nimat Amani Nour from infesting the planet."

"I can help with that." offered a low voice. Leaning against the wall behind them was a tall cookie, "My name is Caelan, I work here and I know where the cookie cars are."

"Why aren't you possessed?" Cassie asked, "The possibility of that is 2.34720%."

"Oh yeah, that. I looooove Vishnu!" Caelan said. Edward looked over to Parnethlope, Cassie and Adriane and saw all three of them muttering indistinct words. However, Edward could have sworn Parnethlope muttered something like, "liar." Edward looked at Adrienne and saw her eyeing Caelan suspiciously.

"Well, this should just be a blast!" Cassie shouted and ran after Caelan who was already halfway down the hall. Soon Parnethlope ran after Caelan too.

"Edward, a word?" Adrienne asked.

"Yeah sure," Edward replied.

"So what's wrong with Cassie and where is Derek!? Who is Caelan and what is this place! What is Parnethlope doing! WHY CAN'T I REMEMBER ANYTHING AFTER THE CLIFF INCIDENT?!"

"Uhh, I was hoping you knew the answers to all those questions!"

"You know what, nevermind! We need to make sure we don't get in trouble." With that, Edward and Adrienne ran after Cassie and Parnethlope.

"Wait!" Edward yelled, "We can use the dragons to get to the Asylum!"

Part I: Edward Chip

"Oh yeah, about that..." Cassie said, shifting her gaze to an imaginary speck of dirt on her shirt. Edward turned around expecting to see two enormous dragons behind him, but dragons seemed to have disappeared.

"I may or may not have shrunken them by a scale factor of 1/9000" Cassie said shifting her gaze from her shirt to Caelan, "then I gave them to Caelan to set free in the wild. Well Oopsy ME!!!" Cassie's confidence and her happiness level grew every second she looked at Caelan.

"No..." Edward said, quite shocked.

"Oh yes." sneered a now stone-faced Caelan, "Dragons are quite dangerous! They will be executed soon. Anyways! Let's get those cookie cars!" Caelan's voice became cheerful again but Edward couldn't forget the way Caelan's voice sounded when he became unhappy. They followed Caelan until they reached a large garage.

"Here we are meh meh meh meh meh meh meh meh awesome Blah blah blah blah! What's for dinner tonight! Take over THE WORLD!!!!!! I mean stop the bugs?" Caelan suddenly looked sick. As Edward watched Caelan, his face shimmered looking like melted cheese. Edward blinked and Caelan looked normal again.

"Are you Ok, Sir Lord Master??" Cassie asked.

"Yeah yeah," Caelan straightened up, "just excuse me for a bit." With that the cookie cop ran off and something fell out of his pocket as he hurried away. Edward checked to make sure no one was looking and casually walked to the object. He looked again at Parnethlope, Cassie and Adrienne, they were all

58

inspecting the cookie cars. He reached down and picked up the object. He didn't look at it, but it appeared to be a small capsule closed shut with a cork. As he went to stand back up, Edward made eye contact with Tiriaq and put a finger to his lips. Tiriaq nodded and understood the message.

"Hiya guys! I'm back!" Caelan stood at the entrance of the garage. Quickly stuffing the capsule into his pocket, Edward turned around.

"Yeah hi," Edward mumbled.

"Well let's choose which car to use!" Caelan said, gesturing grandly to the assortment of cookie cars.

"I like this car." Adrienne said looking at the oatmeal raisin cookie car next to her, "I checked it over and it is safe to drive in."

"No no no," Parnethlope said pointing to an M&M cookie car, "this one is better! It goes faster, is a convertible, and runs on pure sugar alone!" Parnethlope winked at Caelan.

"Then it's settled" Caelan shouted, "M&M it is!"

"But I th—" Adrienne was cut off by Parnethlope honking the horn to the car, "Let's go Adrienne!"

"Fine" grumbled Adrienne and walked over to the car. Edward followed Adrienne. Caelan took the wheel and Parnethlope sat in the shotgun, leaving Cassie, Edward, Tiriaq and Adrienne to sit in the back despite there being only three seatbelts. Caelan then proceeded to turn on the car and pressed a sequence of buttons and before Edward or Adrienne could protest, the car was cruising on the freeway.

Part 1: Edward Chip

Edward started boredly out the window of the car. He couldn't help but notice fewer and fewer dessert items were around. The chocolate chip road was turning into something more slippery. Like the icing in the North Popsicle but it was organic-tan and had many streaks of blackish-brown in it. After another couple of minutes loud and large stomping could be heard followed by howls. When Edward asked Caelan about the sounds he just laughed and kept driving. Edward leaned over to Adrienne, "What are all the moans about?"

"I don't know," Adrienne replied, "but that sounds like words." Another low voice sounded. Edward tried to listen to the moans but Caelan announced that they had arrived at the Athaliahus Asylum. Adrienne jumped out of the car and rushed up to the door of the asylum. The asylum was made of burnt gingersnap and squashed gummy worms. A large gray storm cloud swirled over the top of the asylum flashing lightning and raining blueberry gumdrops. Suddenly high pitched screams came out of the attic of the asylum.

Edward shuddered as Adrienne tried to open the door. It stubbornly remained shut. From behind Edward, Triaq and Cassie made her way out of the car but then, Cassie tripped and fell face first into the ground. Tiriaq knet down to help Cassie up but Caelan pushed him out of the way. Caelan leaned over Edwards' friend and muttered, "Something wrong with the spell... hmmm..." Edward tapped on Adrienne's shoulder, "Look at Cassie!" Adrienne turned around and turned as white as sugar. "No," she said, "Caelan wouldn't be able to cast that spell. Only dinner foods can do that."

Part I: Edward Chip

"What is it?" Edward asked, but Adrienne wasn't listening. Silently, she crept up behind Caelan, moved Tiriaq away from the cookie and quietly chanted. Caelan noticed Adrienne too late. His skin rippled, and soon, before Edward, stood Captain Burrito. Tiriaq gasped in horror.

"You're still alive?!" Edward snarled.

"Yes, I am," Captain Burrito responded, "after the ETM failed his mission, I was sent to take over it. And now that I have you here... Parnethnope, will you do the honors?" Captain Burrito crackled as Parnethnope opened her arms and lightning flashed. Out of the blue, dinner foods dropped from the sky as if summoned by Parethnope's spell. The burrito spacecraft reappeared in the Dessert's atmosphere and flew towards the ground, reached out a claw hand, and snatched Cassie from the ground. The spacecraft flew back into the sky.

Adrienne turned to Edward, "I will go into the Athaliahus Asylum and find this dragon to stop the Ayomide Nimat Amani Nour. You stay here and stall for time." With that, Adrienne shot a purple light at the door to the asylum and ran inside.

Edward stood dumbfounded at the mass of dinner foods around him as he formed a plan. "Ok let's do this thing!" Edward yelled as he, naively, charged into battle.

Part 2: Adrienne

Adrienne ran inside the asylum not knowing what to expect. In fact, she wasn't even sure what she was doing. When she first made contact in Edward's mind and helped him unlock his abilities, she didn't think she'd get in so deep. But nevertheless, for now she just needed to gain his trust, and the trust of everyone around him. The asylum was dark as a black hole. Adrienne reached up and summoned a ball of light above her hand and looked around the room she was in. The asylum had ample amounts of gray cotton candy, and the walls were dripping with flat soda. A "Missing Food" poster had been placed by the entrance for several potatoes.

The whole place smelled of moldy ice cream and gave Adrienne the creeps. Adrienne had been anywhere and everywhere, so something seldom scared her or made her nervous. She turned into a hall and was suddenly lost. She turned around only to find the hallway she had entered through was now gone. *Ok,* she thought, *keep calm, don't panic.*

She managed to stroll for five seconds when suddenly she heard a low growl behind her. That's when she lost all control and ran off screaming her head off. Adrienne ran left and right until she was thoroughly lost in the labyrinth of halls.

Part 2: Adrienne

She came across a staircase that seemed to emanate the sounds of festive bells jingling and an old man screaming, "HO HO HO!". Adrienne immediately ran in the opposite direction because she didn't know what *HO HO HO* meant, but she was sure she knew a battle cry when she heard one. She leaned against the wall for support.

All of a sudden, from the door across from her, she heard sobbing. She walked over to the door and pulled it open. Inside there was a thing of rolled rice cream in the shadows. It was crying so much that there was a puddle underneath the dessert.

"Hello?" Adrienne said, "Who are you?"

"Go away!" The rolled ice cream emitted a female voice.

"Don't worry, I'm a friend!" Adrienne said

"That's what *they* said."

"Who?"

"Not tell'n!"

"Ok, you don't have to."

"Really?"

"Yes, I can."

"What's the catch?"

"I need to find a lemon drop dragon. A race of bugs is on the loose and will eat everything if we don't stop them. I believe the dragon is the key."

"Deal," the dessert, she couldn't have been much older than Adrienne, stepped out of the shadows, "I'm Ginny Gelato, follow me." Then Ginny ran off. The name Ginny Gelato rang some bells in Adrienne's mind and something told her she would need Ginny's trust as well. With that in mind Adrienne ran after Ginny having resolved to break her out of the asylum.

Adrienne had been following Ginny for quite some time and her legs were starting to ache. After passing endless quarters Ginny spoke up, "Are the rumors true?"

"What rumors?" Adrienne replied

"The ones about the cookie, his name is something like Edger... no... Eragon no that's not right either."

"Edward?"

"Yes! That's it!" after a pause Ginny continued, "So are they true?"

"Yeah, they are."

"Cool! We just won the bet!"

"Who is we?"

"Oh," Ginny looked down then replied shakily, "he's my baby lemon drop dragon."

"Oh," Adrienne looked down too, "I worry, we'll get him out."

"I hope so. His name's Saibou."

"That's a nice name."

"We're here." Ginny pointed to a wooden door line with gray cotton candy, "this is where I last saw the burrito guards drag him to." Adrienne nodded then brought her fist up to the door.

"DON'T KNOCK! We need an element of surprise."

Part 2: Adrienne

Adrienne nodded, then she placed her fist on the door whispered, "PenO slylenteĕ." The little brown door opened. Adrienne peeked inside and gasped at what she saw. The only light in the small room was a hole in the roof. Saibou was locked in a cage that was suspended over a fire, dangling by chains covered in cobwebs. Adreinne wondered how long Ginny and Saibou had been there for. To either side of the cage were burritos. They carried churros with peanut brittle at the end. The weapon resembled something like a scythe and Adrienne was reminded of how much she missed her scythe. Ginny peeked in the room with Adrienne and gasped,

"Saibou!" A burrito saw her and a jet of fire rushed out of a flamethrower it was holding. Adrienne went to shove Ginny out of the way, but she was too slow. Ginny sidestepped the fire just barely to avoid being toasted. But the heat was still too much and she began to melt. Adrienne fell into a fit of rage and grabbed the nearest thing, a rock, and threw it. The burrito had a stone stuck in its forehead before it could even do anything. The burrito lay knocked out on the ground. Saibou woke up with a jump, startled from the sounds. Then he looked down at the dying face of Ginny Gelato. She whispered quietly to the dragon, "Defeat the Supreme Leader. I'll always be with you... BLEEEEEHHHHHHHHHH."

Then, after drawing out the "bleh" noise to last an uncomfortable amount of time, Ginny fell silent and melted away. Saibou howled a cry of anguish and shook the cage in an attempt to get out.

Part 2: Adrienne

"She died honorably—" Adrienne tried to say, but was cut off by the last Burrito.

" NO!" The burrito glared at Adrienne, "That was my BROTHER! What's your problem, you witch?"

Then Edward flew and crashed through the wall of the asylum.

"Adrienne! Help now! Not only are there literally all the dinner foods ever, but the Amy— the Ayomide Nimnim— the *bugs* are here too as well and eating the ground under our feet! The dinner foods seem to be controlling them somehow!" Adrienne nodded to him and Edward jumped back out of the room.

With more light in the room, Adrienne could see the room was covered in chains and bones. Filled with rage the burrito flung itself at Adrienne. Adrienne ducked, but not quick enough. The tip of the peanut brittle grazed her arm leaving a stinging sensation that itched.

"Look," Adrienne yelled at the burrito, "I'm sorry I killed your brother!"

"That is OK," the burrito yelled, "I like yelling random words!"

"What?!" Adrienne asked.

"The burrito you killed was actually my evil boss!" the burrito yelled, "I feel no remorse for his death! BWA HA HA HA HA HA HA HA HA HA HA H-" the burrito went into a coughing fit. Adrienne saw her chance and tackled the burrito and stole his churro and peanut brittle scythe.

"Hey!" the burrito protested, "that is not fair!"

Part 2: Adrienne

"I'm really sorry about this!" Adrienne muttered, and threw the burrito into a cage and locked it with a wave of her hand. She ran up to Saibou and blew the door to the cage off its hinges. The glossy yellow dragon fell to the ground, dazed but still alive. The dragon expanded until he was the size of the room and nuzzled Adrienne appreciatively. She got a strong whiff of citrus as she gawked at its lemon slice scales crusted with grains of sugar and its back where instead of spikes, it had various colors of lemon drops.

"Come on," Adrienne told the dragon, "let's get out of here." Saibou burst into the air, breaking the walls of the Asylum all around him and they dove into battle.

As soon as Adrienne saw the battle raging in front of the now burning asylum, she felt sick. Tiriaq was backed into a corner, as a bottle of vinegar waved a toothpick in his face. Evil foods had surrounded Edward and were circling around him like a hurricane. It was very clear now that the desserts were in way over their heads. Adrienne ordered the dragon to sweep over Tiriaq and she was able to grab him and throw him on Saibou's back. With a point of her finger, she was able to get the dragon to land right beside Edward. When Edward saw the dragon, he almost tripped over his own feet.

Adrienne would have laughed except for the fact that she was in battle now. She asked the dragon to shrink and reside in her shell and it obeyed and nestled into the shell. Now, Edward, Adrienne, and Tiriaq were

Part 2: Adrienne

all backed up into a circle surrounded by what felt like millions of evil dinner and breakfast foods.

The extraterrestrial eggs, Evil Taco Man, Captain Burrito, Swiss S Cheese, Unruly Urnebes, the Hostile Hamburger, Malicious Malt Vinegar, The Cheese Wizard (who somehow got out), just to name a few. Many of the evil dinner foods had decided to bring kitchen knives, forks, spoons, and even chopsticks to fight with. All the bad guys were also equipped with onion bombs that would make you double over crying for hours. Then she looked into the distance, and sure enough, just as Edward had warned, the Ayomide Nimat Amani Nour were encircling the whole battle. Occasionally, when the ETM would order it, the bugs would jump in and swarm Edward until he ran far enough away. If the ETM was the one controlling the bugs, then the ETM needed to be taken out.

"Surrender stupid amigos!" boomed the ETM.

"Never!" Adrienne screamed, and grabbed a rock.

She hurled it, The ETM saw this attack coming and quickly teleported to safety. Adrienne grabbed her new peanut brittle tipped churro and charged at the new location of the taco. Her attack was met with an onslaught of hot sauce and a tornado of tacos. The scythe wasn't made to take this kind of onslaught and promptly snapped in half after a nasty collision with a flying taco. Sugar and cinnamon sprayed off the broken weapon and shards of peanut brittle went flying. When she recovered from her weapon breaking, she saw just for a split second that the ETM appeared to be throwing pies into a mass of bugs. Of course the Ayomide Nimat Amani Nour was following his command, they were being compensated for their services!

Now that she knew how the bugs were being controlled, she knew how to stop them.

"Edward, Tiriaq?"

"Yes?" the two boys responded.

"See the ETM throwing the pies? Don't let another pie touch the Ayomide Nimat Amani Nour." Adrienne ordered. Edward and Tiriaq nodded and ran to intercept the pies. As they did that, Adrienne pulled the shrunken Saibou back out and expanded it to full size. Now the mob of bugs were getting angry having not been fed a pie in over ten seconds. Edward and Tiriaq were actually adept at what she asked them to do. Then Adrienne mounted Saibou and got him to hover above the center of the agitated mass of bugs. With a well timed shout, Adrienne told Saibou to shoot a fire at the bugs. It was more than anything she could have hoped for. The jet of fire that erupted from the dragon's mouth was not only blinding and hot, but filled the air with lemon juice causing the unfortunate dinner foods below to hide from the acid raining from above. The Ayomide Nimat Amani Nour cried a sound that seemed like a cross between a ghost and a thousand dice rolling on a table. The bugs that weren't killed by the blast began to skitter away.

"Take that you bugs!" Edward shouted.

"Yeah! And dwon't even twink about coming bwack!" Tiriaq added.

Part 2: Adrienne

"Can you do that again, but this time aimed at the dinner foods?" Adrienne asked the dragon. Saibou shook his head. It appeared that the jet of fire was a once a battle move.

"That's fine," Adrienne said, "we'll just have to destroy the dinner foods another way." Adrinne landed on the ground and Saibou shrunk back up to get some rest inside Adrienne's shell. Across the battlefield, she heard Edward formulating something in his mind.

"What is it?" She asked him with her mind.

"GOSH! It's still so weird to have you read my mind!"

"Ok, but I know you're thinking something" Adrienne sliced several tacos out of the air and dodged a jet of hot sauce.

"I'm just wondering why it is that we hate the foods so much and why it is that they hate us!"

"Are you doubting their evilness!? The ETM literally bombed your school!" A golden net from Edward's cookie blaster soared over her head and landed on the Hostile Hamburger who promptly got tangled and collapsed on several eggs.

"No, no. It's just, it seems stupid that we continue to bash each other senseless. I've only been active in this century-long conflict for several days but—"

"But you're wondering if they are really evil!"

"It's just that when I watch some of these 'evil' foods. They don't seem to enjoy this anymore than we do! There's this one food, Swiss S. Cheese, he hesitates every time before he attacks someone!"

Part 2: Adrienne

Adrienne sighed and decided to do something she had never done before. With a single snap of her fingers, she concentrated on the memory. Both she and Edward experienced the memory in its full length, but only a second of time had passed by the time the experience was over:

Adrienne was on the far north of The Dessert, where there lived a tribe of macaroons and cream puffs. The ground and air were coated in layers of ice and the entire area smelled of popsicles. Rickety structures made of ice packs and empty ice cream cartons stood to function as houses. She'd been here to retrieve one thing, an artifact known as "The Plastic Cherry." It was really just a maraschino cherry but was fabled to have great powers of the unknown. This was back when she worked for King Ice of Cream as an assassin, before she realized what a monster he was. It was then that she had realized that not all desserts were good.

But, at this time, she didn't know any of that. She had a mission and she was here to complete it. She began her search, scythe in hand. She knocked on several houses to see what they knew of The Plastic Cherry, but few even knew such an item was real. Among the citizens she questioned was a small macaroon family; the mother and father kept their young child behind them as they answered Adrienne's questions. The young child seemed to be clutching a fistfull of Candy Blox, LEGO blocks made of candy.

Part 2: Adrienne

However, it wasn't long before ruckus ran rampant throughout the small town. A blinding white glow shot out from all sides and the houses were all blown over. From the glow emerged a large object: it was thick and meaty with five lengthy tendrils wiggling around. It looked like a demented claw. The UFO reached into the small town and whisked up an ice cream carton and half the population. With the object came these words. Words that still haunted Adrienne to this day:

"Honey? Have you taken out the trash yet?" Among the captured population was the macaroon family, their limbs flailing hopelessly against the grip of the large claw. Adrienne tried to save them, but the object with the sausage-like tendrils was too fast and soon disappeared from the sky. She turned around to see the wreckage of the macaroon family's house and saw that only a small child remained. From the wreckage stood the leader of The Diner, Supreme Lord Mac-N-Cheese; his Kraft cup body glimmering in the fires that had erupted around him. His notorious deeds were well known throughout the entire foodiverse and at once, Adrienne assumed that it was he who had summoned the sausage object. Supreme Lord Mac-N-Cheese laughed evil and said something about how it turned out he didn't need to do anything and his work was done.

"LIAR!" Adrienne screamed as he vanished into thin air. The small macaroon child was shaking vigorously but still holding his blocks when she bent down and asked what its name was.

Part 2: Adrienne

"Tiriaq!" The macaroon replied. Adrienne tried to calm the child down to no avail and soon arranged a creampuff couple to take care of the child and she left the town and went to report back to King Ice of Cream.

Edward gasped as the memory faded from his mind,

"I've heard of the dessert disappearances, but I've never seen one in person! That claw that stole Tiriaq's parents, that must be the same one that took Jelly Jim! It's the cause of all the "Missing Food" posters around The Dessert. And that evil food! That Supreme Lord Mac-N-Cheese orphaned Tiriaq!"

"I told you!" Adrienne retorted inside of her mind as she knocked the ETM unconscious with the butt of her churro spear. Parthenope quickly took his place in engaging the fortune cookie in combat. Their conversation ended there as both of them were suddenly attacked by the dinner foods who had abruptly gained new bravado.

"For the missing desserts you captured!" Adrienne heard Edward shout as he fought back valiantly, firing as many nonlethal projectiles out of his cookie blaster as he could.

"No! You disgusting desserts are the cause for the missing food cases back on the Diner!" Captain Burrito sneered at Edward, slapping him with a corner of his vampire cape.

Part 2: Adrienne

"N-wo! That's wong!" Tiriaq argued back, "I was there when Supweme Lord Mac-N-Cheese kidnapped my entire famiwy!"

"Arggg! He did no such thing!" the Pizza Pirate jumped into the argument, "He was only there to set the town on fire as revenge for the kidnappings you desserts did!" Adrienne was so distracted by the conversation that Parthenope was able to gain the upperhand and shove her down.

Her sister raised her arms up, preparing to fire a fatal blast at Adrienne's head, who raised her hand to defend herself when a large tortilla chip impaled Parthenope. Parthenope looked down just before she met her demise. She slipped off of the blade and fell to the ground dead.

Behind her stood Ginny Gelato. "Turns out the basement of the asylum is super cold. When I melted, I fell through a vent in the ground and was able to refreeze down there. Sorry it took me so long to get out."

Adrienne jumped up and hugged her. She heard a cracking sound. Parthenope the fortune cookie had cracked open. A slip of paper was there.

"Holy crêpe," Adrienne said looking at her sister's corpse, "she's really dead this time."

"I'm sorry," Ginny said, placing an arm around Adrienne, "I know she was your sister."

"That's ok, we never really got along. She first tried to kill me when I was four years old and she was seven... ah, those were the days."

Part 2: Adrienne

Ginny looked at Adrienne, concerned,"I'm not sure those *were* the days. It sounds like you have some really severe childhood memories you should deal with."

"Shush! I'm having a moment!" Adrienne retorted, "Besides, I did deal with it! I became a master of Vishu and took up jujitsu!"

"Whatever you say..." Ginny shrugged, although Adrienne heard her mumble under her breath something about therapy.

Adrienne turned the ground behind her and willed a hole to dig itself in the ground. She then leveitated her sister into the air and placed her in the grave. Soon, with the fortune cookie buried in the ground, Adrienne placed the fortune that once rested inside her sister as a gravestone. Together the group read the fortune out loud:

Take a rest, you deserve it.
LEARN CHINESE: - betrayal/turncoat
變 (biàn) 節 (jié)

"Yeah, we do deserve a rest, don't we?" Ginny said.

"Oh yes." an evil voice behind them said, "How do you feel about a permanent one?"

Ginny and Edward turned to face the thug who threatened them. The Cheese Wizard stood behind them with all the dinner foods surrounding them along with a few guards—one who looked very familiar. The Cheese Wizard laughed as Adrienne realized that the

Part 2: Adrienne

dinner foods had defeated Edward and Triaq, both who lay knocked out on the ground.

Ginny noticed one of the burrito guards and pointed an accusing finger at him, "Hey! You killed me like, twenty minutes ago!"

The burrito guard cowered in fear and muttered something that sounded like, "Dang it, she remembered."

The Cheese Wizard menacingly pulled out a breadstick sword and swung it. Adrienne grabbed a toothpick out of a burrito guard's hand and stabbed the Cheese Wizard with its peanut brittle point. He screamed and held the place where there was now a tunnel through his chest. Cheese oozed out but soon stopped because the tunnel was now filled with string cheese. The rest of the foods charged them. Ginny screamed in rage, snatched the breadstick bat from the guard that killed her, and swung at his head. It was all slow motion.

The guard's head disconnected from his body, and beans, onions, and cheese flew out. His contents spilled out and now he was just a deflated tortilla. She used the breadstick as a lance and charged the other guard who had dropped his weapon and ran. Ginny was faster than him, though. He got impaled and deflated himself. But, the two of them were no match for the remaining enemies.

"I have an idea," Ginny said. "Adrienne, give me Saibou." Adrienne bit her tongue, and hesitantly, she pulled the dragon out of her shell.

Part 2: Adrienne

"Give me the vile, whoever you are," Ginny demanded to Edward, but soon realized he was still passed out and pulled a capsule out of his pocket. Ginny then, in one swift motion, dumped the contents of the capsule, two shrunken down dragons, onto Saibou's head. The lemon drop dragon glowed a brilliant bright light and the onslaught of dinner foods stopped in their tracks. Adrienne averted her eyes and when she could look there was a three-headed dragon sitting in front of her; part lemon drop, part gingersnap, and part chocolate.

Adrienne gasped. The dragon was utterly beautiful, topped with sleek, sliced almond scales. The three heads nuzzled against each other, clearly something had separated the being together and it was a great joy to see them reunited. All together, not including the chocolate chip topped lemonheads that served as spikes on its back, the dragon was ten feet tall sitting down. The lemon drop head roared, shooting a jet of golden fire from its mouth. Adrienne always knew what to do instantly.

"Get on!" She yelled, grabbing a passed out Edward and throwing him onto the back of the dragon. Ginny followed suit and clambered up and grabbed a spike on its back.

"Wait!" Adrienne cried, "Where's Tiriaq?" She turned around and saw him lying face down about to be trampled by the Hostile Hamburger. The dragon saw this quickly and snatched the macaroon child from the ground.

Part 2: Adrienne

The Cheese Wizard stood with his jaw hanging down to the ground. "It's the dreaded Saibou! All hope is lost!!!"

The Saibou produced a jet of white fire, melting the Cheese Wizard, a now screaming puddle of yellow goop, on the ground. The Saibou went airborne, leaving the angry mass of dinner foods behind.

"Wahoo!" Ginny whooped. "Never thought I'd be doing this!"

"I didn't either!" Edward, who just woke up, shouted through the prevailing winds.

Adrienne wondered aloud, "Can I still call the dragons Meliton and Lilith?"

"No, please do not refer to us that way again. We are the Saibou now. In fact, even separately, all of our names were Saibou," the Saibou calmly said. Adrienne shivered. Saibou's voice was so calm but very powerful. It sounded very wise.

"We need to travel back to the land of desserts!" Edward said, "We need to regroup."

"Agreed, Edward Chip, resident of Sugarcane." The Saibou responded, "We will take you there." Adrienne was very tired from the day's events and after Saibou finished speaking, she promptly fell asleep. Her last thought as she closed her eyes was that after saving everyone from that giant battle, they should all trust her a lot. And that was very good.

Part 2: Adrienne

Being a fortune cookie meant that Adrienne had fortune telling magic in her DNA. It was this magic that also allowed her to perform Vishnu at the expert level that she did. And when she looked out at her surroundings, she knew this wasn't a normal dream:

The ground was a strange green and consisted of little blades of some sort of vegetation. Giant birds made of something other than food soared through the skies. Then all around her, foods, dessert and dinner alike, were dying left and right. Several were snatched up by birds while others met their demise on the soles of many large and stinky feet. Then the scenery changed. Five spices walked out of a large brown door and gave Cassie Cake several deep bows as they sang in perfect harmony,

"Welcome to The Crumb." Supreme Lord Mac-N-Cheese burst through a white void inside of a giant robot suit. Derek and Edward ran from a giant monster that roared a menacing "Mew!"

Then a large sausage looking claw plucked a banana off the ground right in front of her and Adrienne could see what looked like short hairs on the claw. Adrienne shrieked and looked to defend Tiriaq. The banana was now falling and met its doom. The fruit was smashed to the floor, its head collapsing under its body as one large banana pancake. A booming voice shouted,

"Honey, have you taken out the trash yet?" and Adrienne screamed in her dream.

As always, the dream ended with an aphorism:

Part 2: Adrienne

NOT EVERYTHING IS AS IT SEEMS

YOUR LUCKY NUMBERS ARE: *14, 210, 16, 6979, 2*

Adrienne woke up in a daze and found herself sitting in the living room of some random house.

"Morning you!" a girl cookie said, "I'm Chipette!"

"Chipette, don't harass Adrienne, she just woke up!" Another cookie said. Adrienne immediately jumped to her feet and pointed her nearby scythe at her apparent captors, "How do you know who I am?" she questioned accusingly.

"Edward told us!" Chipette spoke happily, "Is it true that you found the Saibou!!!" Adrienne was confused,

"You mean the Saibou isn't here?"

"Nope, Ginny took them and went to go save Derek and Cassie," Edward replied, appearing from behind a doorway.

"I've been practicing my abilities," Edward said, "conjuring fireballs is just one of the skills I have mastered in the three days you were asleep." He waved hands around wildly, like a blind food swatting flies. Then, after spinning around three times, he managed to summon a large fireball and the house erupted in flames.

"I don't even want to know what else you learned while I was asleep."

Part 2: Adrienne

"Another thing I know is shapeshifting." He turned into the Cheese Wizard with a sharp **CRACK!!!!** and then back again. Adrienne thought it was pretty amazing, but she wasn't about to admit that she couldn't do that herself.

"What else have you learned???" She asked, trying to keep the awe out of her voice.

"Well just to name a few, super jumping, glowing, and making banana splits!" Edward said cheerfully.

"How will making banana splits help us, Edward?" Adrienne asked.

"In case we get hungry in battle, duh!"

Adrienne sighed. Chipette was very excited to have Adrienne. She emerged from the flames surrounding the cooking area holding a waffle smothered with syrup, the butter barely visible, and to top it off Chipette dramatically dumped a bag of gummy bears on the top. Out came the whipped cream. Forming a nice spiral, Chipette tossed the now empty can behind her. She took a big canister of sprinkles and went crazy. Then she poured a glass of fondue and brought it over to Adrienne.

"Here's your breakfast, cool lady!" Chipette squealed.

"Thank you sweetie, but I'm not hungry. I'll—"

She was interrupted when Chipette shoved a piece of waffle into her mouth. "Eat up!" She tried to breathe in between bites, but then the next piece came. Adrienne had had enough.

Part 2: Adrienne

She spat out the waffle resentfully, "**HashO Anura!**"

Chipette shrieked as her arms and legs turned into frog limbs. Her eyes got big and buggy, and she turned into a pure chocolate frog. Adrienne walked out of the room and closed the door. Chipette tried to open the door. Thankfully, it was locked from the outside.

"Clauditis premintibus!" The door clicked. She tried to shout but there was only a croak. Then Edward came down the hall with a banana split and gave it to Adrienne.

She wolfed it down. "That's a lot better than Chipette's waffles," she said.

Edward looked around, "Where did Chipette go anyways?"

"Oh, nowhere, she probably went to the store or something." Adrienne shifted in her chair uncomfortably.

"She shouldn't have." Edward said with a frown, "I'll call her cell phone." Adrienne watched as Edward pulled out his cookie blaster and shapeshifted it into a cookie case. Soon a faint *RING RING!!!* could be heard from the other side of the door along with many croaks.

Edward glared at Adrienne and opened the door. Once he saw the frog he quickly changed it back to Chipette. He faced Adrienne and turned into Supreme Lord Mac 'N Cheese. With an evil laugh, he said, "I'LL BE WATCHING YOU!!!!!!" and lunged at Adrienne…

Part 2: Adrienne

Adrienne woke up for real this time, trembling, still trying to shake off the nightmare. As she lay with her eyes closed she overheard some desserts talking.

"Are you sure we can trust her?" a voice asked.

"Yes I'm sure." Edward said.

"And she just, like, popped in your head and gave you magic?" a different voice asked

"Yes!" Edward said again.

"Then she randomly shows up at the burrito ship and tries to kill you. Right?"

"Yes. I mean no!" Edward sounded exasperated, "It wasn't like that, I promise."

"I don't know. Seems, like, kinda sketchy." Then the voices fell silent and Adrienne figured that they knew she was awake now so she sat up and opened her eyes, trying not to feel offended by the conversation she just overheard. It would just be more foods to get to trust her. Who knew this would be so much work?

When she looked around, she found herself sitting in the living room of some random house.

"Morning, you!" a girl cookie said, "I'm Chipette!"

"Chipette, don't harass Adrienne, she just woke up!" Another cookie said. Adrienne gasped and fell out of the chair she was sitting in, "Are you alright???!" Edward asked, appearing from behind a doorway.

"Yes," she replied, "just a little bit of Déjà vu." She paused. "You're Chipette," pointing a finger at the girl cookie in the room.

"Hi!" Chipette spoke happily. "Is it true that you found the Saibou!!!"

Part 2: Adrienne

Adrienne was confused "You mean the Saibou isn't here?"

"Nope, they went with Ginny to go save Derek and Cassie," Edward said, however, Adrienne said it at the same time as him. Edward frowned. Adrienne looked down for her scythe and realized it wasn't there, she had forgotten that she lost it. Adrienne noticed another cookie standing in the kitchen that seemed to be glaring at her.

"Whose that?" Adrienne asked, pointing to the cookie.

"Oh that's just Sugar Cookie my other sister. Don't mind her, she's in one of her moods." Sugar Cookie rolled her eyes and stormed away.

"So, I've been practicing my abilities in the three days you were asleep," Edward explained, trying to change the subject, "so far conjuring fireballs is just one of the skills I have mastered in the three days you were asleep." Again, Adrienne reflexly spoke the same words in sync with Edward. Then Edward said, "Here, watch this." He waved hands around wildly, like a blind food swatting flies. Then, after spinning around three times, he managed to summon a tiny fireball, no larger than a jelly bean. It was a very pitiful attempt really, but Edward was proud of himself and she didn't want to burst his bubble.

"What else have you learned???" She asked, trying to keep her amusement out of her voice.

"Well, so far just making banana splits!" Edward said cheerfully.

Part 2: Adrienne

"How long was I asleep?" Adrienne murmured, not bothering to ask how banana splits would be helpful (she had a feeling she already knew the answer).

"Three days. I already told you!"

"Geez, ok, chill!" Adrienne rolled her eyes, annoyed.

"Sorry, I'm tired and irritable. I was up for a while and didn't get much sleep."

"Oh sorry. Didn't know."

"Don't apologize— my fault."

A large static filled the air and a giant voice was heard outside, and the gang ran outside to gawk at the sky

"Ingredients Ascertained. Target's located. Consequences pending in 3, 2, 1." . A robot suit made entirely of dried noodles descended from the burrito ship.

"This again!?" Sugar Cookie gasped at the mention of the Ingredient Ascertainer. Adrienne had forgotten all about the warning, apparently so had Edward.

"Ingredient Ascertainer?" Edward asked.

"An Ingredient Ascertainer scans your genetics; each dessert is unique in the retrospect that they are made of varying amounts of different ingredients. The ascertained marks your unique genetics and uses it to track you down later. The burrito ship must have a sensor targeted at The Dessert searching for us," Adrienne explained. A giant aluminum foil hand reached for the group of desserts. Sugar Cookie managed to pull everyone, except Adrienne out of the way. The claw tried to adjust for this sudden motion and ended up ripping the shortbread roof off of Edward's house.

"Surrender Edward Chip, and nobody gets hurt," the voice from earlier spoke from inside the noodle mech. Tiriaq appeared next to Chipette having pulled out an old cannon from the closet and lit the fuse. The two children let out a loud battle cry as the cannon fired. It hit the burrito mech's power source on its chest, and it fell backward into the Churro park. The churro children screamed at the top of their lungs as the enormous mech started falling on top of them.

"THOSE CHILDREN ARE GONNA GET CRUSHED" Adrienne screamed. She dashed out of the house and summoned all her strength. She caught the mech just in time. Adrienne screamed as her arms burned from carrying the weight of the heavy robot. Suddenly the weight lessened. Adrienne glanced over to see Edward next to her, chocolate pouring down his face. Just as quickly as it lessened, the weight suddenly became too much for both of them.

"Ha! I really did plan for everything!" The dictator from the cockpit laughed. "My meatloaf magnets will rip all your homes out of the ground and you will be crushed under the weight of your own town!" A deafening BOOM! sounded off and the mech was blown to smithereens.

From the wreckage, Tiriaq and Chipette could be seen dancing around their cannon with an astounded Sugar Cookie behind them taking a video on her phone.

Part 2: Adrienne

"Play nicely, kids!" a voice came from inside Edwards' now wrecked house.

"Aw, man!" Edward cried, "My mom's gonna kill me!"

"Why?" asked Tiriaq

"Because we just paid off that house!"

"Why?"

"So we don't have to pay the mortgage anymore!"

"Why?"

"I'm just a middle schooler! I don't know how the world works!"

"Why?" Tiriaq was starting to get on Edward's nerves.

"Wait, I'm lost." Adrienne interjected, "what is going on?"

"MY HOUSE!" Edward's mom (also known as Mrs. Chip) screamed, "AND I JUST PAID IT OFF!!! **EDWARD!!! IF MY HOUSE IS DESTROYED AGAIN I WILL GET THE HUMANS TO COME FOR YOU!**"

"Gosh! She always uses that fairy tale to try and scare me into behaving," Edward sighed.

"OOOh, I gwet it now!" Tiriaq exclaimed.

Adrienne quickly thought up a spell and waved her hands. The rubble of the house began to fly into the air and put itself back together. Edward winced as his mom continued to protest. Adrienne also couldn't help but notice that Mrs. Chip seemed to be talking a lot louder now.

Edward groaned, "I might as well start writing my will. Tiriaq, do you want my Super Chip action

Part 2: Adrienne

figures? Adrienne can have my tiramisu teddy bear. Derek, promise you'll pass down my favorite book and read *The Prophecy of The Last Course* ever so often. The book even has the original Human fairy tale." Adrienne tapped on her friend's head, causing him to look at his house.

The squeals of Mrs. Chip could be heard, "Oh thank goodness! For a second there I really thought—"

She was cut off when the voice sounded above them, "Thank goodness I only had a hologram of myself in that mech! Allow me to introduce myself, I am Supreme Lord Mac-N-Cheese, the food behind the brainwashing of the SCL. Now, you children are a nuisance to my plan for foodiverse domination and have been proven to be really hard to catch. So, I figured I'd just do it myself." With that, a tortilla crashed into the house and wrapped its coarse bread around her. Adrienne looked up and realized a bowl-shaped spacecraft had emerged from the clouds.

"I thought you could be reasonable!" Boomed the loud voice of Supreme Lord Mac-N-Cheese from inside the spacecraft, "It looks like you need more incentive!"

"To do what?" Adrienne cried.

"Wait just one second," Supreme Lord Mac-N-Cheese muttered, "I appear to have lost the cue card for that question." Adrienne and her friends stared blankly, wondering what was happening.

"You guys still there?" the ever loud voice of Supreme Lord Mac-N-Cheese, "All right, let me start over." The tortilla containing Edward's mom lowered from the sky and placed the bewildered cookie back inside the wreckage of the house.

"Ok, I got this," Supreme Lord Mac-N-Cheese continued, "COME TO THE CAPITAL OF FOOD LAND WHERE WE CAN DISCUSS YOUR EVIL DEEDS!"

"Our evil deeds!" Adrienne scoffed. "You're the one kidnapping and destroying our town!"

"I THOUGHT YOU COULD BE REASONABLE!" Boomed the loud voice of Supreme Lord Mac-N-Cheese. "IT LOOKS LIKE YOU NEED MORE INCENTIVE!" The tortilla still hovering in the sky proceeded to drop back onto Edward's mom. Edward's mom looked up and tried to swat at the tortilla but missed and ended up running away screaming.

"Wait! Wait!" Chipette added, confused. "Didn't you just say that, Mr. Cheese?"

"Umm, no. Totally not. You heard nothing at all!!!" an irritated Supreme Lord Mac-N-Cheese added, "And it's Supreme Lord Mac-N-Cheese! Not Mr. Cheese! You have to say the whole thing!"

"Yes I know that!" teased Chipette, "We went over this after you captured me and Sugar Cookie during the first burrito invasion."

"So that's what you guys were doing there!" Edward mused.

"OH SHUT UP ALREADY AND STOP BULLYING ME!" Supreme Lord Mac-N-Cheese screamed through the speaker.

"But Mr. Cheese!" Chipette protested

Part 2: Adrienne

"IT'S SUPREME LORD MAC-N-CHEESE, YOU IDIOT DESSERT! IS YOUR BRAIN CRUMBLING?" the enraged lord continued to scream.

Chipette pulled a baseball out of her dough and hurled it at the speaker, breaking it while yelling, "Thanks for letting me distract you!"

Adrienne bewilderedly looked around and was shocked to see Sugar Cookie sitting on top of the tortilla that once encased Edward's mom, typing away on her phone.

"Sugar Cookie! Get off of there! You're going to get hurt!" Adrienne cried

"Like, oh my Gourd shut up! I'm, like, using this, like, food tech to hack into the dinner food's security system. So, like, chill."

"WHOA! You talk?" Chipette, Edward, Tiriaq, and Adrienne all said at the same time.

"Yeah, you haven't said much the whole story!" Chipette added

"Speak for yourself, Little Sis." Sugar Cookie replied, "Let me and Chipette explain what Chipette and I were doing while you guys were off defeating the Burrito Bison, ETM and others..."

Part 3: Sugar Cookie

SEVERAL DAYS EARLIER:

It was a dry, dreary day as the sun beat down on the sidewalk of the town Sugarcane. Sugar Cookie was on her way to Brownie High. Sugar Cookie didn't know what it was, but she felt tension in the air. Something big was going to happen. She had just finished walking Chipette and Edward to school, their mom didn't trust Edward and Chipette to find their way to school without getting distracted and/or lost. But now that she had rid herself of siblings, she could finally begin thinking about all the projects she had to do for today. That was until her best and only friend Tammy Tart showed up and started gossiping in her ear.

"Ok, you'll never believe this!" Tammy started, "so, Bubble Gum Bobby took Jelly Bean Jill out for a date and then the two ran into Bobby's ex, Jello Julie, who of course hated seeing Bobby out with another dessert that wasn't her. So then, when Bobby and Jill went to the movies the following day, Julie found one of Jill's ex boyfriends, Bob the Bread, to stalk them into the movies, of course Bobby wasn't too happy about this and became super agitated throughout the entire movie. This led to mounting social tension which ended up with Bobby punching Bob in the face for trying to kiss Jill. But, it turns out that Bob and Julie were secretly

Part 3: Sugar Cookie

dating this entire time, so when Bob got punched, Julie, who had been watching the whole thing from afar, went completely ballistic on Jill and Bobby. Jill got thrown into a popcorn machine, breaking it (the parents of those sprouting kernels were not happy), Bob and Bobby tackled each other down a flight of stairs, and Julie tried to stuff an entire roll of movie tickets that were printed on Fruit-roll-ups into Jill's mouth.

"That scuffle resulted in all four of them being banned from the movie theater for life. And the cherry on top is that Jill decided that she didn't like seeing the violent side of Bobby and broke up with him. Bob also decided that he didn't like the crazy side of Juile and broke up with her, too." Tammy was gasping by the time she finished her story as she had not taken one breath throughout the entire thing. Sugar Cookie just looked at her friend with great concern.

"Why and how do you know all this?" She asked.

"You got to stay in the loop with all the texting chains!" Tammy explained, "Susan Softserve told Ronda Rolo who told Carly Crumble who told-"

"All right I, like, get it," Sugar Cookie said, "we are like, almost at school anyways." When Sugar Cookie and Tammy arrived at the school entrance, they could tell something strange was going on. Everyone seemed to be very somber and quiet. The lively chatter of highschoolers that normally filled the school's chocolate hallways was abnormally absent.

"Tammy," Sugar Cookie said, "do you, like, know what's happening?"

"No, I'm just as clueless as you are!"

93

Part 3: Sugar Cookie

"Excuse me students," the loudspeaker boomed as their principal came on the loudspeaker, "as many of you know, the middle and elementary schools in our school district were victims of terrible attacks from a race of foods from the planet, Diner. Exploding tacos have been reported destroying the schools. Now I don't mean to cause panic, but it is rumored this is only phase one of a large-scale attack on dessert-kind. As of right now our school is on lockdown. Please stay calm and whatever you do, don't run around screaming and waving your hands in the air like maniacs."

With that, the loudspeaker clicked off and simultaneously, as if on cue, the electrical circuits fried and all the lights in the building flickered off. All the students completely freaked out. They started running around screaming at the top of their lungs waving their arms and hands in the air. It was complete chaos, Sugar Cookie couldn't move for fear of being trampled and the sounds of hundreds of screaming desserts echoing throughout the halls was deafening.

"I have to get out of here!" Sugar Cookie shouted to Tammy.

"WHAT?!" Tammy asked, "WHY?!"

"I NEED TO CHECK ON MY SIBLINGS, I DROPPED THEM OFF AT SCHOOL AND I NEED TO MAKE SURE THEY AREN'T DEAD!" Tammy nodded to this response and told Sugar Cookie that she had a plan to help her through the crowd of panicked students and get out of the school building. Tammy proceeded to hoist herself into a table near the entrance of the room and shouted, "I HAVE SOME JUICY GOSSIP! BUT YOU CAN ONLY HEAR

Part 3: Sugar Cookie

IT IF YOU SHUT UP!!!" At once, all the desserts fell silent, even the teachers.

"Now," Tammy said, walking away from the entrance of the school, everyone's eyes following her, "so, Bubble Gum Bobby took Jelly Bean Jill out for a date and then the two ran into Bobby's ex..." Everyone was so enthralled by Tammy's "juicy" gossip, Sugar Cookie swore that she heard many of the teachers gasp when they heard that Bobby and Jill ran into Bobby's ex.

With the crowd's attention solely on Tammy, Sugar Cookie was able to sneak out unnoticed by everyone except Tammy, who winked at her as she left. As soon as Sugar Cookie made it out of the building, she sprinted back to Chipette's school, Lil'Sweets Elementary School. She arrived there within minutes as Chipette and Sugar Cookie went to school only a few blocks away.

The elementary school was in terrible shape, half of the windows had been shattered and the entire north side of the building was peppered with holes and the playground was riddled with exploded tacos and taco fillings. Sugar Cookie spotted Chipette boarding up the holes in the walls. Sugar Cookie smiled, Chipette had always been good working with her hands and fixing and building things.

"Chipette!" Sugar Cookie shouted, as she ran over to her sister, "are you, like, ok?"

"Yeah! Just trying to secure this school, we got attacked! It was the most exciting thing to ever happen at school!" Chipette said enthusiastically. Sugar Cookie then sought out Chipette's teacher, Mrs. Maple, and asked to take her sister home. Mrs. Maple was more than happy to let Chipette go with her. as the Mrs. Maple was swamped taking care of the other children and answering calls from worried parents.

Sugar Cookie and her sister then proceeded to Edward's school, Dessert Middle School. When they got there, very out of breath, (it had been years since they had both had ever run) Sugar Cookie saw to her dismay that the entire building had been reduced to just piles of crumbs and Edward was nowhere to be found.

Chipette noticed some footprints leading up to the French Toast Forest but the trail was soon lost as two other sets of footprints covered up the original set of footprints after a few yards. Several shrieks suddenly sounded behind Sugar Cookie and Chipette. They spun around and saw a group of desserts trying to get out of the doors of a nearby store, Sweets-R-Us.

"Let us out!" an elderly couple shouted at Sugar Cookie through the windows, "the windows are too thick and the doors are jammed" Sugar Cookie and Chipette ran up to the front doors of the store and sure enough, the doors were sealed shut with super sticky strawberry flavored jam. Inside, several desserts waved around frantically, a bundt cake seemed to be bossing everyone around.

"Amigos!" a voice said, "welcome, I hope you're not trying to break these civilians out! Because I am on a mission today. First, I successfully infiltrated the SCL twice! (Only both times it turned out to be the wrong building and I destroyed some schools by accident.) This is exactly what my dead wife warned me about. That I would get sloppy and mess up like this. Hopefully I can successfully hold these several desserts hostage in their own supermarket! Then I shall be redeemed!" Sugar Cookie looked up to the direction of the voice and saw a taco with a very weirdly well groomed mustache. The taco disappeared in a flash of shredded cheese and reappeared seconds later behind the old couple that was trying to escape the store. The Evil Taco Man began to throw explosive tacos around the store, causing panic among the twenty or so shoppers trapped inside.

"We need to get inside that store!" Chipette said as she watched in horror.

"First we need to remove the jam as much as we can, and quickly!" Sugar Cookie responded. The two girls quickly searched the surrounding area for something, anything to scrape the jam off. Sugar Cookie spotted a lone Peanut Brittle walking down the street and ran over to it.

"Sir or ma'am," Sugar Cookie said, "We need your help, there are innocent desserts trapped in that store! Do you think you could help us scrape the Jam that is sealing the door shut?"

Luckily, the Peanut Brittle agreed after correcting Sugar Cookie on its pronouns (they/them) and used its triangle shaped hand to remove the sticky jam with ease. Once the door was free, Sugar Cookie tried to open the door but it still budged shut.

"I don't understand, all the Jam is gone!" Sugar Cookie said.

"Dum Dums," the Peanut Brittle said, pointing to a keypad hanging on the wall next to a poster with a

missing lollipop on it, "it's password locked. Now you'll
have to type in the right code."

"Can you help us do that?" Chipette said.

"Nope, I'm out of here!" With that, the Peanut
Brittle ran off.

"What the heck will we do now!?" Chipette
asked. Another explosive taco went off inside the store.

"I have an idea," Sugar Cookie said, "I once took
a hacking class at school, it was one of those
unauthorized after school activities you always hear
about."

"I've never heard of that," Chipette eyed Sugar
Cookie skeptically. Sugar Cookie took out her phone and
opened an app she had downloaded that opened up a
code input screen. She then started furiously typing in
code.

"It should be about... done!" Sugar Cookie said,
and her phone dinged with the "Code Complete"
screen. She then pulled a wire out of her pocket and
connected it to the keypad. The keypad made a whirring
sound and then the lock clicked open. Success! Sugar
Cookie and Chipette pried the doors open setting the
trapped and exasperated desserts free.

"Couldn't you have hacked faster!" the snotty
bundt cake named Karen said, "I'm speaking to the
manager of your hacking company!" Chipette tired to
tell the bundt cake that they didn't work for a hacking
company but Sugar Cookie shushed her saying,

"There is no arguing with a Karen."

Part 3: Sugar Cookie

"Excuse me sonny," an old dessert said, holding his wife, "are you really going to take on that taco invader by yourself?"

"Yes we are Mr..." Chipette said, then trailed off as she didn't know his name.

"Madeira," the Dessert's wife said, "Mr. and Mrs. Madeira."

"You can't possibly defeat that Mexican food all by yourselves!" Mr. Madeira said, "we will help you. Right hon?" Mrs. Madeira turned to her husband who nodded in return.

"We can't possibly ask you to do something like that!" Sugar Cookie said, "You should get out of here while you still can!"

"We are staying and that is final," Mr. Madeira stated firmly.

Chipette tried to retort back but was cut off by an exploding taco, which flew in between the conversation and promptly exploded behind Sugar Cookie.

"Enough of this chatter, *amigos*," the ETM said (Sugar Cookie decided to call this Evil Taco Man the ETM for short).

"What are you going to do?" Chipette said, "It's four of you against one of you." Chipette and Sugar Cookie nodded to each other, and together they changed the ETM. Right before the two sisters impacted the ETM, he disappeared into a cloud of shredded cheese and reappeared behind them.

"HA HA HA!" the ETM gloated, "you'll never be able to catch me! I can teleport! Suckers!" Chipette was

about to charge the ETM again, but Sugar Cookie
stopped her for Mr. and Mrs. Madeira were already
there, punching the ETM in his self-righteous shell.

The ETM teleported several feet away and
collapsed on the ground, the wind knocked out of him.
Mr. and Mrs. Madeira high fived each other. Chipette
looked around and began to construct a small cage
(made of various granola bar pipes she had borrowed
from toilets in the bathroom) around the ETM.

"I hope no one needs to use the bathroom,"
Chipette told her sister, "there'd be nowhere to flush!"
Chipette finished her cage within two seconds, but she
wasn't fast enough; when she looked at her handy work,
the ETM was gone.

"You didn't think it would be that easy to catch
me, amigo!" The ETM laughed and revealed himself to
be standing just outside the cage.

"What the-" Chipette said.

"Witchcraft!" Mr. and Mrs. Madeira shouted.

"How did you make yourself invisible!?" Sugar
Cookie asked.

"A magician never reveals his secrets!" the ETM
said, "just kidding! I have an invisibility cloak!"

"Everyone!" Sugar Cookie said, "We need to get
to that cloak!"

"Not so fast!" the ETM said as he vanished in
plain sight.

"Let me take care of this," Mr. Madeira said,
rolling up his sleeves, "I've dealt with twenty children
and all of their grandchildren! There isn't a trick this evil
food can pull on me and my wife!" The old married

Part 3: Sugar Cookie

couple both closed their eyes and meditated for a couple seconds, then synchronously, they moved into a corner of the room and grabbed a space in midair. They both pulled and revealed the ETM, cowering in the corner, Mr. and Mrs. Madeira holding the invisibility cloak.

"ARGH!" the ETM shouted, "how did you find me?"

"Our family is from a line of Professional Hide and Seek champions," Mrs. Madeira explained, "that's why everyone knows who we are. Unfortunately, the game of Professional Hide and Seek was banned after a group of players went missing in the middle of an IKEA and were never found again."

"Also the twenty children thing..." Mr. Madeira mumbled under his breath.

"Well," the ETM said, "you may have defeated me this time, amigos! But I will be back!"

"What do you mean?" Chipette said, "we have you apprehended!" The ETM just smiled and teleported away, but not before he grabbed his invisibility cloak. And then, he was gone.

"Well," Chipette said, "that was eventful."

"It sure was!" Mrs. Madeira agreed. "I think my husband and I should go home and rest."

"Yes," Mr. Madeira agreed, "I may have thrown out my back!" Sugar Cookie and Chipette agreed to help the biscotti to the nearest oven to rebake and as soon as he was situated, then they go and find Edward. When they arrived at the hospital the new station was playing and Sugar Cookie noticed Reily Rolo the reporter say,

"...and this 'Evil Taco Man' was supposedly captured by a group of middle schoolers." A brief picture of Derek, Cassie and Edward's school pictures were shown on the screen, "...now pie police and questioning the popsicle police about the failed detaining of the ETM. Stay tuned for more details."

"Oh, so Edward's, like, fine." Sugar Cookie said.

"Of course he gets all the credit for this," Chipette scoffed, "I bet they even gave him a cookie blaster for his deeds."

While they were heading back home, they passed a mess of Popsicle Police in the Pastry Plains all talking about how they had let the ETM escape literally two seconds after a Edward and his friends helped the police catch him.

"This police branch is terrible!" A pie dressed in a police uniform was telling the Popsicle Police chief. "The highly secret government officials at SCL labs are ordering a full disbanding of the Popsicle Police and they are to be replaced with the Pie Police!" Several Popsicles nearby started to cry.

"I still can't believe Edward caught the ETM," Chipette said.

"Me neither TBH," Sugar Cookie said.

"TBH?" Chipette asked.

"To be honest."

"Ohhhhhhh. Ok. That makes sense."

Part 3: Sugar Cookie

Sugar Cookie smiled at her sister, "Come on, let's head home."

"RACE YOU!" Chipette said, already sprinting away.

"OH YOU ARE SO DEAD!" Sugar Cookie shouted as she chased her sister, laughing.

Two days later, Sugar Cookie and Chipette sauntered to Sweets-R Us, their local shopping mall, with their brother Edward Chip. All was quiet despite the dramatic attack from the ETM earlier that week. Sugar Cookie had told Edward that they were going to the shopping center so she could look at dresses for an average time of four to five hours, but Chipette and she knew the real story.

They were meeting their new friends Mr. and Mrs Madeira to discuss how the rebuilding of the damaged school buildings and mall were going. (Sweets-R Us was the old couple's favorite place to go despite being ten miles away from their house). As Sugar Cookie walked with her siblings she listened to Tammy's latest "juicy" gossip over her phone.

"... so then, Bubble Gum Bobby told Jelly Bean Jill, 'it's over Jill, I'm in love with someone else' and Jill was like, 'HOW COULD YOU DO THIS TO ME!' and Bobby, get this, Bobby says, 'I never loved you,' and Jill goes, 'what about all of our history together! We make such a great couple!' and Bobby says, 'Made, Jill, we *made* a great couple. But I just don't see us going anywhere! We don't have a future together, at least not one I want to be part of.' At this point, Jill is flat out crying, then sobbing she asks, 'So who are you in love with?' Bobby pauses and says, 'I'm in love with Bob the Bread.' And Jill's all like, 'YOU'RE IN LOVE WITH MY EX!' and Bobby just was like, 'yes.' and Jill was like, 'THAT'S IT! *I'M* BREAKING UP WITH *YOU!*' so then Bobby was like-"

"Wait," Sugar Cookie said, cutting Tammy off, "I thought Bobby and Jill broke up after the movie theater scuffle!"

"Yes, that's true," Tammy said, "but they got back together like three hours later."

"This sounds like that one Soap Opera on TV I watch all the time," Sugar Cookie said, "what's it called, *Days of Our Lives*?"

"You mean, *Danish of our Lives*?"

"Yeah that one," Sugar Cookie said.

At this point they had arrived at the Sweets-R Us and Chipette had run inside the store before Edward and Sugar Cookie and had gotten a free cupcake.

She ran out eating it delightfully, when a nearby grandpa cupcake yelled at her, "Cannibal!" They finally were at the mall and Sugar Cookie told Tammy that she had to go. She and Chipette split up with Edward to "look at dresses" and headed to the spot where they were meeting Mr. and Mrs. Madeira when, before they even got inside the mall, they heard a loud BOOM and several "Missing Food" posters fell dejectedly to the ground. Edward's friend Sarah Smoothie burst out of the doors of Sweets-R Us running and screaming. One of the displays behind Sarah had flooded with burrito beans. Many shoppers who were about to go inside the store stood outside, not injured at all, but trembling vigorously.

"It's the ETM!" Chipette told Sugar Cookie in a voice barely above a whisper.

"No," Sugar Cookie said, "The ETM uses explosive tacos, not burritos. This is someone new." Beans were flooding out of what used to be the doorway of the mall, and a giant tortilla had descended from the sky and was floating above Sarah, who was still running toward him. The tortilla dropped on Sarah, curled into an impenetrable ball, embracing her and took off at least 90 miles per hour.

Sugar Cookie and her siblings could only watch in horror as the ball flew towards a giant, floating burrito shaped ship hovering over the sugar planet. A circular hatch in the bottom opened up, allowing the tortilla ball containing Sarah to enter. The hatch closed, separating Sarah from the outside world. Another torpedo looking object dropped from the back of the Burrito Ship. Edward pulled out his Cookie Blaster (Sugar Cookie wondered when Edward got a Cookie blasker but there wasn't time for that) and yelled out, "Pull your blasters out!"

The cookies pulled out their cookie blasters, including Sugar Cookie, who had earned her cookie blaster by saving some Brownie's child from falling into a skate park and getting run over by malicious teens and their murderous boards on wheels. The donuts pulled out their donut blasters, and so on. They all sprinted towards a second tortilla that was falling from the ship and knelt down abruptly so they could try firing at it to stop it from landing on Mr. and Mrs. Madeira, who had finally arrived to meet Sugar Cookie and Chipette.

Unfortunately, despite the civizens group efforts, the tortilla seemed unaffected by this attack. Seconds later, a flying tortilla ball, containing Mr. and Mrs. Madeira, soared towards the burrito ship. The desserts wondered who would be next. Everyone started to panic, there was screaming and lots of running around. A few desserts tried to rob the mall in their terror but were swiftly stopped by the newly instated Pie Police.

"Everyone!" Sugar Cookie shouted, "get to your homes and hide!!" Soon there was a mass of desserts running for their cars and other transportation, the desserts inside the mall seemed to have heard her as well as they started pouring out of the doors to the mall, wading through a mess of beans on the way. Sugar Cookie then proceeded to grab Edward and Chipette and they raced home, hoping they wouldn't get kidnapped by a flying tortilla.

The next few days no torpedoes dropped down on Dessert Planet, but desserts were still aware of sudden drops. The giant ship was still hovering in their atmosphere. Sugar Cookie was spending her lunch period with Chipette, (both of their schools happened to have lunch at the same time and Sugar Cookie couldn't eat with Tammy, her only friend because Tammy was always too busy talking to all the popular desserts and gossiping).

"I am so bored in my woodshop class," Chipette complained, "we never get to build cool things like laser cannons and gaming consoles! Instead we are forced to build useless things like clipboards and crayons made of wood!"

"Crayons made of wood?" Sugar Cookie said, "why?"

"That is what I'm talking about! Who the heck is going to want a wooden crayon! 'Here's your present! It's a crayon, but you can't draw with it. CAUSE IT'S MADE OF HECKING WOOD!' "

"Woah, Chipette," Sugar Cookie said. "Calm down, I'm sure you'll build tons of cool things in the future. Heck, maybe one day you'll fulfill your dream of fixing up a spaceship!"

Chipette looked like she wanted to say something but was interrupted by several first graders screaming. Sugar Cookie and Chipette quickly abandoned their lunches and raced over to the playground where the screaming came from. When they arrived they saw that a first grader had just fallen off the monkey bars and thought the drop was longer than it actually was. After checking in with the child, Sugar Cookie and Chipette went back to their lunches. As soon as they tried to start another conversation, more screaming was heard.

"I'm sure another kid just dropped off the monkey bars," Sugar Cookie told a worried Chipette.

Part 3: Sugar Cookie

"HELP US! A TORTILLA IS TRYING TO TAKE SUSIE SHAKE!!" Chipette and Sugar Cookie ran back over to the playground where, sure enough, a tortilla had descended from the sky and was trying to take a small kindergartener who appeared to be a Milkshake. The tortilla would have flown off with the child, but the smart child had found a tree nearby and was gripping it for dear life. Sugar Cookie ran over to the child, but was too short to reach the part of the tree trunk the child had latched her arms around.

"I can reach it," Chipette said, "just give me a boost."

"What if you get taken instead!?" Sugar Cookie asked.

"Trust me, I won't." Sugar Cookie gave Chipette the boost up. Chipette grabbed the Milkshake's torso and managed to pull it free of the tortilla and the three fell to the ground. Chipette barely had time to recover as the tortilla swooped down and attempted to grab her. Sugar Cookie threw herself over Chipette and the tortilla grabbed her instead.

"NOOOOOO!" Chipette shrieked as Sugar Cookie began to rise away from the ground. Chipette then proceeded to grab onto Sugar Cookie's leg, which was hanging out of the tortilla ball. The sisters quickly flew away from the playground.

"You are an idiot," a muffled Sugar Cookie told Chipette, "you should have escaped when you had the chance."

"I'm not leaving you," Chipette said, "plus we don't do this much anymore, it's been quite some time

Part 3: Sugar Cookie

since we were last kidnapped together. I miss these one-on-one moments with you."

Sugar Cookie grunted in response. The tortilla ball quickly ascended to the spaceship above the sugary planet and into the cotton candy cloud sky. Sugar Cookie couldn't see anything but heard the metal grinding noise as a hatch opened up to allow the tortilla ball inside the spaceship. The tortilla spilled Sugar Cookie violently onto the cold floor of the spaceship as Chipette landed softly next to her and somersaulted into a standing position.

"Ahhhh. So there's two of you this time!" a lone burrito guard holding a whip made of cooked spinach leaves walked into the room. Sugar Cookie noticed a sticker name tag on the burrito that read: **HELLO! MY NAME IS:** BRENDA.

"Stay away from us!" Sugar Cookie said, standing up.

"No," Brenda stated flatly. Sugar Cookie began to charge the burrito guard and managed to disarm her.

"BACKUP REQUESTED!" Brenda managed to shout as she tried to fend off Sugar Cookie. Twenty or so burrito guards holding various weapons marched single file into the room. Sugar Cookie saw out of the corner of her eye that Chipette's hands imminently went up in surrender.

"I can take all of these guys!" Sugar Cookie thought to herself. Unfortunately, she couldn't, and one of the guards managed to hit her on the head with its Cheeto staff, knocking her out.

Part 3: Sugar Cookie

Sugar Cookie's last thought before she fell to the ground again was, "Oh crêpe.

Part 4: Chipette

Chipette was freaking out as the burrito guards dragged her unconscious sister away. As the burrito guards advanced on her, she knew she would have to go and save her sister. This meant she couldn't get captured. Quickly, without thinking, Chipette punched one of the burritos in the face and its tortilla unwrapped, spilling its fillings out. Chipette grabbed the tortilla and wrapped herself up in it. The rest of the burritos poured into the room but didn't notice her. Chipette's disguise worked.

"Where is the intruder?!" one of the burritos asked.

"I swear Brenda, if you called us in for a fake intrusion..." another burrito said.

"I promise," the burrito who appeared to be Brenda said, "there is another cookie in our midst." Chipette slowly started backing away.

"THERE SHE IS!" a voice came from the pile of unwrapped burrito fillings, "that is the cookie!" The burrito guards turned their weapons toward Chipette and encircled her. There was no way out, the burritos had her trapped. Or so they thought.

Chipette realized she was standing on a vent, and in one fluid motion, removed the grate, jumped into the ventilation shaft, and returned the grate. As soon as Chipette's feet touched the ground, she took off running.

112

Part 4: Chipette

As she ran away, she heard one of the burritos say, "There is an imposter among us..."

Chipette crawled through the ventilation shaft unsure where she was going. All she knew was that she had to find her sister. She had been following the sounds of the burrito guards dragging Sugar Cookie on the ground above her but now, no sound was heard. She quietly sneaked over to the nearest grate and lifted it up. She then, making sure the tortilla still concealed her identity as a cookie, crawled out of the vents. She breathed in a deep breath of fresh air.

The ventilation shaft had not been comfortable. As the shaft ran throughout the ship, it changed its size, sometimes being large enough for Chipette to stand comfortably and other times being just barely large enough for her to army-crawl through. Either way, the air quaily sucked down there.

Chipette was pretty sure that the ventilation shaft vented the dusty air (created from a poorly made engine room out of the ship) away from the main control room of the ship. This created the effect that the farther Chipette got from the control room, the dustier the air got. Overall, the entire ventilation system smelled of sulfur.

Chipette looked around at her new surroundings. She appeared to have emerged from the vents into some sort of library, except instead of books on the shelves, there were small jars each with an individual sprinkle inside of it, looking sad and dejected, all alone. These sprinkles didn't appear to have faces, but Chipette could tell that they were living, for some of the sprinkles crawled around in their small cages, like the gummy worms below the soil on The Dessert.

"What is this place?" Chipette asked the nearest Sprinkle. The red sprinkle merely turned what Chipette assumed was its head and regarded her with mild interest.

"What are you doing here?" a voice said. Chipette was taken aback, she hadn't expected the Sprinkle to respond.

"What the-" Chipette said, "how can you talk?"

"With my mouth dum-dum!" Chipette realized the voice was coming from behind her and turned around. She came face to face with a burrito and almost fell over.

"What are you doing here! I don't remember any guards being stationed in Captain Burrito's personal sprinkle collection."

"Excuse me?" Chipette said. Then remembering that she was in disguise added, "oh yeah, um... I was um.. asked to watch over some particularly troublesome Sprinkles who were trying to escape." The burrito looked at her and Chipette felt him start to see through her lie.

"What is your Order Code?"

"My um... Order Code?"

"Yes, give me the six numbers of your order."

"Five..."

"Yes? Continue."

Part 4: Chipette

"six, seven, eight..."

"Go on,"

"nine... ten?"

"Are you sure that is your Order Code?"

"Yes..."

"Hmmmm, I don't see those numbers in the database. Oh I see, there are only six numbers in the order code and you gave me seven."

"No, I only gave you six!" Chipette protested.

"5-6-7-8-9-1-0," the burrito read outloud, "that's seven numbers right there."

"Ummm..." Chipette started, she was beginning to sweat under the tortilla outfit that was concealing her identity.

"Possible identity theft, we have an imposter on the loose," the burrito guard's radio crackled. The burrito's eyes widened and he reached for his radio,

"I think I've found the—" Chipette punched the burrito in the face, knocking him out, before he could say anymore.

"Hello? Barney? Is everything ok?" the voice on the radio spoke once again.

Chipette cleared her throat and deepened her voice,"Everything is fine. I thought I saw an extra sprinkle roaming the ship, but it was just a crumb."

"Roger that, and Barney? Stop using the radio unless you have something real to report!"

"Roger that," Chipette said, and then she took the radio and left the library. On her way out, she "accidentally" opened all the containers, setting all the sprinkles free.

Part 4: Chipette

"Flee! Save yourselves! Meet me under the south wing in the ventilation shaft! I'll get you off this ship." Chipette slipped out the library doors and her radio spoke:

"A cookie named Edward has blown a hole in the landing port. Casualties: four burritos were knocked out. Bring backup."

"Who is this Edward?" Chipette asked over the radio, she couldn't help herself.

"Edward Chip, the only dessert to capture the ETM." Chipette immediately redirected her course. If her brother was here then maybe he could help save Sugar Cookie. She ran through the hallways until she reached a dead end, at the left was the hole Edward had made by exploding it, to her right there was a sign that read: **CONTAINMENT ROOM ↘**.

Chipette sprinted down the staircase, and found herself in a large room full of cages containing all sorts of foods, desserts, and even drinks. Edward was already down and he seemed to be wearing some sort of armor. Her brother quickly rushed over to a cage that contained Derek Donut, Mr. and Mrs. Madeira and to Chipette's great relief, Sugar Cookie who was holding her phone, but still passed out. Chipette noticed Sugar Cookie's coding app up on her phone screen and realized Sugar Cookie must have been trying to hack her way out but was then knocked out a second time.

Then, a burrito larger than all the burritos and dressed in what appeared to be a vampire halloween costume, stormed into the room. This vampire-dressed burrito then promptly strutted up to Edward and tased him with an electric spear. Edward's now unconscious body fell to the floor and a group of regular sized burritos dragged his body into one of the cells and chained him to the wall. Chipette decided it was better to stay in the shadows for now and jumped back into the ventilation shaft through the nearest vent. She proceeded to wait for the burritos to leave but they didn't. They seemed intent on waiting for Edward to wake up.

Chipette sat down. If she knew her brother, which she did, it was going to be a long time before he woke up. So she sprinted to the south wing in the ventilation shaft and saw that the sprinkles were waiting for her there. She then proceeded to load them into a nearby spacecraft, one that Edward must have ridden here on, and set their ship's course for The Dessert. The sprinkles thanked her profusely and began a celebration aboard the ship. As the spaceship disappeared off into the distance, Chipette scrawled a small "IOU" note onto the back of a nearby "Missing Food" poster for a corndog. Then, Chipette made her way back to the containment room.

When Edward finally woke up he seemed delirious and unstable.

"It won't end like this," Edward whispered to no one.

"Or will it?" The large burrito in the vampire cape, who had been waiting for him to wake up,

Part 4: Chipette

sneered, "I am Captain Burrito. Your disintegration will begin in five seconds. Five... Four... Three.. Two... One..." Chipette was halfway out of the ventilation shaft as she was going to try and save Edward, but then, Edward pressed a button on his armor and completely disappeared from sight. The shackles that once held Edward hostage fell, clattering to the ground as burritos looked around dumbstruck.

Chipette then noticed a smaller version of Edward running across the ship. Chipette estimated him to have shrunken to approximately 7.78 inches tall. Unfortunately, Captain Burrito seemed to notice Edward had shrunken and proceeded to raise his foot above Edward in preparation of crushing Edward to smithereens. Chipette practically threw herself out of the ventilation shaft and across the room. She rammed the side of her body into Captain Burrito's shoulder, pushing him in front of his disintegration machine.

Captain Burrito yelped and a second later beans and cheese fell to the ground where Captain Burrito once stood. Chipette glanced around and was relieved to see that Edward had escaped. She then looked up to see that the other burrito guards in the room were looking at her with very concerned faces.

"Are you ok?" one of the guards asked.

"Forget that! That burrito killed our leader! Attack!" another burrito shouted and the ten or so burritos left in the room all rushed at Chipette at the same time. Chipette turned around to run away to find Captain Burrito slowly reforming himself.

Part 4: Chipette

"Take... me... to... my... rewrap... room..." Captain Burrito managed to say. The burritos stopped charging at Chipette and ran to help their leader. They quickly dragged away the remains of Captain Burrito leaving Chipette in the room by herself. Just before they left the room Chipette heard Captain Burrito say with much pain,

"I will find and... hunt... you down..." Chipette stepped outside to watch as Captain Burrito was taken away but was knocked back into the containment room by a gust of the wind. Chipette looked up to see Edward flying on a chocolate dragon that flew clumsily throughout the ship, knocking into a wall almost every two feet.

"Explain yourself, you imposter!" a burrito shouted at Chipette. Chipette looked down and saw that her tortilla disguise had been torn revealing her true identity as a cookie.

"Nevermind," the burrito quickly said, "it doesn't matter. I'll have to detain you!"

"Oh really?" Chipette said raising her fist, "I've defeated so many burritos today, I doubt you can take me down." The burrito just smirked and pulled out a bazooka from its pocket.

"Haha," the burrito said, "I'm super prepared for this!" with that the burrito shot a giant avocado out of the bazooka.

Chipette attempted to dodge the avocado by jumping up, however, the avocado was too fast. Chipette flew through the air and impacted the wall. Stars flew through her eyes and her vision doubled. The

Part 4: Chipette

burrito took advantage of Chipette being temporarily incapacitated and locked Chipette in one of the cages next to her sister.

Just at that moment, Edward and his dragon burst into the containment room and flew over to the burrito that locked Chipette up. Chipette tried to get Edward's attention but he seemed otherwise occupied by trying to get his dragon to pick up the cages.

"Edward!" Chipette tried to shout, but when the dragon picked up the cages, it sent an unconscious Derek Donut, whom she shared a cage with, flying into her face so her shout ended up being muffled and barely audible. Chipette managed to shove Derek off of her just in time to see Edward lift a burrito off the ground, hold him by the scruff, and demand,

"Where's the ship's weak spot?"

"The power generator is in the center! Fly down the south hall, and you'll find it!" the burrito squeaked.

Edward was so frantic in his attempt to go to the center of the ship that when the dragon lifted off, they accidentally dropped the cages which slid through the halls of the ship and fell out of the hole Edward had blown in the side of the ship. Chipette swore she heard Edward shout,

"I'll come back for you!" as the cages fell back to Chipette's home planet, The Dessert.

As the cages fell through the air, Chipette tried to wake up her cell mates. Derek Donut, a can of soda, a gingerbread man, a slice of blueberry pie, and Mrs. Madeira. She looked around her; it was no wonder that

Part 4: Chipette

Edward's dragon dropped the cages, there were at least six cages almost filled to the brim with prisoners.

"*We need to land softly,*" Chipette thought, "*Otherwise, we die.*" Chipette didn't have a plan and she didn't have anything to build with. Out of the corner of her eye she saw the cage that contained Sugar Cookie.

"SUGAR COOKIE!" Chipette shouted, trying to wake up her sister. A lone thin mint noticed Chipette shouting and proceeded to shout directly into Sugar Cookie's ear. Sugar Cookie's eyes flew wide open and instinctively punched the thin mint in the face.

"SO SORRY ABOUT THAT! THANK YOU FOR YOUR HELP!" Chipette shouted at the dazed thin mint.

"OH CHIPETTE! WHAT'S HAPPENING!" Sugar Cookie yelled at Chipette.

Chipette attempted to fill in her sister on their situation but Chipette was sure that most of her words were lost in the wind. The planet below them was getting closer. "WE ARE GOING TO DIE WHEN WE IMPACT THE PLANET'S SURFACE!" Chipette shouted.

Sugar Cookie smiled and whipped out her phone and did some furious tapping. Chipette wasn't sure what texting was going to do in a situation like this but she figured she'd give it a shot. Sugar Cookie, stopped typing, put her phone away and gave Chipette a thumbs up.

When the cages impacted the ground of The Dessert, they landed in one of the largest tubs of Jello

Part 4: Chipette

Chipette had ever seen. One, two, three, for, five, six, seven cages all crashed down into the orange jello. Sugar Cookie immediately set to hacking the digital locks on all the cages setting all the citizens captured in them free.

Mr. and Mrs. Madeira and many of the other desserts stopped by Sugar Cookie and Chipette to thank them for saving them. The Thin Mint, who worked at the bank, even told Sugar Cookie that she could borrow money from the bank anytime she wanted, free of charge. Derek Donut told the sisters that he would stay and help them in any way he could.

"What the—" Chipette started to say turning to Sugar Cookie, "how'd you know we would land in Jello?"

"I texted Tammy Tart who told her friend Timmy Taffy, who told his dad about our situation. Timmy's dad was in high standing with the mayor of Sugarcane, who owed him a favor. Long story short, the mayor, Madam Madeleine, pulled a few strings at the nearest Jello factory so that we wouldn't die on impact!" Sugar Cookie explained.

"Guys! Over here!" Tammy Tart screamed from in front of the nearby MilkShake Mart (Proud sponsors of Sweets R Us), "the mayor wants to meet you!"

Sure enough, standing right beside a "Missing Food" poster that was plastered by the entrance of the store, was the madeleine cookie herself. Before Chipette and Sugar Cookie even got within six feet of the mayor, a sudden static ringing filled the air and the sound of an intercom clicking on was heard,

Part 4: Chipette

"Ingredients ascertained. Two targets acquired. Consequences pending in 3... 2.. 1..." Chipette and her sister exchanged looks of confusion before a giant Kraft mac and cheese cup burst out of MilkShake Mart, grabbed Tammy and the mayor and retreated inside. Chipette, Sugar Cookie and Derek all sprinted inside Milkshake Mart.

"Wrong targets acquired," the voice of the intercom said as it flung Tammy and the mayor into the wall. Two churro guards quickly ran to the mayor and Tammy Tart and began to hold them hostage.

"Leave us," Tammy cried to Sugar Cookie, "don't risk your lives to save us! You just escaped from a burrito spaceship!"

"No! No no no no," the mayor interjected, "please save us! I need to pick up my coffee order at Starburst-bucks! It's an iced white chocolate mocha! WE CAN'T LET THE ICE MELT!!!"

"Don't worry," Chipette said, "I've got this."

"No Chipette! Don't!" her sister said. Chipette ignored her and stepped forward.

"Excuse me, um— Mr. Mac and Cheese," Chipette told the Kraft cup, "But it's not really all that nice to hold our friends hostage, so, if you could kindly let them go please." The Kraft cup considered what she had said then responded,

"No, I am the Supreme Lord of the Foodiverse! I shall not take orders from you! I am here to take over this planet, something my father and his father before that has failed to do! I will go down in history as the GREATEST CONQUEROR OF THE ENTIRE UNIVERSE!"

Part 4: Chipette

Chipette sighed, "Mr. Cheese, is it ok that I call you that? I was really hoping we wouldn't have to get violent here but you leave me no choice. "

"EXCUSE ME! WHAT DID YOU JUST CALL ME!"

"Ummmm, Mr. Cheese?"

"HOW DARE YOU! Just for that! I'm taking the mayor and this random tart hostage aboard my ship!" Supreme Lord Mac-N-Cheese started fiddling with a teleporter he was wearing around his wrist.

"Yeah," Sugar Cookie said, triumphantly holding up her phone, "you're not going anywhere with that teleporter. Not with the virus I just downloaded onto it." Supreme Lord Mac-N-Cheese huffed,

"Guards! Attack them!" At Supreme Lord Mac-N-Cheese's command, approximately 67.5 (one of the burritos was missing his top half) burritos and churro guards jumped out from hiding, all holding various weapons.

Just at that moment, Cassie Cake walked inside the store saying, "Yeah Mom, I know, just get the airhead balloons from the store and nothing else! ... I *am* responsible! ... No! I didn't bring extra money! ... Yes! I am going to try and get a discount!" Cassie abruptly stopped talking and her eyes widened as she registered the scene happening inside the store.

"Mom," Cassie said into the phone, "I am going to hang up now. Ok bye." Cassie turned off her phone and shoved it in her pocket then turned to Sugar Cookie and said,

"Mind if I help you in taking down these baddies?"

Part 4: Chipette

"Yes please!" Derek said, nodding vigorously.

"ENOUGH WITH THE DISTRACTIONS!" Supreme Lord Mac-N-Cheese bellowed, "ATTACK, MY MINIONS!" The churro guards and the burritos launched into action and the four desserts grabbed the nearest things they could find. Supreme Lord Mac-N-Cheese began dragging the mayor and Tammy away from the battle scene.

Chipette grabbed a crowbar off the nearest shelf and began bashing the enemy foods in the head with it. Derek and Cassie were standing back to back firing their donut and cake blasters at any food that attacked them. Sugar Cookie made a lunge for Tammy and Madam Madeleine to free them of their guards but several burritos tackled her. Upon seeing this, Chipette whacked the nearest enemies and jumped on their heads and launched herself at Supreme Lord Mac-N-Cheese's back.

"GAAAAH!" the evil tyrant screamed when Chipette landed on him.

"Take that Mr. Cheese!" Chipette said bring the crowbar down on his head.

"I am not Mr. Cheese! Stop being *rude* and *disrespectful*!" Supreme Lord Mac-N-Cheese spun around and grabbed the crowbar. The two struggled neither one wanting to let the other retain control of the weapon.

"RUN TAMMY!" Sugar Cookie screamed from across the room. The tart grabbed the mayor and the two ran out of the back door.

"Mr. Cheese," Chipette grunted, trying to pull the crowbar from Supreme Lord Mac-N-Cheese's grip, "*you* are the one being rude and disrespectful!"

125

Part 4: Chipette

"That's it!" Supreme Lord Mac-N-Cheese yelled as he let go of the crowbar and kicked Chipette backwards, "I am going to kidnap two desserts today to test my brainwashing serum whether you like it or not!" Supreme Lord Mac-N-Cheese grabbed the nearest dessert, Chipette, and tapped a button on his teleporter.

"No!" Sugar Cookie yelled, "how did you get past the virus I put on your teleporter!" The Kraft cup merely just winked evilly. Suddenly, Cassie and Derek, having just bashed two burrito's heads together, charged at Supreme Lord Mac-N-Cheese. They rammed into him as his teleporter began to hum. Chipette was pushed out of Supreme Lord Mac-N-Cheese's grasp seconds before he teleported away, taking Derek and Cassie with him.

"No! Cassie! Derek!," Chipette screamed then turned to Sugar Cookie, "we have to go after them." A sudden ringing of a phone was heard over the intercom, then, it sounded like the mac and cheese cup picked up.

"Hello? Who is this? I'm in the middle of a dessertnapping!" Supreme Lord Mac-N-Cheese demanded.

"Sorry sir, it's Captain Burrito. I just wanted to inform you that operation Brainwash-All-of-the-SCL has been completed, just as you requested."

"Ah, yes! Finally someone who can do his job. Do me a favor and tell the ETM that he's demoted."

"With pleasure sir."

"Oh and hand tight at the SCL, I want to try a new spell on two very special desserts. Be on the lookout for a cake and a donut arriving to you very soon."

126

Part 4: Chipette

"Copy that sir."

"Wait a second,"

"Sir?"

"Ah, fishsticks! I forgot to turn the large intercom off!" Supreme Lord Mac-N-Cheese must have absolutely destroyed the intercom after that because there was a loud screeching and the call was ended.

"We have to save Cassie and Derek!" Chipette said.

"Let's take these enemy foods down first," Sugar Cookie said, cracking her knuckles. The evil burritos and churro guards still inside the market looked at each other nervously. Chipette gripped her crowbar.

"Reinforcements!" a churro called out and hundreds of extraterrestrial eggs beamed down into the supermarket. Chipette felt a knot tighten in her stomach, they were outnumbered.

"Run?" Chipette asked.

"Run." Sugar Cookie agreed. The two sisters sprinted out of the supermarket, a horde of enemies behind them. Chipette knew they couldn't outrun all the guards and eggs chasing them, but she didn't know how they would get away. Then, seeing the pile of broken cages outside, a plan hit her.

"Cover me," Chipette told her sister and handed her the crowbar. Sugar Cookie protested saying that she couldn't possibly keep the horde at bay for very long.

"I have a plan," Chipette said reassuringly, "just give me a couple minutes." Sugar Cookie nodded. Chipette ran back inside MilkShake Mart and grabbed a set of welding tools in the store window display, several electrical wires and three gallons of maple syrup that functioned as gasoline, Sugar Cookie smashing evil foods away from Chipette all the while. She then set to work, connecting the bits of cage together, making a small compartment, wings, engine and truster. Soon her masterpiece was done. Masterpiece being a strong word, the rocketship she had created was shoddy-looking at best, but hopefully it would work.

"Get in!" Chipette told Sugar Cookie, hopping on the ship. Sugar Cookie crammed herself inside and Chipette flicked the switch to turn on the thrusters. The rocketship flew forward, running over several burrito guards. She then pressed a button and the wings on the ship flexed. They began to gain altitude.

"Where are we going!?" Sugar Cookie asked.

"We need to save Edward," Chipette said. "We are going back to the burrito ship! He's still there!"

"How did he even get on the Burrito Ship? Shouldn't his vehicle still be there?" Sugar Cookie pointed out.

"Well, about that... I may have sent his ship off the burrito ship filled with sprinkles that Captain Burrito had captured."

"Are you serious!?" Sugar Cookie probably would have continued scolding Chipette but the ship began to shudder and creak. They were starting to leave the atmosphere of The Dessert. The burrito ship loomed in the distance and soon, Chipette saw the strangest thing.

"What," Chipette said, "the heck." Through an opening inside the burrito ship Chipette saw there were just two dragons flying around, Edward on one of them

Part 4: Chipette

and some random fortune cookie lady on the other, also what appeared to be a child was on one the dragons as well. Chipette shushed Sugar Cookie and flew the ship closer to them.

"Sorry, Edward." Chipette heard the fortune cookie lady say as she swung her scythe at him . Chipette gasped and watched Edward duck just in the nic of time. Chipette sped her ship inside the burrito ship and Sugar Cookie sprang into action. She rolled down her window just as Edward yelled,

"Traitor!"

"Edward! Duck!" Sugar Cookie shouted from inside their homemade ship. Sugar Cookie then proceeded to throw her phone from inside the ship. The tool flew through the air, hitting the fortune cookie lady smack dab in the eye and bouncing right back into Sugar Cookie's hand, just like a boomerang. The lady shrieked in pain.

"Must've been possessed." Chipette heard the fortune cookie say. Chipette threw herself out of the window of the spacecraft and flew up to Edwards' attacker and kicked her. Right as it happened, the dragons and Chipette's pod exited the burrito ship. The fortune cookie lady went flying into empty space. Her dragon dove after her, accidentally knocking everyone off the platform— including Edward and his sisters— into the endless space. Edward's dragon saw it's rider falling and it shrieked and dove, Edward landed smoothly on the dragon's back and steered his dragon into a steeper dive and caught the fortune cookie lady, stopping her fall. Chipette noticed that the dragons tried

to dive to catch Sugar Cookie and herself but they were falling too fast and the dragons soon faded out of Chipette's vision. Sugar Cookie noticed this too and pulled out her phone. She tapped several buttons and Chipette homemade pod came swooping underneath them, catching them, stopping their fall.

"You gave my ship autopilot!" Chipette said once inside the pod. A massive thundering sound emmenated overhead and Chipette craned her neck to see what it was. Just as she did so, the Burrito Ship that resided in The Dessert's atmosphere shot off into hyperspace.

"Good riddance!" Chipette cheered.

Sugar Cookie nodded then said, "Let's go home."

"But what about Cassie and Derek?" Chipette asked.

"We need to rest up first. Look at us, we're starting to crack and crumble from all this activity. We need to rebake and redecorate ourselves first. My icing got a little bit dented and there's this blue icing that I've been wanting to put on because I think it would, like, look so good on me. Then after all that we can go after them." Chipette agreed and the sisters then steered the ship to their house on The Dessert. But they never made it to the SCL, because right when they were about to leave, Edward burst in with a passed out Adrienne and Chipette went to make waffles for the guests.

Part 5: Adrienne

After Sugar Cookie and Chipette finished telling their story, Edward, Tiriaq and Adrienne stared at them, mouths gaping.

"Huh," Edward said, "that explains why you guys were in those cages, and how you were able to save me when Adrienne was possessed!"

"Possessed?" Chipette asked, "it didn't look like you were—"

"Let's like, keep our suspicions to ourselves for now," Sugar Cookie said, cutting Chipette off.

"But I had to kick—" Sugar Cookie covered Chipettes mouth with her hand.

"Wait so you hack stuff with your phone?" Adrienne asked in disbelief

"What's it to you?" Sugar Cookie scoffed, still trying to hack the tortilla she sat on.

"All this time," Edward mused, "and I just thought you were on your phone texting Timmy Taffy, your crush."

"OMG! I thought he was cute for like three days and that was only because I liked the way he wore his hair and the six-pack abs he had gotten from working out. So when Tammy accidentally told him he was like, 'Ew get away! I will never be your boyfriend!' So like yeah."

Part 5: Adrienne

"Wow." Tiriaq said, "Gowing to high school swounds compwicated."

"Now," Sugar Cookie said, "I'm almost done hacking this tortilla so we can escape from Supreme Lord Mac-N-Cheese, so no more questions!"

"THAT WAS A VERY INTERESTING STORY," the voice of Supreme Lord Mac-N-Cheese boomed over them.

"Wow," Adrienne sassed to the supreme lord, "how *kind* of you to wait until they finished telling their story."

"WHY THANK YOU!" the supreme lord almost seemed flattered by Adrienne's sarcastic remarks.

"Oh," Chipette said, "I totally forgot you were there *Mr. Cheese.*"

"I AM NOT CALLED MR. CHEESE! NOW I WILL DESTROY YOU! USING MY SECRET WEAPONS!" At that announcement, the mac and cheese cup emitted a scream and started shooting globs of melted cheese at the group.

"Ok actually, why didn't Supreme Lord Mac-N-Cheese attack us earlier?" Edward wondered out loud while sidestepping a cheesy projectile.

"Don't question it," Adrienne said, dogging a glob of cheese, "just appreciate that Sugar Cookie and Chipettes stories were so entertaining he got very invested in them."

"AHHHG! THIS ISN'T WORKING!!! I'M GOING TO SEND DOWN MY OTHER EVEN MORE SECRETER

Part 5: Adrienne

WEAPONS!" Supreme Lord Mac-N-Cheese declared, "YOU'VE LEFT ME NO OTHER CHOICE!"

Suddenly Sugar cookie laughed, "I successfully hacked it! Everyone hop on the Tortilla Express!" Everyone looked astounded but quickly hopped on the thin flaky bread, for extraterrestrial eggs just beamed down from the spacecraft still hovering above them.

"Gwo Gwo Gwo!" shrieked little Tiriaq as the green, garlic-smelling eggs tried to grasp the edge of the tortilla.

"Wait! What about Mom?" Edward asked Sugar Cookie.

"Ummm... she will be fiiiine." Sugar Cookie responded with uncertainty, dodging an egg that had launched itself at her. The Tortilla Express continued to soar through Edward's town as eggs continued to slash and grab at the back of it. They viciously bit and shrieked, attempting to tear it apart. It was all Adrienne and Edward could do to keep them from attacking the group while Sugar Cookie was steering the ride. Tiriaq and Chipette were otherwise occupied by grabbing items as they zoomed by them for a contraption they were making. When the two smallest desserts managed to finish their contraption it looked to be some sort of slingshot to Andrienne but she wasn't sure. Together, the pair started pulling road signs out of the ground and ripping the rice paper sign part off until only the chopstick pole remained.

"READY!" Chipette shouted once there were plenty of chopsticks in their arsenal.

"W-AIM!" Tiriaq shouted in return.

Part 5: Adrienne

"FIRE!" the both of them shouted as they pressed the trigger button on the machine. Immediately the contraption started propelling chopsticks that flew into the faces of the extraterrestrial eggs, causing them to faceplant into the road unable to stand back up. Edward tried to summon something to use as a projectile and only managed to make a banana split appear; which he threw dejectedly at the mac and cheese ship in the sky.

Needless to say, the bowl of ice cream and banana missed its target by several hundred feet.

"I should warn you about something," Adrienne said, "I'm lactose intolerant and I forgot when I was eating that waffle earlier." Then Adrienne farted, the musty fumes filled the air behind them and all the extraterrestrial eggs fainted. Edward and Tiriaq gagged while Sugar Cookie mumbled,

"Of course you are."

"NOOOO!" Supreme Lord Mac-N-Cheese shouted, "YOU'RE ASKING FOR IT NOW! PREPARE TO MEET MY OTHER OTHER SECRETEST WEAPON! DEVILED EGGS!" A hatch opened up from the side of Supreme Lord Mac-N-Cheese's ship and three hard boiled eggs dropped out, their faces seemed to be decorated with paprika as war paint and their teeth seemed sharper than any sword Adrienne had ever seen.

Chipette and Tiriaq turned their weapon up to the sky and shot chopsticks which Adrienne and Edward began supplying through similar methods used earlier, into the open hatch. A particularly lucky chopstick rammed into the hinge of the door causing the door to get stuck and be unable to close. As they continued to launch the pairs of chopsticks down the hatch, one of the sticks bounced off the stuck hatch door and smashed into the engine room, causing a side of the ship to erupt in a fiery explosion.

Supreme Lord Mac-N-Cheese screamed in rage and immediately pulled his ship away, back into the atmosphere of The Dessert. The three deviled eggs touched down on the group and immediately started chasing their ride. The machine that Chipette and Tiriaq had built flew off of the tortilla and slammed into all three of the eggs, successfully knocking two of them out. One of the deviled eggs, however, managed to get close enough to the tortilla ship and shot a potato chip missile at them. The egg was so light that the force of the missile leaving the weapon it was holding caused the egg to fly backward several blocks.

The tortilla chip missile hit the side of Adrienne and her companions' ship and they went spinning and crashed into the sign saying: Now leaving Sugarcane! Their flying tortilla went rolling down the street. The ship caught fire and everyone flew off. The entire company soared through the air and smacked into another sign that said: Welcome to the Fondue Fountains!

Chipette's chips were partially melted and Sugar Cookie was missing sprinkles. They all coughed and some threw up liquid dough, their throats scorched. Edward had gotten toasted. He wouldn't be surprised to see burnt marks everywhere. All of a sudden, a small mechanical hum filled their ears. A robot made entirely of chocolate candy walked over to them. His joints seemed to be made of Hershey's kisses while his body was a large yellow rectangular box labeled:

Milk Duds
Candy Made with **Chocolate & Carmel**

"Hello, my name is MilkDudBot 1.0! May I be of assistance?" the robot said.

"No, you noob!" Chipette screamed and shoved a melted chocolate chip over his eyes, which quickly melted into him. He stuck out his arm, and a lighter shot out and he melted the handicap off his eyes.

"You cannot inconvenience me!!! That is bullying!!!" He let out a horrible mechanical screech and SHOT Chipette IN THE ARM! Chipette screamed, she fainted dead away. Adrienne saw Sugar Cookie's look of dismay and placed a hand on Sugar Cookie's shoulder.

"I've this," Adrienne said, "Trust me." Then went up and started beating the robot. The robot kicked her and she went flying half a mile. Literally. Adrienne felt weightless, also miserable, so much for a brave act to win over Edward's older sister. Adrienne crashed through several layers of thin wafer cookies and found herself on the floor of a Milkshake Mart and saw an Adrienne-shaped hole in the ceiling. She wasn't too surprised to find that the robot's shoe size was stamped into her dough. 8½. The robot didn't look that big! Adrienne didn't feel like getting up. Everything hurt. She decided to retire to the floor for just a couple minutes.

Adrienne woke up from her "short nap" in a cold sweat. She had had the dream again. The one that ended with a banana being killed by the sausagey looking claw. The words *"Honey, have you taken the trash out yet?"* still rang in her head. Adreinne rubbed her eyes and was horrified when she looked at her watch. She had been asleep for twelve hours! Adrienne felt like she might fall apart. She looked around and realized she was in a white cot. Starched white sheets were wrapped around her, a marshmallow pillow beneath her head.

"Sorry about that!" MilkDudBot 1.0 appeared out of thin air, "I sense your unease around me. If it helps, I am now MilkDudBot 1.1 because my hostile functions have been eliminated. Except for special occasions. Let me tell you my story!"

Adrienne rolled her eyes. This was going to take awhile. And MilkDudBot 1.1 didn't seem like he was about to just let her leave.

The Long Short Story Of MilkDudBot 1.0 (1)

"It all started when my creator, Dr. Wally WhippedCream, created me. He worked night and day, just to finish me. He said I was the son he never had. I hoped to make him proud one day. So, I packed my wafer suitcase and left to provide money for my Master. But then, I lost my way tragically in

the Maple Syrup Marsh. When milk rain began to beat down on my weary body, my chocolate started to fuse together making me all stiff and I had to stop, I grabbed my remaining belongings and took shelter in a rock candy cave—"

"Hold it!" Adrienne interrupted, "There just happened to be a rock candy cave IN THE MIDDLE OF THE WOODS?!"

"Yes," replied an annoyed MilkDudBot 1.1, "Can I finish my story now?"

"Fine." Adrienne huffed. What a drama queen, SHEESH!

The Long Short Story Of MilkDudBot 1.0 (1) Continued:

"So anyways, before I was so rudely interrupted. I took shelter in a rock candy cave in hopes of coming back home when the rain stopped. However, fate did not want me to go home. It rained for hours and the hours turned into days and the days turned into years—"

"Wait!" Adrienne interrupted again, "If you stayed in the cave for that long, what did you eat?"

"Well," MilkDudBot 1.1 replied, "in reality, it was only 37 and ½ minutes, BUT it felt like years."

"Ok. That makes more sense!" Adrienne stated, "Continue!"

The Long Short Story Of MilkDudBot1.0(1) Continued Again

"Once again! It rained 37 and 1/2 minutes and I sat inside the cave shivering—"

"Not all the boring stuff! We're not interested in that! When did you get out?" Adrienne said.

The Long Short Story Of MilkDudBot1.0(1) Continued still

"I decided to make a run for it. I sprinted with my rigid limbs but eventually, I gave up and fell in the mud. I rolled down a big hill, unable to move. When I finally stopped moving, I realized I was inside the ruins of my Dr. Wally WhippedCream's house! I mourned the loss of my master for eleven minutes, then tried to move. I was found by burrito scouts hours later. They loosened my limbs and I was able to move once again! Then they forced me into a labor camp to build a giant ship for a Super Mac-N-Cheese guy.

"There I learned, through listening to the labor camp gossip, that my master Dr. Wally WhippedCream was actually the Cheese Wizard. I got so mad I kicked many camp guards a half a mile to release my anger, then I was immediately taken down by the burrito guards. I was brought before the evil ETM who sentenced me to life in prison. 2.67 minutes later I was thrown into a raw sausage jail cell. Then I felt a fire within me and Hostile Mode was born! It was like another robot within me.

"I felt evil, powerful, and needing someone to share my glorious strength and power. I stood there dramatically for exactly 3 minutes and 24.5 seconds. I was even more glorious and stronger than I had been already (as impossible as it seems). I had a strong urge to go and find a sweet dessert to show off my groovy new powers to, but I had to focus on the problem at hand. I screamed my heart-wrenching battle cry and pried the bars apart.

"I proceeded to defeat burrito guards with such finesse, it would put Craigolas from Lord of the Ring Pops to shame! Shame, I tell you! I ran by, absolutely mauling all the burrito guards. I passed a girl MilkyWay Bot and flashed her my best smolder. I'm still not exactly sure why she looked at me funny. She probably just didn't know what to think of my handsomeness.

"After my victory against the burrito guards, I ran far away from the camp and decided to bunk in an old broom closet I found in a supermarket. I felt suddenly empty, I needed a master, someone I could serve. So I took to the Fondue Fountains, there I found a small house with locks on the outside where many desserts claimed to have been kidnapped by evil foods. I set them free and tried to get one of them to be my new master, but none obliged and they ran back into town. I sat down on the porch of the house in defeat.

Part 5: Adrienne

I sat there wondering what to do with the 498,395,209 hours I had left before my battery died. I sat there for many days until I came upon the lovely Chipette cookie girl. I thought I'd found my master/mistress. But then she called me noob, there was no way I could possibly be that. Being in hostile mode, I just had to stop her from insulting me. I will admit, for the first time in my life, I had a regret. I regretted shooting her in the arm. I was then beaten endlessly by a beautiful fortune cookie whose eyes sparkled like the stars and whose—"

"Nooooooo! I get it! Please don't continue!" Adrienne frantically shouted, covering her ears as if that would save her from embarrassment. She did have to admit, it was nice being complimented in such a way. Maybe this robot could convince Sugar Cookie to trust her, "So who did you choose to be your master/mistress?"

"The little one," MilkDudBot 1.1 replied.

"Which one?" Adrienne asked again.

"THE LITTLE ONE!" MilkDudBot 1.1 insisted, "Like about this high." MilkDudBot 1.1 held a robotic arm up to about where his knee cap was.

"You do realize that describes all of my friends, and me?" Adrienne asked.

"I know right! You guys are all so cute and tiny!" MilkDudBot 1.1 grinned like a child receiving a new puppy.

"Oh shut up, you hunk of metal!"

"Chocolate! I'm MilkDudBot 1.1! Duh!"

Part 5: Adrienne

"Where are my friends, anyway?" Adrienne asked

"I have taken you and your friends to the house I found in these Fondue Fountains."

"You mean, the house that you found the kidnapped desserts in."

"Oh don't worry about it!" I'm sure the evil foods forgot all about this place," MilkDudBot 1.1 said.

"Hi Adrienne!" Edward's cheery voice was heard, "Isn't this place amazing!?"

Adrienne looked around just in time to see Chipette shriek in delight and dive into one of the various lakes of chocolate fondue. She came out wiping the melted chocolate off of her tongue and gagging,"I didn't realize that it was dark chocolate!"

Edward retorted, "Well, it's not like there's going to be a sign telling you!"

"Really?" MilkDudBot 1.1 stated. "The sign is right there!"

Chipette turned around as best as she could to see the sign and screamed in rage, "YOU NOOB SIGN, YOU WEREN'T THERE WHEN I LOOKED!!!!!"

"Neither was I." Captain Burrito appeared behind them, "Oh and by the way, welcome to my summer vacation lake house!! Supreme Lord Mac-N-Cheese sends his regards."

Adrienne was so shocked by this that she actually punched Captain Burrito. Unfortunately, the burrito just disappeared and reappeared several feet back, unscathed.

Part 5: Adrienne

"You didn't think that was actually going to work? Did you?" Tiriaq charged before Adrienne or Edward could stop him. Tiriaq prepared to slam into the burrito as a look of rage that Adrienne had never seen passed over his face. However he passed right through and fell down.

The burrito mysteriously levitated 10 feet above the ground. Adrienne hurled a knife at the apparition but it passed through him again and lodged itself in a nearby rock made of a Reese's peanut butter cup. Edward moved his hands and shot a fairly decent sized fireball out, he was getting better at this. A ring of fire surged outward, Edward as the epicenter, all the chocolate in the area was melted, including the peanut butter cups, whose liquid quickly joined that of the lake, leaving only several waxy wrappings behind. Once again, Captain Burrito wasn't harmed.

"Ha ha ha!" The evil food laughed. "Is that all you can do to defeat me? Well guess what? NEWS FLASH! It's not working! Cheese Wizard, make me fly higher!" The burrito levitated higher into the sky and seemed to grow in size at the same time, his vampire cape flapping magically in the wind.

"The Cheese Wizard must be here!" Adrienne shouted. "Captain Burrito is not this powerful!"

"If that evil Cheese Wizard is here," MilkDudBot 1.1 roared, "I will tear this place apart just to smash him to smithereens!"

"We can't have that!" the burrito laughed. "Activate Hostile Mode!"

Part 5: Adrienne

"Wait, no!" the sound of the Cheese Wizard's voice was heard, "I actually came here to make amends!" But it was no use. MilkDudBot 1.1's eyes turned from the normal blue to a bright shade of cherry red.

"NOOO!" the robot screamed, "I don't harm desserts now!" The robot seemed physically pained.

"Sorry robot," Captain Burrito sneered, "my friend the Cheese Wizard gave me an override!"

"No I didn't!" the Cheese Wizard shouted from his hiding place behind the house. This was quickly followed by a loud clang and the magic illusions of a giant Captain Burrito flying above them vanished. Adrienne just barely glimpsed the Cheese Wizard's body go flying through the air, presumably having been thrown in a fit of rage.

"Shouldn't have brought him along!" Captain Burrito growled, as he stepped out from behind the house.

Meanwhile, MilkDudBot 1.1 fell over to his knees, struggling to maintain control of his body. Tiriaq looked sympathetic and went to comfort the robot when spinning Oreo buzzsaws appeared in both of his hands.

"Oh cwêpe," Tiriaq shrieked.

The robot stood up abruptly and Captain Burrito clapped his hands in delight. MilkDudBot 1.1 aimed his eyes at Sugar Cookie, who was furiously typing on her phone, complaining about how she couldn't get past the

Part 5: Adrienne

Firewall. He spewed red-hot liquid marshmallows at her feet.

She cried out and tried to move, but couldn't.

He advanced towards Sugar Cookie with his blades spinning, ready to slice.

Sugar Cookie screamed and tried to push a button on her phone, but the robot swatted her cellular device aside. The mech kicked her down so she was lying down in the marshmallow. He stepped on her and started to push on her chest.

Sugar Cookie screamed, but that was promptly cut off by marshmallow goo filling her mouth. MilkDudBot 1.1 started to lower the blades towards her dough. She thrashed and flailed around. The blades touched her and started to cut. She tried to shout out.

All of a sudden, he stopped. His eyes went blank and he fell down. Chipette stood behind him, holding several gummy wires that apparently once resided in the robot's back. Edward ran over and pulled Sugar Cookie out. Sugar Cookie shuddered and picked up her phone and inspected it for any scratches before looking down to see the damage that the mech had done to her. She was pleased to find the only injury on her was a dent on her side.

MilkDudBot 1.1 lay lifeless. Edward looked over at Chipette, who looked shocked.

"It was the only way," Adrienne shook her head, "We had to shut him down." Chipette ran up and hugged Edward.

"NO!" Captain Burrito screamed. Then he ordered, "Cheese Wizard, fix it! Fix it!" When nothing

146

happened Captain Burrito seemed to remember that he had thrown the Cheese Wizard into the distance. "Stay here," he told the desserts, "I'll be right back to finish you off. Don't you guys dare move!" Then he took off running in the direction the Cheese Wizard had been thrown.

"He was a half-decent robot." Sugar Cookie sniffed, looking down at the body of MilkDudBot 1.1, "Even if he, like, had no Instagrahamcracker followers." She began to cry and yelled, "Nobody ever liked his posts!"

"Not the time for lamenting, Sugar Cookie!" Edward said. "We need to get out of here, Captain Burrito is still attacking us!"

"Where swhould we go?" Triaq asked.

"We can't stay on The Dessert," Adrienne stated. "If we stay here, Captain Burrito will just keep attacking us and bring destruction with him. You all heard him when we first arrived, we are all wanted by Supreme Lord Mac-N-Cheese. And especially with the stupid DNA tracking, these dinner foods won't stop until we are eliminated. Our loved ones might get hurt in the process."

"That, like, only leaves us one option," Sugar Cookie said, wiping her eyes. "We have to leave the planet." Everyone agreed.

"But we need a mode of transportation." Chipette said, and Triaq nodded.

"I have an idea," Adrienne said, pulling some of the chopsticks and rice paper they had salvaged earlier out of her shell. "Chipette, Tiriaq, can you build the frame of a ship from these?"

"I thwink so," Tiriaq said, "bwut we don't have an engine or awnything."

"I will do that, you just worry about building everything else," Sugar Cookie told her sister. The young desserts set to work creating a ship frame while Sugar Cookie pulled some wires and technology panels out of the lifeless robot and fiddled with them with one hand and typed on her phone with the other. At one point Chipette and Tiriaq ran inside the house and returned several minutes later carrying sewage pipes.

"There's got to be a way to build ships without using sewage pipes," Sugar Cookie scolded her sister. Chipette just shrugged and mentioned something about the heart wanting what it wants. Adrienne and Edward used their abilities to turn the sewage pipes into sheets of metal and weld them together.

Twenty short minutes later, the group had built the most epic ship they had ever built. Sugar Cookie set to wiring the ship with her makeshift engine and soon it hummed with energy. The group climbed inside the ship and Sugar Cookie pressed a button. The ship started the climb into the sky.

"Whoa! This ship is so much better than my last ship!" Chipette said.

"That's because I helped this time," Sugar Cookie responded

"No! This is a work of my creative genius mixed with my impressive engineering!"

Part 5: Adrienne

Captain Burrito, dragging a passed out Cheese Wizard behind him, stumbled back into the area just in time to see their ship begin to rise up. After exiting the atmosphere on their new fancy ship, Adrienne looked down and saw Captain Burrito shaking his fist shouting, "I TOLD YOU TO STAY PUT!" but the dessert comrades had already reached safety in space.

Sugar Cookie sat down and started watching *Stranger Cakes* on her phone while Chipette and Edward argued over who had done more to help on this wild journey while Edward manned the ship. They were peacefully cruising through space when they were rammed by an unidentified object. Adrienne rushed to the windows to see a colossal flying pizza saucer ship with the name *Olive Destruction* painted sloppily on the side.

"Arrg, scrap!" a triangle shaped food screamed at them as he passed by. Adrienne was astounded by the amount of acne on his face when she realized it was actually pepperoni.

Coming to this conclusion, Adrienne determined that the being was a pizza slice and yelled, "PIZZA PIRATE!!!!! RUN FOR YOUR LIVES!" Then she ran into Tiriaq who tripped and promptly face-planted into a wall. " Chipette rushed over to Tiriaq and helped him get up.

"Load up some weapons!" Adrienne yelled. The ship rocked back and forth as the Pizza Pirate slammed the side of their ship with his own. Adrienne grabbed the driving console from Edward, who was still flying the ship, and started tapping furiously. She didn't know what buttons did what and started tapping random ones. With a tap of a button, a screen appeared on the phone: Weapons system engaged. Adrienne sighed and handed the phone back to Edward and instructed him to continue flying the ship.

"What did dat do?" Tiriaq questioned Adrienne. "The Pizza Piwate is still after wus!"

"I have no idea," Adrienne stated, "but it said, 'Weapons system engaged,' so..." A mechanical whirring was heard. Adrienne rushed over to the window and saw a mechanical hand expand out of the side of their ship. The hand reached back past a sign that said: Storage Room! and disappeared from everyone's sight. When the hand reappeared it was holding a ten foot tall can of whipped cream. A metallic screech behind them sounded and everybody turned around. A computer had flowed from the ceiling and spoke in a robotic voice,

"Welcome to the weapons system! Vanquish your enemies or just harm them." Chipette ran over the screen but was too short to use it. She was suddenly boosted up by Tiriaq and hit her head on the screen.

"Chipette! What did you—" Edward shouted, but was cut off by the pleasant robot voice, "Now aiming at hostile enemy." An image of the Pizza Pirate was shown on the screen with a giant X over his face. Soon a loud static noise was heard outside quickly followed by screams of shock and minor shouting,

Part 5: Adrienne

"Curse these fish finger desserts and their whipped cream wickedness! Those desserts shall pay! ARG!" Adrienne looked out the window to see the bottle of whipped cream covering the Pizza Pirate's entire ship in it's white foam. It seemed to be working really well until the Pizza Pirate retaliated. A cannon emerged from the back of his ship and shot a large meatball at them.

Chipette shrieked and dove for cover under the controls as Tiraq covered his ears. The sound of metal crushing sounded like nails on a chalkboard amplified with thousands of microphones. A large dent in the ship formed behind Sugar Cookie, who was oblivious to what was going on because she was still watching *Stranger Cakes*. A jet of whipped cream shot out towards the pizza saucer but was soon torn apart by a volley of meatballs. One meatball hurtled toward their ship. The mechanical hand attempted to stop it but was torn apart by the meatball.

"Time to abandon ship," the friendly robot voice said, "the escape pod is ten steps to the right of the control panel, quickness is advised." Edward jumped down from the control panel and grabbed Tiraq and Chipette. Adrienne rushed towards the escape pod, only to look back and see Sugar Cookie STILL watching *Stranger Cakes*. Adrienne ran over to Edward's sister and ripped the phone out of her hands and threw it at the window. The phone merely bounced off the glass, miniscule cracks sprouted in the glass and the entire window broke off the ship, and flew back into Sugar Cookie's hand.

Part 5: Adrienne

"What the—" Adrienne gasped, "how does your phone do that?"

"You bully!" Sugar Cookie screamed, ignoring Adrienne's question, "I was just about to find out what happened to Eleven!" An earth shattering BOOM! sounded as the shards of the broken window embedded themselves into the Pizza Pirate's meatball cannon. Sparks flew out from the weapon and the cannon was soon shorted out.

"Oh," Sugar Cookie said, finally noticing what was happening, she then turned to Adrienne and said, "Thanks for potentially saving my life!"

"Let's go!" Edward shouted from the escape pod, "Our ship's gonna blow!"

"No problemo!" Adrienne replied to Sugar Cookie as they started zig zagging through the wreckage of their ship. If this didn't win Sugar Cookie's trust, Adrienne didn't know what would. The two were soon aboard the pod and about to fly away when a meatball soared at them.

"Nope!" Edward shouted, "escape the escape pod!" Everyone sprinted out to the escape pod just as it was torn off the side of the ship. Tiriaq turned around and fell off his chair. When he got up he pointed behind them. Adrienne glanced back and saw the Pizza Pirate following close behind them weapons at the ready.

"Feast your taste buds on my Burrito Torpedoes mateys!" the greasy triangle shouted. Two more cannons sprouted from the side of his ship and fired. Two bulging burritos shot out towards the tiny pod black beans and rice trailing behind them.

152

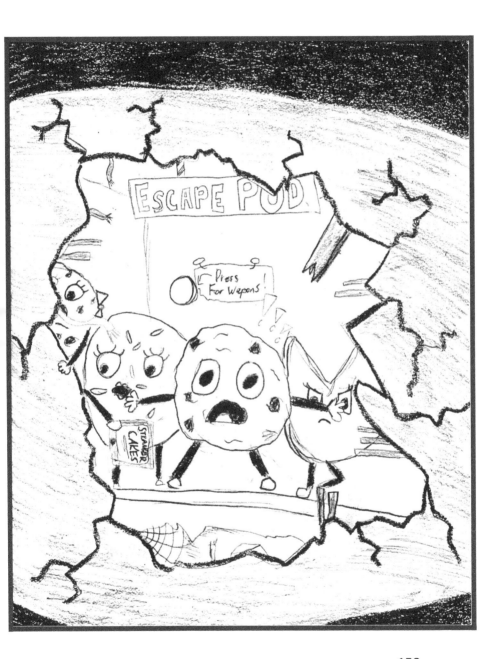

Part 5: Adrienne

"We need to defend ourselves!" Edward shouted.

"On it!" Chipette and TIriaq said at the same time. They both ran to the living room in the back of their pod and started disassembling the sofa. Within minutes the chair was in pieces on the floor and was reassembled into a giant spoon.

"How's that gonna help us!" Adrienne shouted.

"We can use it as a catapult to fling stuff at the Pizza Pirate!" Chipette proceeded to bend back the spoon while Tiriaq threw on some marmalade to the back of the spoon.

The two children were about to fling the marmalade off the spoon when Edward screamed, "WAIT!"

Chipette and Tiriaq paused.

Edward pressed a button on the side of the ship. and a large hatch opened above the spoon, giving the children a clear shot of the Pizza Pirate's spaceship.

"Now you can do it!" Edward said. Chipette let go of the spoon head and it sprang forward. A transparent orange glob hurtled through space. A moment later a loud squish was heard.

"Arrg! Me ship be jammed!" The Pizza Pirate shrieked.

"Wrong!" Tiriaq shouted, "It's marmalade!"

"Marmalade be a jam!" the Pizza Pirate argued.

"Nuh UH!" Tiriaq retorted, "Marmalade is a conswerve."

"What be this conserve you speak of?"

"Conswerves are similar to jam but are pwoduced by combining fwuit with the occasional waisins, nuts, and coconut. Marmalades are usually made of citrus fwuits and contain pieces of the fwuit peel inside."

"ARRRG! YOU SNICKEROOGLED THAT ON YOUR PHONE!"

"WRONG!"

"NOT WRONG"

"YES IT IS!"

"NUH UH!"

"UH HUH!"

"NUH UH!"

"UH HUH!"

"GUYS STOP IT!" Adrienne shouted, "We are leaving!" With that Adrienne pushed the booster button on the mangled consol. The spaceship blasted off leaving a baffled Pizza Pirate behind them shouting, "I WAS RIGHT!!!!!"

Part 6: Tiriaq

Tiriaq could not believe the day he was having. After escaping the evil Pizza Pirate, Chipette and Tiriaq realized they both had a talent for building objects. Together, they could give the ship some much needed major upgrades. Pretty soon they commenced taking apart all the furniture in the spaceship.

Hours later the two stopped and took a lunch break, but that's not a key part of the story. Anyways, when Chipette and Tiriaq had finished building, the ship was equipped with: a giant retractable whisk, a lunch room, a skybox, and a plethora more boosters. Everyone thought that Chipette and Tiriaq did a great job. They decided that the new boosters would help them track down the Saibou. Sugar Cookie installed a new app on her phone called: **Find My Friends**. This was all exciting and all but it was also exhausting. Chipette fell asleep at noon and Tiriaq fell asleep soon afterwards.

Tiraq woke up to a peaceful morning and it was smooth cruising. However, halfway through the day, angry peas and baby corn (in tiny pods) started pummeling the spacecraft. They were mad about something, but no one was paying attention to that, their issue remained a mystery. The peas and corn cracked the satellite dish on the top of the ship, making Sugar Cookie's **Find My Friends** app go berserk.

Edward pulled out his cookie blaster and started firing it at the vegetables. This was a mistake which ended in twenty-some massive holes in the stern of the ship. Chipette and Tiriaq were sent to work to repair the holes, but they couldn't fix the holes fast enough. Baby corn zoomed past them into the ship with peas following closely behind. Soon the ship was infested with angry, but surprisingly cute, baby veggies. The whole team tried their best to fend off the vicious veggies but to no avail.

In no time at all everyone was all backed into corners of the ship because none of them actually wanted to hurt the baby vegetables. The corn and peas had stepped out of their pods and started poking and prodding the desserts with their toothpicks. Tiriaq glanced over at Adrienne long enough to see her nod her head towards the door that led to the closet between them. Adrienne stared at Tiriaq and mouthed the words, "One, TWO, THREE!" On three they both jumped over their captors (who were quite small) and dashed for the closet, their new enemies at their heels. Adrienne flung the door open to the closet and quickly slammed the door behind Tiriaq. There they cowered in the dark space for what seemed like days.

Suddenly the door burst open and Sugar Cookie emerged into the light and told them it was ok to come out. When Tiriaq stepped out into the light he was baffled at what he saw. Sugar Cookie's phone was hooked up to a projector and was currently displaying

Part 6: Tiriaq

Candy Crush with Chipette playing the game. The baby corn and peas were nestled in cotton candy and happily exclaimed "Ooo" and "Ahhh" every time the announcer of the game belted out words like, "Tasty!" and "Sweet Combo!"

"This is such a different scene from when Adrienne and I fled into the closet," Tiriaq exclaimed. He asked Edward how many days he had been hiding in the closet. Edward looked at Tiraq, puzzled, and explained to Tiriaq that the beginning of the invasion of the baby veggies was only nine minutes ago.

Over the next few days Tiriaq and my friends managed to get some info out of their new… friends(?) Apparently, the ship's engines were so loud that they woke up the veggies from their slumber party. The veggies, of course, were furious about this and reacted the way any normal food would, with violence (as was the norm ever since the great war 200 years ago). Tiriaq and his friends entertained their new guests as Edward drove all the veggies back home. When the vegetables departed the ship, a small pea handed Edward a small slip of paper. The pea then explained to Tiriaq and his friends that it was the pea's business card and the pea wanted us to call him if we needed help.

The pea leaned in closer and whispered, "We are assassins in training." With that, the small pea ran back to his home leaving Tiriaq very confused. He tried asking

Part 6: Tiriaq

Adrienne what she knew of these infant assassins but she had naught a clue.

Now undistracted, Chipette and Tiriaq were finally able to fix the satellite dish on top of their spacecraft. With it back in order, Sugar Cookie's **Find My Friends** app was back to normal. After a couple seconds of searching, the app alerted the team that the three headed dragon known as the Saibou was currently residing in the SCL lab on The Dessert but due to complications with the navigation (them getting lost while fighting the Pizza Pirate) they would have to make a pit stop on the newly found sister planet of "The Dessert", "WisSweetsVille".

"That's where Prince Cream of Ice Lives! Do we get to meet him?" Chipette exclaimed. Sugar Cookie rolled her eyes and explained that Chipette had a mega crush on the cone. Chipette glowered at her sister and pushed her sister's arm.

"It's also where King Ice of Cream lives," Adrienne grumbled, grabbing a chalkboard, "Moving on, I found WisSweetsVille. All we just fly this path.":

Part 6: Tiriaq

"Ok," Edward said, "I understand not wanting to travel close to the spaghetti monster in between us and WisSweetsVille, but why can't we go through the space village?" Edward walked up to the board and drew another path:

"And if we go your way we might not reach the Saibou before they take off again!"

"I'm sorry, but no." Adrienne stared at Edward

"Why?" Edward asked.

"There's a civilization of the most dreaded food ever."

"What is it?" But before she could answer, a loud thump was heard.

A voice everyone dreaded bellowed into the team's ears. "I'm back, Amigos! And I've brought some friends with me."

Part 6: Tiriaq

"Ah SCRAP! It's the ETM!" Chipette exclaimed, "Fire the thrusters!" Sugar Cookie pushed a giant blue button and the spaceship hurtled through space.

"You can't escape me!" The ETM laughed. Tiriaq yelped as the ETM materialized in front of him in a cloud of shredded cheese. Edward yanked his cookie blaster out and started firing while Chipette and Tiriaq started to grab chairs to throw at the ETM.

"You're probably wondering how I got on your ship," the ETM sounded bored, "Before I tell you that, I'd like to introduce you to Swiss S. Cheese, Unruly Urnebes, the Hostile Hamburger, and Malicious Malt Vinegar."

Four evil looking foods stepped into the light. Swiss S. Cheese was a flat, square shaped food. He had holes all over his face and wore a leather jacket containing slices of swiss cheese. The Hostile Hamburger was massive compared to the ETM. Each sesame seed on his top bun was an eye the size of Sugar Cookie's phone. The meat and the lettuce seemed to form a mouth on the Hostile Hamburger's face with a juicy red tomato tongue lying in between. When the hamburger moved, eight giant french fries, two times the height of Tiriaq, would appear under the hamburger allowing it to move. Tiriaq then turned his attention to Malicious Malt Vinegar. She was rather small in stature but looked fierce beyond belief. She was a salad dressing bottle with black flowing hair that seemed attached to the bright red cap on the top of her head. Unruly Urnebes seemed to have no shape due to the fact that she was a type of salad made of cheese and hot chili peppers, with salt and other spices. Her entire being was bright orange-ish-red and when she moved her body took the shape of a sphere and she rolled around.

Tiriaq brought his attention back to the ETM who had continued speaking, "Just so you know, Unruly Urnebes can't talk as she has no mouth and Malicious Malt Vinegar has taken an oath of silence in support of her friend. You've all met. . . right?" The ETM scanned the dessert's faces. Some of the desserts must have looked confused because the ETM said, "You know, during that terrible battle in front of the Athaliahus Asylum."

"Oh I remember them now!" Edward exclaimed. The rest of Tiriaq's friends muttered in agreement.

"Wait!" Tiriaq said, "I don't remember this battle!"

"Neither do we!" Chipette and Sugar Cookie exclaimed. Edward and Adrienne filled them in on what happened.

"Are you done?!" the ETM sneered when Tiriaq, Sugar Cookie and Chipette were all caught up.

"I think so," Edward replied, "Please, continue your evil speech!"

"No," the ETM sighed, "you stupid desserts ruined the mood." All ten foods stood awkwardly inside the spaceship. This lasted for a couple of minutes, that seemed like an eternity.

Abruptly the ship scraped against the side of something. Sugar Cookie practically sprang up out of the

Part 6: Tiriaq

awkward circle in which they were standing and dashed for the window.

"Well, we have reached the space village." Sugar Cookie happily reported. The ETM's face turned the color of marshmallow.

"Only a mad food would travel here..." Tiriaq heard Swiss S. Cheese mutter.

Hearing this, Tiriaq did the only logical thing. "Why?" he asked.

"Because here lives a terrible species known as—" Swiss S. Cheese was cut off by a thump on the top of our ship, followed by the sound of metal ripping apart. Everyone craned their necks to see what was making the noise. Suddenly, the roof gave-way and a hideous monster peeked through the hole.

The monster was unnaturally green and had a round cylinder body as thick as five Edwards stacked on top of each other. The monster donned a wild afro that looked like millions of tiny leaves. The monster bared its teeth which were as sharp as knives and jumped into the ship, landing on its head and bouncing upright.

"BROCCOLI!!!" someone (who might have been Tiriaq) screamed.

"Wait!" Adrienne stopped Tiriaq from running away, holding out her arm, "Maybe it's friendly?"

The monster teetered over and stood upright. Its tiny hands reached up into its afro and pulled out two wicked sharp knives. The monster grinned and howled like an animal. Suddenly, more monsters poured into the ship, each gripping their own set of knives.

Part 6: Tiriaq

"NOPE! NOT FRIENDLY!" Edward screamed as all ten of the currently non-hostile foods freaked out and ran away. Not very far though, as the ship was rather small, despite all the expansions built by Tiriaq and Chipette.

"Every food for themselves!" The ETM screamed.

Tiriaq was the first to react as he pulled out a chair and started bashing broccoli on the head, rendering them unconscious. To Tiriaq's left he saw Adrienne had created a transparent dome around her. A broccoli gathered up its courage and poked that dome. As soon as it did, it caught on fire and the poor broccoli ran around trying to extinguish the fire on top of its head.

To Tiriaq's right, Edward fired his cookie blaster and a golden net shot out and entrapped several broccolis under its treads. Then, suddenly, a new wave of broccolis jumped in and untangled their friends from the net and threw the net on top of Edward. Edward sighed and put away his cookie blaster. Edward shouted something about needing a weapon and two glowing blue knives fell into his hands. Edward cut the net and the knives turned into freeze ray guns. Edward jumped on top of a broccoli and used his freeze rays to close the hole in the top of the ship with ice. Tiriaq stumbled out of his daze just in time to see a broccoli flying towards him. The broccoli was soon bombarded with a series of burrito torpedoes. Tiriaq turned and saw the ETM shouting,

"Are you going to help Amigo?" Tiriaq nodded and grabbed a nearby ladle that once doubled as a joystick to drive the ship. The console sparked where the ladle once resided while Tiriaq engaged the next broccoli who attacked him in combat.

The broccoli tripped and Tiriaq yelled, "See you ladle!" and bonked it on the head, knocking it out.

"Duck!" an Italian voice shouted from behind Tiriaq. Tiriaq obeyed and a slice of swiss cheese flew across the room, impaling itself on a broccoli's forehead. Tiriaq turned around to see his savior. It was Swiss S. Cheese and he was holding cheese slices in his hands and throwing them like ninja stars.

"I have a plan, but I need to be undistracted by broccoli!" Sugar Cookie yelled over all the comotion. The Hostile Hamburger scuttled over to Edward's sister, crushing broccoli under its enormous french fry legs. The Hostile Hamburger laid down and gestured with a fry leg for Sugar Cookie to climb on its back. When Sugar Cookie was all settled, the Hostitle Hamburger resumed smashing the giant green monsters.

Unruly Urnebes shape shifted into a giant cylinder and started bulldozing any broccoli that dared to attack the Hostile Hamburger. Tiriaq jumped up and started grabbing chairs and stacking them around Sugar Cookie, forming a barricade. The broccoli, however, started to pile on top of each other in a vain attempt to steal Sugar Cookie's phone.

One lucky broccoli managed to get close to the Hostile Hamburger. Within a split second, the broccoli opened its mouth and chomped on the burger's fry leg. The burger screamed in pain and used its last resort attack. It had not been used in ages. He screamed so

Part 6: Tiriaq

loudly that all of a sudden his patty started squirting juice in all directions dissolving the broccoli but drying himself out in the process.

The once savory and juicy Hostile Hamburger fell to the floor screaming, "I'M DRYING, I'M DRYING!" He gasped one last breath of air before falling to the ground and cracking into five pieces.

All of the broccoli cheered and they turned their attention back to Sugar Cookie's phone and charged. Swiss started throwing cheese shards and incapacitating broccoli left and right. Soon, the broccoli had an idea. They all started stacking up together and soon formed the shape of a broccoli about 40 feet tall. The giant broccoli made up of hundreds started striding forward slowly and crushing everything in its path.

Soon the broccoli outgrew the ship and the massive weight made the ship rock like a canoe on rough waters. Tiriaq screamed and ran to the steering wheel of the ship. He reached the console and found the ladle that drove the ship to be missing. Realizing that he had too hastily pulled the steering mechanism out earlier, he pulled on a spatula that doubled as a lever marked "Emergency Landing"and the ship shuddered and headed down to the nearest planet at an alarming rate.

"We're going to cwash!" Tiriaq shouted just as the ship impacted the ground. The sudden stop in movement threw everyone out onto the new planet with a loud SQWISH!

As Tiriaq lay on the ground he suddenly thought that it didn't make sense for the Broccoli to just attack them out of nowhere. Maybe when they accidentally flew through their village they were angered by the engine like the baby corn and peas. The two incidents had to be connected somehow. Tiriaq didn't have time to contemplate this thought because he noticed that the giant made of broccoli had recovered before the others had even stood up and snatched Sugar Cookie off the ground.

 Tiriaq jumped to his feet and grabbed the nearest thing to him—the dashboard to their now destroyed ship. A bent spatula was the only thing left connected to it. Edward pulled out his cookie blaster but found it had been smashed during the crash. He then summoned the blue knives to find that they were both reduced to useless scrap as well. He threw the weapons aside and raised his fists. Tiriaq wondered what his fist would do against the giant monster. Swiss started twirling rapidly like a ballerina chopping and spun all the way to the foot of the Broccoli giant. Soon he was chopping up the shins of the titan veggie. The giant monster emitted a low and rattling scream and promptly dropped Edward's sister and the titan bared its teeth at Swiss.

 "Wait! ST-WOP!" Tiriaq screamed as he came to a sudden realization. The baby corn and peas and the broccoli attacked. It was definitely connected. But it was too late. Swiss threw a knife at the giant broccoli. However, the broccoli was learning quickly and sidestepped the knife. The knife went flying and spinning through the air but it was too late.

Part 6: Tiriaq

Sugar Cookie fell right into it, the knife penetrating her outer layer of dough. She stumbled and fell. She had trouble breathing. Edward ran over sobbing. "S-sugar?" Tiriaq took the opportunity and stopped all the other foods from attacking the broccoli,

"G-wuys, I th-wink I'm ont-wo something," Tiriaq informed them and started walking up to the titan veggie.

"Oh no you don't!" Adrienne protested and tried to hold Tiriaq back.

"*Stooop it!*" Tiriaq said, "I'm wold enough to s-wolve some pwoblems on my w-own! Give me a b-wit wof space!"

"When did you become such a teenager!" Adrienne gasped, then she shed a single tear saying, "they grow up so fast." Tiriaq wrenched his arm free of Adrienne and marched up to the fallen broccoli giant. The titan quickly disassembled at Tiriaq's approach and bared their teeth.

Tiriaq help up his hands to show them that he wasn't armed and said,"We didn't kidn-wap the baby vegetables."

The broccoli stopped being hostile and the largest one confronted Tiriaq."Then where are they!? You dessert crumb!" it said in a raspy voice while holding up a knife. Tiriaq felt a bead of sweat fall down his face and he stumbled to find words. The lead broccoli placed the tip of its knife against Tiriaq's chest. "Speak or die!" the broccoli demanded, its sour smelling breath wafting over Tiriaq's face.

Part 6: Tiriaq

"Are you okay honey!" Adrienne shouted, "Need me to help you?"

"*GOOOOSH! SHUSH UP!*" Tiriaq shouted over his shoulder. Adrienne turned her face down in defeat.

He then gathered his courage and spoke to the broccoli. "They boarded our ship for a bwief pewiod duwing their sleepover all angwy and attacking us," Tiriaq explained, "We almost were over run and I h-wid in a closet!" The broccoli all cheered at this and muttered about how they taught their apprentices well. "And th-wen, we distwacted them by p-wutting on a game of Candy Cwush!" The broccoli let out disappointed sighs and several even pulled out notepads and wrote, "resistance to Candy Crush training" on their daily agenda.

"B-wut, they didn't stay long," Tiriaq continued, "soon they up and weft! We never saw them again." The lead broccoli put down his knife and the broccoli behind him put away their notepads.

"You better be telling the truth," the lead broccoli said, tracing Tiriaq's face with its knife, "otherwise, we will kidnap everything you love and maybe return them to you in eight to ten business days!"

"Not eight to ten b-wusiness days!" Tiriaq said, horrified, "the waiting will be so torturous!"

"Exactly," the broccoli said. With a final nod to Tiriaq, the entire broccoli fleet used their superfood strength and jumped out of the planet's atmosphere. After they jumped, Tiriaq could have sworn that he heard the planet groan in pain below his feet but

Part 6: Tiriaq

immediately dismissed the thought. Tiriaq noticed, as he walked away, that there was a marking where the broccoli had jumped off from that read, "The Vegetable Assassin League (VAL) was here."

"How'd it go?" Adrienne asked Tiriaq when he returned to the main group.

"Good," Tiriaq responded, "the bwoccoli are out of this world."

"They are pretty cool, eh, amigo?" the ETM said.

"No, I mean they weft the planet."

The ETM just responded with a soft, "Oh".

Tiriaq quickly turned his attention to the injured Sugar Cookie. Edward and Chipette were trying to help her while Swiss. S Cheese stood slightly afar, a look of remorse on his face.

"Edward. I-I n-need," Sugar Cookie was saying. Edward ran, trembling, up to his injured sister.

"We need to find an infirmary!" Adrienne said, her voice shaking.

"W-where?" Edward asked.

"Take her here," two voices ordered behind them. Tiriaq turned around and saw two meatballs standing with spears made of toothpicks pointed at them. Edward refused, but Sugar Cookie was getting weaker by the second.

"This might be the only way for her to survive," Adrienne pointed out. Before anyone else could react,

Part 6: Tiriaq

the two meatballs swiped Sugar Cookie up and carried her limp body away.

"NOOOOOOO!" Edward and Chipette screamed as she disappeared into the sunlight. They both turned to Swiss, glaring like never before. They both charged at him. He fell backward and bounced multiple times as he fell to the ground. Before he had time to scream, Edward and Chipette tied him up.

"You are a danger to this entire party!" Edward shouted, "We can't let you harm, or worse, kill someone else!" Tiraq tried to stop them but there was no reasoning with Edward and his little sister. They solemnly, on the outside but concealing their anger and sadness, dug a hole in the ground.

"Are you s-wure you want to do this?" Tiriaq asked. Edward and Chipettete looked at Swiss and nodded.

"No, guys, don't do this! We can talk this out! I'm sorry!"

"You might have murdered our sister." Chipette seethed.

Edward grabbed him and threw him in the hole. Without another word they silently walked away, leaving Swiss in the hole. Tiriaq was mortified but he couldn't make himself move. Tiriaq ran back to the wreckage of the spaceship. He was about to go inside when a vibrating noise caught his attention. Tiriaq looked down and gasped. It was Sugar Cookie's phone. The screen read "Incoming call from: Unknown Caller." A voicemail message appeared. Tiriaq wiped the tears from his eyes, picked up the phone and pressed the voicemail button.

172

Part 6: Tiriaq

"Hey SC!" It was the cheery voice of Ginny Gelato, "I hope you don't mind but I'm using your phone to track you guys. And, just to let you know, the Saibou and I located Derek and Cassie inside brainwashed the SCL. Did you know that the SCL is corrupt? Anyways I'm going to drop Cassie and Derek off with you guys so that the Saibou and I can go back and decorrupt the rest of the facility. The Saibou was able to unbrainwash Cassie and Derek; luckily there wasn't much brain damage. Anyways, see you soon! Alrighty! Bye!"

The message ended, filling Tiriaq with newfound hope. He ran to go tell Adrienne but tripped on something. Tiriaq tired to get up, but he was trapped under the same something. He looked back. It was a greasy spaghetti noodle with a large eye at the end.

Staring. Right. At. Tiriaq's. Face.

Part 7: Swiss S. Cheese

Swiss S. Cheese was mortified at what he had just done. Sure the desserts were the enemies, but he wasn't a ruthless killer. He stood there, shocked at what he had done, and could only watch Edward and Chipette rush over to help their sister. When Edward and Chipette tied him up he didn't resist very much.

"Sure, being buried alive was pretty bad. Nothing I can't escape, though," Swiss thought to himself. After the desserts left, Swiss started to try and escape. He used an old tactic. He melted himself so he was liquid cheese running through the soil. He was flowing through the ground so fast that he hit a layer of stone. He heated himself up even more and burnt through the stone. Swiss thought he would eventually hit the core of the planet and be boiled.

There was nothing he could do now. This was the end for Swiss S. Cheese. Or so he thought. Abruptly, Swiss shot out of the hole and landed on his feet. When he looked up he came face to face with colossal spaghetti noodle with a large white eye at the end. Then Swiss's pale cheese face turned to the color of asiago cheese for he just realized that the planet he was on wasn't a planet. It was the Spaghetti Monster.

The yellow greasy noodle made a sound like chittering bugs and retreated into the distance. The call of the noodle was answered back and seven dark shapes soon were sent flying all around Swiss S. Cheese.

Part 7: Swiss S. Cheese

They all landed within close proximity of Swiss, each one making a "SQUISH" sound as they impacted the ground.

Soon the dark shapes came into the light. Each one was another tiny meatball dripping with red sauce, just like the two that had whisked Sugar Cookie away. They had eyes as red as strawberries and their teeth… Disgusting! All seven meatballs studied the terrified Swiss but didn't make a move on him. Three loud SQUISHes behind him alerted the Swiss that more meatballs had arrived. Swiss cautiously turned around to face two new meatballs. The three meatballs looked like the other meatballs behind him. Except one of the meatballs wore a pair of round, blue, glasses.

"Now, sir," said the meatball with the glasses, "I have been instructed to welcome you and your friends to the Spaghetti Monster, and I hope that you will enjoy your painful demise."

"Wait, *what!*" Swiss exclaimed.

The meatball with the glasses frowned, "Perhaps you didn't hear me the first time. I have been instructed to welcome you and your friends to the—"

"No, no. I get that. But—"

"Ah!" the meatball said, "You, like your comrades, do not understand the 'painful demise' part. Correct?"

"First," Swiss said, "the desserts are not my friends. Second, yes the 'painful demise' part is 'slightly' confusing."

"Well, I have some explanation.'' The meatball said, "First, one of the desserts is your friend because it fired one of the ship's guns next to the spot you were

175

buried, causing you to shoot out of the ground, saving
you from certain death. Second, the atmosphere of the
Spaghetti Monster becomes filled with an unknown gas
that forms irrational thoughts of action in the occupants
of the Spaghetti Monster's mind when the monster is
greatly annoyed. So when occupants get so angry,
they're likely to explode, hence the 'painful demise'."
*The ship crashing onto the monster must have released
the gas. And the gas must have caused Edward's and
Chipette's outburst.* Swiss thought.

"Who saved me?" The Swiss asked.

"The dessert that goes by the name of Tike and
the fortune cookie."

"Tiriaq and Adrienne?"

"Ah. yes. I believe those were their names."

"Do you know where the other foods and
desserts were taken?"

"Yes!" the meatball with the glasses said. "They
were kidnapped and taken to the holding cells just like
what's about to happen to you." Before Swiss could
react, the meatball with the glasses whistled. On the
command the nine other hideous meatballs closed in on
Swiss and hoisted him onto their backs and started to
roll him away.

"YOU'LL NEVER GET AWAY WITH THIS!" Swiss
yelled. Tomato sauce was splashed over his mouth
preventing him from talking any more.

As Swiss was rolled away, he finally began to
notice his surroundings. The ground was made of
meatballs. No surprise there. The sky was a sickly pale
orange and cloudless and the air had a scent of tomato

sauce much like the febreze Swiss used inside the bathroom of his house on The Diner. There were little physical landmarks except for the small indents in the surface of the meatball and the mesas and buttes of spaghetti surrounding him. Out in the distance lay the remains of the dessert's ship.

Swiss smiled, satisfied at his handiwork, but then snapped back to reality. He couldn't communicate verbally and knew nothing about the environment he had been placed in. He desperately looked around, but couldn't see any opportunity for escape due to the girth of his captors waists.

Suddenly, a giant black temple could be seen on the horizon. His eyes widened as he saw the green walls of celery and carrots sticking out all around it each covered in a layer of grease and grime. It was at this moment he realized what he was seeing. This was the legendary Food Pyramid. He didn't realize Supreme Lord Mac-N-Cheese had already built it. That wasn't supposed to happen until the SCL was thoroughly taken over. Swiss came to the conclusion that since the Food Pyramid was recently built, Supreme Lord Mac-N-Cheese must be inside. But why was the supreme lord capturing him? Unless... Swiss felt a wave of terror wash over him. As the armored meatballs dragged him into the pyramid, Swiss resolved to find the supreme lord and demand him to explain himself.

"Your doom awaits here!!" One of the carrots screamed as Swiss was rolled into the chamber. He looked around and saw many foods from all backgrounds screaming and flailing. Meatballs everywhere whipped them and armored them. Soon it dawned upon him what he had to do.

He was going to be forced to fight to the death. It was then that he knew Supreme Lord Mac-N-Cheese didn't care about anyone but himself. All that talk about dinner foods being superior was pure baloney. And now, Swiss S. Cheese would have to fight another food for the supreme lord's enjoyment.

A buff meatball with ten pack abs seemingly etched out of its torso walked over to Swiss and grumbled, "It's your turn. And why are there so many bullet holes in your body?"

"Shut up! I am a slice of Swiss cheese!" Swiss replied.

"Right." smirked the buff meatball as he started taking measurements to match him up to a fitting rival. He started shouting into a walkie-talkie. After a minute or two of talking, the muscular mass of meat responded. "You're against some dude named Meatloaf Master or something along those lines. I don't care. I do this job 'cause I get paid. Like really paid. Like a ton of ketchup packets an hour."

"Ok beef ball, shut up! I don't need your life story; you aren't that interesting anyway," retorted Swiss.

The muscular meatball glowered and punched Swiss in the gut.

He didn't have much time to regain his full strength before the meatball threw him into the arena with a bow and a quiver of toothpicks. He raised his head and saw his opponent towering over him. It was a giant hunk of meatloaf. The meatloaf smiled, revealing rotten teeth.

"Welcome to the Food Pyramid! To begin our first fight of the day we have: SWISS S. CHEESE!" a voice over the loudspeaker said. One person in the audience cheered but quickly realized their enthusiasm wasn't shared by the crowd and tried to pass it off as a cough.

"Against the legendary, master of magic, MEATLOAF, JR.!" Loud cheers and applause erupted all over the stadium. Swiss, feeling hopelessness, knelt down and punched the ground out of anger.

As the two faced off Swiss thought to himself, "*I just have to fight this guy, and once I defeat him, I'll look for a place to escape, find the supreme lord, and end this all.*"

"SHIELDY-O!" Meatloaf Jr. shouted. Meatloaf Jr.'s voice was very high pitched, making Swiss's eyes water. Suddenly a golden circle of runes appeared around the meatloaf and started spinning rapidly. The meatloaf stood up and started levitating. Columns of meat burst out of the ground all around him.

Swiss stared in amazement and shock and started running.

The columns started gliding towards him. Soon, he was encircled by pillars of Meatloaf Jr. blocking his vision.

The crowd chanted.

The pillars of meatloaf closed in slowly.

Swiss started panicking. He had no idea what would happen if he made contact with one of the columns. He noticed all the walls were covered in

Part 7: Swiss S. Cheese

built-in grills covered in grease and the remains of dead
gladiators. So he made the jump. He leaped into the air,
turned sideways, and had just enough room to clear the
pillars.

He stuck the landing. The crowd went *wild*.
Swiss took a toothpick, knocked it, and fired at the
meatloaf. It went straight into his leg. The meatloaf
screamed in pain and fell to the ground. The columns
disappeared from around Swiss and he was able to see
clearly once more.

"Are you ok!?" Swiss shouted remorsefully,
forgetting that he was in a fight to the death. The slice
of cheese knelt down and lent a hand to help the
meatloaf up. It bellowed and grabbed Swiss's hand with
such force that he was flung across the stadium. Swiss
stood back up, greatly angered that his gesture was not
reciprocated. It was like going to high-five a friend and
having them ignore you. Swiss knocked a toothpick
arrow in his now dented bow and fired at the meatloaf's
head. Meatloaf Jr. snapped his head in Swiss's direction
and caught the arrow in mid flight. Swiss didn't waste
another second and began to rapidly fire the rest of the
arrows out of his quiver. Surely his opponent couldn't
catch them all.

Swiss couldn't have been more mistaken.
Instead, Meatloaf Jr. just sprouted more arms out of his
back and snatched each arrow sent his way. Swiss
gulped. The loaf of meat let out another growl and
returned all the arrows to their owner, pointy ends first
and at 100 miles an hour. Thank goodness Swiss had
holes already pre-punctured into his body. He jumped

180

up and rotated, all the arrows passed through his holes harmlessly and impaled themselves in the wall behind him. He looked behind him as the toothpicks impacted the grill wall of The Food Pyramid. Jets of fire shot out from the wall incinerating the toothpicks. This gave Swiss an idea.

"Hey! Meatbutt!" Swiss shouted. Meatloaf Jr. glared at him. "That's right you greasy sack of protein, I'm talking to you! Straight to your ugly face." Meatloaf Jr. placed all of his now countless hands against the ground. "That's right, come and get me."

Meatloaf Jr. used the combined power of all his arms to fling himself into the air and land several feet away from Swiss. As the meatloaf charged at Swiss, he grabbed himself one of his cheese slice throwing stars and ditched the bow on the ground. Once Meatloaf Jr. was inches away, Swiss threw the star. As anticipated, the meatloaf just used one of his arms to shield his face from the projectile. But this blocked his vision and Swiss was able to fall over, his body completely flush with the ground. Meatloaf Jr. barreled right over him and crashed straight into the wall. Swiss stood up.

"Listen to me," Swiss said, "if we stop fighting, we can escape from here!" Meatloaf Jr. seemed to consider this. But before an answer was given, the flames jetted out of the grills on the walls and Meatloaf Jr. was no more. The crowd screamed and cheered in approval.

Swiss began to look for an escape route but the announcer came on again before he could muster as much as 1% of a plan, "SWISS S. CHEESE, YOU HAVE

BEATEN THE PREVIOUS CHAMPION! YOU ARE NOW THE
CHAMPION!" The crowd whooped and shouted and
held up foam fingers.

They threw screaming baby peppermints into
the arena chanting, "EAT UP! EAT UP! EAT UP!" Swiss did
his best to run around and toss them back to their
parents, who caught them graciously.

"Now for Swiss's next opponent: THE EVIL TACO
MAN!" The announcer screamed. Swiss suddenly
realized that he had heard that voice before. It was just
as he predicted, but he never thought that the supreme
lord would take such a central part in the slaughter.

The announcer was Supreme Lord
Mac-N-Cheese.

"YOU TRAITOR!" Swiss yelled at the announcer.
"YOU DEVILISH STEAMING CUP OF DRIED UP ELBOWS! I
KNOW IT'S YOU, SUPREME LORD MAC-N-CHEESE!"

"Oh, scrap," the now exposed Supreme Lord
Mac-N-Cheese said.

"I was wondering when you would make that
conclusion, *Amigo*," a Mexican accent said. Swiss turned
around to see the ETM, and everyone that was on the
ship including the still scowling Edward and Chipette.

"Here's the plan," the ETM whispered to Swiss,
"all of us dinner foods decided that we don't want to
work for the supreme lord any more, especially after he
betrayed us like this. Plus, we don't even get dental or
medical coverage!" Swiss nodded. A fiery rage filled his
chest. No one cut dental out of Swiss S. Cheese's
insurance plan!

Part 7: Swiss S. Cheese

Part 7: Swiss S. Cheese

"This place is the perfect base, if we can just get Supreme Lord Mac-N-Cheese out of here, we will have enough resources to take on the rest of his army," the ETM continued to explain, gesturing to a hallway behind the battle area where it appeared the rest of the gang was being held captive.

Swiss quickly glanced around to locate the announcer's booth. He saw it and fired an arrow quickly through the window. It penetrated the glass and there was a distorted scream over the microphone. The guards quickly started firing on Swiss, but the ETM dove over to him, hugged him, and created a forcefield of refried beans surrounding them.

"WAIT!" Supreme Lord Mac-N-Cheese screamed. The guards held their fire. "The count of foods I've captured is off. Edward, Chipette, Adrienne, Tiriaq, Swiss S. Cheese, ETM, Unruly Urnebes, Malicious Malt Vinegar and WHO IS THAT?" Only now did Swiss notice the tall figure with them that he had never seen before.

"Hello. I am the ETL, Evil Taquito Lady."

"Honey!" the ETM shouted, staring unbelievingly, "I thought you to be dead."

"Who is that stick?" Tiriaq inquired.

"My wife. Who I thought was dead."

"You just said that last part," Swiss pointed out. The ETM glared at him.

"Well honey, I'm alive! I know right! Now we can take that vacation to the living room like we've always dreamed of!" The ETL squealed excitedly.

Part 7: Swiss S. Cheese

"That was mainly your idea, but ok." The ETM said flatly.

"Um. GUYS! I WAS RIGHT IN THE MIDDLE OF MAKING A BIG SPEECH!" Supreme Lord Mac-N-Cheese screamed.

"Oh right. Continue! Mr. Cheese!" Chipette squealed.

"I AM NOT MR. CHEESE!" Supreme Lord Mac-N-Cheese screamed some more, "I'M SUPREME LORD MAC-N-CHEESE."

"Yeah, sure. Whatever." Chipette said, rolling her eyes.

"Children!" Supreme Lord Mac-N-Cheese grumbled, "Anyways, surrender to me or I'll make sure that Sugar Cookie perishes! HA HA HA HA HA!"

"No!" Edward screamed.

"Oh, yes," Supreme Lord Mac-N-Cheese said with a hint of delight, "I have her captured right here." Seeing Edward and Chipette's confused looks, Supreme Lord Mac-N-Cheese continued to explain, "By 'here,' I mean that after my meatball guards took her into an infirmary and had her laceration rebaked shut, I had her locked up in this Micro-wa-vey I built." Supreme Lord Mac-N-Cheese gestured to a big black box with gray buttons to cook the prisoner in different ways. On the front of the box was a window where Swiss could see Edward's sister stuck to a plate being turned slowly. Swiss gasped. The Micro-wa-vey was only something read about in fairy tales about illusive giants, called humans, who ate foods. Often, these stories were used to scare younger foods into good behavior, but Swiss never thought one of them would manifest before his eyes, even if it was the Supreme Lord's creation.

"Set her free!" Swiss demanded.

"Why do you care!?" Supreme Lord Mac-N-Cheese returned

"Well, I accidently almost killed her, so. . . I would like to prevent that from happening again."

"You were always too soft and melty," scoffed Supreme Lord Mac-N-Cheese. "KILL THEM!" Meatball guards charged at the group, then stopped suddenly.

"WHAT ARE YOU WAITING FOR?" screamed Supreme Lord Mac-N-Cheese.

"Well, sir," one of the braver meatballs started, "We're not quite sure who to attack. Do you mean the desserts, the dinner foods, or the foods in the audience who are all glaring at you?"

Swiss looked around, and sure enough, the entire crowd was glaring at the booth from which the supreme lord sat.

"Fine!" Supreme Lord Mac-N-Cheese screamed, "I'll do it myself!" With that, he started firing elbow macaroni at the meatballs. Swiss and the ETL ducked for cover and were able to remain unscathed due to their thin width. The ETM wasn'tso lucky and received several chips to his shell along with losing a ton of lettuce. Several of the members of the crowd who weren't paying attention were completely blown senseless and caught by their friends. The noodles started bouncing all over the walls and knocking soldiers out left and right. The crowd went wild and began to chant Swiss's name. The audience once again began throwing baby peppermints into the arena. This time it was ETM and his wife who threw them back to their parents. When Supreme Lord Mac-N-Cheese revealed himself and started making a bolt for the gate, the crowd applauded and one corn dog even shouted,

"Marry me Supreme Lord Mac-N-Cheese!"

Swiss heard Adrienne mutter a Vishnu spell and the lot of them burst out from confinement. Edward and his party quickly chased down the supreme lord. Supreme Lord Mac-N-Cheese started shooting liquid cheese behind him, causing the crew to slip and fall. Swiss, fortunately, was made of cheese and continued running.

Supreme Lord Mac-N-Cheese had one more trick up his sleeve. He summoned a spoon with a flash of light and chucked it at Swiss like a javelin. Swiss took the blow in the head and was blown back to Edward. They all stood up, looking grimly at the now sprinting cup of instant mac. Then a three headed dragon appeared on the horizon.

"It's the Saibou!" Tiriaq shouted. The team watched as the dragon picked up Supreme Lord Mac-N-Cheese and cheered. On the Saibou's back, Derek Donut, Cassie Cake and Ginny Gelato waved triumphantly. The dragon dropped Supreme Lord Mac-N-Cheese in the middle of the arena. On a closer inspection, it was clear that Supreme Lord Mac-N-Cheese was leaking melted cheese from scratches on his face.

"You'll never catch me!" Supreme Lord Mac-N-Cheese snarled, and he started glowing.

Part 7: Swiss S. Cheese

"Somebody STOP HIM FROM TELEPORTING!"
Swiss yelled. At this, the entire crowd jumped out of
their seats and started to sprint towards the teleporting
food. Swiss looked around hopelessly, knowing that the
crowd would never reach the Supreme Lord in time.
That's when he noticed Chipette and Tiriaq whispering
to each other. Suddenly they both dashed away into the
armory. Seconds later they came around the corner
holding a large fork on their shoulders.

"WONE!" Tiriaq shouted.

"ONE!" Chipette responded.

"TWO!" Tiriaq continued.

"TWO!" Chipette responded.

"THREE!" they both cried. At the same time the
ETM and ETL teleported to where the supreme lord was
and went to sock him in the nose. Meanwhile, Swiss
threw a cheese slice and Adrienne and Edward threw
fireballs. The fork was launched from their fingers and
flew through the air like a javelin. The cheese slice and
fireballs connected midair and the fireballs melted the
cheese, causing it to drip everywhere and spray the ETM
in the face.

Supreme Lord Mac-N-Cheese's eyes widened as
the ETM attacked him, but the punch that the Mexican
foods landed on him was unbalanced because of the
cheese spray and their fists missed his face by an inch.
The attack was uncoordinated and sloppy, everyone had
been trying to do their own attack and there was no
team work whatsoever.

Part 7: Swiss S. Cheese

"Oh, Flaxseed!" Supreme Lord Mac-N-Cheese screamed as the fork neared his face and punctured the side of his cup. Then he vanished, fork and all.

Then silence. Really. Long. Silence.

Everyone knew that had the attacks been more fluid and coordinated, maybe they would have ended the supreme lord right there.

Edward glared at Swiss and muttered,"You messed everyone up!" while the ETM and ETL tried to put out the fire that had combusted on their faces.

The crowd went absolutely wild over this, still thinking it was part of the show, and Edward took the opportunity. He reached down and placed some melted cheese on his finger and wiped it on his face like war paint. Swiss, understanding what Edward was doing, followed suit and so did his comrades. They threw their arms in the air and the crowd was silent. After a moment, they erupted in the loudest cheer ever heard and resumed throwing baby peppermints.

They were flowing over the edge of the arena and copied the war paint. They had an army now. They gave the civilians forks and toothpicks. They started training the crowd in the arena immediately.

Swiss, Edward and Chipette quickly located the fastest way to the micro-wav-ay and bounded towards Sugar Cookie and hugged her. Sugar Cookie embraced her siblings but awkwardly shook off and pushed away Swiss S. Cheese. Who hung his head.

"I'm terribly sorry Sugar Cookie." Swiss said.

Part 7: Swiss S. Cheese

Sugar Cookie's face softened. "I know you are."

"Sugar Cookie. He is a psycho dairy chunk. Don't get too close to him again." Chipette warned her sister.

Swiss retorted, "You do realize that you also have dairy products in your dough. More than me, actually."

"Not the point, cow scrap. Now stay away from my sisters or I'll see to it personally that you will get a couple of extra holes. Made with a sharp toothpick." Edward said as he picked up one nearby.

"Pwease! Stop the fwighting." Swiss turned around to see Tiriaq holding Sugar Cookie's phone, "Swugar Cookie, hwere's your phone bwack." Tiriaq continued and handed her the phone reluctantly.

"Thanks, you're my new favorite living being with dairy," Sugar Cookie said, glaring at her siblings and Swiss.

Edward ran up to Cassie and Derek, who had been standing by the Saibou in shock at what had just happened. "Oh, gosh guys! I'm so sorry I left you there hypnotized and whatnot I just—"

"It's ok," Cassie said, patting his back, "you did what you had to do. Plus, we heard all about Parnethanope and her shenanigans." Derek nodded in agreement.

A picture of Supreme Lord Mac-N-Cheese, tied up with a licorice, was hung in the great hall to inspire the foods who really did not like his presence. Dinner foods and desserts alike threw baby peppermints at the photo (which had surprisingly wicked sharp teeth to bite the Supreme Lord) as target practice. There were also

Part 7: Swiss S. Cheese

foods assigned to throwing the children back immediately after being chucked. The parents knew there was no danger of losing their child so they threw it, had it returned to them, and then stepped back in line to throw their son or daughter again. Edward and Adrienne were training the foods and desserts. Derek Donut and Cassie Cake supervised the baby peppermints when they were not being thrown at Supreme Lord Mac-N-Cheese. Ginny Gelato, after freeing the prisoners that were previously being held to fight, said that she had to take The Saibou back to the SCL to try and decorrupt the facility for good.

"I left SCL in a bad place, I think with just a bit more work I can un-hypnotise the rest of the workers and restore everything there to working order" she explained. Swiss S. Cheese and the evil Mexican foods attended to hyper civilians. Tiriaq and Chipette were put in charge of the rebuilding and decoration team in hopes of bringing a more homey vibe to the Food Pyramid. Unruly Urnebes was put in charge of keeping moral standards up, although many of the foods got excited about fighting and practiced on their friends. Malicious Malt Vinegar was put in charge of stopping the foods who practiced on their friends, and for providing medical care to the friends who they were practicing on.

Swiss attended a training just to brush up on his skills as a talented swordsman, knifeman, ninjastarman, and archer. Everyone was doing fine except for one half-brown banana. His name was Barry. Barry the banana. He constantly questioned everyone's knowledge and was always talking about somebody accidentally slashing his peel. One time, Swiss threatened to peel him if he didn't stop holding up the training. Barry, hearing this, promptly took off his peel and stood there naked. Because of this, he got a beatdown from the Evil Taquito Lady.

"Nice gentle-banana-men do not strip themselves of their peels in public!" She scolded while intensely beating him with a pillow. "Why take it off when you have no muscles to show?"

"ETL!" Adrienne cried, seeing the scene, "What did I tell you about beating foods up?" The ETL rolled her eyes but set aside the pillow.

"Run along *Barry,*" the ETL grumbled as the banana quickly scampered off. Edward, who had been watching from a newly installed bench, came up to Swiss and the ETL.

"Was that really necessary?" Edward asked.

"Well. . ." The ETL started, probably about to defend herself. However, after seeing Edward's disapproving face, she said: "No."

"Call a meeting of your food friends then meet me in the armory," Edward instructed Swiss. "We need to discuss the rules." The ETL started whining so Swiss turned to her and told her to shut it. Swiss then quickly rounded up the ETM, the ETL, Unruly Urnebes, and Malicious Malt Vinegar. Then the four of them quickly proceeded to the armory.

Part 7: Swiss S. Cheese

Edward was already at the armory along with Sugar Cookie, Chipette, Tiriaq, Cassie, Derek, and Andriene, when Swiss and his friends arrived.

"Good, you actually made it." Edward said when he saw Swiss.

"What's that mean?" Swiss respond defensively.

"It's just you being a criminal and I didn't think you would follow through with what you said."

"EXCUSE ME!" Swiss said, exasperated. "I am no longer a criminal! In fact, all of my friends have decided to leave that life behind!"

"WE HAVE!" Shouted the ETM and ETL simultaneously.

"Duh!" Swiss shouted, "Why else are we cooperating with the desserts!"

"Cause we have a common enemy," Edward retorted.

"No, we swear, all of us have decided to change. Even Unruly Urnebes and Malicious Malt Vinegar agree with me." Swiss looked over to see the two foods nodding like bobble heads.

"ANYWAYS," The ETL said, clearing her throat loudly, "We are here to talk about rules. Remember?"

"Yeah, *Edward!*" Chipette said.

"Right. Anyways," Edward said, wiping the sweat from his forehead, "rules."

"I'll start!" Sugar Cookie said, saving Edward from melting on the spot. "First of all, no, like, harming foods or desserts unless they are evil and like attack you for no reason. Second, listen and follow the first rule.

Third, follow the second rule. Fourth, follow the third rule. Fi—"

"I think we get it." Swiss said.

"B-b-but I had likd five more of those!" Sugar Cookie cried. Unruly Urnebes and Malicious Malt Vinegar looked at each other and ran to comfort Edward's sister. Swiss looked over at Adrienne who looked like she wanted to say something. Then she farted.

"What's wrong with you!" the ETM screeched, "Disgusting!" Suddenly the ground started rumbling.

"I'm sorry!" Adrienne cried, "I just had a sip of milk from the milk fountain over there!" Swiss looked to where she was pointing and sure enough, shaped just like a water fountain, was a contraption that spewed milk.

"FEE FO FI FUM! I SMELL THE FART OF A DESSERT-MON!" A deep voice boomed.

"I needs to tell you the important info!" someone shouted from outside the door of the armory. "Let me in! It's Barry Banana!" Swiss rushed to let the fruit in as the ETL rolled her eyes.

"The Spaghetti Monster has awakened! Your senseless bickering has angered him deeply!" Barry sheirked. At this news, all the citizens that were living on the Spaghetti monster ran around screaming. A few level headed mints and their babies managed to open up the secret shed built in the side of the temple. With the help of Edward Chip and his friends, the citizens were gathered into secret burger patty shaped bunkers.

Part 7: Swiss S. Cheese

"There's not enough room for us," Edward said to Sugar Cookie.

"We'll figure something out," Andreinne, who had overheard him, said. The ETM and ETL tried to sneak down into a bunker by throwing some baby mints out, but received several smacks from the Mints' parents, and the two mexican foods were kicked out of the room. Barry Banana tried to hide in a bunker as well, but ended up slipping on his peel. All the rooms filled up as he tried to get up.

"Mind if I hang with you guys for a little while longer?" Barry smiled sheepishly.

"Oh BOLLOCKS!" Swiss exclaimed, "I swear if I'm killed by a giant meatball. . ."

"I'd be completely fine with that," Edward sneered, "and that's just because you are such a— "

"Do you think the Spaghetti Monster will like the renovations we have done to the battle arena?" Chipette asked, not letting her brother finish his sentence.

"ARE YOU KIDDING ME!" The Spaghetti monster boomed, hearing Edward's sister, "WHY WOULD ANYONE WANT A BUILDING ON THEIR BUTT!"

"I thought it was smelly in here," The ETL complained.

"No," Andrienne replied, "that was my fart."

"Wait," the ETM interjected, "you can tell what your farts smell like?"

"OH MY GOURD!" The Spaghetti Monster said, "ARE YOU GUYS SERIOUSLY TALKING ABOUT FARTS!"

"I'm not!" Barry said happily, receiving glares from everyone around him.

"YOU KNOW WHAT?!" The Spaghetti Monster said, "I. DON'T. CARE. JUST GET OFF OF ME AND ARGUE SOMEWHERE ELSE!"

"Well, we can't exactly." Sugar Cookie said.

"WHY NOT!!!!!!" The Spaghetti Monster was getting irritated.

"Cwas our ship bwew up." Tiriaq stated.

"UHG! FINE I'LL GET YOU OFF MY SELF!" The monster yelled. With that the entire armory was whacked apart by giant spaghetti noodles. Then one particularly colossal noodle picked everyone in the destroyed armory up, including Barry Banana. The noodle connected to two other noodles forming a slingshot to the Swiss and his friends in the middle. Then all the noodles went taut.

"ANY LAST WORDS?" The Spaghetti Monster asked.

"Yeah," Chipette said, "How can we hear you if we are on your butt?"

The Spaghetti Monster sighed, "THERE ARE GREAT ACOUSTICS ON THIS SIDE OF THE FOODIVERSE."

"I have another question," Chipette started again.

"NOPE!" The Spaghetti Monster said, "NO MORE QUESTIONS TODAY! BYE!" Then all the noodles released and the gang was slingshotted away, traveling at light speed. Then everything around Swiss went completely dark.

Part 8: Cassie Cake

     Cassie Cake felt like she had been flying through space forever since her and the gang's rough departure from the Spaghetti Monster. Also, there was this annoying high pitched sound in her ear ever since she started flying through the air. Maybe the flight had impaired her hearing somehow. Oh. Wait. Nevermind. The high pitched sound is just Tiriaq screaming. Sorry. It's not Tiriaq. He's right beside Cassie pretending he's one of the soup can birds that resided on the Spaghetti Monster. Whoa. That's the ETM's high pitch scream! Cassie hoped she wouldn't have to deal with the ETM screaming the entire time.

FIVE HOURS LATER:

     Turns out the ETM could scream for a long time. The ETM literally screamed for three hours, without taking a breath, before passing out. The silence had allowed her to reflect on her past adventures. She had been hypnotized, escaped countless dangerous situations, befriended several dinner foods, learned a little Vishnu, and none of it was known by her parents. From early on in Cassie's childhood she remembered her parents pushing her to be great, to do great. But then, as time went by, they seemed disappointed that she wasn't doing as much as she could. Suddenly

Part 8: Cassie Cake

straight As in school and all the extracurriculars in the world wouldn't appease her parents' hunger for an ultra successful child. She wondered what her parents would think of her now. Would they be proud of her finally? Or would it still inevitably not be enough?

Anyways, Cassie had noticed that her surroundings were starting to brighten up. Instead of seeing only pitch black, she was surrounded by light gray and a bright swirly light could be seen far ahead of her.

"It looks like we are finally going to land!" Cassie shouted to her best friend Derek Donut.

"WHAT!" he shouted back.

"IT LOOKS LIKE WE ARE FINALLY GOING TO LAND!" Cassie shouted again.

"HEY CASSIE," Derek shouted, "THAT BRIGHT SWIRLY THING IS GETTING CLOSER! I THINK THIS MEANS WE ARE GOING TO LAND SOON!"

Cassie sighed. Derek could be so dense sometimes. A surprisingly negative trait for a donut. She was going to shout something back, but then she noticed that the white swirly thing was approaching at a much faster rate than before. As she was about to go inside the light, Cassie held her breath involuntarily.

Cassie was soon blinded by the white light for a couple of seconds. Then, there was an abrupt. loud "POP!" and Cassie could see again. The moment Cassie looked down, she regretted it. Instead of flying through an endless void, she was now hurtling toward the ground. Adrienne and Edward both tried to use their Vishnu powers to slow their descent to no avail. The ETM even tried to teleport and that failed as well.

198

Part 8: Cassie Cake

Adrienne cursed in ancient cookienese and the ETM woke up and started screaming in a high pitched voice again.

Cassie tried to calculate the likelihood that they would survive the fall, but it appeared her Vishnu powered math magic wasn't working. She started to panic; she had grown fond of her ability and really wanted to use it on a math test if she was ever able to go back to school. Then she reminded herself that that would be cheating and her parents would never be proud of her if she cheated. At the sound of the ETM's voice, many small multicolored candies looked up and formed a giant landing pad under Cassie and her falling companions. Upon closer inspection, Cassie determined that the candies were a gaggle of gumdrops. Then Cassie hit the candy and bounced to her feet.

Other members of the group weren't so lucky. Edward fell on his side and chipped a chocolate chip, the ETM spilled lettuce and cheese everywhere while Barry Banana fell on head and another brown spot started forming where he bruised himself. As the foods struggled to get up, Cassie looked around and counted everyone:

1. The ETM
2. The ETL
3. Unruly Urnebes
4. Malicious Malt Vinegar
5. Edward
6. Sugar Cookie
7. Chipette
8. Tiriaq
9. Derek
10. Adrienne
11. Barry
12. Swiss S. Cheese
13. and herself.

Part 8: Cassie Cake

"THIS IS ALL YOUR FAULT!" Edward screamed at Swiss S. Cheese, who glared at him.

"Are you kidding me!" Swiss retorted, peeling himself off the metallic cold ground. "This is as much your fault as it is mine! Just face it! You were never keen on the idea of working with *dinner foods!*"

"Amigos! Calm down!" The ETM interjected, stepping between Edward and Swiss, who promptly yelled at him to shut up. "Geez, I was just trying to help! But if you don't appreciate it, I'll just leave!" With that, the ETM marched over to what appeared to be a nearby wall and attempted to scale it. The surface was slick and the ETM came crashing down. The ETL and Adrienne went to try and help him, but he shoved Adrienne away, who fell into Sugar Cookie.

"Like, excuse me!" Sugar Cookie glared at Adrienne. Chipette came running to aid Sugar Cookie, but due to the slick floor, she slid into the ETM.

"Hey! Back off my husband!" the ETL shouted to Chipette.

Cassie looked around. They seemed to be encased in a sort of bowl that housed a blade inside a giant hole in the center. Chipette was currently in a standoff against Unruly Urnebes and Malicious Malt Vinegar, as she had slipped on Barry and skidded into the pair of them. In true Derek fashion, he seemed overwhelmed by what was happening and had backed himself and Tiriaq into a corner in an attempt to avoid conflict.

Part 8: Cassie Cake

"YOU WANNA GO!" Cassie heard Edward shout to Swiss, his hands up in fists, "LET'S GO!" He launched himself at Swiss, who proceeded to launch five cheese slices into the air from his leather jacket. Meanwhile, The ETL and ETM were arguing fiercely with Chipette,

"I was just trying to help!"

"Oh *sure* you were! Just like you were trying to help when you and your brother buried Swiss!" the ETL retorted as she punched Chipette in the mouth. Meanwhile, Adrienne and Sugar Cookie had begun to grapple with one another.

"All I do is try and win over your trust," Adrienne was screaming, "time and time again I save your worthless life, and you do nothing to acknowledge it! Not even a thank you!"

"Well, excuse me for not trusting some dessert who was, like, trying to kill my brother when I first met them!" This was getting out of hand real quickly. Cassie didn't need her math powers to know she had to stop the fighting and looked up, trying to see if there was anything to use. There seemed to be a dispenser above them connected to a lever, and right next to it, on the wall, was a switch labeled: Garbage Disposal.

Cassie had no idea what either of those things were but decided to give it a shot. When in doubt, press all the buttons. Right? She sprinted across the floor and grabbed Derek by the leg. He protested very loudly but his complaints weren't heard over the chaos around them.

Part 8: Cassie Cake

"Sorry, Derek!" Cassie said as she spun him around and, using the nearby gumdrops as a bounce pad, bounced him into the air where he flew like a frisbee. Her donut friend went flying through the air and smashed in the lever before sliding back down the smooth walls of the bowl.

"Why do foods keep throwing me around?" Derek groaned. The effect was instantaneous and was more than she could have ever hoped for. Water flooded out of the dispenser and filled the metallic bowl. All of the foods who had been fighting abruptly stopped. Swiss, mesmerized by the water, accidentally let one last ninja star cheese slice fly. The cheese slice flew through the air and smacked straight into the switch, flicking it on.

A loud grinding sound was heard, emanating from the hole in the center of the bowl, and to Cassie's horror, she saw the blade inside of the hole was now spinning. The water filling the bowl began to form currents clockwise around the bowl. The foods began to spin around faster and faster. It was all Cassie could do to stay away from the hole in the center. The gumdrops weren't so lucky, and were sucked into the center of the forming hurricane; their screams were cut short as they entered The Garbage Disposal.

Momentarily, as the blade tried to move through their gummy bodies, the whirring slowed down, but soon picked back up when the candies were shredded. Everyone flipped out, all panicking as the waters rushed higher and spun faster. Derek was whisked up by the current and was launched out of the bowl into the unknown.

"Not again!" Derek screamed as he fell away.

This gave Cassie an idea. She paddled as best she could and linked arms with the nearest food, the ETL.

"EWWWW! Get away from me!" The ETL shouted, and tried to shake off Cassie's grip.

"You have to trust me!" Cassie yelled back, "Unless you want to die!" The ETL rolled her eyes but complied when Cassie motioned for her to link arms with Sugar Cookie. Sugar Cookie linked arms with the ETM, who linked with Adrienne, who linked arms with Unruly Urnebes and Malicious Malt Vinegar. Pretty soon, all of the remaining twelve foods had linked arms and were spinning around the bowl as a group with Cassie at the end of it. Then, after estimating the group's total mass, velocity, and radius, she flung herself and everyone towards the edge of the bowl, hoping that the rising water and centrifugal force would do the rest.

They went flying through the air and soon were crashing down onto a new surface, below the silver bowl they had just left. Landing with a splat, the group spat out water and tried to reform the parts of their bodies that had gotten soggy. Derek was already sitting on the floor, rubbing a dent on his head. Barry was trying to stand up, but with him being soaked, he kept falling over.

"You all are supreme idiots," Cassie gasped, reshaping her icing.

Part 8: Cassie Cake

"You are right, amigo," the ETM said, breathing heavily.

"I shouldn't have let my anger get to me," Edward said, "it almost killed everyone! And those poor gumdrops! Oh gosh, their deaths are our fault."

"We have to work together better," Adrienne was sitting on her knees. She looked like she might puke. "I'm so dizzy."

Of course Adrienne would say that. Cassie could never trust Adrienne. She just kind of popped in out of nowhere and decided she was part of their group. And now here she was, preaching about working together. Something about that fortune cookie didn't sit right with her. However, they had more pressing issues, so Cassie pushed the thought out of her head.

"That was, like, worse than the spinning teacups ride at Danish Land!" Sugar Cookie held her stomach, an imprint of her hand was on her icing.

"I promise you guys," Swiss vowed, "I'm on your side, I—"

"No need to explain yourself, I believe you," Edward stood up and offered the cheese slice a hand to stand up with.

With everyone having completely calmed down from their recent daring escape, Cassie was finally able to look around at her surroundings. They appeared to be on some sort of hard plank of... something brown. Cassie had no idea what it was. Above them strange buildings towered from every angle and there was a tiny doorway in the bottom of one of the walls. Cassie squinted as she looked through the doorway and could've sworn she saw beady eyes staring at her. Closer inspection yielded no pertinent findings and Cassie chalked it up to being tired.

"So, what now guys?" Edward asked.

"What a great question," Derek responded.

"I know it is. But does anyone have any thoughts?" Edward said.

"Well, what do we know so far?" Swiss mused.

"We know that we are, like, fugitives of the foodiverse with that mac and cheese guy hunting us."

"Are we 'like fugitives' or are we fugitives Sugar Cookie?" Edward teased.

"You know what I, like, ment!"

"We alswo know th-wat we aren't in the foodiwerse any more. Nothing here is made of fwood," Tiriaq piped up before Sugar Cookie could argue back.

"Should we even consider going back to the foobiverse? Would it be worth it?" The ETL asked.

"Should we consider going anywhere? I want to take a nap right here," Barry contributed. Everyone shouted at Barry to shut up.

"Being in this new area might be a good thing," Adrienne said, "it will give us a chance to regroup, come up with a plan of attack against the supreme lord, and rest."

"You make some good points, amigo. But how can we rest if we don't even know if the area we are in is safe?"

Part 8: Cassie Cake

"We should for sure go back eventually. I can't in good health leave the foodiverse while it is fully possible that Supreme Lord Mac-N-Cheese will just take it over while we are gone." Cassie said.

"So, it sweems like we should just expwore this area."

"Tiriaq's right," Chipette said, "there might even be something here that we can use to build a device that will help us defeat him once and for all."

"I really wish we had coordinated that attack on the Food Pyramid. We could have been done with this by now," Edward sighed.

"There's no point dwelling on what could have been, let's focus on now." the ETL picked a speck of dirt off of her shell.

"Well, there is that doorway in the wall over there," Cassie pointed to the opening she noticed earlier, "we should take a look in there." The group nodded in agreement.

"Noooo. I don't wanna do that. I still want a nap."

"SHUT UP BARRY!"

They walked into the dark opening one by one unsure what to expect. They poked around for several minutes but they could only find cobwebs and the smell of mold. They decided to return to the main area. As the foods exited the doorway, one by one, a giant gray blur ran back and forth. No one seemed to notice it until

Part 8: Cassie Cake

Cassie, who was at the back of the line saw that with each food that stepped out, the gray blur zoomed by and they were taken away. One by one they were taken, Edward stepped out in front of her and Cassie shouted at him to wait but it was too late. Cassie stepped out finally. When the gray blur came for her, she jumped up, the blur streaking under her feet.

"Who are you? And how did you escape the Garbage Disposal?" a voice demanded when Cassie landed.

"I could ask you the same thing, " Cassie said, then quickly added, "except the Garbage Disposal part."

"Turn around and put your hands up!" the voice demanded again. As Cassie turned around she heard five other voices instruct the same thing to her friends. Now that Cassie was facing the other way with her hands up she could totally see her captors. They were five jars of spices with green lids, and they were all girls.

"We are the Spice Girls," the lead Spice said, staring her cold eyes into Cassie. "I'm Ginger Spice and these are my sisters, Cinnamon Spice, Allspice, Nutmeg, and Pumpkin Spice. But Pumpkin Spice is an idiot, so ignore her!" All of the spices laughed except Pumpkin.

"Um. Okay." Cassie said.

"So," Ginger Spice said, "you are going to tell us what you want, what you really really want."

"Oh!" Cassie said, "I'll tell you what I want, what I really really want!"

"So what is it?" the spices asked

"I want to know where you are taking my friends."

Part 8: Cassie Cake

"We took them to the Cabinet to use as leverage against you in case you turn out to be evil," Pumpkin Spice stated.

"Pumpkin!" Allspice shouted, "You've ruined the plan!"

"Dang, it's not like I saw a gray blur or anything kidnap them literally a minute ago," Cassie said sarcastically.

"Really?" Nutmeg said, "You're not going to go mega raging mode?"

"No, Why would I do that?" Cassie replied.

"Cause we just kidnapped all of your friends." Pumpkin Spice said.

"First of all Barry Banana is not my friend. He's too annoying. Second of all, why didn't you kidnap me? I literally just jumped out of the way and y'all didn't care." Cassie said

"Girls, you take it from here," Ginger said, "I must make sure our *guests* feel welcome." Then Ginger walked away.

"Well, to answer your question—" Pumpkin started as soon as the leader left, but she was cut off by Nutmeg.

"Shut up, Pumpkin! You won't ever explain it more correcter than I. You still idioty. So much idiot since you ruined our master evil plan to escape this weirdy place! You cannot be brainer within five miles of a second ago! SO HA!" Nutmeg said.

"Oh my gourd!" Allspice interrupted, "You will never be able to explain it with that grammar, Nutmeg!"

Part 8: Cassie Cake

"Mind the business of your own! You're like an idiot actually!" Nutmeg shouted. With that, all five of the spices started arguing. Cassie thought this was very stupid and knew that if she wanted to get the information that she wanted, the Spices would have to be getting along.

"Girls, girls! You are *all* pretty." Cassie shouted over the noise. This got the Spices' attention.

"Thank you!" all the Spices said in unison, except for Nutmeg who added a "the" in the middle of "thank" and "you."

"Haha! Idiot!" screamed Pumpkin Spice.

"Shut up Pumpkin! You're dumb. You're only here because our moms told us to be nice to you!" They all giggled. Pumpkin Spice scowled and smacked Nutmeg upside the head.

"Ow! Shut up your hands!" yelled Nutmeg. "My the body is paining!"

"So what was the point of all that?" Cassie said, interrupting the fighting. There was just so much drama today! Cassie thought she would explode if literally any more drama took place.

"The group which I am a part of is always looking for true warriors. You are a true warrior."

"What makes me a warrior? Why not Edward?"

"You are so much better than that wuss Edward! Plus we heard you and you're quick thinking up in the Kit-Chun Sink. You were the only one that kept a level head.

"I guess that's true... Where am I?" Cassie asked, half trying to change the subject (she never took compliments well) and half baffled by the topography. Nevertheless, she tried not to gloat inside. This was the first time anyone besides her friends had recognized her for something she had done. If only her parents could see her now,

"Finally," Nutmeg said, "Someone taller smart than Pumpkin! Haha! Pumpkin so much idiot, right I am?"

"Can I answer the question please!?!" Pumpkin said, jumping up and down.

"Fine." Allspice sighed.

"OK," Pumpkin started, "You are on Planet Crumb! Also known as The Kit-Chun Floor (made of wood). Did you know that us five spices are actually less than 1% of our family? But that's beside the point. The point is that there are monsters that live here of all kinds and they all destroy foods. In fact this place is called Planet Crumb, because after foods leave here, there's nothing left of them but crumbs! Long story short, you and your friends, no Barry Banana, are kind of doomed!" So much for no more drama.

"Well then," Cassie said, "what is up there?" Cassie gestured to the weird buildings surrounding them.

"Well it's the—" Pumpkin started, but Ginger, who had returned, cut her off.

"I think you've done enough for now. We don't want to scare the new arrivals too much." Ginger said. Then she looked at Cassie and continued, "Those are The Shines of Silver-Where and the place of the butchering of the foods."

Part 8: Cassie Cake

"Oh my Gourd," Cassie gasped, "are those the hideous towers called the Counters with the Drawers."

"Unfortunately, yes. They are not only a horror story." Ginger said.

"We have to get out of here!" Cassie exclaimed, "Where's the nearest exit?"

"No." Nutmeg responded.

"What do you mean, no?" Cassie asked

"We can't leave Planet Crumb," Ginger responded

"Why?"

"The only exit is through there," the lead spice said, pointing to a vast dark opening in between the towers of Counters with the Drawers.

"Let's go then!" Cassie said.

Ginger gently caught her arm, "I'm telling you we can't go there!"

"Why not?"

"It's guarded by an evil machine at great devastation. The Vacuum Cleaner. It's only one of the many great dangers that Pumpkin Spice was telling you about." Then, as if summoned by its name, a great rumbling was heard in the distance.

"No oh!" Nutmeg screamed, "The Vacuum Cleaner is the coming! And bringing mega death to the group of us!"

"RUN!" Pumpkin shrieked.

"Quick! Follow me! I'll bring you to your friends!" Ginger said, leading the group towards one of the doors below The Shines of Silver-Where as quickly as she could. The group of girls sprinted across the wooden

Part 8: Cassie Cake

floor of Planet Crumb, and within seconds, they reached
their destination. Quickly, the spices hoisted one
another on top of each other so they could reach the
bottom of the door. Pumpkin, being at the top of the
spice tower. jumped up, shoved the door open, and
landed gracefully inside. Pumpkin then grabbed each of
the spices and Cassie by the arms and pulled them to
the safety of the room behind the door. Seconds later
they heard the evil monster hit the wall behind them.
Everyone stood still.

"Don't. Move." Ginger whispered. It seemed like
an eternity, but the monster eventually went away, its
roaring growing fainter every second. All the girls let out
a collective sigh of relief, and Ginger told the other four
Spices to bring Cassie's friends to them. Cassie, no
longer being under attack for the present moment,
looked around, her eyes adjusting to the dark light.
What she saw, she was not prepared for. The room was
made of the same stuff the Kit-Chun Floor was made
of— wood. The dark room smelled of mold and wasn't
particularly spacious. There were stale bagels and
withered fruits everywhere. When Cassie asked Ginger
about them, she called them the veterans.

"We have been at war with gross obese giants
that call themsleves Human Bea-ins." The lead Spice Girl
explained, "these giants will reach into the Free-Idge
and grab any food they want to obliterate them with
sharp stones they call Teeth." Cassie shuddered and
remembered the bedtime stories her parents would tell
her about Humans eating desserts that didn't
overachieve.

Part 8: Cassie Cake

"The Free-Idge?" Cassie asked, feeling the new word on her lips and trying to block out the memory.

"Yes," Ginger said, "it's the boxy portal you came through. How did you get through the portal anyways? We haven't had any visitors in years." As Ginger said this she pointed to a giant rectangular box with a large handle against the wall across the way. It emitted a low humming sound that was rather pleasant.

"Yeah, about that. We were thrown off the Spaghetti Monster after my friends mistook it for a planet on their way to WisSweetsVille to meet up with Derek, The Saibou, and I."

"So let me get this straight," Ginger said, "your friends got lost and you were with the Saibou?"

"Yes."

"You merged the three dragons?"

"Yes." Cassie said, growing tired of the questions.

"How?"

"It's too long of a story to tell right now, besides— AHHHHHHHH!" Cassie shrieked when she looked over. There was a large beastly being carrying her tied up friends on its back. It had small beady red eyes and a pointed face. At the end of its face there was a large black nose. Its body was round and cylindrical in shape and covered in matted gray fur. It was four legs with large paws at the end and long claws that gleamed even in the low light. At the end of its body there was a large, pink, whip-like tail.

"Don't be of screaming mode!" Nutmeg reprimanded Cassie, "Ronald the Rat it this dude! You're paining his ears and doing the scare on him! Him ears no

Part 8: Cassie Cake

are superman juice!" Cassie stopped screaming. Ronald the Rat slowly approached Cassie, sniffing her face intently. Cassie worked very hard to stifle a scream. Within a second, Ronald started prancing around Cassie and showing off his big buck teeth.

"How?!?" Allspice shrieked, flabbergasted, "Ronald only does that to Ginger!"

"I told you she was a true warrior." Ginger said to the spices with a knowing smile. Nutmeg sat down in a corner and started pouting. Ginger stepped up to the rat and held up her hand. The rat instantaneously stopped moving and lay down. Ginger motioned to the other four spices and produced to unload Cassie's friends off the rats back. Pretty soon, all of Cassie's friends were sitting on the ground. They all seemed awake except Edward.

"Does he pass out a lot? 'Cause he went out quickly." Ginger asked Cassie, motioning to Edward.

"You don't even know." Cassie responded.

"That's ok. We have a way to wake him up. Allspice, the Fee-ther please," Ginger ordered. Allspice nodded and sprinted around the corner, out of Cassie's sight.

"What's a Fee-ther?" Cassie asked.

"It's a white stick with fluff on the sides of it. When foods come in contact with it they will either start laughing or sneezing. It is known to wake foods up from deep slumber." Ginger said.

"The more bester thing is the Fee-ther!" Nutmeg shouted, sending a scared Ronald Rat crying out of the

215

room. Ginger sighed and told Pumpkin and Nutmeg to track the rat down.

Cassie and the remaining two Spices stood there in awkward silence for a couple of long minutes. Finally a quiet voice spoke up:

"If you go back through the Free-Idge Portal, can I come with you?" Cassie turned around startled to see Cinnamon Spice speaking for the first time since Cassie met her.

"What's the Free-Idge?" Cassie asked. But she was ignored and Ginger started repremeneding Cinnamon Spice,

"You know we can't go there! It's only a one way ticket! The desserts are stuck there unless they can summon the power of the Plastic Cherry! It's a miracle they got here without using it! How did you manage such a big feat?"

"I know, I just thought..." Cinnamon started again.

"No. And that's final." Ginger said.

"EXCUSE ME! I ASKED A QUESTION!" Cassie raised her voice. She was getting quite annoyed.

"Yes, I'm sorry. What did you want?" Ginger asked tiredly.

"First, what's the Free-Idge?"

"It's the magical silver box that holds all the planets that you know of."

"Wait, so you said that we were stuck here? Does this mean that I can't go back to my home planet?" Cassie was panicking.

"I'm so sorry." Ginger said

Part 8: Cassie Cake

"Um, Ok. Th-that's fine."

"So, the Free-Idge… how far is it?"

"There is only but one entry point. But you have to get past the giants. They like to take food out of there and eat them." Cassie didn't believe Ginger for a second, then she remembered cases of missing desserts in her town Sugarcane back in the Free-Idge. The cases were never solved. Cassie wasn't sure she wanted to know the truth, but it was too late now. Cassie was consumed with only one thought. She was a resident of the Free-Idge.

"Wait, so it wasn't the dinner foods that were responsible for the dessert kidnappings?" Chipette asked.

"That's what we've been trying to tell you!" Swiss S. Cheese exclaimed. "Dinner foods didn't start kidnapping desserts until Supreme Lord Mac-N-Cheese ordered it. And that was only weeks ago."

"Wait, so the claw I saw when I first met Triaq..." Adrienne started.

"I'm sure that claw that you saw was just a human hand," Ginger explained.

"So the hwumans still stealwing foods fwom the Fwee-Edge?!" Tiriaq asked.

"Yes, unfortunately."

"We have to go back then," the ETM shouted, "I mean look at us. We are a strong group of foods. We can save them!"

"No, no," Ginger said calmly, "now you're thinking like Cinnamon Spice over here. She's been obsessed with rescuing foods from there forever."

"But—"

"No!" Ginger said, "It's too dangerous!" Cassie was about to retort when she noticed Allspice come around the corner, dragging the white Fee-ther behind. Unfortunately, Nutmeg and Pumpkin Spice came back with the rat at the same time. Ronald saw the Fee-ther and immediately took off towards it.

"NOOOO! STOP HIM!" Ginger shouted, waking some of the sleeping veterans. The Spices and Cassie started sprinting to intercept the rat, but before anyone could reach him, the rat grabbed the Fee-ther out of Allspice's hands and ran off again. Nutmeg and Pumpkin sighed, turned around, and jogged in the direction the rat left in.

"Well," Ginger said, turning to Cassie, "we won't be able to wake your friend Edward for a while now."

"Actually," Cassie said smiling, "Let me try something." Ginger looked skeptical but motioned for Cassie to try.

Cassie nodded and walked up to Edward's ear and yelled, "GET UP TO LAZY COOKIE! IT'S TIME TO SAVE OUR PLANETS!" Edward stirred slightly, but it wasn't enough. He yawned. Opened his eyes, sleepy. Closed them.

"YOUR MOM IS ASKING WHY THE HOUSE IS DESTROYED AGAIN!" Cassie tried shouting into his ear. His eyes snapped open.

"NO! She just paid it off! Wait, why was I sleeping?" Edward asked.

"You fainted at the sight of Ronald." Ginger explained with a smirk.

Part 8: Cassie Cake

"You always liked scary things." Edward said, but seemed mildly embarrassed that no one else had fainted.

The group was very hungry and Edward tried to use his abilities to create banana splits for everyone to eat. They were all excited to taste them except Barry, who glared at Edward and called him a banana murderer. Unfortunately, Edward soon found out that the extent of his abilities did not reach beyond the Free-ldge.

"So maybe that ability is useful!" Andrienne gasped, recalling when she doubted Edward's new found abilities.

"How did you know that would wake him up?" Ginger whispered to Cassie.

Cassie smiled and merely replied, "He's my best friend." Then, after some thought, she added, "Also, his mom is really attached to their house." They waited a good 20 minutes before Cassie turned to Ginger to ask a question.

"No." Ginger said.

"I didn't even say anything!" Cassie said.

"You had a question forming on your lips. I already know the question. The answer is no."

"But—"

"No."

"Come on!"

"NO."

"You said something about a Plastic Cherry?"

"What?"

Part 8: Cassie Cake

"You were talking to Cinnamon and you said that we needed to summon the power of the Plastic Cherry."

"Yes. The Plastic Cherry. It's rumored to have many powers. Among the rumors are that it entices all of the giants. Especially the ones they call Kiddos and Teen-agers. If we have one of those, we can get out of the Kit-chun Floor and step out to where the giants call Out-side and finally be free. But we don't have the Plastic Cherry, so that's impossible."

"What about the other rumors?" Adrienne asked from the corner, suddenly interested in the conversation.

"Some foods on Plant Crumb believe that it is the key to opening the Free-Idge from the other side, other foods believe that it will vaporize humans at sight."

"Where can I find a Plastic Cherry?" Cassie asked.

"WisSweetsVill. The Ice Prince of Cream holds the last one left in the universe."

Cassie smiled, "I have a friend, her name is Ginny Gelato. I'm sure she'll be happy to help us."

Cinnamon's face brightened, "Can you contact her?"

"Sure," Cassie said, "one condition."

"What is it?" Ginger asked eagerly. Cassie could tell that Ginger would accept anything.

"We save all the beings in the Free-Idge."

"WHAT!" Ginger said.

Cassie waited a long time for a response, because this was a tough eternal struggle for Ginger.

Part 8: Cassie Cake

Finally, after looking at Cassie and Cinnamon's hopeful faces, she gave in.

"Fine," Ginger said. Cassie and Cinnamon let out a celebratory laugh and hugged each other. Ginger let out an exasperated sigh before joining in on the hug.

Cassie then turned to a groggy Sugar Cookie, "Can you contact Ginny Gelato and the Saibou and ask them to travel to WisSweetsVille to bring the last Plastic Cherry here please?"

"Of course." Sugar Cookie said, and opened her texting app on her phone and put in the message and sent it. After a few moments, Sugar Cookie nodded to Cassie, indicating that Ginny said she could do that.

"Ginny said she will be here in as soon as she could." Cassie said.

"Ok," Ginger said, "Now that everyone is awake, we have something to show you." The spice girls stood together and sang in harmony to the group,

"Welcome to the Crumb!"

Most of them just stared blankly at the Spice Girls, but Adrienne gasped and mumbled, "My dream! It's coming true!"

Cassie grinned and thought, *"Take that Mom and Dad, now I'm going to save the whole foodiverse. Bet you didn't see that coming."*

Part 9: Ginny Gelato

Ginny flew through the air on the Saibou just after a close escape from the SCL. There were many brainwashed cookies and explosions in the process of de-corrupting the facility, but the job was done and the facility could finally get back to helping desserts. They had been flying overnight since Cassie had texted her to get The Plastic Cherry, and Ginny was feeling the effects of the battle at SCL. Her head often rolled from side to side as she drifted off to sleep.

"You should get some rest," The Saibou's calm voice emanated from below her. "It's ok. I know where I'm going. You should go to sleep now."

Ginny nodded, barely able to keep her head up.

When Ginny woke, a colossal snow cone was heading for her face. Ginny shrieked and ducked as they were intensely barraged by snow cones.

"Thank goodness you were just sleeping and not dead.," The Saibou said, flying breathlessly.

"What?" Ginny asked loudly. "That doesn't make any sense."

"When you were hit with that snow cone, I thought for sure you weren't going to make it. But then I thought, '*Saibou, it's just a snow cone! Why are you worried?*' But then I noticed you were melting a little

Part 9: Ginny Gelato

so..." Ginny looked down at herself. Sure enough, she was covered head to toe in sticky colored liquid.

"I'm not melting now, am I?" Ginny asked.

"No, I flew you higher up in the sky because it's colder there for some reason."

"Sweet, thanks!" Just at that moment, a snow cone smacked the Saibou in the face, blinding him for a second. The Saibou's body lurched to one side, sending Ginny off of the dragon's back. The dragon shook the snow cone shavings off himself and dived down to catch Ginny as she fell.

Unfortunately, another particularly large snow cone slammed into his side and knocked him backwards and away from Ginny. She fell through several layers of cotton candy clouds and tasted blue raspberry. Gross! Ginny glanced back at the Saibou as he frantically tried to reach her.

"It's ok," she shouted to the dragon, "I'll get down safely, you fly away and find a different way down!" The Saibou looked at her with all six of its kind eyes and nodded and flew back up. Ginny then focused on her cylinder body and began to do something she hadn't done in years. She unrolled herself. Now, instead of a cylinder torpedoing toward the ground at top speed, she was a flat round sheet of ice cream and floated down to safety. She adjusted her body position frequently to avoid the flying snow cones. She swooped and swerved, dived and dodged. Soon the clouds cleared and Ginny spotted a majestic Graham Cracker Castle in the distance.

Part 9: Ginny Gelato

It was flawless, save for about 50 "Missing Food" posters all apparently being for foods that used to be butlers. She immediately altered her body and sailed fluently through the air, now in the direction of the castle. The entire castle was covered in light fluffy powdered sugar and its eminence made the candy cane forest around it seem miniscule. After a few moments she had glided over to one of the large chocolate chimmys. Within a split second, she had rerolled herself and dove into the large opening.

Ginny landed on the ground with a muffled thud. Thank goodness she hadn't landed in a fireplace and instead had landed on a scoop of ice cream who protested loudly. Quietly, she kicked a small indent into the ice cream, rolling the cherry on its head slightly to the side, and told him that if he didn't shut it she would break his cone. With the ice cream subdued, Ginny looked around and saw pictures of another ice cream being with a crown on its head, smiling idiotically, covering every pink waffle cookie wall.

The ice cream in the pictures appeared to be strawberry flavored, like her, and was always pictured with an enormous blood red cherry. Nothing about this cherry seemed natural, its face shined like ice and instead of a normal green stem, the cherry wore an unnaturally red stem.

Alarms blared, startling Ginny out of her thoughts. She turned around and glared at the ice cream in the corner of the room.

Part 9: Ginny Gelato

"I didn't!" the ice cream cried, "I swear to Gourd!"

Ginny scoffed, "You're coming with me!"

"But I—"

"I don't think I can trust you!"

"Said the dessert who is breaking and entering the most highly protected castle!"

"I haven't broken anything!" Ginny exclaimed. Right at the moment, two gummy bear guards armed with toothpicks kicked down the door. The door ripped off its hinges and flew across the room.

"The door wasn't even locked," one of the gummy bears scolded the other. Without missing a beat, Ginny grabbed the nearest thing, a chair made of licorice, and snapped it in half. She jumped on top of a table and leapt into the air. The gummy bears stared in awe, but not longer than a couple seconds, for the chair came crashing down on their heads, knocking them out cold.

"Haven't broken anything have we?" the ice cream queried. Ginny rolled her eyes and tied the ice cream's hands together and marched him out of the room.

The hallway that lay outside the room had the same annoying pink walls and wasn't furnished at all. The floor was made of hardened caramel that showed a clear reflection of Ginny when she looked down. Every step she took emitted a loud click against the floor that echoed around the halls. The hallway branched into another hallway, which led to several more hallways that all looked the same. Soon Ginny and her captive

Part 9: Ginny Gelato

were lost deep within that labyrinth of the Castle of WisSweetsVill. They turned corner after corner, but they only seemed to get deeper and deeper in the castle.

"Wait, this looks familiar," Ginny said, and she peeked inside the room. Inside the room there was a broken licorice chair and table, and two Gummy Bears knocked out cold.

"Diddly darn it!" Ginny exclaimed, "All I've done is walk around in a giant circle!"

"Well," the Ice Cream siad, "It's too bad you don't have a person who knows the castle right by you at the moment."

"Wait a second," Ginny said, "You live here! You can show me around the castle! You better do what I ask!!!"

"Oh goodness no!" The ice cream replied, "I know nothing about this castle! Well how could I? I only live here! Nothing else! How could I know the way around my— I mean, the castle!" Ginny grabbed the frozen dessert and shoved him back into the room she started in. She grabbed the dismembered chair and used its bendable licorice strips to tie the Ice Cream up.

"Now will you show me around?" Ginny demanded more than asked.

"Well, it seems I am quite tied up at the moment, but if you don't kill me right now, I guess I'll do it."

Ginny untied the ice cream just enough so that his hands were still bound and ordered him to show her around, and soon they were on their way. The ice cream led her across the room to some of the paintings of the

226

Part 9: Ginny Gelato

Prince Ice of Cream and The Cherry and removed one of them. Behind the painting was a small tube-like slide that led to a room covered in neon yellow icing.

"Right this way," The ice cream said, smirking. Ginny jumped in the tunnel and went to bring the ice cream up with her, but he dodged her arm and shoved her down the steep tunnel. Ginny slid all the way to the bottom and landed with a soft THUD. Behind her she saw the ice cream place the painting back over the opening. Just as the ice cream disappeared from Ginny's view, she saw something. Just a glimpse of it. But there was no doubting what she saw. In the dent where Ginny kicked the ice cream, there was a bit of an unnatural red object showing and to accompany it, the end of a bright red, fake, stem.

The ice cream that she had been holding hostage *was* Prince Ice of Cream.

The room Ginny was locked in was completely neon yellow. The floor, the walls, even the ceiling had the awful neon icing dripping off of it. Ginny stuck a finger in the wall and tasted the icing—lemon flavored. She needed to figure out a way to get out. That's when she noticed the figure in the corner of the room. The figure was also yellow and almost blended in perfectly with the walls and floor.

"You okay?" Ginny asked, holding out her hand to help it up. The figure took her hand and stood up.

"That three headed dragon isn't here with you is it?" the figure asked.

Ginny gasped. "Cheese Wizard?"

Part 9: Ginny Gelato

The Cheese Wizard sighed. "Yes."

"You're not going to try to kill me, are you?"

"No, my killing days are behind me. Plus, I'm too out of shape to kill you anyways," the Cheese Wizard gestured to himself. Sure enough, the once shiny, bold can of Cheez Wiz, was dented and disfigured.

"What happened to you?" Ginny asked, "I didn't think someone as powerful as you could be destroyed so plainly."

"Well," he said with a glare, "it all started after I tried to save MilkDudBot . . ."

The Long Short Story of The Cheese Wizard:

Captain Burrito had assigned me to help him with a secret mission in the Fondue Fountains. He said it involved a robot I had previously made by the name of MilkDudBot and I decided to go with him in order to retrieve the bot and make amends. I had ditched it in a bad place and felt guilty ever since. We went to the forest and began a small skirmish with Edward Chip and his friends. That's when I realized that Captain Burrito was trying to destroy my robot even more! I couldn't let that happen and tried to protest but was swiftly knocked out with a frying pan that the burrito had brought for that exact reason.

I woke up hours later in my bedroom chambers with a note from Supreme Lord Mac-N-Cheese saying to meet him and all the other

Part 9: Ginny Gelato

foods at our secret base for a meeting. I ran to the
secret base (no I won't disclose the whereabouts of
our base) but the door was locked and the secret
password wasn't opening the doors. I quickly cast a
spell that let me slip in by walking through the door.
Alarms blared and I shouted,
"No! I'm a friend!" but it was to no avail.
Thousands of cookie cops with vests labeled: SCL
jumped down from the ceiling. I was being held at
cookieblasterpoint.
"Put your hands on your head!" someone
yelled.
I complied.
"No tricks here," a burly cookie stepped
forward, his chocolate chip beard swinging from side
to side, "right?" I shook my head, sweat pouring
down my head. I feared for my life.
"Please, don't melt me again," I pleaded, "I
can't do that again!"
"I'm not going to melt you! I'm going to
arrest you!" the cop said, "I let the others get away,
I'm not going to make that mistake again."
I knew I had to do something.
"Petrifus Striarmus!" I bellowed. A burst of
yellow smoke exploded outward from my hands. The
effect was instantaneous. The cookie cops had been
frozen, even the ones currently jumping down from
the ceiling had been frozen in midair.
"You will let me go and take your entire troop
back to the SCL base where you belong." I told the
frozen cookie cop with his eyes glazed.

Part 9: Ginny Gelato

I quickly dashed out and ran.

It was when I had been running for fifteen minutes that I realized something. One: I could have just teleported away, and two: if I had wanted to just freeze the cops I should have just said "Petrifus" but I said "Petrifus Striarmus" which freezes the cops and leaves the minds open for brainwashing (I had taught the supreme lord this exact spell to aid him in brainwashing the SCL and also some random cake and donut). I quickly teleported back to the base to restore the cops' minds. But, when I got there, all thousands of the cops were gone. I had just completed the corruption of the SCL. (I had only brainwashed that one facility, all the cookie cops that were out in the field had been spared).

Now, I am not fond of the SCL for they have locked me up multiple times, but they have stopped my arch nemesis and twin brother, Chizz Whees, from expelling me to another dimension. So, I figured I owed it to the SCL to free them. Through a series of teleporting and spells I managed to get the SCL headquarters. I looked through one of the windows to find that all the cops were now brainwashed. It was a horrifying picture: Supreme Lord Mac-N-Cheese was standing on a pedestal made of the bottom part of a chair and all the cookie cops were bowing down to him, eyes glazed.

That's when I knew I couldn't work for someone as cruel as he, and I knew I had to do

Part 9: Ginny Gelato

something. Quickly I shapeshifted my body into the shape of a cookie and walked in, pretending to be mind controlled. I followed Supreme Lord Mac-N-Cheese's orders for three hours until he ordered all the cookie cops to stack themselves into the stairs so he could paint a mural of himself on the ceiling.

I stacked myself at the very top of the stairs. When Supreme Lord Mac-N-Cheese went to step on me, I grabbed his legs and flipped him on his back. The move was very effective, for he slid down to the bottom of the stairs, taking almost all of the cookie cops down with him.

"WHO IS THIS INSUBORDINATE COOKIE!" Supreme Lord Mac-N-Cheese shouted, and pointed at me, "SEIZE IT!"

All the cookie cops turned around and looked at me with glowing red eyes. I quickly bolted for the door, all the cops chasing me into the street. I figured I could lead them into the forest behind the SCL laboratory.

"STOP!" Supreme Lord Mac-N-Cheese shouted, "I have just been informed that Ginny Gelato riding the Saibou has been spotted! She and her three headed dragon will terrorize us again! As if it wasn't enough that she robbed me of my first brainwashing victims, Derek Donut and Cassie Cake. And from the looks of it, she is coming from the living planet, THE SPAGHETTI MONSTER! If she can survive that monster then we must prepare for war!"

Part 9: Ginny Gelato

All the hypnotized cookies ran around and grabbed weapons and started boarding up doors and windows.

"You!" Supreme Lord Mac-N-Cheese pointed straight at me, "You fooled me at first with your disguise! But now I see you, Cheese Wizard. Now, you're going to help me kill that ugly sheet of ice cream called Ginny!"

"No!" I shouted, shifting back into my own body, "I was once like that, but seeing your cruelty towards the cookies here and to my robot has taught me that being evil only results in my own pain!"

"FINE THEN!" Supreme Lord Mac-N-Cheese raged, "YOU SHALL DIE IN SPACE!" The Supreme Lord Mac-N-Cheese snatched me up and placed me in an oversized slingshot and pulled back on the seat, slowly increasing the tension in the Fruit by the Foots that were being used as the "sling" part of the slingshot. I closed my eyes and awaited my doom.

With a loud SNAP, I hurtled out of the SCL laboratory, creating a big hole in the ceiling and into the sky. I would have flown straight into space and died if I hadn't hit the Saibous' wing. When I struck its wing, I was smacked back down to the ground with such force that I created a new hole in the ceiling of the car garage of the SCL labs. For some reason, one of the M&M cars was gone, which was strange because everyone knows that the oatmeal raisin cars are more durable. That didn't matter though,I knew I couldn't take a car because Supreme Lord Mac-N-Cheese and his cookie goons would find

Part 9: Ginny Gelato

me in a second, I knew then that I had to leave the planet. Then, in the corner, I saw my rescue vehicle—the flying pizza saucer that once belonged to the Pizza Pirate. I hopped in the saucer and fled the planet at top speed.

I had been (poorly) flying in space for a while when I spotted a pink planet. The radar on my ship identified it as WisSweetsVille. I tried to land on an island on the planet, but officers down on the planet just identified the ship as belonging to the Pizza Pirate. So, they shot it down with a marshmallow cannon. I crash landed into the middle of (what I found out later was) Prince Ice of Cream's castle. Donut officers boarded the ship and dragged me out.

"You thought you could infiltrate the castle eh?!" One of the officers said, glaring at me.

"No sir, I just—" I started but was cut off by the other officer telling me to "SHUT IT!" The two donuts conferenced with some other foods via the radio on what to do with me. The consensus was that I was to be thrown in jail forever. So that's exactly what happened. I sat in the jail cell for what seemed like years, only being fed twice a day with drugged food to strip me of my powers. Then, one day, someone slid into the cell. It was you, Ginny.

"Cassie told me about MilkDudBot1.1 and, well, from what I know about the robot, you and it tell stories about the past very similarly." Ginny remarked.

"I should hope so," the Cheese Wizard replied, "I did make him. How is he, by the way?"

"Oh yeah, he's dead. He was corrupted and tried to crush my friends with his foot. So Sugar Cookie had to disable him. Only I don't think Edward and them re-enabled him so he is most likely dead."

The Cheeze Wizard looked crushed. "Well," he said, "I'll help you get out and attack Prince Ice of Cream for the Plastic Cherry, but we are making a pit stop at The Dessert as soon as we get out."

After hours of planning, replanning (the Cheese Wizard kept accidentally dropping melted cheese on the plan so they couldn't see what they had written down), and strategizing, Ginny and the Cheese Wizard had come up with a five phase plan.

Phase one:

"HELP ME!!!" Ginny shouted at the entrance of the cell, "I'M MELTING! OH NO, THE PAIN! I'VE USED MY TELEPATHIC POWERS TO TELL MY FAMILY TO SUE YOU!" Ginny heard the sound of someone running above.

"You don't actually have telepathic powers, right?" The Cheese Wizard asked.

"Of course not!" Ginny said, "but the cops don't know that." Five minutes later a hidden door in the side of the cell flung open.

"DON'T SUE US," a skinny donut cop gasped, "We are broke as it is!" Ginny nodded to the Cheese Wizard, who was crouching in the corner of the room.

Part 9: Ginny Gelato

He sprang up and wacked the cop on the head, knocking him out cold. Ginny grabbed his keys and used his own handcuffs to lock his hands together behind his back.

"Donny donut?" the cop's radio crackled, "is everything all right?"

The Cheese Wizard casually picked up the radio and responded in a low voice, "Uh… yes, everything is fine."

"You sure? You sound a little different…"

"You must be hearing things, maybe the signal is weaker all the way down here, it must be getting scrambled."

" 'Down here'? What do you mean 'down here'? The cell is on the second highest floor. "

"Oh no!" The Cheese Wizard gasped, "I'm losing signal! I—" with that the Cheese Wizard threw the radio on the ground, smashing it to pieces.

"Losing signal?" Ginny asked.

"I'm sorry! I panicked," He responded.

"Well, now guards will be coming to us, so we better hurry up and get out of here!"

Phase two:

Ginny and the Cheese Wizard ran through the halls. They figured since they were at the top of the castle that they should go down to reach Prince Ice of Cream's room. They quickly located a long spiral staircase in the middle of the lobby right outside their cell. Ginny unrolled and the Cheese Wizard sat down on top of her. The pair slid down the staircase, knocking

Part 9: Ginny Gelato

over several groups of donut cops running up the steps to arrest them. When they reached the bottom, Ginny promptly rolled herself back up and contemplated on how she was going to find the exact location of Prince Ice of Cream's room.

As she was beginning to think of a plan to find the room, mainly involving stealing cop radios and splitting up to search the entire castle floor, the Cheese Wizard shouted,"Over here Ginny! I found a map of this place." Ginny sprinted to his voice. Sure enough, there was a giant map printed on the side of the castle wall right by what appeared to be the main entrance.

At the very bottom of the map there was a big green dot that stated: You are here!

"It appears Prince Ice of Cream's room is about 50 feet behind us," The Cheese Wizard pointed out. Then, he grabbed Ginny's hand and led her at a full sprint to Prince Ice of Cream's royal chambers.

Phase three:

When the pair reached His Royal Highness' chambers, they saw that it was being guarded by almost twenty donut cops, all armed with electric spears made of licorice and peanut brittle. Quietly, Cheese Wizard explained how he thought they could get past the guards. After hearing his plan, Ginny nodded to him, giving him the green light to start. The Cheese Wizard closed his eyes and intently began chanting under his breath. Normally, casting a spell wouldn't take this much effort for the Cheese Wizard, Ginny thought, but months of not using magic had taken its toll.

"ASPA BUTA NOCTURNUS," The Cheese Wizard shouted. A blue light (made of many glowing and fastly materializing particles) appeared in his palm. The Cheese Wizard then brought the light to his lips and ate it. The donut cops had not ignored the sudden flash of blue light and led an investigation behind the wall which Ginny and her companion were hiding.

The Cheese Wizard motioned Ginny to move to Prince Ice of Cream's chambers, now only guarded by five cops. Ginny sprinted at the doughy men and punched one the cops in the face, leaving a big dent and breaking the once perfect glaze that was on the cops skin. The other four cops moved to arrest her, handcuffs out. She quickly evaded them and dodged their pointed spears.

Behind her, the Cheese Wizard let out a humongous sneeze, followed quickly by another flash of blue light. Ginny glanced behind her and saw glowing blue snot everywhere and a pile of donut cops on the floor, all sleeping peacefully and sucking on their thumbs. Ginny turned around and jumped up to avoid two electric spears from piercing her legs. Another cop tried to impale her from behind, but she quickly spun around and grabbed its spear and jabbed at the cop's butt, causing him to fall down due to lack of feeling in his legs. In one swift movement, Ginny jumped up and twirled in the air, successfully hitting all three of the remaining cops in the noggin, knocking them all out cold.

Part 9: Ginny Gelato

"Wow," The Cheese Wizard exclaimed from behind her, "That was amazing!" Ginny turned around to see him sitting on top of the sleeping cops, happily munching on a bucket of popcorn.

"Mmmhmmm," Ginny groaned, "big help you were."

"Hey! Do you not see these guys," The Cheese Wizard gestured to the cops pinned down under his butt.

"Ok, well, whatever. Let's just get to kidnapping the prince already."

"Fine," The Cheese Wizard said, "Just let me do something first." With that, the Cheese Wizard farted on the cops he was sitting on.

The fart was very stinky and woke up several of the cops, who complained and shouted out, "Seriously!?" and "EWWW WHO FARTED?"

"I bet it was Jeremy," another cop said

"It wasn't me!" Jeremy said.

"Well it was someone!"

"It kinda does smell like one of Jeremy's signature farts."

"IT WASN'T ME!" Jeremy shouted, "AND I DON'T HAVE SIGNATURE FARTS!!!"

"Yeah, you kinda do." That comment was followed by many murmurs of agreement. Jeremy screamed in anger.

"HAHAHAHAH" The Cheese Wizard laughed, "It was me. I cut the cheese, (pun intended)."

Part 9: Ginny Gelato

"Ewww. Gross man," One of the cops said. The Cheeze Wizard laughed and released another louder, stinkier fart that knocked the cops back out again.

"Are you done?" Ginny asked, hands on her hips, very disappointed in the Cheese Wizard.

"Yeah yeah," The Cheeze Wizard said, "You're such a party pooper." And with that, the Cheeze Wizard got down from his throne of donut cops and joined Ginny in infiltrating Prince Ice of Cream's royal chambers.

Phase Four:

Ginny, still holding one of the cops' electric spears, and the Cheese Wizard, still laughing about farting on the donuts, burst into Prince Ice of Cream's room. To Ginny's absolute horror, the prince was changing clothes (More like changing scoops. His strawberry scoop that Ginny saw him wearing was tossed on his bed, slowly melting, while he donned a vanilla one on his head.)

"AHHHHHHHH!" Ginny screamed, "YOU'RE NAKED!!!!"

"AHHHHHHHH!" Prince Ice of Cream screamed, spinning around in shock, "I'M NAKED!"

"AHHHHHHHH!" The Cheese Wizard screamed, "WHY ARE WE SCREAMING?! HAVE WE NEVER SEEN A NUDE ICE CREAM BEFORE!?"

"EXCUSE ME!" Prince Ice of Cream shouted, "GET OUT! You mustn't see your royal highness in less than

Part 9: Ginny Gelato

fabulous clothing! Now get out of my room, I'm in the middle of something between me and my guards!"

"You guards aren't coming." The Cheese Wizard smirked, "They are all sleeping outside, AND I farted on them!"

Prince Ice of Cream gasped, "You *farted* on them? What are you? FIVE YEARS OLD?"

"*Excuse me,*" The Cheese Wizard interjected, "Just because you don't get my superior humor doesn't mean you get to talk bad about it!"

"BOYS," Ginny said over the shouting, "You're both idiots. Now, Prince Ice of Cream, we are taking this," Ginny held up the Plastic Cherry which she had stolen from Prince Ice of Cream's bed (he had to take it off to change) while the prince and the wizard were arguing.

"RUN," Ginny shouted to the Cheese Wizard. The pair took off for the door. Prince Ice of Cream tried to follow them but quickly realized he was still naked and ran back into his room to put on a scoop.

Phase Five:

"How are we supposed to get off this planet again?" the Cheese Wizard asked as they both burst out of the castle.

"I have an idea," Ginny replied, and whistled as loudly as she could. She waited for a response but none came.

Part 9: Ginny Gelato

"*That* was your big idea?" The Cheese Wizard
scoffed, "whistling and calling attention to ourselves.
Niiiiiice."

"He should have heard it!" she replied, "I
wonder what is keeping him."

"Who is our supposed savior?"

"The Saibou!"

"Oh, well I don't see him anywhere!"

"*Really?*" Ginny said sarcastically.

"STOP, THIEVES" a voice shouted from behind
them. Ginny turned around to see a now fully clothed
Prince Ice of Cream driving a waffle cone shaped truck.

"HE'S BACK!" Ginny shouted, and the Cheese
Wizard and her sped up. However, their legs did not
compare to the speed of the prince's truck.

"GIVE ME BACK MY CHERRY!" Prince Ice of
Cream shouted as he slowed his truck alongside them as
they ran.

"NEVER!" Ginny said.

"OH COME ON!" the prince said, his truck barely
reaching seven miles an hour. "THIS HAS GOT TO BE THE
LAMEST CHASE SCENE EVER!"

"OH REALLY?" Ginny said, spotting a black
shadow in the sky, "HOW ABOUT NOW?"

Ginny grabbed the Cheese Wizard, turned them
off of the main road, and jumped over a bush. Actually,
Ginny was able to jump over the bush while she dragged
the Cheese Wizard through it. Just then, the black
shadow swooped down and destroyed the prince's truck
in a fiery explosion.

Part 9: Ginny Gelato

"YEAH SAIBOU!" Ginny shouted as the three headed dragon landed in front of them.

"Come on! Let's leave this planet!" she shouted. The Saibou lay down and allowed Ginny to climb up.

"I'm not riding that thing!" The Cheese Wizard cried.

"Really?!" Ginny asked, "Now you get cold feet? You're not even supposed to be refrigerated.Your feet should never be cold."

"Hey! That monster almost killed me!"

"Well too bad! Either come on or we are leaving you here."

The wizard hesitated, looked over his shoulder, and then consented. "Fine!"

"Are we leaving the prince here?" The calm voice of the Saibou emanated from below Ginny.

"Yeah," She responded, "why would we take him with us?"

"Because," the dragon began, "he might tell more cops to follow us throughout space and then it will be considerably harder to deliver Cassie Cake the cherry."

"Fine." Ginny grumbled as she climbed down off the dragon and wrenched Prince Ice of Cream out of the burning wreckage. The poor guy was half melted. Ginny tied his hands behind his back with a gummy worm she pulled out of the ground and marched him onto the back of the Saibou.

With all three of them on board, the Saibou gently took off.

Part 9: Ginny Gelato

"What took you so long?" Ginny asked once they were steadily up in the air.

"I fell asleep." the Saibou responded matter-of-factly.

"Of course," Ginny said, rolling her eyes.

"What?! Even powerful creatures need their sleep! Now where are we going again?"

"The Spaghetti Monster," Ginny said, "we need to get to where Edward and the others are."

"EXCUSE ME!" The Cheese Wizard said loudly, "Aren't you forgetting something?"

Ginny smacked her head, "Right! I have a promise to keep. To Sugarcane!"

End of Plan

After flying for several days, The Dessert was in sight. The Cheese Wizard was getting super excited.

"-and me and MilkDudBot1.1 will be best friends!" he was saying.

"Are you sure that MilkDudBot1.1 will even like you? I mean you did pretend to be a whipped cream, and then you left and his house got destroyed, and then he found out that you were the Cheese Wizard, so... " Ginny said.

"Hmmm, that does provide a problem," the Cheese Wizard said, "Oh well, I'll figure out what to do about that when I see him."

"Ok..." Ginny said.

Part 9: Ginny Gelato

"Alright guys," The Sibou said, "I'm landing now, you might feel some popping in your ears as the air pressure changes."

"Thanks for the warning," Prince Ice of Cream said sarcastically, "could've given me a warning before YOU KIDNAPPED ME!"

"Shut up you whiny soft serve!" Ginny said.

"I'm sure my father is looking for me right now!" the prince said.

"Well I know for a fact you don't have a father, because you were made in a machine! And you're only the prince because of the brand of ice cream you are, Royal Cream."

"Ugh. You know nothing! In fact my father is so real that he banished me from the kingdom entirely over a love affair! You are right about our brand being Royal Cream, though."

"I don't even want to know." Ginny said and ignored the rest of Prince Ice of Creams complaints. By then, the three headed dragon had successfully landed on the outskirts of the town Sugarcane.

"All right guys," the Saibou said, "Let's all meet back here in five hours. Then we leave for the Spaghetti Monster."

"Can I stay on the dragon?" Prince Ice of Cream asked.

"Sure, but only if we tie you to the dragon." The Cheese Wizard said.

The Prince thought about it and decided that he didn't want to be around Ginny any longer than he had to, and was quickly tied to one of the spikes on the Saibou's back.

"Alright," Ginny said. "If what Cassie told me was true, MilkDudBot1.1 should be right by the nearest Milkshake Mart."

"Well then," the Cheese Wizard said, sliding off the dragon, "let's not keep my creation waiting!" The Cheese Wizard started walking forward.

"Ummm, Milkshake Mart is in the other direction." Ginny said, and the Cheese Wizard turned about and continued to walk happily. Ginny hoped this side quest wouldn't take long. What she really wanted to do was get back to Cassie and Edward as soon as possible. She knew that they wouldn't ask her to make such a long journey to grab the Plastic Cherry and head to The Spaghetti Monster if it wasn't necessary. And something else didn't sit well with her about Adrienne despite the fact that she saved Ginny's life. Everything the fortune cookie did was almost too perfect, too coordinated, and too helpful. Ginny had a sneaking suspicion she had met Adrienne before but couldn't remember it.

When Ginny passed the "Now Leaving Sugarcane" sign, she knew that they were getting close. She checked her watch: they had been walking for an hour. The walk back was also going to be an hour long, so that only left three hours to locate the robot and fix it up.

"I SEE IT!" The Cheese Wizard shouted, breaking into a sprint as the black blob of Milkshake Mart appeared on the horizon. Ginny quickly followed him. Within a minute they had arrived at the door of the supermarket. The place had been utterly trashed. There was an Adrienne shaped hole in the ceiling, the sliding glass door had been shattered, and the lights were flickering.

Upon closer inspection, Ginny saw bits of burrito everywhere. Something about it felt wrong, and she felt a snake of fear creep up her back."We need to get out of here," she said, suddenly alarmed. "This is a trap!"

"What are you talking about?" The Cheese Wizard asked, "Nothing bad ever happened in any abandoned supermarket, anywhere!"

Just at that moment, extraterrestrial eggs dropped down and surrounded the two of them. Their slimy bodies glowed green as they encircled Ginny and the Cheese Wizard. The smell of garlic filled the air as the eggs opened their abnormally large mouths and barred their wicked sharp teeth.

"Give me your hands," Ginny told the Cheese Wizard.

"What? Why?"

"Just do it!" Ginny snapped, and with no time left to argue, the Cheese Wizard placed his hands in Ginny's.

"Get ready to be dizzy," Ginny said, and she started spinning the Cheese Wizard around. The momentum of the spinning lifted the Cheese Wizard's feet off the ground, causing them to flail around. As the Cheese Wizard spun, his feet managed to hit every single garlic smelling egg in the face.

Part 9: Ginny Gelato

Ginny stopped spinning the wizard and managed to lead him inside the wreckage of the building, the sound of screaming eggs behind them. Ginny dragged the wizard to the back of the shop, where he promptly threw up.

"Never, ever, ever, ever, ever, ever, ever, spin me again," the Cheese Wizard said.

"Well, I did tell you it was a trap, and you didn't listen to me." Ginny retorted.

"Whatever. Now that we know that the extraterrestrial eggs are here, that only means one thing, that Captain Burrito is here."

"Why is that?"

"Because they are his henchmen. Either way, we need to defend ourselves," the Cheese Wizard said. Ginny looked around. They appeared to be in the school supply section of the supermarket.

"Well," Ginny said, handing the wizard a stapler, "guess we'll just have to use what we have." The ground rumbled and the rest of the roof fell, revealing a giant mech in the shape of the burrito.

"HELLO PUNY FOODS," the voice of Captain Burrito boomed over a loudspeaker, "You will pay for what you have done."

"Ummmm... what have we done?" Ginny asked.

"I don't— I don't actually know." Captain Burrito said, "Let me think about this..."

Ginny turned to the Cheese Wizard and told him to go and find MilkDudBot1.1,"I'll distract Captain Burrito and his mech."

Part 9: Ginny Gelato

The Cheese Wizard ran off, leaving Ginny staring up at the massive mech. She looked around and grabbed the first thing she saw, a stack of ten composition notebooks made purely out of rice paper.

"OH! I REMEMBER NOW!" The voice of Captain Burrito rang out once more, "I KNOW WHAT YOU DID!" he seemed almost excited at the fact that he had remembered what they had supposedly done wrong.

"So," Ginny invited, "what did we do wrong?"

"WELL, IT'S THAT— no that was Edward's doing. WELL THERE WAS THAT ONE TIME WHEN— no, Sugar Cookie and Chipette did that. UMMMM..."

"So I've done nothing wrong," Ginny said. "I'm literally just friends with Edward."

"THAT'S IT! YOU ARE FRIENDS WITH EDWARD, THAT EVIL, ARROGANT, SMUG COOKIE!"

"So, I've done nothing wrong except be friends with a good dessert."

"DID YOU NOT HEAR WHAT I JUST SAID! EDWARD IS EVIL, ARROGANT, and SMUG!"

"I WILL NOT LET YOU INSULT MY FRIEND LIKE THAT!" Ginny shouted.

On an impulse, she started throwing the composition notebooks in her arms like ninja stars at the mech. Nine out of ten of the notebooks just bounced harmlessly off the chest of the robot. One notebook, however, managed to lodge itself in a chink of armor on the robot's stomach.

"YOU THOUGHT YOU COULD DEFEAT THE AWESOMESAUCE CAPTAIN BURRITO WITH SOME NOTEBOOKS!" Captain Burrito laughed.

Part 9: Ginny Gelato

"No," Ginny said, getting an idea, "but your armor is made of dark chocolate, right?"

"ONLY THE STRONGEST CHOCOLATE WAS ACCEPTABLE WHEN MAKING THIS BEAUTY OF A MECH!"

"Got it, thanks!" Ginny grabbed one last notebook and took off though the store in search of some matches.

"I TOTALLY SEE YOU LOOKING FOR MATCHES DOWN THERE!" Captain Burrito said, "LUCKY FOR YOU, I HAVE ALL THE MATCHES RIGHT HERE!" Ginny stopped and looked around, and sure enough, the match aisle of the supermarket was empty. Ginny looked up, seeing Captain Burrito's mech holding all the shelves containing matches in its enormous left hand.

She looked behind her, trying to come up with a Plan B. There was just the vegetable aisle; no, she couldn't pelt the mech with vegetables. There were only two more aisles behind her, the diaper aisle and an aisle labeled in rainbow colors:

TOTALLY ILLEGAL FIREWORKS STORED HERE!!!

She doubted that the robot needed changing, so fireworks it was. She ran to the fireworks, but unfortunately, Captain Burrito seemed to figure out her Plan B and started shooting at her with his hand burrito blasters and tortilla chip missiles. Burritos smashed to the ground behind her, flinging beans and potatoes everywhere. Ginny was two feet away from the fireworks when a large tortilla chip struck the ground in front of her. The chip had struck the floor of the supermarket with such force that it cracked the tile and stood upright, blocking Ginny's path.

"HAHAHAHAHAHAHA!" Captain Burrito laughed gleefully, "YOU'LL NEVER GET TO THOSE FIREWORKS NOW! HAHAHAHA!"

Ginny ran up to the chip and managed to jump and karate kick it, a move she didn't know she could execute. With a satisfying CRACK, the top half of the chip snapped off where the notebook impacted it. Ginny jumped over the chipped remains of baked tortilla. Ginny managed to grab one fireworks before Captain Burrito fired down on the aisle.

The hot sauce inside the burritos he fired was literally hot. One of the burritos impacted a firework and lit it. Before long, all of the fireworks in the shop had been lit by each other. Fireworks started zipping all around the shop, exploding in firefly sprinkles against the walls, floors, and shelves of Milkshake Mart. Ginny somehow managed to escape just before the entire store exploded behind her. Sizzling hot sprinkles of all sorts of colors rained down and she began to feel herself melt from the exposure to all that heat.

"YES! I WON! I DEFEATED—" Captain Burrito stopped short when he saw Ginny emerging from the smoke, "OH. MY. GOURD. YOU GUYS ARE SO HARD TO KILL!"

"Yes we are," Ginny said, "but you're going down."

Part 9: Ginny Gelato

She pulled out the last unexploded firework and lit it using some leftover hot sauce on the ground. Then she threw it.

Captain Burrito screamed as the firework came closer and closer to him. The firework hit the composition notebook that was still lodged in the mech's chest. The notebook caught fire and started melting the surrounding chocolate that made up the mech. This allowed the firework to bury itself deeper inside Captain Burrito's robot. Then, in a fiery and chocolate explosion, the once impressive robot was reduced to a puddle of dark chocolate. Even more burning sprinkles rained down as well as some, now thoroughly heated, chocolate. Ginny had to take cover to keep from melting completely. Her vision started blurring and she began to feel light headed, Just before she fainted from the heat, she saw the shape of the Cheeze Wizard and a much larger shape beside him.

"Come on, we need to get her out of here or she'll die! " someone said.

"Allow me, Master." Ginny was lifted up, and then she blacked out.

Ginny woke up with a start. The air was cool and fresh. She patted the ground around her; it felt like dragon scales. She then proceeded to see if she had all her limbs. Arms? Check. Legs? Check. Head? OH NO! Ginny realized as she patted her head, she was at least two inches shorter.

Part 9: Ginny Gelato

"Yeah, sorry about that," Ginny turned around to see the Cheeze Wizard talking to her, "You had melted big time before we were able to get you up to the colder air in the sky so you wouldn't die."

"I helped too," A cheery voice beside her said. Ginny turned and saw a robot flying next to the Saibou. "Howdy, I'm MilkDudBot 1.2."

"1.2? I thought it was MilkDudBot 1.1." Ginny said.

"Master had me upgraded so that I could fly. I was too heavy to ride on the dragon's back," MilkDudBot1.2 said sadly.

"There was no way we would have made it to the Spaghetti Monster with all four of you on my back." the Saibou interjected.

"Are we there yet?" a very flustered Prince Ice of Cream asked.

"Not since you asked two minuets ago." The Saibou said. Ginny could tell he was getting annoyed with the Ice Cream.

"Anyways," Ginny said, turning to the Cheese Wizard, "how'd you find MilkDudBot1.2 and convice him to come with us?"

"Oh yes! I can tell this story also?" MilkDudBot1.2 said.

"Well," the Cheese Wizard started:

The Long Short Story of How The Cheese Wizard Found MilkDudBot1.2 and Convinced Him to Come With Him:

When I ran off, I—

"Can I just stop you right there," Ginny said, "we are almost there to the Spaghetti Monster and I don't think we have time for an entire long short story, nor do I want to listen to another one. So, can I just get the important details please?"

"Fine," the Cheese Wizard sighed and turned to a disappointed MilkDudBot1.2. "It's ok, buddy. I'm sure you'll get to tell someone else a long short story someday."

Just The Important Details (Because We are Almost There to The Spaghetti Monster and We Don't Have Enough Time for an Entire Long Short Story and Ginny Also Doesn't Want to Listen to a Long Short Story) of How The Cheese Wizard Found MilkDudBot 1.2 and Convinced Him to Come With Him:

- *When I (the Cheese Wizard) ran off to find MilkDudBot 1.2 at first I didn't know where to look.*
- *Fast Forward 10 minutes, I spotted a crater behind MilkShake Mart*
- *MilkDudBot 1.2 was in the Crater.*
- *He wasn't moving, but most of his parts were there (thank goodness)*

Part 9: Ginny Gelato

- I woke him up using magic and my awesome mechanical skills
- He hated me when he woke up and tried to kill me
  - but then I told him that I was working with Edward's friend, Ginny
- He said that it was nice that I was working with the good guys and forgave me
  - Plus he wanted to apologize to Chipette for how he reacted to her calling him "noob"
  - He also wanted to apologize to Edward, his sisters, and Adrienne, and Tiriaq for trying to kill them.
- We ran back to Milkshake Mart to find it completely exploded and Captain Burrito's mech ruined
- Ginny was melting quickly so MilkDudBot 1.2 picked her up and we sprinted back to the Saibou
- As we ran off we heard Captain Burrito sobbing over the loss of his mech
- We made it to the Saibou
- The End

"I don't know guys," Ginny said, "that was still kind of a long recap." The Cheese Wizard and MilkDudBot1.2 groaned.

"The Spaghetti Monster is in sight guys," the Saibou interrupted. "Strap in, this is going to be a bumpy ride."

Part 9: Ginny Gelato

"Strap into what?" Ginny asked. "This isn't a car."

"Some of us are friggin tied to the dragon," Prince Ice of Cream grumbled.

"Hey! It was your choice to stay back on the dragon," The Cheese Wizard and Ginny pointed out at the same time. The Saibou angled its body toward the large food entity. As they neared the Spaghetti Monster, the air became warmer and more humid. Ginny and Prince Ice of Cream began melting again so the Cheese Wizard cast a spell that allowed them to adjust their body temperature at will.

Soon they landed on the oily ground of the Spaghetti Monster. It was strangely quiet and no noodles were anywhere to be seen.

"Maybe he's still sleeping?" Ginny suggested.

"Welp," Prince Ice of Cream said, "guess we won't be leaving this dimension for the other dimension your 'friends' are in. Let's go home." Just as he said that, MilkDudBot1.2, who had fallen behind the Saibou during the descent, crashed into the ground, making a giant robot shaped dent in the ground.

"RAWWWWWWWWWUUUUUGGGGHH!" the scream of the Spaghetti Monster was heard, "WHO HAS LANDED SO RUDELY ON MY FOREHEAD?"

"Ah, poo," Prince Ice of Cream said, "it's awake now."

Giant noodles erupted from the ground all around them. "WHAT DO YOU WANT?" The Spaghetti Monster asked.

"Um, Mr. Spaghetti Monster," Ginny said, "I had some friends who landed here and then you threw them

Part 9: Ginny Gelato

into another dimension, and we'd like to go there please."

"Hmmm, why would I want to throw such nice foods off into another dimension?"

"Ummm. One," Ginny said, "our robot made a giant dent in you and I can insult you if that would help you throw us off."

"Hmmmm," the Spaghetti Monster thought, "throw me some insults."

"You're fat," the Cheeze Wizard said.

"I bet you get so much acne because you're so oily." Ginny threw out.

"NOOB!" MilkDudBot1.2 shouted, then added, "I learned that one from Chipette!"

"I'M NOT GETTING ANGRY!!!" The Spaghetti Monster said.

"Step aside, losers," Prince Ice of Cream said, "let a pro do this."

"You can try..." The Spaghetti Monster muttered, "I'm just not in the angry mood today."

"Let's get started," Prince Ice of Cream grinned, "I envy foods who have never met you. In fact, you are so depressing, you make onions cry and red pepper's eyes water. I will try to forget that we have met today, but the image of your face is seared into my mind. I'm sure I'll have nightmares later tonight about it."

"ENOUGH," the Spaghetti Monster yelled, "BE GONE, MEANIE HEADS." With that, the giant noodles that were surrounding them lifted them up and threw them into an abyss. As they hurtled away, Ginny shouted, "Thank you Mr. Spaghetti Monster!"

Part 9: Ginny Gelato

"THANK YOU FOR NOT BUILDING AN ARMY CAMP ON MY BUTT." the Spaghetti Monster yelled back. With that, Ginny was on her way to Cassie, with the Plastic Cherry.

Part 10: Edward Chip

Down on the Planet Crumb, Edward Chip and his friends had taken shelter in a Cabinet and they were in one of the most intense games of Go Fish ever with an old human deck of cards they had found in the Cabinet. Each card was as big as Edward's face and smelled musty, but he didn't mind. Ronald the Rat was winning the round, though he hadn't said a word himself. Cinnamon spoke for the rat, and Edward thought that she must be looking at everyone's cards because she would often walk around the table very conspicuously. Derek was getting very frustrated because Ronald the Rat kept eating Derek's cards right out of his hand, making it impossible for him to make any matches. Barry, who was also playing, kept slipping on his peel and falling off his chair.

"Do you have any sevens?" Edward asked Derek.

"No, the stupid rat just ate all my sevens, go fish." Just as Edward was about to "go fishing," a big gust of wind blew all the cards around them. The ground shook and Barry fell off his chair and Ronald got scared and ran out of the room.

"The Free-Idge is opening!" Ginger screamed, running into the room. Cinnamon ushered Edward and Derek quickly outside. Cassie, Andreienne, and Tiriaq were already outside, staring as the Free-Idge rumbled and shook uncontrollably.

"Guys!" Ginger shouted, "get over here. You're going to get crushed there!"

"Yeah guys," Nutmeg, who was standing next to the Spice Girls' leader, said, "the most crushed your bodies will be with you there standing."

"What's happening, amigos?" The ETM holding the ETL's hand emerged from another Cabinet.

"Everyone over here!" Ginger shouted again. The group followed her orders. Seconds later, the front part of the Free-Idge burst open and a bright white light shot out of the metal box temporarily blinding Edward. Just as suddenly as the Free-Idge opened, it closed, leaving a smoldering pile of bodies in the middle of Planet Crumb. The entire group ran up to the bodies. Cassie sighed in relief when she saw that Ginny was there, then she screamed when she saw the Cheese Wizard.

"AH! IT'S THAT NOOB ROBOT! MILKDUDBOT1.1, WHO TRIED TO KILL US!" Chipette said, appearing behind Cassie.

"Look!" Nutmeg said, "'tis the Saibou arrived too, stuff of the legend!"

"and Prince Ice of Cream," Ginger shouted, "but, where is the Plastic Cherry?"

"Alright guys," Adrienne said, "we need to get these foods inside before the humans see them on the ground and kill them using the Vacuum Cleaner." The group was able to pick up and carry everyone (except the Saibou) to the makeshift medbay that Chipette and Tiriaq had built for Sugar Cookie to work in.

"Unruly Urnebes," Ginger called, "we need you to help move this dragon." The blob of grains rolled up and managed to flatten herself against the ground and slide under the enormous dragon. She then moved the dragon across the planet using herself as a conveyor belt.

"All right!" Ginger said once all of them were in the makeshift hospital, "get the Fee-ther, we need to wake the new arrivals."

Once everyone was awaked, the Spice Girls introduced themselves. Prince Ice of Cream tried to run away but ended up running into the Spice Girls.

"Your majesty, it's an honor." The Spice Girls sang going into deep curtsies.

"Well. Um. Yes. I wish I could say the same for you. But I was kidnapped by a scary girl and tied to a dragon so…" The Prince Ice of Cream faded into inaudible mutters while throwing nervous glances at Ginny.

Ginny smiled, unfazed. "I'm terribly sorry about that but it was the only way to get the Plastic Cherry off of your head without you screaming for your guards." She offered the Prince a somewhat sympathetic smirk. He cringed away. Ginny turned towards the Spice Girls and rolled her eyes at the Prince's behavior. Edward watched as Ginny and Cassie's eyes found each other across the room.

"Cassie, how are you? I've missed you so much." The two of them ran and met halfway in a tight hug.

Part 10: Edward Chip

"I do hope it's ok that I brought the Cheese Wizard and MilkDudBot1.2." Ginny said, "They are good now, they saved my life!"

"I thought it was MilkDudBot1.1!" Edward said, confused.

"Yeah, we couldn't get him to fit on the Saibou's back, so we had to make him fly in a new update."

"WE!" The Cheese Wizard exclaimed, "I recall you being gone while I made that update!"

"Fine," Ginny said, rolling her eyes, "you did the update while I was risking my neck fighting Captain Burrito!"

"WHERE IS THAT NOOB ROBOT!!" Chipette burst into the makeshift hospital room, "He is NOT safe to be around!"

"Hello I am MilkDudBo—" MilkDudBot1.2 said, emerging from one of the hospital beds. Before he could say anything more however, Chipette launched herself at him and tried to incapacitate the robot.

MilkDudBot1.2 fell down and screamed, "NOOOOO! I'M TRYING TO APOLOGIZE!"

"Excuse me?" Chipette said, suddenly stopping her attack.

"I'm so sorry for the way I reacted to you calling me 'Noob'. I realize now it is a complement, and I won't try to kill you and your friends anymore."

"Huh," Edward said, "you know, calling someone a 'Noob' isn't really a comp—"

Adrienne shushed Edward before he could finish and said, "do you really want him to try and kill us again?!" Chipette fortunately didn't hear this because she was already distracted by the presence of Prince Ice of Cream.

"Ohmygosh! Is that His Royal Handsomeness!" Chipette squealed and ran up to the prince and began talking one hundred miles an hour at him,

"Ohmygosh, ohmygosh, OH MY GOSH!" Chipette said, fanning herself with her hand. "I-I'm such a great fan of yours! I have all of your posters and calendars and scented candles and Prince Ice of Cream branded light bulbs!"

Prince Ice of Cream looked confused and said,"Wait, are you Icecrreamlover55? The only food to buy anything I have ever tried to sell. I've made over $6,000 from that user alone."

"YES! Yes she is!" Edward and Sugar Cookie interjected.

Chipette blushed and yelled at her siblings to shut up. Derek stood in the corner staring at Prince Ice of Cream. Edward wasn't sure why though and waved his hand in front of Derek's eyes. Derek blinked, blushed and looked down, leaving Edward confused about his friend's behavior.

"Yeah," Cassie said, turning back to Ginny, "I'm sure it's fine that you brought the robot and the wizard. They will fit in just fine here."

"Did we get the Plastic Cherry?" Ginger asked, appearing behind them.

"Yes," Ginny said, pulling the sacred object out from the center of her roll. Everyone suddenly turned to look at the Cherry at once, and they all cheered simultaneously.

Part 10: Edward Chip

"SHUTTING UP YOU GUYS!" Nutmeg screamed out, "THE HUMAN EARS WILL BE THE SCREAM AND LET THEM KNOW LOCATION OF US!"

"Huh?" Ginny said, "does she have brain damage?"

"No no," Ginger said, "The humans really enjoy nutmeg around the winter months and due to her diminishing fillings, she hasn't been quite sane. I fear Nutmeg won't last another Christmas. What she means to say is that we need to be more quiet because the humans might hear us and our cover will be blown." BOOM! BOOM! BOOM!

"Oh Scrap," Edward said, "that isn't the..."

"HUMANS!" Barry screamed, and started running around in circles. He then tripped on his peel and fell flat on his face.

"Ok, everyone," Edward said, "we aren't prepared to fight off the humans, so we need to hide. Sugar Cookie, you've planned for something like this right?"

Sugar Cookie nodded."Yes, I have, like, designed a secret compartment in the back of the Cabinet, if I just open the app, enter the combo code, and..." she trailed off as she started typing furiously on her phone. A message popped up on an illuminated screen behind her saying:

WELCOME TO SUGAR COOKIE'S HIDEOUT, ESTABLISHED WITHIN THE LAST COUPLE OF DAYS.

Part 10: Edward Chip

A metal part of the wall suddenly sank into the ground, revealing a large room decorated with fairy lights and soft couches made of dust bunnies. Ronald the Rat was already inside the room, sleeping in the corner by a small plant labeled, "Thyme."

"Come on everyone!" Sugar Cookie said, "we will be safe here!" All seventeen foods plus the five Spice Girls trumped inside Sugar Cookie's Bunker. They barely all fit, especially with The Saibou in there taking up most of the space and MilkDudBot1.2 sprawled in the middle of the room.

"This isn't very comfortable," Prince Ice of Cream complained, "I barely have room to move around."

"Of course we all don't fit comfortably," Sugar Cookie said, "Lucky for you, I had Chipette and Tiriaq help me build the expansion underneath this room!" With that, she tapped on her phone some more and the couch retracted underneath the floor. Everyone oohed and ahhed.

"Come on, " Cassie said, "Let's get everyone inside. I think I hear the humans coming closer." Sure enough, the booming of human footsteps was getting louder. The majority of the foods jumped down the hole. Suddenly, the humans' footsteps stopped.

"Honey? Have you taken out the trash yet?" Edward heard what must have been a human voice say.

Adrienne immediately lost it and screamed, "We are all doomed!" The fortune cookie tried to make a run to the door to the Cabinet they had taken shelter in but it quickly burst open, sending the cookie lady flying backwards. From the empty space created by the opening of the door, a human hand came through.

"Everyone go now!" Edward screamed to the remaining foods still above ground. The hand was fleshy and pink, its sausage fingers wiggled around as if possessed by a ghost. Edward jumped down into the bunker and turned around. Barry the Banana and Cassie were the last foods above ground. Just as Barry was about to jump down into the hole, he slipped on his own peel. The thick fingers of the human hand whisked him up and began pulling him out of the makeshift hospital.

"NOOOOOOOOOO!" Barry screamed. Cassie ran after the fruit and managed to grab the banana's legs. But it was no use. She began traveling upward with Barry.

"WHAT THE— " Edward screamed, flying out of the bunker with Derek. They emerged from the hole in Sugar Cookie's bunker. The pair grabbed onto Cassie's legs and were able to slow her ascent. But soon, they too were taken upwards. Adrienne climbed back up and screamed,

"Sausage claws!" and instinctively went to keep Tiraq away from the fingers, fearing they would snatch him just like they snatched his parents. The four of them were soon whisked into the light of Planet Crumb, momentarily blinding Edward. The ground of Planet Crumb was so far beneath them and Edward got dizzy looking down. He decided to look up; it was a mistake.

The Human's face was even more terrifying than the hand. With a fleshy pink mouth with lips that moved

Part 10: Edward Chip

like worms. The eyes glistened and shone more intensely than Jawbreakers. The nose, a small mountain that erected from the middle of the face and glistened like vegetable oil. Worst of all, the entire face, except for the forehead, was covered in hairs the size of needles that clustered together in a matted mess of brown. Barry and everyone hanging on below him let out a collective scream of terror.

The Human, upon hearing this scream, screamed as well and dropped the chain of foods. The ground of Planet Crumb came hurtling toward them and Edward knew within a matter of seconds they would hit the ground and be killed on impact. "I'm sorry I'm so clumsy!" Barry cried out, "I hope this helps repay the debt I owe you for getting me off the Spaghetti Monster."

"What are you going to do?!" Edward asked, wind rushing in his face. Barry didn't respond. Instead he flattened his peels, causing him to streamline past Cassie and her friends. Right before he hit the ground, Barry opened up his peels.

His head and body impacted the floor with a sickening squish. Edward, Cassie and Derek landed on Barry's body safely for his peel absorbed the shock of their fall. However, Barry was gone. His entire body collapsed into itself.

They rubbed his mush on the wall in a painting of his face. It wasn't fabulous, but it was enough to commemorate him. They had to keep moving, the human was coming out of the shock induced by seeing living food. The human looked murderous and said something. Unfortunately, Edward understood what he was saying,

"Hey! You were supposed to be my pre-dinner snack!" The human stood up, towering over the three desserts, took a step, and slipped on Barry's peel. Seeing their chance, Edward grabbed Cassie and Derek and the trio fled the scene as the human came crashing down, knocking himself out.

After hiking for hours through the Kitchen and the surrounding area, Edward realized they were lost. He felt terrible about getting lost, they were so close to using the Plastic Cherry to reopen the Free-ldge and Edward felt that his and his friends' abduction had derailed it all. The Cabinet holding Sugar Cookie's base was nowhere in sight. So, they resolved to make camp in the fabled Junk Drawer Ginger had told them about for the night. They chose this place because they heard that the humans never went in this drawer for it was in a place called The Attic.

One problem though: the drawer was on another level of Planet Crumb. The only way to ascend to this level was to climb the Jagged Mountain. This wasn't a regular mountain. Instead of smooth sides, the Jagged Mountain, as its name suggests, was made up of slabs that went all the way to the top of the mountain creating the jagged look. When the slabs were no more and the Jagged Mountained reached a plateau, they would know they were on the second level of Planet Crumb.

Edward decided to call this place The Barren Crumb, because it was a place where no crumbs had ever come back. But, they had to get to the Junk Drawer, it was the only place they would be safe. Working together, the three desserts created a plan to climb the Jagged Mountain without the humans seeing them. They waited for night, when the human activity slowed to a halt, then they set out.

The three desserts reached the foot of the Jagged Mountain over two hours later. It was an uneventful journey. Cassie had to keep sushing the boys, who kept talking when they were supposed to be sneaking around. Edward and Derek stacked on top of each other so Cassie could reach the top of the first step of the mountain. When she was on the step, she pulled Edward and Derek up to the step she was on. They would repeat this step for the next twenty-six steps. Edward goaned a little bit every time Cassie stepped on him, despite having whipped cream icing, she wasn't all that light. He wished he hadn't broken his cookie blaster back at the Food Pyramid, its grappling function would have made this so much easier.

Ever so often, Edward would hear strange noises coming from the top of the Jagged Mountain, loud droning noises, soft pattering, at one point the sound of hydraulics emanated loudly, shaking the ground. Cassie

Part 10: Edward Chip

fell backward and would have fallen off the step they were on if Edward hadn't caught her.

"I had to develop quick reflexes when I learned to fly," he explained to her.

With each step they climbed the three got more and more fatigued. At one point, Edward could feel sweat dripping down his back, causing Cassie to slip as she hoisted herself up. He thought he felt a singular chocolate chip fly off of his back when Cassie slipped, but wasn't sure. Edward didn't think about it then, but later would have wished he paid more attention to this. Then, just when Edward thought he couldn't take being stepped on any more, the Jagged Mountain plateaued. Edward and Derek collapsed on the ground as Cassie massaged her sore arms. The area at the top of the Jagged Mountain was extremely ominous.

A hallway longer than anything Edward had ever seen opened up in front of him. The corridor seemed to be lined with enormous doors. Behind one of the doors he heard the loud droning noise; he peeked underneath the large door and realized that the noise was coming from a smaller human who was sleeping.

"We have to keep moving," Derek said, appearing behind him and tapping Edward on the shoulder. Edward was so startled that he punched Derek in the face on reflex, sending him flying into the wall behind them both. Derek fell to the ground with a muffled thump.

CREEEEEEEEEK

Part 10: Edward Chip

Edward turned around as light flooded the hallway. One of the doors had opened, spilling light out of the room and a small human emerged. Cassie grabbed Derek and pressed them both against the wall hoping the human wouldn't see them.

"This is your fault!" Derek mouthed, rubbing the spot on his head that hit the wall.

Cassie glared back at him. The small human was slightly less grotesque than the one they had met earlier. She was shorter, height and width wise, her brown hair flowed down her back smoothly and flawlessly despite just waking up. The little girl human yawned and looked down the hall perhaps to see what the noise was. She then rubbed her eyes and walked into another room. This room held a Sink much like the one in the Kit-Chen but this one was white. On the other side of the Sink was a shiny bowl. Cassie realized that this was the room called the Bathroom and it was where the hydraulic sound was coming from. The girl walked into the Bathroom and shut the door.

"This is our chance," Edward said, "let's move out." The gang raced to the end of the hallway. To the right, a dead end. To the left, something that appeared to be a smaller version of the Jagged Mountain.

"Please tell me that we don't have to climb up that," Derek said.

"If we want to get to the attic, we do," Cassie said. Edward then proceeded to stack himself on top of Derek so Cassie could climb on top and hoist herself onto the first step.

Part 10: Edward Chip

Edward collapsed at the top of Jagged Mountain Two, exhausted from the night's journey. Derek grumbled about the foot shaped dents in his body while Cassie complained about her sore arms. Edward patted himself down, feeling just a bit lighter than before he started with the journey.

"Do I look different, Cassie?" Edward asked.

Cassie turned to face him, "No..." she said, why?"

"Well, it's just that I feel suspiciously lighter." Edward explained as he continued to check his body for missing pieces.

"C'mon guys," Derek said, having finally rubbed out the footprint in his doughy body, "the Attic is so close!" Edward helped Cassie as she reluctantly got up. Sure enough, Derek had spoken the truth. The entrance to the Attic was merely feet away.

"Wait a second..." Edward said. He patted a spot on his back where a chocolate chip used to reside.

"Oh no," Cassie said, "what is it?"

"I'm missing a chocolate chip, that's why I felt so light."

"Seriously man!" Derek said, exasperated, "we are almost safe and you're worried about cosmetics!"

"Well," Edward said, "it's just that if a human finds it, they might be able to track us here."

"Oh dear Gourd, please don't tell me we have to go back down the mountain we just climbed..." Derek said.

Part 10: Edward Chip

"Well," Cassie interjected, "Edward has a valid point."

"Exactly," Edward said, "we don't want to be found. Right guys?" Cassie and Derek didn't respond, instead they just stared at something above Edward's head, mouths gapping.

"Guys!" Edward said, "Excuse me! Is there anyone inside those brains of yours?!"

Cassie and Derek didn't respond. Instead, they simultaneously pointed at a spot above Edwards head, fingers shaking. Edward turned around and came face to face with one of the scariest monsters she had ever seen.

At first they just regarded each other, the monster and desserts. No one blinked. The monster's giant pointed eyes carried a look of dangerous calm and the slits it had for irises, black as night. The monster was completely covered in orange fur with black stripes on its back that glinted in the low lighting.

"Everyone," Edward whispered, "back away very slowly."

The group began to step backward, lightly, as if walking on thin ice. The monster titled its head as if confused by this action, its tail swaying back and forth.

"Mew." The monster said, yawning.

Derek started trembling.

"Get a grip, Derek!" Cassie whisper-scolded him, "I don't think it's going to hurt us."

"Guys..." Derek interrupted, "look up."

Part 10: Edward Chip

Edward looked up, the monster had its paws over their heads, claws outstretched, ready to smash them all to obliteration. Derek let out an unearthly scream and tore across the floor. The monster hissed and began to launch itself at the trio.

"RUN!" Edward screamed as he and Cassie quickly followed Derek.

The monster reacted just as quickly and began chasing them on its four padded paws. They ran through the dark corridors, not knowing where they were going, the monster claws clicking on and scratching the ground as it chased them. At one point, all Edward knew was that the monster's hot, fishy breath was touching at his neck, putting more fear and adrenaline inside his body. He reached down to pull out his cookie blaster and was reminded that he was destroyed it beyond repair and groaned in frustration.

"Quick! Over here!" Edward said, making a sharp left turn, "I see a potential hiding spot!" Cassie and Derek slid into the turn behind him. The monster tried to execute the turn but slid forward before turning, giving Edward and his friends just the couple extra seconds they needed. Straight ahead, Edward saw a small wooden box—its lid seemed nailed shut, but there was a small crack in the side, just small enough to fit them.

"See that wooden box up ahead?" Edward shouted, "When you get close enough, dive into that crack." He glanced behind him.

The monster had gotten up and was getting closer to them by the second. The tight turn had really angered it, and Edward could see its fangs were dripping in saliva. The wooden box was getting closer now, he could almost jump into safety. He glanced back. Cassie was in front of him, but Derek was never going to make it.

Icing sweat dripped down his forehead, the dents on his dough seemed to be impacting his breathing. Cassie saw him looking back at Derek, Mew (Edward decided to call the monster Mew because it was the first sound it made), was getting closer to Derek, jaw wide open, ready to eat up her friend.

Edward nodded to Cassie. She stopped running and turned around, Edward also stopped running and got down on a knee. Cassie sprinted toward Edward and jumped. As she landed on Edward, he stood up and pushed her back upward with his arms outstretched. Edward watched as Cassie went flying over Derek and straight at Mew's face. She tightened her hand into a fist and smashed into Mew's face, temerparly blinding the monster with the cream cheese frosting that fell off of her body. The monster cried out and emitted a menacing hiss as Cassie rolled off its nose back onto the floor.

Mew used one of its paws to wipe the frosting from its eyes and glared at Cassie.

"RUN, CASSIE!" Edward screamed. He and Derek were standing just inside the crack of the box. Their attack had worked, and Derek was now safe. Cassie took off, running (again) to the wooden box, the furious monster's paws hitting the ground behind her. The monster's mouth was inches from the back of her head.

Part 10: Edward Chip

As she neared the wooden box, the monster managed to get close enough to chomp off a small chunk of Cassie's head. Luckily, it didn't eat any dough and only bit off icing. Despite knowing that she could get it refrosted later, Edward heard himself gasp. If he knew his friend, the thought of her once perfectly smooth icing being ruined would have angered Cassie deeply.

"OH NO YOU DIDN'T!" Cassie screamed, and picked up the nearest thing on the Attic floor, a red pointed stick labeled: Crayon. Cassie spun around and threw the Crayon at Mew in one swift motion. The monster's eyes widened as the red javelin came closer and closer to its face.

"You're done!" Cassie said triumphantly while waving her finger through the air sassily. The Crayon sailed majestically through the air in a perfect arc and impacted Mew's nose... and fell harmlessly to the ground. Edward and Derek gasped again from inside the wooden box. Both Cassie and Mew stood there somewhat stunned, then Mew smiled, an evil, gruesome, fanged smile. Mew was going to kill Cassie and Edward knew he had to stop it. But how?

"I TOLD YOU TO RUN CASSIE! WHY DID YOU STOP!!!" Edward shrieked and ran outside the wooden box.

Cassie was way too close to Mew to run. Edward knew that if she tried, the monster would just eat her up. He looked around and spotted a yellow and green box labeled Crayola. He grabbed the first thing he could from it, a blue Crayon impacted, and threw it at the monster's face. He didn't wait to see if he hit his target and quickly threw a yellow one, and an orange one. Green pink, black, and brown— SWOOSH, SWOOSH, SWOOSH, SWOOSH!

When he was out of colored javilans, he saw several of them smack into Mew's face. The monster looked back and forth between Cassie and Edward as if not sure who to attack, until the last Crayon, colored purple, smacked Mew straight in the eye.

"Bullseye," Edward shouted, quickly followed by an, "oh crêpe!" as the monster launched itself at him. Edward and Cassie sprinted toward the wooden box together, and an even angrier Mew chased them. They both just barely slid through the crack in the side of the wooden box as Mew's mouth snapped shut, almost eating them. Edward and Cassie slid to the floor of the box and just sat and caught their breath, Mew pacing back and forth outside the box and occasionally coming up the crack to hiss at them.

"Hey," Edward realized, "that monster's breath smells kinda like my chocolate chips!"

"Didn't you lose one?" Derek asked.

Edward trailed off feeling embarrassed, "ooops... sorry guys."

"Eh," Cassie said, "shut up, Derek. Just be thankful that Edward and I both saved your butt."

"I would have run better if I DIDN'T HAVE YOUR FOOT PRINTS IN MY DOUGH." Derek retorted. His loud outburst was met with a sharp HISS from Mew outside and a swipe of claws from outside the box.

Part 10: Edward Chip

Cassie glared at Derek and mouthed, "IDIOT!" Edward put his hand on Cassie's shoulder in an attempt to calm her down.

"Guys," Edward said. "If we wanna make it out of this box, then we need to cooperate. Please be nice to each other."

"Look guys!" Casssie said, pointing at a crack in the far wall of the box, "there's a window over there! We can see what is waiting for us outside the front door!"

The trio rushed over to the crack and peeked out. The sun was just rising, they had spent the entire night in utter terror. Hiding from the humans, climbing all those mountains, and running from Mew, Edward just realized how tired he was.

He looked beside him. Derek and Cassie were nodding off as well. Tomorrow would be a better day, Edward decided. When they got back, they could finally unlock the secrets of the Plastic Cherry to reopen the Free-Idge and save the foodiverse. Edward smiled to himself. The last thing he saw before he fell asleep was the warm, golden rays of the sun, just peeking out and dancing before his eyes.

When Edward awoke, he was momentarily blinded by the light of the sun which had risen much higher now. Derek and Cassie were already awake and still staring out the crack.

Part 10: Edward Chip

"Edward! Look over here!" Cassie said, motioning him over, "beyond the front door is paradise." Edward walked over.

What he saw was beyond amazing, beyond magical. It was absolutely perfect. It was any food's dream. A yellow bright circle in the sky warmed the grass, which sparkled from the droplets of morning dew. Red and white checkered patterned blankets had been laid out on top of the grass. On top of the blankets lay brown woven baskets, one for each blanket. As the morning wore on, the baskets started to open and various foods started peeking out into the world.

A couple sandwiches began to step foot on the blanket their basket was on. When nothing bad happened to them, the other foods started coming out of their baskets. A group of grapes started playing tag with various berries. Hotdogs laid down on the blankets and began to tan.

"What is this place?" Derek asked in wonder.

"See that sign?" Cassie responded, pointing to a petit wooden sign in the middle of the peaceful scene playing out below them, "it says Picnic Palace!"

"So this is what awaits us outside the Front Door." Edward said, watching some sushi rolls pretend to sword fight using chopsticks as swords.

"C'mon guys," Cassie said, "it should be safe to go down now. Ginger told me that during the day all the larger adults leave the house for an event called Work and the smaller humans leave the house of a big yellow contraption with wheels. It should be safe to go to Sugar Cookie's bunker now."

Part 10: Edward Chip

"What about that monster outside?" Derek asked.

"I think Mew is asleep for now," Edward said.

"Mew?" Cassie and Derek said in unison.

"Yeah, that's what I'm calling the monster. It was the first sound I heard it make."

Edward and his friends approached the crack in the box from which they had escaped the clutches of Mew cautiously. Sure enough, Mew was fast asleep, basking in the warmth of a beam coming through the window. Silently, Edward, Derek and Cassie snuck out of the wooden box, shimmying through the crack. As they tiptoed around Mew, Edward felt a sneeze coming on. He held it in as long as he could, but as the urge to sneeze became stronger, Edward began to panic. Quickly, he turned herself away from Mew and sneezed as quietly as he could into his elbow.

The trio froze in place and turned slowly to look at Mew. The monster seemed unaffected by the sneeze and continued to snore softly. Edward motioned to Derek and Cassie that he thought it would be ok to continue out the door and the other two desserts followed him. Edward held his breath, determined not to sneeze again. When they reached the long hallway at the top of Jagged Mountain Two, Edward gasped, his face had turned blue from not breathing for so long. Cassie and Derek turned back and looked at him shocked.

"Are you ok?" Cassie asked.

Edward nodded and tried to return his breathing to normal. A shadow passed over Edward's face and Cassie and Derek looked behind Edward in fear.

"WE GOT TO GO NOW!" Derek shouted.

Mew was awake, and wanted revenge.

Abandoning all caution, the group stumbled away from the monster, crashing into walls and each other, just barely staying out of the reach of Mew's fangs. When the trio reached the top of Jagged Mountain Two they barely stopped to consider what they were doing. Derek couldn't even stop running and completely fell over the edge, bouncing on each step as he went down. Edward stopped for just a millisecond and turned himself on his side, rolling down the steps, crumbs flaking off of him. As Edward tumbled head over heels down the steps, he noticed Cassie sliding on a smooth railing to the left of and several feet higher than the mountain top.

Mew stopped at the top of Jagged Mountain to hiss and claw at the railing Cassie slid down. To Edward's relief, she was able to stay upright and didn't go plummeting to her death. Derek and Edward reached the base of the mountain just seconds after she did and they dusted themselves off and turned around.

"HAHA! Take that you stupid monster!" Derek shouted, "such a scary monster, defeated by a mountain!"

Derek laughed some more, seeming abnormally amused by this turn of events. That was until Mew, looking Derek square in the eye, began to descend the mountain, three steps at a time. Derek screamed and

Part 10: Edward Chip

sprinted back towards the first Jagged Mountain, a fearful Cassie and Edward close behind him.

The three soon came upon the first mountain they climbed and proceeded to make their way down the mountain in violent and reckless ways. Three steps from the bottom Edward felt several more chocolate chips fly off of his sides. Mew was catching up to them, the monster was halfway down the mountain when they reached the base. Derek's body was damaged, the glaze on his body was far from perfectly smooth and Cassie's back was still damaged from where Mew bit her. Edward rubbed his throbbing body, feeling the dents caused by the missing chips as he did.

Edward knew that they couldn't possibly make it to Sugar Cookie's bunker, they were all too winded and damaged to make it back there before Mew caught up to them. Still, he had to try to get them to safety. He helped Derek and Cassie to their feet and proceeded to let them use him as a crutch. As they hobbled away, it occurred to Edward that she didn't hear Mew's paws behind them anymore. He looked behind him, the monster seemed completely interested in the chocolate chips that had flown off him. Edward had a personal somber moment of silence for his chips.

"Well, now we know for sure that it was your chocolate chips that brought Mew to us," Cassie said to Edward.

"Hopefully that will hold the monster's hunger for a while," Derek said, "I am so tired my legs might as well be jelly filled!" With that, the three desserts hobbled their way back to the Kitchen and headed back to the Cabinet.

Part 11: The Evil Taco🍪 Man

"Amigos!" The Evil Taco Man groaned, "Why can't we just hire Chipette and Tiriaq to board up this bunker right now! We can't risk the humans getting to us too!"

"Calm down now," The Evil Taquito Lady said, trying to sooth her husband, "let's not get our fillings in a tizzy."

"I'm sorry," Ginger said, "I'm not leaving Cassie out there."

"And Edward," Andreinne, Sugar Cookie and Chipette said in unison.

"We can't leave them outside," Ginny agreed, "and that's final!"

"What's so special about this Edward dude anyways!" Prince Ice of Cream interjected. Everyone except for the ETM and ETL turned to look at the whiny scoop of frozen dairy. A long awkward silence ensued.

"They have probably been eaten already," the ETM said. All the heads turned now to stare at him. "I'm just being realistic amigos."

"Bickering is useless," the Saibou sighed from the corner, "they are almost here anyways." Just at that moment those idiot desserts that had gotten captured by the humans, Cassie, Derek and Edward, burst into the room, severely damaged and tired.

"Oh yeah," Adrienne said, realizing Derek hadn't been in the room. "Derek was there, too." Derek glared at her.

"Where the heck have you been!" Swiss S. Cheese asked them, polishing one of his cheese throwing knives. Sugar Cookie and Chipette ran up to Edward, asking him a billion questions. Cassie was encircled by the Spice Girls and they took her into another room to fix the icing that she appeared to be missing on the back of her head.

After all the greetings and fussing that the ETM hated so much were finally over with, he cleared his throat and tried to speak. Of course, right as he did so, the Spice Girls decided to burst into song, drowning out any attempt of the ETM to be heard. Only the ETL noticed this. He poked Swiss S. Cheese and whispered something in his ear. Swiss S. Cheese threw several cheese throwing stars into the wall above the Spice Girls. A record scratch could be heard, and the startled spices froze in the jazz hands position.

"AMIGOS," the ETM said, "WILL YOU SHUT YOUR PIE HOLES!"

Everyone looked at each other awkwardly. Adrienne covered Tiriaq's ears.

"Oh..." the ETM said, realizing that the phrase 'pie holes' was vulgar, "just... shush."

"We are shushed!" Chipette pointed out.

The ETM shushed her. Then, when he was convinced no one was going to talk, he said: "We need a plan. We can't continue to let the humans eat our kind.

Part II: The Evil Taco Man

There is no way I'm just going to hide in this bunker forever."

Murmurs of agreement spread through the crowd.

"I propose that we fight back. The humans have done enough damage and taken enough lives, and it's time to take them down. We should—"

"Wait!" Edward interjected, "I have some information."

"Very well, spill it." The ETM spat.

"There seems to be a food paradise that lies beyond Planet Crumb, it's called Picnic Palace. Derek, Cassie and I saw it when we were hiding from the humans and Mew in the attic."

"The attic place you were!" Nutmeg gasped in awe. Edward proceeded to fill everyone in on who Mew was, their 'daring' escape from the humans and Barry Banana's death.

"Let's get to the Picnic Palace," the ETM said, feeling hopeful. Maybe there was a way out after all.

"But what about going into the Free-ldge and saving the foodiverse from Supreme Lord Mac-N-Cheese?" Cinnamon asked.

"We can't save the foodiverse by bringing them here if all of Planet Crumb is this dangerous. We need a safe haven. I believe we can make Picnic Palace that haven. We just need to get there first," Cassie pointed out. There were mummers of agreement.

"So, we all know that the humans won't let us out the Front Door that easily, they need to be taken down. That is correct, right Ginger?" Edward continued his speech.

"Yes it is," Ginger responded, "though it will be no easy task. The Front door doesn't open easily, and the human's guard it with a vicious passion. Mew is a completely separate problem. It will snap you into its jaws in seconds, you won't even know what happened 'til after you've died. We will need a plan."

"Oh, I've got a plan alright," the ETM said, grinning, "now, everyone, listen closer."

The foods shifted forward in their seats.

The Plan:

There were several teams sent out. Their mission: Spy on the humans and gather intel and bring weapons back to the bunker, where Sugar Cookie and Chipette would be waiting to build armor and weapons they could use against the humans. Steps are as follows:

1) Edward, Adrienne, and Tiraq covered themselves in dust as camouflage and set out of the bunker, armed with nearby toothpicks and something called a toothbrush. They were to skirt around the edges of Planet Crumb and view the humans from inside a hole in the planet boundary created by Ronald Rat. They were told to record the number of times and for how long the humans entered the Kitchen part of Planet Crumb.

Part II: The Evil Taco Man

2) Derek and Cassie sprinted out of the Kitchen part of Planet Crumb and into a section the Spice Girls called, "the Living Room" and hid under an enormous couch titled "Lays-E-Boy". There they would be hidden from the human eyes, but would be able to track the movements of the humans and Mew all around the house.

3) Ginny and the Cheese Wizard took Prince Ice of Cream to another room where they would attempt to discover the magical properties of the Plastic Cherry and learn how they could use it against the humans.

"You can't take my crown!" Prince Ice of Cream protested as the three of them escorted him into the other room. Even once the door was closed, one could still hear the frozen diary's whiny voice.

4) Swiss S. Cheese, Unruly Urnebes, and Malicious Malt Vinegar set out around Planet Crumb, collecting various weapons and tools that might be useful against the humans.

5) MilkDudBot1.2 and the Saibou remained in the bunker common room, resting. MilkDudbot1.2 claimed that his power was dwindling and that he was in need of a reboot. The robot hoped that in the reboot he would update again and gain better combat abilities without compromising his devotion to protecting species

like desserts. The Saibou claimed that he was going on a dream quest in search of a way to make Vishnu flow through the air again. The battle would be much easier if the power of Vishnu was in their grasp.

6) The Spice Girls went around and told the other spices about their cause. They hoped to get beings known as Salt, Pepper, Cumin, Oregano, and many others to join them in their battle against the humans.

7) ETM and the ETL were to help Sugar Cookie and Chipette set up the intel station. Then they would move onto weakening the Front Door. If they wanted any chance of escaping to the front door and living happy lives at Picnic Palace, this would be the only way.

All foods were to meet back at the bunker by the end of the day. If a food didn't, it was to be assumed that they had been eaten.

"Everyone got that?" the ETM asked after the meeting concluded. Everyone nodded. With that, everyone set out and started to prepare for their tasks ahead. Within five minutes everyone was prepared and about ready to venture out into the open.

"Wait," Chipette said, just as the groups were about to step out, "I have something for you all." Edward's little sister proceeded to hand everyone tiny earpieces.

Part II: The Evil Taco Man

"Sugar Cookie coded these and I built them while we waited for Edward, Cassie, and Derek to escape the humans, this way we won't lose track of one another," Chipette explained.

"Great!" Pumpkin Spice said, "If you guys want, the other spices can fill you in on more human lore. That way we can be even more educated about them."

"Yes, and maybe you'll use the right terminology for human objects!" Cinnamon added, "The Jagged Mountain was literally just human stairs."

"Stairs?" Derek asked, confused. Cassie and Edward seemed equally dubious about this term.

"Haha," Nutmeg shouted, "I am the more taller smart then all of you! The facts on humans lives on in my brains."

"Oh, Nutmeg," Ginger facepalmed. Awkward silence followed.

"Oh my goodness," the ETM's word's cut the air like a knife through a ripe avocado, "come on, are we going to do this plan or are we going to stand around like loco idiots!"

"Yes," the ETL said, "let's head to our stations please."

The foods moved into action. Two to three foods started slipping out of the cabinet at a time and somersaulting away all spy-like. Then only Sugar Cookie, Chipette and the ETM and his wife were left inside the room. (The Saibou and MilkDudbot1.2 had already left for their sleeping quarters.) The four foods walked into the main control room.

Part II: The Evil Taco Man

"Does, like, everybody hear this?" Sugar Cookie said, pushing a button on her ear piece. Through his own ear piece the ETM heard everyone's response, though some were a bit staticy.

"Boost the signal," the ETM said to Sugar Cookie. The dessert proceeded to push a few buttons on her homemade console. "How's the voice clarity, like, now?" Sugar Cookie said into her earpiece.

Everyone responded, agreeing that the signal was much clearer now. Except for Unruly Urnebes who didn't know where to put her earpiece as her entire body was an ever shifting mass and she had no facial features.

"Alright Ginger," the ETM said, "please inform us of any information you have on the humans." The head spice proceeded to launch into a detailed explanation of the human lore. As the spices talked, each chiming in when they had something to add, the ETM and ETL helped Chipette and Sugar Cookie rewire several bits of technology around the bunker. It was hard work, and sometimes unpredictable sparks of electricity shot out, but it was worth it.

Several hours later, the ETM had gained much knowledge about the humans, but he wished those obnoxious Spice Girls would just shut up now! He and his wife had finished setting up the bunker and were now sneaking around Planet Crumb, on their way to the Front Door. When they reached it, the Front Door looked even more daunting than Ginger had described. It was painted sloppily with gray paint that peeled and yellowed at the edges. The door knob seemed to hang precariously by one screw and it was doubtful that the lock worked.

It was the perfect situation, the door would be broken down in no time, the ETM thought. Making a quick gesture to his wife, the ETM sprinted out from hiding and scaled the side of the door using shoes lined with melted gumdrops to stick to the wall. The ETL followed quickly behind using similar shoes. They reached the first hinge on the door and the ETL helped lift the ETM up to the small ledge atop the hinge. Reaching far into his shell, the ETM pulled out a small potato chip which he used as a screwdriver to remove the screws from the hinges. This would allow the door to be knocked over easily. When the first hinge was completely free of screws, the couple moved up to the second hinge. That's when the trouble started.

"ETM? ETL? What is your status? Where are you?" Adrienne's voice cracked over the earpiece.

"We are halfway through loosening the front door," the ETL calmly replied, "is there an issue?"

"You have two humans coming your way straight from the Kitchen doorway on your right," Edward's panicked voice sounded over the radio, "they almost got Tiriaq but we got away."

"Nuts!" the ETM exclaimed, then added, "all teams, return to the bunker!"

"Copy!" Edward's, Adrienne's and Tiriaq's mics all suddenly cut out. The ETM didn't have time to worry about that though. The ETL suddenly lost her footing and the ETM just barely caught her. The two mexican foods were now just dangling from the second hinge of the door. If they fell, the couple would be obliterated in million crumbs from the impact. It occurred to the

ETM that this might be the reason the place was called Planet Crumb.

"Team two can't return to base at the moment!" Derek said, "we tried to leave the Living Room but Mew has found us and is blocking all exits! Cassie and I are trapped for— ARRGGGG!" Derek suddenly stopped speaking into the radio and a loud smacking sound could be heard along with the faint sounds of Cassie cursing.

"Team 4, this is the ETM," the ETM said into his mic, barely stopping himself and the ETL from falling to their death.

"Go ahead ETM," Swiss S. Cheese's voice came on the coms.

"How many weapons have you guys collected?"

"About ten utensils in fair condition, some sharp lids from canned goods and over fifty broken toothpicks all being carried by Unruly Urnebes."

"That will have to work," the ETM muttered, "I need you to come to the Front Door and throw me a knife."

"Copy, heading your direction now." Swiss S. Cheese said. The human's footsteps were now audible from where the two Mexican foods hung, BOOM BOOM. The ETM's hands started sweating, loosening his grip.

Part II: The Evil Taco Man

"You better not drop me!" The ETL warned, still dangling from the ETM's other hand. BOOM BOOM. The floor shook with every step the humans took.

"It's no use!" the ETM shouted, "I've only broken two of the three hinges! We'll never get out of the door *even if* the humans don't eat us up!"

"Shush up!" The ETL scolded the ETM, "I don't want to hear this, 'I'm giving up' talk! We will find another way!"

The ground was shaking even harder now, the ETM was only hanging on by centimeters with his finger tips. A human stomped into the room shaking the ground harder than ever before. The ETM's fingers lost contact with the door hinge and he and his wife plummeted to their dooms. Below them, Swiss S. Cheese, Unruly Urnebes, and Malicious Malt Vinegar ran onto the scene, arms filled with various weapons.

"NOOOO!" Swiss yelled, dropping an armful of toothpicks and sewing needles. The three foods ran to attempt to catch them. The human seemed to notice what was happening and raised its foot menacingly. Urnebes managed to flatten her normally spherical shape into a form of mattress while Swiss and Malicious Malt Vinegar took up arms against the human.

SQUISH!

The ETM and ETL landed on Urnebes' body and quickly rolled to the ground. Luckily, the only damage they sustained were minor chips taken out of their fried shells. Seconds later, the human's foot slammed down into the ground. Swiss jumped to the side, narrowly avoiding death.

"There's five of us, and only one human," the ETM said, "we can take him." Just then, the second human burst into the room.

"Nope," Swiss said, shaking his head, "everybody run!" The group spun around and began sprinting towards the only other doorway in the room. With their great strides the humans got closer to the party with every passing second. They were mere feet from crossing through the doorway when they ran face first into Edward, Adrienne and Tiriaq. The three desserts' eyes were wide with panic.

"WHAT ARE YOU DOING! GET OUT OF THE WAY!" The ETM and Edward shouted at the same time. The humans were getting closer, they had seconds at most before they were caught.

"No! You gwet out of the way!" Tiriaq shouted, fully panicked.

"We have no time for this!" Adrienne shouted. She then grabbed the ETM and Edward by the arm and took a hard left, the rest of the gang quickly running after them.

As they sprinted away, the ETM snuck a quick glance over his shoulder and realized with horror that they were being chased not only by the two humans, but also Mew, who Edward, Adrienne, and Triaq must have been running from. Tiriaq shrieked and the ETM noticed that he was the slowest runner and was centimeters away from being crushed by a foot. The ETM stopped running for a split second and intercepted the small cookie, grabbing him by the arms and tossing him into his shell. The group ran through several more doorways from sector to sector of Planet Crumb.

"HELP!" Derek cried out over the ETM's headpiece, "We've encountered something new, now we are trapped!"

"Heading to your sector now!" Edward replied into the coms.

"The Living-Room is really close by. I know the way," Adrienne said between gasps.

With Adrienne to lead them, they navigated the maze of corridors and soon came upon Cassie and Derek. The two desserts had been backed into a corner by a shiny black disc that emitted a loud droning noise and seemed to be drawing air inside it like a black hole. Half of Cassie's sprinkles had already fallen victim to this metal disc. As the gang burst into the room, the disc spun around, an inscription on the front glinted evilly.

"Wom-buh?" Tiriaq read out loud.

"Roomba." the ETL corrected.

Mew ran into the room from behind them and shrieked at the sight of the circular robot. The monster let out a loud, "MEROWWWW!" and backed away from the robot. The cat's sudden fear and retreat from the robot caused the humans to trip over Mew, and they were sent sprawling on the floor.

The ETM turned his attention back to the oncoming Roomba. "If only I could teleport!" he grumbled under his breath.

Adrienne then leaned over to the ETL and whispered in her ear.

Part II: The Evil Taco Man

The ETL nodded, though she didn't look quite happy with what she was told.

"When I say 'now,' all of you run in separate directions," Adrienne directed the rest of the group, who nodded despite being mildly confused. Adrienne took a deep breath and lifted the ETL off the ground and started to run at the Roomba. At the last second, before the two of them would have become Roomba dinner, Adrienne drove the ETL's head in the ground, propelling the two of them up into the air. They soared high above the Roomba and landed straight on top of it.

"NOW!"

All nine of the edibles sprinted away from each other.

The ETM realized Adrienne's plan. With the impact of the fortune cookie and the taquito on top of the Roomba and the chaos caused by all the foods running in separate directions, the disc quickly spun out of control and began ricocheting across the walls. Adrienne and the ETL were barely hanging on. If they let go they could become mere smudges of dead food on the walls of Planet Crumb.

"IT'S NOT GOING TO STOP!" Cassie shouted.

She was right, the Roomba was only picking up speed. The desserts and foods were running around in a panic, trying to avoid being eaten by the Roomba, but the humans were starting to regain their footing after tripping on Mew. The ETM got an idea.

"I'll attract the robot over to the humans and try to make it run them over. That will buy us time to run away. What I need everyone to do is, after it impacts the humans, all of you run at it and try to keep it from moving!"

The group nodded in agreement and the plan was set into action.

"HEY UGLY ROOMBA! GET OVER HERE YOU DISGUSTING AMIGO!"

The robot turned its attention to the taco who was standing on top of a human's head. VVRRRRROOOM! The Roomba's engine revved and launched itself full speed at the ETM.

It was merely 50 feet away.

25 feet.

10 feet.

Just as the ETM was about to jump off the human, a massive sausage hand gripped the ETM and the human began to stand up. Urnebes noticed the issue and, with a

battle cry, shoved herself under the human's foot. The giant beast dropped the ETM, slipped, and once again came crashing down, kicking Urnebes into the conjoining room.

The ETM heard a loud scream and he barely got a last glimpse of his comrade, right before she and the toothpicks she was still holding flew into a lit fireplace. The ETM whipped around upon hearing the drone of the Roomba get closer. It was inches away from his face, coming at full speed.

What happened next appeared in slow motion to the ETM, and there was nothing he could do to stop it. Edward, Tiriaq, and Cassie lunged to grab Adrienne and the ETL off the top of the Roomba. Derek and Swiss S.

Part II: The Evil Taco Man

Cheese launched themselves at the human's face, holding the can lids Team 4 had scavenged earlier. The second human was also starting to get up and slammed its hand down, narrowly missing Tiriaq and Cassie, who were sent sprawling to the ground. Edward made contact with Adrienne and the ETL and managed to tackle them off of the top of the robot. The ETM tried to run during all this, but there was no time, this was the end of the ETM.

The ETM fell to the ground with a loud thud. Something had pushed him. He turned to look, just in time to see Malicious Malt Vinegar standing triumphantly where he stood.

"RUN!" He screamed at her, but she was already in motion.

She ran several feet. The robot pursued. She wasn't fast enough and the Roomba slammed into her body, shattering it into a million glass pieces. One singular glass shard seemed to hit the Roomba in just the right place and the robot sputtered and shut off.

The two humans were now standing. Derek and Swiss S. Cheese lay in a corner, appearing to have been kicked away by the humans. In fact, everyone lay on the ground in various positions of recovery. Gradually, the foods noticed the humans staring at them and stood up. The humans seemed confused.

"I thought you said we had rats," the first human said to the other.

"That's what I thought we had," the second one, who appeared to be female, said, "I didn't realize that it was flippin' living foods, of all things."

Part II: The Evil Taco Man

The ETM was surprised to be able to understand the humans so well. Previously it had been a struggle to make out syllables because the human's speech sounded so slurred. But now, he must have been on The Crumb for a decent amount of time for his hearing to change.

"Everyone," the ETM whispered, "begin to back away. We've already lost two foods to the humans, we can't afford to lose more." The group of edibles began to walk backward very slowly.

"What should we do with them?" the first human said, "now that we know they are alive, we can't eat them."

"Hold up," the second one said, "we should capture them and sell them to scientists! We could make so much money!"

"Yes..." the first human said, drumming its fingers together evilly, "We could sell them to children all around the world as pets! Make special dog treats! Imagine! Treats that your dog will have to hunt for!"

"We'll be millionaires!" The humans stopped talking and seemed to notice that the ETM and other edibles were starting to get close to leaving the room.

"Hey!" the second human said, "they are starting to leave!"

"Oh no you don't!" the first one said, and it lunged at the ETM.

"RUN" Edward screamed, and the remaining foods took off. One of the humans grabbed a nearby vase off of a table and, spilling the flowers and water it held, began chasing the edibles. The second human followed suit, grabbing a box of matches and dumping its contents onto the carpet.

"We can't— go— back— to the base!" Adrienne said in between breaths, "It will—endanger our only safehouse— on The Crumb!"

"We need to split up!" Derek said.

"No!" Cassie yelled back, "that's what got us in this mess!"

"She's right," Adrienne said, "we're stronger together."

"Well th-wen," Tiriaq piped up, "where are we even wunning to!?"

"We could send one person back to the base to get reinforcements!" Derek said, breathing heavily. The sound of the humans behind them was getting louder.

"Derek," Edward said fondly, "that is the first good idea you have had in a while!"

"Derek," the ETM said, "since this was your idea, you get to go back."

Dereked nodded.

"I'll go with him," Tiriaq said, "we're stwonger together. Just wike you said"

The ETM nodded at the small cookie, "We will cause a distraction, during which time, both of you slip away."

They both nodded. The group ran for several more feet, and then, the ETM and Edward shoved over a trashcan. Used tissues, crumpled on pieces of paper and the corpses of oranges, lemons, eggs and a banana peel, that the ETM recognized as the one that once belonged to Barry, all tumbled recklessly out of the silver container. As the humans stumbled, trying to avoid the sudden obstacles, the ETM saw, out of the corner of his eye, Derek and Tiriaq hide behind a nearby mop. One of the humans came crashing down, having, once again, slipped on Barry's peel. The group of edibles quickly continued running to the next room. This room held a shiny white bowl and a giant hollowed out brick made of porcelain. All of this sat snugly against the walls on a blue and white checkered tile floor.

"Oh no," Adrienne said, "Everyone knows there's no way out of The Bathroom, except for the way you came in."

"We're trapped," the ETL said.

The humans stumbled into The Bathroom Doorway. "Go get a jar," the first one said to the other. The other human ran off and came back with the largest jar the ETM had ever seen. The label was still on the jar despite it being empty.

"Oh no," Edward gasped, "That's where Jim Jelly went."

"Who?" Cassie asked.

"He was in our 1st grade class, he went missing a couple years ago. Everyone thought he just rolled into a ditch and got stuck because he was so fat," Edward explained, "guess not..." The humans advanced forward, jar in hand. There was no escape.

"There's got to be a way out of this," the ETM said, "maybe... we could flush ourselves down The Toilet?"

"No time, plus we'd fall apart, drown, and die," Adrienne said.

Part II: The Evil Taco Man

"This can't be the end..." Edward said.

One of the human's large sausagey hands reached down. The edibles were backed, quite literally, into a corner.

"Humans stupid! We are to be arriving at your faces now!" a familiar voice shouted.

The humans seemed unphased by the voice and swiped Swiss S. Cheese, Edward, and the ETL. They were then dropped roughly into the jar and the lid was closed.

"There soon! Prepare to starting paining!" the voice screamed again, louder this time. The second human grabbed another jar, this one marked "Applesauce" and shoved the ETM, Adrienne, and Cassie in this second jar.

The ETM could hear Edward's muffled voice, "This really is the end..." Just at that second, the voice spoke again,

"My face has view of you through eyes of mine!"

"Shut *up* Nutmeg!" another voice said.

The ETM was filled with hope. A swarm of spices soared into the bathroom, all riding paper airplanes. The original Spice Girls were there: Ginger Spice, Cinnamon, Allspice, Nutmeg and Pumpkin Spice. Behind them, a fleet of multicolored paper airplanes flew, each had a spice riding on top. Salt and Pepper, an infamous dynamic duo, managed to land their plane ride at the nose of a human. The human swatted the plane away with both hands dropping the jar it was holding to the tiled floor. Derek and Tiriaq rushed in dragging the largest rug the ETM had ever seen and just barely in time, the jar landed on the rug, preventing the death of its contents.

The remaining human standing began swatting spices out of the air. Paper airplanes crashed all over the place and the spices began to attack the air in front of the humans as they fell. The smell of cumin and oregano filled the air, followed by rosemary, thyme! Garlic power! Flaxseed! Sage! It wasn't until a combined effort from Paprika and Red Pepper Flakes that the human dropped the other jar, tears streaming down its face and eyes red and irritated from exposure to the abrasive spices. The air was so thick with the particles of different spices that the ETM could barely see one foot in front of him. The second jar landed roughly on the rug. The humans both ran out of The Bathroom screaming something about pouring milk on their eyes. The ETM cringed, that poor carton of milk.

"Let us out!" the ETL said, "We are running out of air here!" Once again, the ETM remembered his days of teleporting and he only hoped the Saibou and MilkDudBot would be able to pull through.

The Spice Girls reacted quickly. Cinnamon climbed up to the top of a cliff in the bathroom known as "The Bathroom Sink". Cinnamon then threw a small metal object down, which Pumpkin Spice caught with one hand.

She then used it to pry the lids off of the jar. When the ETM asked Ginger what the object was, she merely replied, "Humans call it Nail File." With all the foods out of the jars, they tried to decide what to do next.

306

Part II: The Evil Taco Man

"I'm tired of running from the humans!" the ETL said, "I want revenge for all the murders they have caused."

"I hear you, but there's no way we can defeat them," Adrienne pointed out, "we've only barely escaped with our lives during every encounter!"

"And they're not just trying to eat us! They are trying to trap us!" Cassie passionately added, gesturing to the empty jars that still lay on the rug.

"What if," Derek started, "we didn't run. But we moved the battlefield to the part of the Crumb known as the Kitchen. We have more tactical advantage there, and then we can send someone to activate MilkDudBot1.2 and the Saibou, who are by far the strongest among us. If we are going to win, we need their help."

"But won't that endanger the s-wafehouse?" Tiriaq asked.

"Wait," Swiss S. Cheese said, "this could work, as long as no one enters or exits the bunker while the humans are there, they won't ever know it exists."

"Derek," the ETM said, "you are finally having good ideas, amigo. Keep 'em coming."

Derek beamed.

"We have to move fast," Edward said, "the humans are probably already on their way back."

The group advanced to The Kitchen. Turns out, The Kitchen lay adjacent to The Bathroom, so their journey was short lived. The humans were already there. One of them was holding a jar in each hand and was still blinking the tears out of its eyes. The ETM dubbed that human Jar-Jar Blinks. The other human held a meat cleaver in one hand, the largest fork the ETM had ever seen and wore an apron that read, "don't be afraid to take whisks." The ETM dubbed this human, Forking Scary.

Both humans turned and saw the foods and the swarm of spices enter the Kitchen and frantically put on what appeared to be swimming goggles. There was no time to call for MilkDudBot1.2 or the Saibou. The humans let out a battle cry and began charging at the foods. Swiss S. Cheese brought out a fresh stack of cheese slice ninja stars and everyone else picked up whatever they could find. The trashcan was still knocked over from earlier and the ETM snatched up a metal kabob skewer and brandished it menacingly. Just as the humans were about to collide, the ETM noticed a smaller human at the top of the nearby Jagged Mountain One (as Cassie had named it). The human saw the ETM looking at her and gave him a small wink. The smaller human then proceeded to dramatically and loudly fall down the stairs. Jar-Jar Blinks and Forking Scary stopped in their tracks and rushed over to the smaller human.

"Mom! Dad! I fractured my leg! OOOOOH THE PAIN!! IT HURTS SO BAD!" the smaller human wailed.

"Honey, you're fine! Come on and get up! Your dad and I are kind of in the middle of something," Forking Scary tried to comfort the small human and Jar-Jar Blinks tried to pull the small human to its feet.

"NOOOOO! You don't understand! I really hurt myself! I need a DOCTOR!"

Part II: The Evil Taco Man

"I think she's really hurt," Forking Scary told
Jar-Jar Blinks. Taking one last look of distaste at the
group of edibles, Jar-Jar Blinks proceed to pick up the
small human, leading to more wailing. The three
humans rushed to the Front Door. Forking Scary
violently threw open the door in its haste and, because
of the ETM and ETL's loosening of the hinges, the door
flew right off the door frame and across the floor of the
Crumb. Forking Scary gave one last glare at the group of
edibles who were all standing in shock at this turn of
events, and left. Cautiously, the ETM crept up to the
remains of the Front Door and peered out.

"It's Picnic Palace!" Cassie said in awe.

"Just like what we saw in the attic!" Edward said.
But something didn't feel right to the ETM. That's when
he noticed it.

"Amigos..." The ETM said, "Picnic Palace is worse
than the entirety of The Crumb."

"Why?" Tiriaq asked. The ETM with a shaky
finger, just pointed.

Picnic Palace was invaded by around thirty
humans, all of which were sitting on red and white
checkered blankets, mercilessly devouring different
foods, seeming indifferent to the screams as they
traveled down the humans gaping mouths.

"Oh crêpe," Edward said. No one else could make
a sound.

Part 12: Derek D⬤nut

Derek knew that they couldn't possibly go into the Picnic Palace because the blissful scene they had witnessed above in the attic was but a charade placed there to trap them. But those poor foods, they were being murdered right before Derek's eyes. A couple of sushi rolls tried to run away but were pierced by the same pair of chopsticks that they had once dueled each other with. The rolls let out a loud scream and disappeared down the gullet of a human.

"We have to help them," Derek said defiantly.

The thoughts of being eaten or smashed ran through Derek's head. What could they really do against humans? They were dozens of times their size and dozens of times stronger than they were. This was a suicide mission. He had signed himself and the other foods up to die. He had inspired hope in the desserts, and couldn't back down now. The plan was simple.

Step 1 - Harness the power of Mew (method: TBD)

Step 2 - Obtain armor + weapons

Step 3 - Transport desserts to battlefield

Step 4 - Sneak in and out with foods

"I have a plan," Derek said, "let's regroup inside the base."

Part 12: Derek Donut

"It sounds easy in print. But how easy is it really going to be?" the ETM said after Derek finished telling everyone his plan.

"It'll be easier if we, like, only send out a small party," Sugar Cookie said nervously chewing on a pencil.

"Well, who are you going to take? It's your plan," Cassie said.

"Maybe just take two foods," the ETL suggested, "If Mew starts eating, at least only the three of you will die, and the rest of us can still fight the humans."

Sugar Cookie's pencil suddenly snapped in half and Chipette quickly supplied her sister with another pencil to chew on. Derek nodded and chose Adrienne and Edward. Cassie gasped and looked at Derek, betrayed.

"We are going to need to carry heavy things, and Edward and Adrienne are the strongest," then Derek leaned in and whispered, "if you dieded it would be too sad for me."

"Died," Cassie corrected, "but still, are you sure we can trust Adrienne? Like what do we even know about her backstory?"

"Cassie," Derek said, "we've been over this many times. Adrienne has done nothing to show us she's a bad dessert."

"Seriously," Edward gasped, placing a hand to his chest "what if I died?" Derek stuttered and struggled to answer,

"Well it's just— Edward we have— Um— I'd be sad if you died— what have I done?"

Part 12: Derek Donut

"Come on boys," Adrienne said, "you can bicker on the way there." As they walked out, Derek heard Chipette start to give all the new spices a tour of the bunker.

After walking around for a few hours, they found a round container with a large fish icon. Underneath the icon it read, "Fake fish bits! Not made with real fish!" They had never seen or smelled a living fish before, not even in pictures. All they had seen was a rotting tilapia in the leftover drawer when they first landed on the Crumb.

A peculiar smell wafted out of this container and filled the surrounding space and Derek decided he didn't like fish. It wasn't a pleasant smell. Using Nail File, they were able to pry open this container. Derek peered over the rim of the container, and saw smashed up dead not-fish. He quickly turned his head as his gag reflex kicked in.

Adrienne and Edward together pushed the container of tuna across the floor of the Crumb. They trekked across the hardwood floor for what seemed like hours.

"Kitty kitty!" Edward yelled, again and again. There was no sign of Mew. Until they heard a soft padding behind them. They turned around to see large, unblinking green eyes lurking in the shadow cast by the large gray bin. The monster had been following them for

Part 12: Derek Donut

who knows how long, but it had been observing them. The thought of that scared Derek so much he almost tripped and fell inside the can of tuna.

"Stay very still," Derek said. "Maybe if we don't appear as a threat, Mew won't attack us."

Mew and the desserts regarded each other, Mew with an expression of distaste and the desserts filled with paranoia. Derek slowly approached the monster and grabbed a chunk of fake fish. The monster stepped out of the shadows and started sniffing the air.

Cautiously, as to not make any sudden moves, Derek set the meat on the floor and backed away muttering, "That's a nice cat..."

Mew bent down and nudged at the cube on the ground and melodramatically picked it up and ate it. Derek motioned for Adrienne and Edward to give him more food and the two began tossing more cubes to Derek. Mew kept eating, cube after cube getting closer and closer. Then, there was no more food. Mew looked at Derek expectantly, who, in turn, looked back at Edward and Adrienne. They shook their heads and showed him the empty food can. Derek turned to face Mew sheepishly. The monster probably would have been fine with this turn of events, if Adrienne hadn't farted. Mew got a wift of the toxic gas and gagged so forcefully it coughed up several small hairballs. Edward turned to Adrienne,

"What is your issue!?" Edward said.

"I'm sorry! You know I'm lactose intolerant!" Adrienne said.

Part 12: Derek Donut

"When have you had lactose!? WHEN!?" Edward shouted.

"Guys..." Derek said, watching Mew, "we might want to—"

"IT'S A MEDICAL CONDITION" Adrienne shouted back at Edward.

"Seriously guys," Derek said as Mew stopped coughing and took a step in their direction.

"You're a medical condition!" Edward retorted.

"What does that even mean!?" Adrienne yelled.

"I don't know! I was struggling to find a retort to your comment!" Mew suddenly bared its fangs and Edward and Adrienne abruptly shut up.

"RUN!" Derek screamed.

Mew bounded towards them. Edward and Adrienne finally heard Derek and took off behind him. As the monster gained on them, time slowed down for Derek. He began analyzing the situation. They had a spoon, Nail File, and nothing else. He has to act fast otherwise they would be deader than— . Mew swiped his paw, sending Derek falling and sliding to the ground. Derek quickly threw Nail File down into the ground. His momentum sent him spinning around 180 degrees until he was facing Mew.

"Hang on Derek! I have an idea!" Edward shouted, and Derek saw Adrienne boost Edward up onto something out of the corner of his eye. As Mew opened his jaws to consume him and his friends, Edward yelled and threw down something from a podium above them. Derek scrambled to catch the object. Derek's arms were outstretched and the object fell down in slow motion. It was a can but Derek couldn't read the label. The can smacked into his arms and the lid popped off. Millions of dried green, crumpled up leaves showered out onto the floor and all over Derek's body.

Mew stopped. He walked up to Derek and lowered his head and glared. Derek was breathing heavily and quickly. A drop of sweat rolled down his head as the monster seemed to regard him once more. Mew began to lick Derek. He kept on licking him for several minutes until what remained of Derek's glaze was almost all gone. Edward and Adrienne hopped down from the podium and Adrienne rolled the can over exposing its label.

"Ohhh, Catnip!" Derek said. He had heard a lot about this from Pumpkin Spice. Mew started rolling around in the catnip on the floor while purring contently. Edward, Derek, and Adrienne watched for around ten minutes before Mew lost interest in the catnip and began rubbing itself affectionately on Derek.

Derek was beyond proud. Mew was tamed, and it was his leadership that had led to this victory. Using an old human neck decoration he found in the corner, Derek was able to ride Mew like a honeycomb horse. He rode around the house, rallying support from the other foods. A new species of fruit was found in a separate area of the Crumb. Soon apples, oranges, grapes and several papayas joined the army along with a singular watermelon. Their army began to grow.

Hundreds of snacks, desserts, and other foods alike began to march together. Even the withered fruits from under the Cabinet known as veterans had shown up in support for the cause. He had been assigned to gather support and food to fight, while Edward and Sugar Cookie made the plan. He returned to the designated meeting point: The Coffee Table. Why was it called The Coffee Table? Derek sure didn't see any coffee. Edward said he had heard the humans point to it and call it that, so he accepted it. Derek jumped off of Mew and climbed up the leg of the coffee table to meet Edward. Ronald Rat, who was in the crowd, saw Mew and hid under a surprised tortilla. His friend looked absolutely awestruck by the militia Derek had put together. Derek began to feel that they had a fighting chance now.

"FOODS OF—"

They were cut off by screaming. Derek quickly looked into the crowd and saw a large black disk making its way through the crowd and sucking crumbs in.

"Do not, like, fear!" Sugar Cookie yelled. She then frantically started typing on her phone. The disk sputtered and began moving around slowly and sporadically. Sugar Cookie ran through the crowd, recklessly shoving foods left and right shouting,"Excuse me! Pardon Me! So sorry!"

When she reached the disk, she reached down and triumphantly pressed a button on the Roomba and the robot skidded to a stop. Then, with the press of a button on her phone, she made it spin around.

"It's, like, a mindless cleaning thingy. It can't hurt you, I have control over it now."

The gathered foods cheered loudly and looked relieved, but still kept their distance from the black disk.

"As you may know," Edward continued, "unknown foods are stuck outside of this world. They are in a dangerous dimension called Picnic Palace at the mercy of the humans. They are to be eaten! Are we gonna let that happen to them?"

There was a thunderous cheer. "NO!" They all yelled. They banged on the legs of the table, some raising toothpicks and forks up and down.

"That's what I thought!" Derek yelled.

"All these years of feuding with each other," Edward continued, "and for what! Some old and long dead foods tried to take each other's throne? All this time, desserts like me have blamed the residents of The Diner for the state of the foodiverse! But it wasn't true! All around us, food went missing on a daily basis. And yes, some of the missing foods were casualties in the feud, but most of the missing foods were taken mercilessly by the evil humans! Why are humans set on killing us? Who knows? What we do know is that if we don't stop this madness immediately, the humans will only devour and capture more of us. Let today be a celebrated day in history. It shall be the day the foods unite and fight back! No two hundred year old feud is going to stop us! It ends today! Let all kinds of foods unite! Residents of Veggie, Fruity, The Diner, and The Dessert, we are one kind! Food-kind!!!"

This got a large cheer from the crowd, the foods began stomping in unison and chanting things like, "Foods for Life! Foods for Life!" and "We're number one!"

"Who are we!" Edward yelled at the crowd.

"Foods!" the crowd shouted back.

"What do we want!?"

"Freedom!"

"From who!?"

"FREEDOM!!!!"

"No-no-no no, that's what we want," Edward said, "*Who* do we want freedom *from?*"

"THE HUMANS!" The crowd applauded and cheered, every single one of them fired and ready for battle. They chanted for the downfall of the humans and Derek felt adrenaline rush through his entire, now unglazed, body.

"LINE UP HERE!" Chipette and Tiriaq yelled, dragging in a cart of bubble wrap, duct tape, tin foil and saran wrap . Every edible formed two lines in front of them to be fitted with bubble wrap and tin foil armor that they had made during the taming of Mew. Adrienne was passing out forks, knives, toothpicks, and chopsticks.

As Derek continued to look around, he heard Cassie go up to Edward to tell him, "It's 'from *whom*'. Not 'from *who*'. Learn grammar."

Edward replied with a look of confusion and Cassie sighed and walked away. All the desserts seemed to have lined up behind Edward and Adrienne. All the Spices, behind Ginger. The Diner foods seemed to have lined up behind the ETM and the ETL. MilkDudBot1.2 and the Saibou were still on their sleep quest to bring Vishnu to The Crumb. Ginny Gelato and the Cheeze Wizard had shown up as well. Ginny later told Derek that Prince Ice of Cream refused to go out in public as they had had to remove the Plastic Cherry from his head and give it to the Saibou.

"I'll get him, we need everybody on the battlefield," Derek said, "can you send out a group of foods to get the color javelins that Cassie talked about earlier?" Ginny nodded and scampered off in the riled up crowd. The scene was almost identical to the battle on the Spaghetti Monster except for one key difference. In the battle of the Spaghetti Monster, Diner foods were attacking desserts. In fact, almost every encounter Derek had had with Diner foods had been hostile, up until they were united by fighting broccoli. The whole idea of desserts and diner foods working together was unfathomable to Derek, and, despite seeing it with his own eyes, it still felt surreal.

Derek proceeded to walk into the Cabinet and down into the bunker. As he walked through the dark corridors he passed a sleeping MilkDudBot1.2 with a screen on his chest saying:

Update: 84% complete

Part 12: Derek Donut

Derek hoped that the update would finish soon. As he had said earlier, they would need every food in the upcoming battle. In the following room, the Saibou lay snoring loudly, a luminescent purple fog emanating from the Saibou's entire body. The Plastic Cherry floated above the middle of his three heads spinning. Every two seconds the three headed dragon would twitch and moan as if pained by the dreams it was having.

Derek quickly left so as to not disturb the Saibou. Derek really missed feeling the power of Vishnu flow through his dough. Ever since he'd learned it, it had been a strange source of confidence for him. Hopefully the Saibou would be able to bring it to this realm. They would need it against the humans. It was at this point that Derek came upon Prince Ice of Cream's room. Now when Ginny had mentioned that Prince Ice of Cream needed coaxing to come out of his room, Derek was ecstatic. He played it off just as him wanting to be helpful but couldn't help but feel that they would have a pretty good connection. His heart raced as he reached to knock on the door. What would he say? What if the prince didn't like him? Derek shoved those thoughts away and knocked softly on the door. A muffled voice inside shouted at him to go away. Derek took a deep breath. Quietly, Derek opened the door and stepped inside.

"I told you to go away," the Prince said.

"We could use you out there." Derek said.

"I can't show my face ever again!" the Prince said, covering his face.

Part 12: Derek Donut

"Why not?" Derek said as he took a seat on the floor.

"I'm hideous! That cherry on my head was my only claim to fame!"

"Come on, you're not hideous. And plus, just because you don't have the Cherry doesn't mean you're no longer a Prince!"

"You don't understand, I'm not even the rightful ruler of WisSweetsVille. I had taken a big gamble and lost my entire kingdom one night when I visited Vanilla Vegas. Now the castle and throne will only belong to my father and the guards are technically owned by the Victorious Victor Vanilla of the vile Vanilla Vegas. That cherry was the one thing I had left."

"Dang," Derek placed his hand on the cone's back supportingly, "that sucks man. But you know what? That cherry is going to help us win the battle against the humans. Foodkind will forever remember you for this generous contribution."

"What, are you talking about?" Prince Ice of Cream shrugged Derek's hand off of him, "the cherry was taken forcefully from me!"

"Ok," Derek said, "I'm not saying to lie, but, what if everyone thought you wanted to contribute Cherry all on your own."

"How do I accomplish that without lying!"

"Well, for starters, you can tell me if you know of any magical happenings with the Plastic Cherry and then I can tell everyone how helpful you were with the usage of the Plastic Cherry. Maybe you'll even get your kingdom back, because this kind deed will be sure to gain you supporters."

"That won't be enough supporters to gain my kingdom back," Prince Ice of Cream slumped into a corner of the room solemnly.

"But what if they saw you fighting valiantly for the cause of saving all of foodkind from the humans!"

"Do you really think that will work?!" the prince perked up.

"I honestly have no idea," Derek said, "but it's worth a shot. Don't you think?" The prince pondered this and paced the room for several minutes.

"It's a suicide mission," Prince Ice of Cream finally concluded. Derek felt crestfallen, he had really thought he'd convinced the prince.

Derek turned around to leave the room when the prince said, "But, it's a noble cause..."

Derek spun around. "So... you'll help us?"

"I..." the Prince paused, "I can't believe I'm saying this but, yes. It's time for me to shine, and this is how I'll get my kingdom back. I'll do it." Derek was so excited, he pumped his fist in the air and tried to high five the Prince.

"No," the prince said with disgust at Derek's hand lingering in the air, "don't make me regret this."

"Yeah, yeah. No, that's cool," Derek awkwardly put his hand down and the two stood there in silence for a couple minutes.

"Sooo, you wanted to hear about magical events involving the Plastic Cherry?" Prince Ice of Cream said, shattering the icy silence.

Part 12: Derek Donut

"Oh! Yes! Definitely!" Derek stumbled in his
reply, "we going to do that now or..."
"Now?" the Prince said.
"Yeah, sure that works. We got a bit of time,"
Derek responded. Prince Ice of Cream cleared his throat
and began to speak.

The Long Short Story Of That One Time the Plastic Cherry Acted Magical (by Prince Ice of Cream):

I was in my royal chambers, preparing for a
visit to the local casino when the event started.
What seemed as a small event at first, quickly
spiraled out of control.

This small event was putting on my favorite
sprinkles to look my handsomest when I leave. This
was when I noticed a blinking red light in the corner
of the room. I had never noticed it before but it
seemed very suspicious. I ventured a look and found a
black Oreo themed camera. I didn't know how long it
had been there but there was a thick layer of gray
cotton candy dust so, using my world renowned
detective skills I got from an online class (20% off
with code Hershey Holms), I deduced that the
camera had been there a long time.

"What the heck!" I said to myself, and
summoned my butter butler named Bartholomew to
investigate the camera for me. Bartholomew greeted
me with a bow and, after explaining the situation to
him, he agreed to the job, winked, and left without

another word. Now, I couldn't be bothered with the camera anymore. I had money to gamble!

So, I walked through the halls of my lavish mansion, slowly meandering my way to the exit when Butler Butter Bartholomew ran up from behind me, panting hard. "Sir," he gasped in his British accent, "you won't believe what I have found."

"Butler!" I shouted in his face, "Can't you see, I'm trying to get to my secret happy place!?"

"You mean the casino?"

"SHHHHHHH! No one is supposed to know darn it!"

"It's not really a secret sir—"

"SUSH! I'm leaving!"

"But wait!" Bartholomew grabbed my shoulder and lowered his voice, "it's about the camera."

"Can't it wait?!" I pleaded. The urge to gamble was getting stronger by the second.

"No," Bartholomew's voice was deadly serious, "it's about us, and your father. King Ice of Cream." Bam. Just like that. I didn't want to gamble anymore. My butler saw this look on my face and motioned for me to follow him. I complied.

Bartholomew closed the door behind us and turned the lock,

"Your father knows," he said. "That camera, it's been uploaded to the Royal USB drive. It has all the evidence."

Part 12: Derek Donut

"Oh crêpe." I said, "If King Ice of Cream knows. . ."

"That means you'll never be the next King, under violation of the Relations Act of Four Years ago." The Relations Act of Four Years ago or, RAFYA for short, clearly stated that any dessert in line for the throne of WisSweetsVille must not date any dessert unapproved by the dating community, and must especially not date any food from the Diner. Now this wouldn't be an issue except for the fact that the dating community was headed by King Ice of Cream, a known abolitionist of royals fraternizing with "the help".

"No," I could barely breathe.

"You knew this relationship was a gamble." Bartholomew said.

"I know, I know, and gambling is my favorite!" I started massaging my temples, a headache coming on. Bartholomew put his arm around me. A loud banging on the door startled the both of us and Bartholomew quickly took his arm away and stepped back. The King burst in.

"How dare you!" King Ice of Cream shouted, "I noticed the camera I placed in your room was moved so I checked the footage for the first time since placing the camera down! You! Dating the butler!"

"Dad, it's—" I tried to interject.

"No! I don't want to see your face again!"

"Sir, if I might interject-" the butler tried to say.

Part 12: Derek Donut

"Shut up! And you're fired by the way!" the King shouted, then turned back to me, "you can say goodbye to getting the throne to WisSweetsVille! Gosh, you disgust me!" The three of us stood there in awkward silence then the king said, "Why are you two still standing here! Get out of my castle! You have fifteen seconds before I set the guards on you!"

"Fifteen seconds!" I protested, "that's not enough time to even—"

"Time's ticking!" the king interrupted.

Quickly, I looked at Bartholomew. We reached a shared agreement. Together, we collapsed hands and ran off down the hallway, headed for the casino.

It wasn't long before we had an entire force of donut cops chasing after us, all yelling at the tops of their lungs.

"Quick!" My boyfriend said, "I know a shortcut!" He then lifted off a painting from the wall and threw it behind him, knocking over several donut cops. Where the painting once hung was a small hatch that I recognized as leading to the prisoner cells. We quickly climbed inside and shut the door behind us. Bartholomew led us through a maze of empty cells (we don't get many convicts) and soon we passed the one cell that was occupied.

The Cheese Wizard yelled at us as we passed by telling us that we would pay for this! I had no idea what he was talking about. At the other end of the passageways was a vent. Bartholomew kicked the vent off and revealed a slide, which we clambered

Part 12: Derek Donut

onto and slid crashed into the freedom of the casino
but we also smacked into Victorious Victor Vanilla of
Vanilla Vegas.

Victor was a rather large brown bottle of
vanilla extract, his silhouette alone was enough to
intimidate any food. His narrow eyes sat atop his
head, a black cap, always judging whomever they
were starting at. Below his eyes, a soft feathery
mustache that covered his entire mouth. Whenever
Vitor talked, the mustache just vibrated from side to
side.
    "Well, well, well," Victor said, "back to lose
more money, eh?"
    "Normally yes," said I, "but I'm kinda busy at
the moment." Just at that moment, a plethora of
donut guards burst into the main entrance of the
casino.
    "I know he's in here! Guards, fan out, we'll
find him!!" the lead guard shouted. Bartholomew and
I tried to run away but Victor grabbed us, the vanilla
extract inside him sloshing around rather noisily.
    "OHHH no you don't, I can't let you get
away! The King surely will reward me for this...
unless you have a better offer," Victor said.
    "WHAT!" I shouted, but I knew there was no
time for arguing, "fine, what do you want? I'll give
you anything." Bartholomew shook his head at me
with a look that asked what the heck I was doing.

Part 12: Derek Donut

"Anything, eh?" Victor mused, "I want everything you own in this kingdom, the guards, the riches, even the butter butler."

"You can have it all, except for Bartholomew."

"No deal then, I'll just wait for the king to capture you."

"You don't understand, I was fired literally five minutes ago." Bartholomew said, "I no longer work for anyone." The guards were nearing our location as Victor pondered this news.

"Fine, everything BUT the butler I own, even your loyal subjects." Victor said. Seeing as I was no longer wanted in the kingdom by my father, I agreed and we shook on it. Victor dropped us to the floor and escorted us out of the casino through another side door in the wall. I was starting to wonder why my castle had so many secret passageways.

Bartholomew stopped in front of me and pushed on the ceiling. A hatch opened and we climbed out of the floor into Bartholomew's bedroom.

"We should be safe here, at least for a couple of hours," he said. Boy, was he wrong. Literally six minutes later, while we were still haphazardly throwing things in our bags so we could live on the run, King Ice of Cream found us.

"You thought you could hide from me!" the king fumed, "I thought I told the both of you to leave!"

"What the fork?" I said, "How did you find us?"

Part 12: Derek Donut

"Tracking device, duh," he replied, motioning to the back of my cone and picking off the world's smallest Oreo I'd ever seen.

"Now both of you are going to jail for this!" the King waved his hand and most of the donut guards in the castle stampeded into the room. They grabbed my and Bartholomew's arms and restrained us manually. It was no use to fight back. Suddenly, I felt a small vibration coming from the top of my head. The Plastic Cherry.

I don't know how or why, but the fruit had been activated and was now humming with energy! A bright flash of white emerged from the stem of the cherry and I was abruptly unhandled by the guards, who groaned and covered their eyes. KIng Ice of Cream saw this and quickly took cover by leaving the room. The Cherry flew off my head and bounced off the tops of every guard in the room. Soon they all had blank stares.

"Why are we here again?" the lead guard asked.

"Not sure," another guard said. It soon became clear that the guards didn't know each other anymore and they even didn't know who I was! I couldn't believe my luck. I grabbed Bartholomew and yelled at him to run. I started to run but he didn't move.

"Come on!" I yelled at him, "this is our chance! LET'S GO!"

Bartholomew stared at me blankly, "W-who are you?"

Part 12: Derek Donut

"What do you mean!?" I asked urgently.
"Where am I?"
"Come on!" I pleaded, "quit playing around Bartholomew! We have no time!" The king came back into the room, laughing,
"Ha! You don't even know the power you have on top of your own head!" he jeered. I grabbed Bartholomew and tried to pull him out the door with me.
"Let go," the butter said, his voice cold. The warmth in his eyes when he looked at me was gone. I dropped his arm, tears welling up in my eyes, and left the room, shoving past the king on my way out. King Ice of Cream stopped laughing for a millisecond to call a new batch of guards, this time they were gummy bears armed with toothpicks, to capture me. I didn't have the will to fight back. I was restrained and dragged roughly down the graham cracker halls into a spare room. Then, I was thrown inside and the door was closed behind me.

I looked around and there was only a chair, a window, several paintings of myself, and a lit fireplace in the room with me. I then realized my father's plan. I would melt and die here. I went to the window, stared out at the vast, waffle cone littered landscape I was to call my kingdom. If the events of the day were what being royalty was all about, I wanted nothing to do with it. I didn't have time to ponder the workings of the cherry on my head because then, there, up in the sky! There was

Part 12: Derek Donut

something hurtling straight at me! It appeared to be
a serving of gelato? BAM! I was knocked to the
ground as the gelato landed right on my head.
"WHAT THE HECK LADY!" I screamed, (the
gelato appeared to be female).
She, in turn, kicked my head and said, "Shush your
face-mouth right now or I'll break your cone."
Alarms rang out and I assured the frozen
dessert lady that I wasn't to blame. We bantered
back and forth, me being very angry given prior
events, and the gelato decided to kidnap me and
force me to show her around the castle. It appeared
she didn't know that I was the ex-prince of the
kingdom. Just then, the gummy bears outside, having
heard the commotion inside, broke the door down.
"The door wasn't even locked," one of the
Gummy Bears scolded the other. Seconds later, both
gummy bear guards were unconscious on the floor.
The gelato had broken the chair in the room over
their heads to subdue them. This was not a dessert
to mess with, I decided.
So I followed her around the castle for a long
time, then led her around the castle when she
realized she was lost. I managed to trick her at some
point by shoving her down the secret passageway
into the jail cells Bartholomew showed me earlier.
The thought of him pained my heart but I had to
keep going and try to escape the castle. With Crazy
Lady out of the way, I could resume my escape plan.

Part 12: Derek Donut

Yeah, nope. That didn't happen. Instead I was almost immediately recaptured and thrown in my bedroom with at least three bakers dozens of donuts standing guard outside my room. Minutes later, after the sounds of fighting and farting outside, Crazy Lady walked in with, to my horror, The Cheese Wizard. I was really only horrified that the castle no longer had any prisoners.

Lots of events happened after that but long story short, I ended up on the back of a three headed dragon sitting with Crazy Lady (whose name turned out to be named Ginny) and the Cheese Wizard. And now I'm on Planet Crumb.

"Huh," Derek said as the prince sat there breathing heavily. He had barely taken a breath during that entire story.

"Yeah," Prince Ice of Cream said, "it's pretty wild. I actually hadn't thought much about it before now."

"It seems that the Plastic Cherry is some sort of memory wiper," Derek mused.

"That's what I'm thinking now, but I still have no idea how to activate it." Prince Ice of Cream said.

"Amigos, you must figure that out at another time. The time to strike is now!," the ETM said, having stuck his head into the room. "Are you fighting with us, young prince?" The ETM gestured at Prince Ice of Cream and to Derek's relief, he nodded his head.

Part 12: Derek Donut

When Derek arrived at the surface of the bunker, he found the food army assembled in orderly lines. He was somewhat dismayed at the fact that even though they had over fifty different foods all fitted with armor and weapons, the humans were still far more powerful.

"Derek!" Edward said running up to him from behind, "I'm glad you could make it, the majority of the humans are snoozing under the sun. If we want to save the other foods, we have to go now."

"There's no way we have enough food to keep off the humans," Derek said.

"We should be ok, I called a few reinforcements," Edward explained, showing Derek a business card that read: The Vegetable Assassin League (VAL), "I got this card from a pea when we disrupted his friends' and his sleepover. I decided to call them in, as a favor to me."

"Huh," Derek said, "maybe we do have a chance..."

"Everyone in position!" Ginger called from standing on a plastic cup in the front of the Cabinet, "Tiriaq, Chipette? Armor ready?"

"Yup!" Chipette shouted as she fist bumped Tiriaq.

"Weapons distributed?"

"Almost there! We have a few more foods to give these to," the ETL said, gesturing to the armful of forks the ETM was holding.

"What about the colored javelins named Crayola?"

Part 12: Derek Donut

"Armed and ready," Adrienne shouted from behind a homemade looking cannon, a turquoise javelin protruding from the mouth.

"Roomba programmed and ready?"

"Affirmative!" Sugar Cookie yelled, waving her phone in the air.

"Is Ronald Rat still scared of Mew?"

"Nope! We solved that minutes ago," Cassie said, sitting atop her mighty steed, ahem, rat.

"Alrighty then, battling will be commencing now!" Nutmeg screamed from the mob of troops.

"Shush!" Ginger glared at Nutmeg. "Disregard her statement! We want to avoid hand to hand combat with the humans at all costs. Because why?"

"Because they will eat us!" the crowd shouted in unison.

"Correct," Ginger resumed, "so, our battle plan is as follows; there is a path that leads from the back of Planet Crumb to a place in Picnic Palace called The Playground. We will send scouts, Edward and Adrienne, ahead. They will lead foods around the currently sleeping humans to a place within The Playground called Sandbox. Now Sandbox is the perfect place to bury foods for a short time. From there, we will send out groups to retrieve the hidden foods and smuggle them away from the humans into The Cabinet.

"Now, we will be sending foods to the Sandbox in five minute intervals so it is very important that each group gets in and out within that five minute period. Otherwise, it is more likely the humans will notice us. As a safety precaution, Derek will ride around outside in the shadows on Mew and Cassie will be on Ronald. If anything goes awry–" Ginger looked right at Derek and Cassie for this, "–ring the bell on Mew's collar, shout, holler, anything to warn our troops in the field then help with the evacuation of the slower foods.

"Any questions?"

The room was silent.

"Good, let's go," Ginny said, and stepped down from the red cup and motioned at Edward, Adrienne, Cassie and Derek to head out.

Right before they left, Ginger stuck her head out the door to the Cabinet and said, "If you find yourself under attack without any place to retreat to, go for the crotch. It's a universal weak spot."

Cassie mounted her rat and the other three desserts climbed aboard Mew. Sugar Cookie handed each of them headsets and bid them good luck, especially Edward. The four friends set off, away from The Cabinet, away from their other friends— nay— family, and most of all, away from safety. The quartet rounded the bend. Mews paws padded softly on the floor formally exiting the area called the Kitchen for, what Derek thought must be, the last time. The infamous Front Door lay ahead now and its gaping mouth seemed to dare Derek to go through. Derek urged Mew to slow to a trot and the group stopped right before the exit of The Crumb. They looked at each other, an unspoken communication between the four of them.

And they stepped out into the open.

Part 12: Derek Donut

The first thing Derek felt was the heat. Not a scorching heat, but enough to make him uncomfortable. He looked up. The sky here was blue, unlike the light pink that lay splattered on The Dessert. Smack dab in the middle of the sky, was the brightest light Derek had ever seen and he groaned and quickly averted his eyes. It appeared to be the source of the heat Derek felt. He blinked several times and the spots that were dancing before his eyes quickly vanished. The ground here in Picnic Palace seemed to be blanketed in a green substance made of leaves that danced when the wind blew. *Grass,* Ginger had called it. There were trees everywhere as well, but they looked different than Derek had ever seen before. The rough brown shell that coated the trunk was so unlike the smooth and bare candy cane trunks that Derek knew and loved.

The leaves seemed just like bigger grass and danced in the same way when the wind blew. Cassie gestured at Derek, waving her hand in front of his face and he pulled out of his thoughts. The Sandbox was near and Derek stopped Mew. Adrienne and Edward hopped off and hid behind the frame that held the sand in. Sand, Derek thought, was even stranger than Grass. It didn't seem to have a purpose other than sitting there and sometimes blowing around in the wind. He watched as Edward and Adrienne tried to walk in it and sank down a bit with every step, the sand shifting like clay beneath their feet with every step. When they were situated, Cassie and Derek rode off and hid in several bushes.

Part 12: Derek Donut

The first troop was dispatched. Led by Swiss. S. Cheese, a group containing an apple, orange, and three saltine crackers marched timidly out the Front Door. Derek watched as they all looked around in bewilderment at their new surroundings. Swiss refocused them as Edward tiptoed to them from the Sandbox. The cookie led the first troop to the nearest foods laying on checkered red and white blankets. So far so good. The human on the blanket Swiss and company were on was still deep in its nap.

Swiss cautiously flipped open the lid of a grass woven basket where the foods were being concealed. Swiss reached his hand in and helped a ham sandwich out of the basket. He then motioned to the other foods in his group to follow suit. The apple reached in and pulled a bunch of grapes out. The orange, a juice box and each cracker helped out several bags of chips. When all the foods were free of the basket Edward led the group back to the Sandbox and gestured that Adrienne would lead them back into The Crumb.

The plan had worked flawlessly; Derek remembered to breathe. Only about fifty more baskets of food needed to be freed, they could do this! Adrienne returned to the Sandbox and the second troop was dispatched, this one led by the ETL.

Quickly, the second group freed another group of foods. This time it was several hotdogs, buns, and ketchup packets from a metal box. Soon the third troop was dispatched, then the fourth, and the fifth, sixth, seventh and so on. Each group managed to free their

Part 12: Derek Donut

designated foods without waking up the slumbering humans. Derek couldn't believe their luck. *No, it wasn't luck*, Derek thought, *it's skill.*

By the time the first troop had ventured outside for the fourth time, Derek could tell Edward and Adrienne were feeling ragged. All the running back and forth escorting escaping foods into The Crumb. Derek was about to suggest they take a quick break, they had freed over half the foods by now, when one of the saltine crackers in Swiss' troop tripped and fell to the ground with a thud. Though the thud was barely audible, it somehow triggered something inside the complex systems of the human.

This human was larger than most others, its stomach protruding from its torso as if trying to escape the ratty shirt and unbuttoned pants that constrained it; bits of hair clinged haphazardly to its skin. The human's many chins seemed to flap in the wind if a breeze strong enough came through. Its breath smelled of garlic and rotting food flesh and its teeth were stained with a yellow so dark, it rivaled the coloring of the sand in the Sandbox.

"ROOOOOOOOOOOONNNNNNNNNNCCCCC!" the obese human snored and rolled over on its side, its tongue falling out of its mouth like a cheese stick left in the sun too long. Everyone froze. The cracker had fallen facedown and now lay perfectly still, its body inches from the human's face. The human emitted another deafening snore and rolled further onto its side, its eyelids now millimeters from the cracker that lay

Part 12: Derek Donut

petrified on the ground. Creatures called birds scattered from trees where they were once hidden. One black bird looked at the scene curiously. Derek stared at it and pleaded with his eyes for it to just leave. The bird made eye contact with Derek and he swore the bird smirked at him.

"CAW!" A flap of wings. A blur of feathers. *Snatch.* The bird flew away with the cracker that once lay near the human's face. Only two beige crumbs remained of the cracker.

"NOOOOOOOO!" Derek screamed before he could help himself. The human's eyes snapped open. They were dark brown and speckled with gray. The black irises widened, then shrunk rapidly, adjusting to the light of the sun.

Swiss S. Cheese didn't waste a second, and shoved the remaining members of his troop far away.Then the group of them sprinted away.

The human sat up and rubbed its eyes. Derek slapped Mew's behind and the monster ran to Swiss and gang's aid. With a single motion, Swiss, the apple, and the other two saltines were on Mew's back behind Derek. Ronald rat was right behind them as Cassie helped the orange on. Edward and Adrienne were already running back to The Crumb alongside them.

"Base, this is Edward," Edward spoke into the radiohead set.

"Go ahead, Edward," Sugar Cookie's voice rang out.

Part 12: Derek Donut

"Code 3! I repeat we have a code 3!" Edward shouted as Derek swung him onto Mew's back behind Swiss S. Cheese.

"All teams! Like, head to base! Like, NOW!" Sugar Cookie shouted through the static of radio chatter. Behind them the human let out an anguished wail and Derek reckoned it had just found out that its food was gone.

"The human's waking up the others!" Cassie shouted from beside Mew. Derek whipped his head around and sure enough, more humans were sitting up, rubbing their eyes and yelling as they found their food missing.

"HEY!" the obese human shouted, its breath wafting through air, still strong enough for Derek to smell it, "they're getting away!" The human's pudgy finger was pointed right at Mew. Humans all around them let out battle cries and jumped to their feet. Several of the more muscular humans managed to run in front of Mew and Ronald, effectively blocking the way to Planet Crumb. Derek looked around and noticed the human ranks consisted of around twenty or so humans.

"Base, it's Cassie, change of plans," Cassie's voice shook a bit as she spoke.

"Go ahead Cassie."

"Reentry to The Crumb is no longer a valid option. The humans have woken up and are now blocking our path."

"Copy that, humans blocking your path. Sending, like, the entire army out now. Godspeed."

Part 12: Derek Donut

"I'm not dying like this," Swiss said, and he pulled out several cheese ninja stars. Derek didn't know where he held them, not that it mattered right now. One. Two. Threefourfive ninja stars flew through the air, each of them hitting a different human square in the chest. Plonk. Plonk. Plonk. Plonkplonk. On impact, each ninja star folded in on itself, bringing absolutely no harm to its targets.

Swiss' jaw dropped.

One of the humans smirked and said,"That's cute," and proceeded to stuff the entire weapon in its mouth and swallow it whole.

"Oh, we're screwed." Adrienne said.

Humans had begun to form a circle around them and Derek could see no exit. Derek motioned at the foods currently riding Mew to dismount and they all complied.

Derek steeled his nerves and looked at Cassie, "Remember, when there's no retreat,"

"Go for the crotch," Cassie finished his sentence. Derek had Ronald the rat climb aboard Mew and he sprinted at the first human he saw, the one with the yellow teeth. The humans must have found the sight of a birthday cake riding a rat, who was riding a cat, steered by a donut, hilarious, because they just laughed and pointed as Mew sprinted towards them. The wind blew all around Derek, making his dough cool to the touch, but filled with a fiery energy. Derek was sure that if he had a head of hair, it would be flowing majestically behind him right then. When they got near enough to the human, Cassie and Ronald rat sprang off of Mew and soared through the air.

CHOMP!

The ugly human's gray speckled eyes widened and watered as it let out what Derek could only assume was a human curse word. Gasps echoed through Picnic Palace as Cassie and Ronald landed back on top of Mew. The human grabbed its crotch and fell over, moaning. Edward and Adrienne cheered. Just then, the sounds of more battle cries echoed from inside Planet Crumb and soon, a horde of foods marched in unison outside armed to the teeth with utensils, toothpicks, staples, thumbtacks, literally anything they could find. And all of it was being led by Ginger and the rest of the Spice Girls.

Derek spotted Prince Ice of Cream in the crowd immediately, and he felt a small warmth in his body as something fluttered inside him. What the feeling was, he had no clue, but it wasn't so bad he decided. Sugar Cookie brought up the back of the army, riding on Roomba, the death vacuum. It would appear that Tiriaq and Chipette had made some adjustments to the circular robot as it now sported several bags of icing.

The ETM and ETL rolled out the homemade Crayla cannon Derek had seen earlier and pushed it over to where Edward and Adirenne were sitting. The next thing Derek couldn't help but notice was that MilkDudBot 1.2 and the Saibou weren't present but everyone else was, even little Tiriaq and Chipette, both armed with some fierce looking homemade slingshots. As they marched in, the Spice Girls led everyone else in the singing this poem;

Now we got the flavour, the bad behaviour,
The rhythm, the melody, the juice for your to
savour,
Rockin' and vibing somebody is jivin',
You need to take a tip, sort it out, get a grip
Whenever I go out, whenever it may be
There never is a Kit-kat stronger than me
you know we'll score, and you'll be the loose in the
battlefield floor
Take a deep breath count 1 2 3

you can't win, you can't win,
you can't win, you can't win,
you won't succeed, you can't defeat us baby
you can't win, you can't win,
you can't win, you can't win,
you won't succeed, you can't defeat us baby

The humans looked at each other in bewilderment and the mass of food took full advantage of it. In something that Derek could only describe was a frenzy of peels, tin foil, and bubble wrap, the foods attacked.

Energized by this sudden turn of events, Mew and Ronald Rat resumed biting and nipping at the crotches of humans. Mew flew through the air, Derek on its back. Whenever a human got close enough, Mew would swipe its sharp-toed paw, jump up and bite, or straight up roundhouse kick the unfortunate recipient in

343

the groin. Wherever they went, humans groaned as they fell to the ground, hands glued in between their legs. Around them, foods started jabbing the humans with their weapons. Sugar Cookie zoomed around on her robot, controlling it with an app on her phone. The disk raced around Picnic Palace ramming into humans and shooting icing in their faces, momentarily blinding them. The humans might have been one hundred times larger than them but they were no match for the sheer number of infuriated foods, at least Derek thought so.

Above Derek, as he and Cassie rode to the human's groin, Ginny swooped over head and kicked a human in the eyes. She had unrolled herself and was floating through the air by riding the winds. In the distance, the Cheese Wizard jumped on humans shoulders and shot some of his artificial cheese filling into their ears, noses, really anything that he could hit to make the humans scream in shock.

"What are you doing!" The human with the stained teeth shouted to the other still stunned humans as he hobbled to his feet, one hand still clamped on his groin, "Stop standing around! Y'all are getting beat up by a bunch of FOODS! We aren't going to take this! DOWN WITH THE FOODS!"

Humans as far as the eye could see shook themselves out of their daze and confusion and shouted a chorus of "Yeah!" and "That's right!" The humans began stomping around in an attempt to crush the foods beneath their feet.

Somewhere to the left of Derek, Adrienne shouted a Vinshu spell then cursed when nothing

Part 12: Derek Donut

happened. *Come on Saibou,* Derek thought to himself as he steered Mew around several humans trying to kick them, *we need the magic back.* Around him foods started perishing faster than a molding peach on a warm summer's day. A set of croutons smacked a human at the knees, bringing the human down to the ground. CRUNCH. A second human smashed them into obliteration. A banana attacked a human with its toothpick. SQUISH. The human stepped on the fruit and proceeded to slip and fall. Adrienne raced by Derek and Cassie firing the homemade cannon at the humans. A red Crayola Javelin soared through Derek's hole and struck a human in the stomach behind him.

"UNLEASH... THE ONIONS!" Ginger screamed, and six onions ran out from The Crumb bare naked, their onion skins removed. These onions all sported haircuts, their juices leaking out. Immediately, the humans in the nearest proximity teared up and started all out bawling. The tear soaked humans stumbled around, their vision impaired. One of the human's tripped and fell to the ground, crushing all of the onions beneath them. Everywhere Derek looked, more death.

Prince Ice of Cream, sporting a handsome peppermint scoop, slid on the ground in front of Derek and jabbed his pair of chopsticks into the foot of a human as it came down on him. The thought of the Prince dying angered Derek greatly. The world should not be deprived of that beautiful waffle cone, each marking etched into it sparkled as the Prince tried to roll out of the foot's way. Derek screamed and charged at the human, Mew's padded feet a blur of orange and white. They jumped. Derek flew through the air and landed roughly on the human's head. Without thinking, Derek grabbed two fistfuls of the human's greasy blond hair and the human shrieked and stumbled backward, seconds before crushing the prince.

Mew swiped its tail under the human's nose as the monster fell back down the ground. The human sneezed, spittle and green gelatinous snot flying out of its mouth and nose. The movement of the sneeze sent Derek tumbling from the top of the human's head and to the ground. He shut his eyes preparing for the impact. Instead he landed in something comfortable and he felt the sensation of feet below him. Derek opened his eyes and Prince Ice of Cream flashed him a devilishly handsome smile,

"I've got you." The prince was carrying Derek in his arms as he ran, avoiding falling humans and foods alike. Derek's stomach fluttered again and he felt the strange sensation once more. "The battle isn't going well," Prince Ice of Cream told Derek as he set him down. A human saw the pair and charged at them. Derek grabbed the Prince's arm and spun him into Derek's chest, narrowly avoiding being trampled by the human. The Prince grabbed Derek's hands and the two practically waltzed around about the grassy field just to avoid being mauled.

The humans started throwing anything they would find, small rocks, twigs, even several foods got thrown by other foods. Derek tossed Prince Ice of Cream in the air, a rock soared over Derek's head and under Prince Ice of Cream. The Prince fell back down and this

time, it was Derek who caught him in his arms. Another set of twigs flew at Derek and Prince Ice of Cream. Derek dipped the Prince down and the twigs grazed the back of Derek's head. The pain was barely registered. Derek was very acutely aware of how close his lips were to Pince Ice of Cream's. The moment was magical, the ice cubes (which Derek had never noticed before) that lay in the Prince's eyes sparkled in the light of the sun. Prince Ice of Cream moved in closer; so did Derek.

A large object impacted the side of two desserts and Derek's vision went momentarily dark. When he could see again, Picnic Palace was rolling around, upside down, then rightside up. Upside Down. Rightside up. Derek realized he himself was rolling on his side, down a hill. It was at this moment that he realized how bad the battle was going. The food numbers were dwindling. Over half of them lay on the ground, smashed, bitten, stomped. Dead.

Sugar Cookie sped past Derek on Roomba and yelled at him to lie down in a push up position. Derek complied, the wet grass soaking his hands. VROOOM! Sugar Cookie steered the robot and used Derek's doughy body as a ramp. As the robot glided over Derek, the sucking mechanism at the bottom lifted Derek up off the ground. Derek screamed and Sugar Cookie pushed a button and the suction ceased, dropping Derek into the branches of a tree.

The Roomba and Edward's sister collided with a human's face. This human was relatively thin, but sported a dark blob of voluptuous hair above its upper

Part 12: Derek Donut

lid. *Mustache.* Sugar Cookie reactivated the suction and the mustache hair strained to escape from the human's face as the human screamed in terror and pain.

Derek turned his attention back to the rest of the battlefield. Dozens of Spices lay dead, their glass bodies shattered, spilling their contents unceremoniously into the ground. Derek couldn't tell if any of the Spice Girls were still alive except for Nutmeg, who kept shouting, "My body is paining! Paining!"

Apples and bananas lay smashed on the cobblestone path that lay down the middle of Picnic Palace. Chips and crackers, reduced to crumbs. Salt and pepper lay unconscious on the ground. At least Derek hoped they were unconscious as they seemed to not sustain many injuries. Edward was running away, sticking forks into the ground, prongs up, as several humans chased him. His friend was looking terrible—chunks of Edward's body were missing and, with every step, it seemed another chocolate chip fell off.

Adrienne was still firing her homemade Crayola cannon, but she had run out of colored javins to shoot out and was currently stuffing grass down the barrel of the cannon and shooting it at humans. Cassie Cake was still riding on Ronald Rat, but the humans had caught onto her crotch biting and guarded their groins whenever she came near. The ETM and ETL were back to back, toothpicks in hand desperately trying to fend off the four humans encircling them. The ETM was missing most of his filling and the ETL was starting to crack along the sides.

Swiss S. Cheese lay stuck to a tree, some humans had stabbed a fork into the tree trunk and dangled him from the fork by one of his many holes. Chipette and Tiriaq had made a sort of grass remover out of a spoon and were chunking bits of ground at the humans. Ginny Gelato, was no longer soaring through the air, in fact, she could barely stand up as she was melting under the sun. The Prince was in a similar predicament, his scoop glistening in the sun. Mew lay on the ground, panting hard, seemingly too tired or hurt to move any more. It was official, the foods were out gunned, outmanned, outnumbered and quite possibly, out planned. They had made their all out stand, and now they would perish.

No, Derek thought to himself, *you can't think like that, Get your butt out of this tree and do something! You are not going to let your fellow foods and most of all friends down!*

Derek shimmied himself down the tree trunk and ran to Mew,

"C'mon, old pal," he told the monster, "one last run and I'll get you some catnip after this is all over." The monster perked up at the mention of catnip and it mewed in pain as it rose to its feet. Derek gingerly mounted the monster and rode it to where Ginger lay, melting. Quickly, while avoiding several flying projectiles, he scooped up his friend and draped her on the monster's back.

Part 12: Derek Donut

Next, he picked up a passed out Prince Ice of Cream, his cone soggy from the drippings of a melting scoop on the top of his head. Derek steeled his nerves once more; he was going to do it. He would travel across the battlefield, into The Crumb, and save his dying friends.

With a nudge of his legs, Mew bolted forward and the landscape became a streaky background. Edward noticed what Derek was trying to do and ran in front of Mew. A human attempted to kick them. Edward tied the human's shoelaces together as Derek dodged the falling human . Flying rocks, headed straight for Derek's face. Edward grabbed a stick and batted them away from Derek. A human managed to grab onto Mew's tail.

Derek flipped himself around and kicked the sausage like fingers as hard as he could. They didn't budge. Edward grabbed a nearby fork and threw it at the human. The flying utensil slapped the human's hand with its four prongs. The human let out a grotesque yelp and tumbled away. Dodge right. Dodge left. Duck. Jump. Stab. Dodge. Stab. Jump. Dodge. Edward was clearing the way for Derek to The Crumb. A bird flew down and tried to kidnap Derek in its sickly yellow claws. The Cheeze Wizard jumped from somewhere on the left of Derek and body slammed the creature off its path of trajectory. A single feather floated softly to the ground. Before Derek knew it, they were stumbling into The Crumb, the familiar sight of The Cabinet growing larger as they slid in front of it. Edward nodded to Derek and proceeded to run back into battle. Derek grabbed the nearest containers he could find, two plastic bags by the name of Ziploc, and shoved the Prince and Ginny each in their own respective bags, seconds before they melted into a sugary puddle on the hardwood floor.

"Come on, come-on, come-on," Derek said to no one in particular, sweat dripping into his eyes, "where to refreeze desserts?" The Free-Idge's white door glinted in the corner of Derek's eye. Derek turned around and attempted to pry the portal open.

The door remained shut as if glued.

Derek looked back in panic at the two Ziploc bags that contained his now shapeless friends. He let out a yell of frustration and slammed his fists down on the Free-Idge out of anger. Instantaneously, the Free-Idge emitted a gurgling sound and began to shake violently, fingers made of bright white light jutting out from the edges.

The Free-Idge was opening.

Like a shot, the door was thrust open by some invisible force and Derek was flung into the air like a ragdoll. Derek was deposited on top of the counter, a giant dent now in his dough, and he looked up. The portal was now fully activated and a giant mass appeared to be thrusting its way through the void. Derek's eyes widened as the mass came closer, its silhouette now crisp and sharp.

The mass stepped through the portal and before Derek's eyes stood a giant robot, almost as tall as a human, made completely of dried noodles. This wasn't good, no it wasn't at all. They were already fighting all the humans, they didn't need another foe.

Part 12: Derek Donut

"Well, don't look so shocked," a cold voice emitted from the cockpit of the robot. A hatch opened in the face of the robot. And there he was, grinning evilly: Supreme Lord Mac-N-Cheese. The robot's tortilla chip cannon charged up and Derek dove into the Kitchen Sink for cover.

Part 13: Supreme Lord Mac-N-Cheese

THREE HOURS EARLIER:

Supreme Lord Mac-N-Cheese sat on his throne in his castle in the epicenter of The Diner, Ediblavia. Countless thoughts ran through his head. Everything that had happened recently left him stressed and on the verge of insanity. He had been chasing that brat of a child, Edward, and his friends for who knows how long. When Supreme Lord Mac-N-Cheese sent the infamous Evil Taco Man to bomb Secret Cookie Labratories he wished he knew that the ETM would have mistaken two different schools for the secrect base! Supreme Lord Mac-N-Cheese wondered how someone with the smarts and military experience of the ETM made such a horrid mistake.

Eventually, Supreme Lord Mac-N-Cheese began to feel interesting feelings regarding the pesky desserts that plagued his quest for foodiverse domination. On one hand, they were so annoying and managed to thwart him at every turn, despite most of them being mere teenagers. On the other hand, however, the Supreme Lord began to realize that he mildly enjoyed the desserts' presence and their interesting quirks. Tiriaq and his speech patterns, Edward's constant need to feel in control. Even Chipette, referring to him as Mr.

Cheese, was quite adorable, though he would never actually admit that to her.

No, he mustn't deviate from the plan. Supreme Lord Mac-N-Cheese looked behind in at the condiment board where, writing in ketchup and mustard, he had detailed his plan;

1. **Take control of Secret Cookie Labs**
   - ☐ Must be done before the rest of the plan because otherwise they will be all over his back and will hinder the progress of the rest of the plan.
2. **Begin creating fear**
   - ☐ Done by kidnapping dessert via tortillas and exposing them to The Bean aboard the burrito ship.
3. **Take out Edward Chip and his friends**
   - ☐ Ingredient Ascertainer activated with Edward, Adrienne, Sugar Cookie and Chipette's unique genetic codes.
     - ☐ Signal of the ascertainer was boosted through use of an SCL satellite as to follow them through space
4. **Build the Food Pyramid**
   - ☐ Used to build a reputation of fear among desserts around the foodiverse.

☐ Desserts will be kidnapped from
The Dessert by tortillas and
brought to compete in games
5. **Big reveal to the foodiverse**
☐ By now, The Dessert should be in
disarray and its defenses weak.
☐ This is the perfect opportunity
to destroy the planet.
☐ Method – TBD

Had Supreme Lord Mac-N-Cheese followed this
plan to a tea, things might have ended up differently.
But he made a grave mistake when he accidentally
forced several dinner foods, his own henchmen, to
compete at the Food Pyramid. He had specially told the
meatballs to capture anyone on the spaceship he'd been
tracking. He didn't realize that the ship contained not
just Edwarnd and company, but also several of his most
loyal followers.

What he should have done was, as soon as he
realized the ETM and others were also on Chipette's
homemade spacecraft, he should have had them
uncaptured. But instead, he continued with the games
and didn't even pretend to act remorseful for his
treatment of his henchmen. It was no wonder they
turned on him.

"Your greatness." A burrito guard knelt low in
front of him, starling him out of his thoughts. "You have
visitors."

"Name?"

356

Part 13: Supreme Lord Mac-N-Cheese

"There are two."

"And, names?"

"John Kraft and Annie Cheese."

The throne room doors swung open slowly, to reveal two cups of mac and cheese, hands joined, walking to the throne.

"Mom? Dad?"

His mom stood beneath him and smiled. She then hit him in the face with her walking stick.

"SONNY BOY! WHAT ARE YOU DOING?!"

"Ouch, mom! That was uncalled for!"

"What are you doing, pal?" His father said, almost sadly. "We didn't raise you this way."

"But Mom, Dad, look at me! Look at what I've built! I have built a glorious empire!"

"Yes, but what have you done? Look what you've caused."

"What…?"

"Look at this pain. You have brought nothing but suffering to the foodiverse."

"We talked about this before! It's only suffering for the desserts, and from what I know about them, they deserve it! But look at our kind. We are above all! We were born to rule the foodiverse! I'm so close, too! As soon as I get rid of that despicable Edward and his friends-"

"Nobody was *born* to rule the foodiverse. We are all foods. And look what you're doing to the desserts."

"But what about our history!" Supreme Lord Mac-N-Cheese said, "We've been trying to take over The Dessert for hundreds of years now!"

Part 13: Supreme Lord Mac-N-Cheese

"You have done nothing but the ripple effect of the terrible actions of your great-great-great-great grandfather, Mac-N-Cheese Senior," his dad said.

"That's right son," his mom chimed in, "Mac-N-Cheese Senior was the cruelest of all the tyrants, and no one knew this until King Ice of Cream Senior attacked The Diner. Mac-N-Cheese Senior was enraged that he became blind to all the harm and pain he ended up causing not just desserts, but all foods."

"So he set his sights on The Dessert and decided he must have it! The inhabitants of The Dessert clearly didn't like this. The two planets fought for ages and the battles never stopped, nor did the conflict get solved. Instead, everyone just pretended like it didn't exist, causing a rift between the two planets," his father finished.

Mrs. Annie brought out her phone and played a news clip. It showed a bowtie pasta bearing a birthday candle, melting a cookie couple. As their chips fell off of their bodies, you could see a cookie child crying under a table. A melted cheese tear began to form in Supreme Lord Mac-N-Cheese's eye. It slowly rolled down his plastic cup. It hit the floor.

"There's tons more videos like this," his mom said sadly.

"You know what!" the Supreme Lord said, wiping the tear off his face in disgust, "Shut up! Shut up! SHUT UP! I don't care about them! Get out!"

"I thought you still had some good left in you." His father smiled weakly. "Clearly I was wrong."

Part 13: Supreme Lord Mac-N-Cheese

"Get out. Right. Now."

"C'mon son," his mother pleaded, "please reconsider."

Supreme Lord Mac-N-Cheese looked his parents square in the eye and belted out, "Guards!" Several churro and burrito guards rushed in. "Arrest them!" The minions turned their weapons on Mrs. Annie and Mr. Kraft.

"Son, don't do this!" The Supreme Lord looked away and ignored the sounds of his parents struggling to escape. Mrs. Annie made a last ditch effort to stop the captors and threw something at his feet. The Supreme Lord Mac-N-Cheese looked, and was greeted with the sight of Mrs. Annie's phone. The large doors of the Supreme Lord's throne room slammed shut and the Kraft cup was left alone with his thoughts.

The phone lay on the ground. *Watch me.* It seemed to whisper. The Supreme Lord refused. *Aren't you just a little bit curious as to what's on me?*

"Shut up." Supreme Lord Mac-N-Cheese snapped out loud. *You know you want to.* The phone seemed to smirk. *Just a teensy little glance couldn't hurt anyone.*

"Stop it!" he yelled out loud. The phone buzzed, moving across the floor in a turtle like fashion. *Just one teensy tiny looksy.*

"I won't give in," the Supreme Lord decided, and steeled his nerves. The phone continued vibrating and crawling in a pitiful attempt to get closer to the Supreme Lord.

Part 13: Supreme Lord Mac-N-Cheese

"No," Supreme Lord Mac-N-Cheese said, and turned around.

DING

He spun back around and saw a little message on the phone's screen. He walked back over to investigate.

```
You have one
notification:
Open up the phone
pretty please!:)
```

"You need to leave," he snapped at the phone, and snatched it up. In a flash, he raced to the nearest window and threw it open.

"Goodbye," he said to the phone, and moved his arm backward to throw it out when it buzzed again and Supreme Lord Mac-N-Cheese accidentally viewed the message being sent to the phone.

It was a small collage of pictures of his childhood. The first picture was a one year old Kraft cup sitting at a table, building a puzzle. The next picture, it was the Supreme Lord playing in a park, probably when he was six or seven years old. In the background, many other foods were also playing in the park. Swinging on the swings, sliding, everything you could imagine to do at a park.

That's when the Supreme Lord noticed something. Several of the foods were desserts. It was just several lollipops, but they seemed happy and were playing quite nicely with several hamburgers. On an even closer inspection, it was revealed that the young Supreme Lord seemed to be smiling at them, as if inviting them to play.

Frantically, Supreme Lord Mac-N-Cheese went back to the first photo. The puzzle he was building seemed to be a picture of some fries and milkshakes at the movies together. The next picture, the second grade Supreme Lord was proudly holding a picture he had drawn of him and his best friend, Paul Pudding, the future Principal Pudding. Gosh, he had forgotten all about his friend. They had been friends for only several weeks due to their school trips to Planet Fruity coinciding. The next picture showed a moody and sullen teenage Supreme Lord listening to some heavy metal music. By looking at the pictures on the CD cases, it was clear that he was listening to Micheal Jelloson, most famous for his song titled, *Bumpy Bandit.*

"Annie, are you ok? Are you ok Annie? You've been hit by— you've been struck by— a bumpy bandit," Supreme Lord Mac-N-Cheese sang under his breath, the lyrics to the song suddenly coming back to him. He swiped his thumb on the phone. The next picture was revealed, and the next one, and the one after that. They were all prominent moments in his life and it became clear that the young Supreme Lord didn't have any aversions to desserts. Then, a picture of a middle schooler Supreme Lord showed up. In the picture, he was being lectured by an ancient looking cup of instant mac. The words of the conversation rang out from Supreme Lord Mac-N-Cheese's memory:

Part 13: Supreme Lord Mac-N-Cheese

"Sit down, boy," Grandpa Mac said, "we need to have a talk."

"About what?" the young Supreme Lord asked.

Grandpa Mac plopped his large circular body down. "I've seen the way you act. I'm afraid it's not correct and sets a bad image on this family. Your ancestors and I have not wasted years, slaving awaying, building this kingdom for you to ruin all of our reputations with your fraternizing with the desserts. I don't care what your parents think, I've decided that they aren't inheriting the kingdom, you are. Their conscience has already been tainted by their empathy for other foods. While you, you are still pure, you still see the value of the dinner foods. You still see how we are far superior than everyone else."

"Y-you're giving the kingdom all to me?" young Mac couldn't believe it.

"Yes, young one. I'm skipping a generation of passing down this entire planet. Just so that it will stay untainted. My father, his father and his father before that have all worked hard for the past two hundred years to make sure that the dessert scum don't come here. They aren't to be trusted. Our entire goal is to one day rule the entire foodiverse. But, I fear I won't live to see that day."

"W-why?"

"I fear I'm getting old. My time is short. I need to ensure that you carry on the legacy of our kind. Can you promise me this? Can you promise me that you won't allow the planet to become overrun with other foods? Will you be able to take all the precautionary measures

Part 13: Supreme Lord Mac-N-Cheese

to make sure that all desserts submit to us? Even if it means eradicating them completely?"

"I guess?" young Mac said, conflicted.

"YOU GUESS!" Grandpa Mac roared, "that doesn't sound like you want this! DO YOU EVEN WANT TO RULE THE FOODIVERSE!"

"Yes! Yes I do! I'm ready! I promise!"

"That's more like it! Your combat and dictatorship training starts tomorrow at noon. You better be there!"

"I won't let you down," young Mac said, nodding vigorously.

Two months later, Grandpa Mac expired. As the newly appointed Supreme Lord Mac-N-Cheese attended a funeral and looked at his grandfather's corpse lying inside a chip bag (party sized), he remembered his promise to him. The hushed whispers of the Supreme Lord's relatives surrounded him, but he pretended not to notice them.

"Did you hear? They appointed the kid as the new leader."

"I know! It's baloney! How is that young child supposed to know what to do with an entire kingdom?"

"I heard his parents passed out when they heard the news in the will reading." Supreme Lord Mac-N-Cheese steeled himself, determined not to let the naysayers' words affect him. He leaned down and gave his grandfather one last kiss on the forehead and turned away. It was time to lead.

Part 13: Supreme Lord Mac-N-Cheese

The memory faded from Supreme Lord Mac-N-Cheese's mind and he was jolted back to the present. Could it be that his reasoning for ruling the foodiverse was tainted? Were the past twenty nine years of his life a sham? Behind him, the condiment board with his plan written on it seemed to loom over his shoulder. As he read through the plan once more, it suddenly seemed ludicrous.

Why had he gone through all this trouble? He'd gotten so caught up in his end goal of foodiverse domination, he forgot his reasoning for all of it. His obsession with controlling the foodiverse had led to two schools being inadvertantly bombed and countless other deadly mistakes where innocent foods had died. He looked back at the phone. A low battery warning flashed briefly across the screen and the phone died. Then, he came to a decision.

"Guards!" The Supreme Lord shouted. Hundreds of varying kinds of noodles as well as several burritos shuffled around, and formed in the throne room.

"I owe the foodiverse an apology. I send you, my companions, on a mission. Spread the message throughout the foodiverse. I will be making a speech at the Spaghetti Monster at dawn tomorrow. If you can be there, please be there. Oh, and take my parents out of jail."

The noodles saluted, and jumped out of the pantry in a single file line, leaving Supreme Lord Mac-N-Cheese standing alone in the throne room, hoping he was doing the right thing.

"I'm sorry, Grandpa."

364

Part 13: Supreme Lord Mac-N-Cheese

As Supreme Lord Mac-N-Cheese arrived at the border to the Free-Idge, he saw hundreds of foods and desserts congregating at the spaghetti monster. Apparently, his burrito minions had spread the message efficiently and the foods were interested as to what he had to say. Quickly, he set his supersized instant noodle shaped spaceship down by the edge of the crowd. Foods shrieked and pointed as he landed. But, they weren't running away or attacking him at the moment. He considered this a win. When the engines of the ship stopped, he climbed out from a roof hatch and stood atop the ship. The foods below fell quiet. With this cue, he began to address the foods on the planet below.

"My edible friends, my confectionary companions. I have come today to apologize for the conflict and pain I have brought to the foodiverse."

The foods on the Spaghetti Monster were absolutely silent. A pin dropped galaxies away.

"Oops! That's my bad," a very distant voice shouted, probably over 10,000,000 miles away, "I won't drop my pin again."

The foods seemed unbothered by this disturbance and shifted around, waiting for Supreme Lord Mac-N-Cheese to continue. He cleared his throat, his heart pounding in his chest. This was the longest he had ever stood before a group of foods, mainly desserts, without trying to kill them. The foods gave him skeptical looks. Among the crowd was Principal Pudding, with several toothpicks embedded in his body. Principal Pudding was for some reason wearing handcuffs, an orange jumpsuit, and was guarded by several pie police.

Supreme Lord Mac-N-Cheese winced at the sight of his old friend and tried to give him a small wave. A large female cookie noticed this and quickly stepped in front of the former principal and shot a glare at the Supreme Lord. Even from a distance he could read the nameplate embedded on her blue blazer: Principal Peanut Butter Cookie. He hadn't even thought about him in forever, but it seemed he was doing just fine. Well, besides the weapons impaled in his body and being a prison inmate. But, it seemed he had met someone who cared about him. He then saw several stalks of asparagus, all impaled together by the tongs of a plastic fork and a very angry looking Sarah Smoothie. He squirmed, as he was uncomfortable. He braced himself for the conversation to come.

"It is my duty to address the violence towards desserts that has taken place in the foodiverse."

He then cast his gaze upon two truffles, melted together. They stared daggers at him.

"This violence was my fault, and mine alone. Therefore, it is my responsibility to bring union to this world, full of turmoil."

The desserts began to relax a bit. Shoulders hunched and legs uncrouched from running positions.

"I am so deeply sorry for the loss of any loved ones you may have experienced during this war. I know one apology cannot fix what has taken place."

The foods began to nod.

Part 13: Supreme Lord Mac-N-Cheese

"From now on, I will—" He was interrupted by the spaghetti monster,

"Sorry to interrupt, but I have seen something. Outside of the foodiverse, there are foods. They are being brutally eaten, ripped out of their home. The greedy humans consume them." Gasps could be heard throughout the foodiverse.

"That can't be true!" someone mused from the crowd.

"Oh it's true alright," the monster replied, "After I launched several foods, including Ginny, Milkdudbot 1.2, Prince Ice of Cream and the Cheese Wizard out into Planet Crumb, the portal between two dimensions stayed slightly open instead of closing up like it normally does. I can see the horror of the Battle of Picnic Palace but can't do anything for I am a planet and too big to fit through the portal."

"This is YOUR fault!" an angry cinnabon screamed from the crowd, "Supreme Lord Mac-N-Cheese is lying to us once again! He didn't come here to apologize! He came to lure us into a trap to feed the humans! He has always been behind the disappearances of our fellow desserts!" Upon hearing this, the other desserts in the crowd agreed and pulled out their various weapons. The cinnabon waved his toothpick in the air screaming,

"GET HIM!"

"What! No! I didn't— Stop! Wait!" Supreme Lord Mac-N-Cheese stumbled backward, dodging rotten tomatoes and other flying projectiles. Several bananas took off their peels and threw them at the cup of Insta

Part 13: Supreme Lord Mac-N-Cheese

Mac-N-Cheese, causing him to slip and fall on his head. The Supreme Lord stared at the stars in a daze as he slid off the top of his ship and onto the soggy, moist ground.

"Stop!" a voice shouted from the crowd, "look at us! What are we doing!?" Objects stopped hurtling at Supreme Lord Mac-N-Cheese's body. He wanted to check to see the severity of the dents to his body but his body refused to move.

"We are all mad at this food, right?" the voice spoke again and a chorus of yeahs and shouting was heard, "And why? Because he hurt the desserts we loved! But look at what you are doing! We are all hypocrites! We are angered when foods like Supreme Lord Mac-N-Cheese resort to violence, but then, what do we do!? *We* resort to violence in the same way! I say we give this food one more chance to explain himself!" Concerned and uncertain murmurs emitted all around the Supreme Lord as the feeling in his legs started to come back.

"What happens when his answer doesn't add up and it turns out he really is here to lure us into a trap!?" a different voice shouted.

"*If* we are unsatisfied with his explanation, well," the original voice resumed, "then, ummmm. I guess we can beat him up then."

The crowd cheered at this. Supreme Lord Mac-N-Cheese's savior walked into his view and stuck out a hand to help him up. Wearily, the once high and mighty Supreme Lord was helped up. As Supreme Lord Mac-N-Cheese dusted himself off he looked up, Paul Pudding stood before him in an orange jumpsuit,

Part 13: Supreme Lord Mac-N-Cheese

"You better not let me down," his old friend whispered roughly into ear.

"You're a prisoner now," Supreme Lord Mac-N-Cheese noted.

"Shush your pie hole and explain your actions" Principal Peanut Butter Cookie, who was hanging onto Paul's arm, snapped.

"I swear on my grandfather's grave, my intentions were nothing but honest. I really wanted to make the wrongs right." Supreme Lord Mac-N-Cheese said, stammering. A deafening silence followed.

"I don't believe him!" The other voice, who came from the cinnabon, shouted once again, "get him!" The desserts before him gripped their weapons and charged at Supreme Lord Mac N-Cheese again.

"STOP!" the voice of the Spaghetti Monster rang out, "I despise this so-called 'Supreme Lord'. But this has gone on longer than we have time for. Do you have any idea what is going on outside of this universe!? Edward and his friends are risking their lives fighting for the freedom of foods they don't even know! That's right, not just desserts, *all* foods. And you guys are here attacking each other, furthering the conflict between desserts and foods!" The cinnabon stared at the ground, mouth agape.

"Yeah, nope," the cinnabon scoffed, "I don't trust either of you. I'm out of here." The desserts all around the Supreme Lord, Paul and his girlfriend, all scoffed and turned their backs. As a group, they climbed aboard their spaceships and flew off into the sky, shouting insults all the way. The pie police shifted uncomfortably

Part 13: Supreme Lord Mac-N-Cheese

as they looked at their own spacecraft, an oversized pie that somewhat resembled an alien ship from children's books.

"Let the pudding go," Supreme Lord Mac-N-Cheese sighed, "I still have some power and I order you to release this dessert from captivity." The police pies nodded and unhandcuffed Paul Pudding, who promptly ran around screaming,

"In your face, world! Suckers! I'm free! I'm free!" The two police pies looked at each other with sad expressions on their faces.

"He played me didn't he," Supreme Lord Mac-N-Cheese sighed. The two police pies nodded.

"Don't worry, he'll settle down eventually." Principal Peanut Butter Cookie said, "then we will both leave."

"What about me!" Supreme Lord Mac-N-Cheese protested, "I need help! How am I supposed to help the desserts on Planet Crumb?"

"That's your problem." Principal Peanut Butter Cookie scoffed, "you really dug yourself deep into this one."

"I've changed! Believe me! Please!"

"Sorry, but if you really want us to believe you... you'll have to do something big," Paul proclaimed. "Now if you will excuse me and my girlfriend, we have to go out on our first date not taking place inside of a jail." Supreme Lord Mac-N-Cheese looked around. Everyone had left even the pie police,

"Please, Paul. Help me. I promise it'll be just like old times. I'm begging you one last time, help me."

Part 13: Supreme Lord Mac-N-Cheese

Principal Peanut Butter Cookie and Paul Pudding started walking away.

"I'll set your first real date, at... um... um... um... Athaliahus Asylum!" He blurted out in desperation.

The couple stopped walking and turned around."Why would we want to spend our first date in an Asylum?" the principal demanded.

"Well, it's more of a five star hotel if you ask me. I only used the first floor though, it was my halloween themed floor and since no one ever visited the hotel. I began to use just the first floor for capturing my most dangerous enemies. I was only, however, able to capture someone by the name of Ginny Gelato and her dragon Saibou. And then I forgot about it until that scum— no, *dessert,* Edward and his *pals* invaded the area. Anyways, the other floors are also decorated for other holidays. Every holiday is represented, I promise."

"You mean there's a Valentine's Day floor?" Paul asked, putting an arm around Principal PC.

"Yes! With jacuzzis, sweet tarts and heart shaped beds and—"

"I'm sold," Principal PC said, cutting him off, "let's do it." Supreme Lord Mac-N-Cheese nodded, relieved, and the three of them boarded his spaceship in search of weapons to aid the other foods in their battle.

"Don't be long," the Spaghetti Monster warned, "you have exactly one hour, forty seven minutes, thirty three seconds and less than ninety two milliseconds before the window of prime infiltration of Planet Crumb closes. Be back before the time is up, or you might arrive upon a battlefield of food corpses."

Part 13: Supreme Lord Mac-N-Cheese

"That's not a lot of time. How do we even know where to look?" the supreme lord pondered out loud.

"I can help with that," the Spaghetti Monster said once more, "I am an entire planet, so I see most things. Here is a map of a few of the most powerful weapons." A noodle shot out of the ground with a flat sheet of pasta that flopped wildly in the wind. Written on the sheet in tomato sauce was a rough map detailing the locations of several of the most powerful weapons in the foodiverse. Surprisingly, the first two were nearby.

"Guys," Supreme Lord Mac-N-Cheese smiled, "we are going to the Spaghetti Monster's butt."

When they arrived on the other side of the planet, the supreme lord was very relieved to see that the Food Pyramid he had built was still standing in all of its grimy and gruesome glory. The dessert couple beside him shuddered as they approached on foot, having already parked the spaceship behind the massive coliseum.

"Alright, Paul and Principal PC, I need you to go into the Food Pyramid and find the weapons and armor rooms. Find the restrooms and then go down that hall, take the first two lefts you see, and then a right, and you should be in the room. Meet me back in the spaceship in twenty minutes."

"Fine," Paul grumbled, "what are you going to be doing?! I'm not doing your dirty work for you!"

372

Part 13: Supreme Lord Mac-N-Cheese

"I will be finding two weapons behind the Food Pyramid, the map says they have been smashed and I plan to use Vishnu to mend them."

They nodded and began to walk into the coliseum, though moaning and complaining all the way. Supreme Lord Mac-N-Cheese turned and teleported away in a flash a gooey cheese. He reappeared seconds later, twenty feet away from a dent in the ground from when Edward and his friends had crash landed on this planet.

Immediately, he found what he was looking for. At his feet lay the shattered remnants of Edward's cookie blaster and his two magical, shapeshifting knives. The supreme lord kneeled down and waved his hand over the pile of scraps and muttered the spell; *réparer*. Slowly, the pieces began to move, as if of their own accord, scrapping and bumbling across the soggy meaty ground when, out of the blue, a foot stamped down, reducing the weapons to piles of scrap once more.

"Now what Eggs-actly do you think you're doing?" A shrill voice demanded as the supreme lord rose from his kneeling position.

"I've come to collect weapons," he said. Then, seeing the skeptical look on the extraterrestrial egg's face, he added: "for the foods on Planet Crumb, they need my help."

"Sure! HA! Who knew! You're a comedian!" the egg scoffed, throwing his hands up in the air.

"Come on, you can trust us! Let us know what you're really doing!" Supreme Lord Mac-N-Cheese glanced around, there were only two remaining deviled eggs and three extraterrestrial eggs. "No, I'm being serious," he tried again. The egg was about throw some more shade when one of the deviled eggs cut him off saying,

"No, I think he's being legit!"

"I am!"

"For real?!"

"Yes! for real!"

The eggs looked at each other unsure so a second, then one of the green eggs decided, "Okay, we're in, how can we help?"

This time it was Supreme Lord Mac-N-Cheese who gasped, "For real?!"

"Yeah, sure! Why not! I mean, we've followed your orders before."

"Alright!" Supreme Lord Mac-N-Cheese couldn't believe it. Apparently, many of his loyal followers were still loyal to him! This gave him an idea, and he leaned in closer to the eggs despite their foul smelling breath. He really wanted them to hear this.

"Okay! Here's what you can do: gather all of my guards, burrito, churro, pasta noodle, every last one. Tell them to bring every weapon they can find to the Spaghetti Monster in," he checked his watch, "an hour and ten minutes." The eggs nodded and sprinted away into the distance.

Resuming a kneeling position, he muttered the spell once more and watched as the pieces slithered back together, forming two glowing blue knives and one seriously decked out cookie blaster. Supreme Lord Mac-N-Cheese wondered if Edward knew how dangerous of a weapon the police had given him when he captured the ETM.

Paul Pudding's high pitched scream emanated behind him from the distance, shattering Supreme Lord Mac-N-Cheese's thoughts. Quickly, he scooped up the weapons and teleported back to the food pyramid.

He materialized in midair and crash landed through the cracker ceiling, collapsing the entire upper left quadrant of the coliseum. He looked around, four meatball guards were aiming baby peppermints at Paul and Principal PC, who were backed in the corner holding armfuls of weapons. Upon noticing the cup of noodles, the meatballs lowered their weapons and kneeled at his feet.

"Your Majesty," the lead meatball said, "what brings you here?"

"I heard the scream of my... ummm... companions," Supreme Lord Mac-N-Cheese said, unsure what to call the two desserts aiding him in his quest for redemption.

"You can't mean that sniveling pile of goo and the cookie?!" another meatball gasped.

"That 'sniveling pile of goo' happens to be a pudding. A pudding with feelings!" Paul whined from in the corner.

"Alright, that's it," the supreme lord demanded, "no more bickering! We are working together now, dinner foods and desserts. There are foods on another dimension called Planet Crumb fighting for their lives against monsters known as humans!"

Part 13: Supreme Lord Mac-N-Cheese

"Dinner foods and desserts... working together?" the lead meatball pondered, "does this mean we have to set the rest of the peppermints free?"

"Yes! My gourd! Let them free!" Supreme Lord Mac-N-Cheese practically shouted. The lead guard snapped his fingers at two other meatballs and they ran off into a hallway behind them.

"Any other foods on this cursed planet?" the supreme lord asked, then added, "No offense," in case the Spaghetti Monster was listening.

"None taken," the planet sighed.

"No my liege," the meatball said, "everyone else left when you did, you know after you got impaled in the face with a fork."

"Twas but a scratch," the bowl of pasta boasted. In reality, it had been a very painful experience in which he oozed cheese out of the three holes for days on end.

Soon, a parade of peppermints, adults and children, came prancing down the hallway. Supreme Lord Mac-N-Cheese checked his watch—fifty eight minutes. Time was slipping through his fingers faster than those two sticks of butter he tried to strangle that one time.

Ah, good times, he thought to himself, but then quickly countered it with: *No, not good times, that was wrong and evil.* Old habits die hard. Quickly, the entire population of Spaghetti Monster (planets not included) boarded Supreme Lord Mac-N-Cheese's large ship.

"Where are we going now?" Principal PC pondered as she browsed the list of weapons.

"The Dessert, Gingersnap Cliffs."

Part 13: Supreme Lord Mac-N-Cheese

The trip took twelve minutes. Too long. They wouldn't have enough time to make another stop after this, they had to make it worthwhile.

"Guys," Supreme Lord Mac-N-Cheese said when they landed, "we are going to need to split up. Principal Paul, PC, and all the peppermints, I need you guys to stay behind on this ship, when the meatballs and I get off. I've set the autopilot to the capital of The Dessert, just press this big green button and it will take you there. Once you get there however, you only have thirty or so minutes to get as many desserts to join our cause. The more the better.

This next part is very important. You must be back on the ship before your thirty minutes is up, because I have programmed it to leave automatically and return here so I can reboard the ship. We'll meet back here in exactly forty five minutes and thirty two seconds. Capeesh?"

All the foods nodded, though a few of the younger peppermints seemed confused. He didn't blame them, it was a lot of information at once. Then, without another word, he and the meatball guards left the ship.

The ground of the Gingersnap Cliffs was cold and desolate. The entire formation was covered in cracks.

Part 13: Supreme Lord Mac-N-Cheese

Black gaping slits peppered the ground, stretching as far as the eye could see. Like some giant spider had decided to run rampant on the cliffs and then was smashed by the fist of a giant. But they weren't here for the cliffs. No, they were here to go to the twizzler rope bridge that lay at the foot of the cliffs. After instructing the meatball guards to hold onto a part of his body, he teleported them all down to the base of the cliff. Supreme Lord Mac-N-Cheese looked up when they rematerialized, just in time to see his ship take off.

"Are you sure this is going to work?" a meatball guard asked.

"Are you questioning my plan?" Supreme Lord Mac-N-Cheese asked. "I am still your commander and ruler."

"N-n-no sir." the meatball stammered. With that, the group walked to the bridge in the distance, shrouded by a wall of fog.

"What weapon are we looking for exactly?" the lead meatball guard asked, "I don't see how anything of any power could be here! The place is falling apart!"

"Shush!" the supreme lord ordered. "I can feel its energy, we're getting close." It was true. There was a kind of electric humming in the air, unnoticeable by most foods, but detectable to those most skilled in Vishnu. He closed his eyes and kept walking, navigating purely by some fifth sense.

The ground changed under his feet and someone tried to warn him of something, but he cut them off with a wave of his hand. Bam! A warm tingly sensation spread all over his body. It seemed as if the radiation was now radiating from, below him! Supreme Lord Mac-N-Cheese opened his eyes. He was standing in the middle of the bridge while the bridge swung back and forth violently. Twizzlers crackled as the massive weight of the Kit-Kat planks shifted back and forth. He teleported back to where the guards were, their mouths agape in awe.

Supreme Lord Mac-N-Cheese didn't understand why, he hadn't done anything impressive yet. With a wave of his hand, the entire bridge collapsed and slid itself over to where he was standing.

Giving two of the meatballs each a strand of twizzler that once fastened the bridge to the ground, he told them, "My life is in your hands. When I tug on the rope three times, pull me up immediately. Not anytime before that, not anytime after that."

"Your royal highness, of course! But, might we know what's down there that's so important?" the meatball on the left asked.

"You'll have to wait till I come back up to find out."

"But what if you perish while down there!?"

"If I perish, it'll be all of your faults," the supreme lord pointed at each of the four meatballs, "because you guys will have dropped the ropes. If that happens and I die, I'll kill you all."

"But if you're dead—"

"SHUSH! I know, I'll find a way!" While they were talking, Supreme Lord Mac-N-Cheese had tied the two sections of rope together and the end of one rope around his waist. Normally he would just teleport down and back up, easy peasy. But because it was a black void, he didn't know how far down it was and he couldn't risk teleporting midway down and falling to his doom.

"Alright," he stepped to the edge of the void, talking mostly to himself, "here goes

nothing." He looked back one last time, all four meatballs had tied themselves to the rope so they were all tied together in a line and bracing themselves against a large chunk of gingersnap that had fallen from the cliffs above them.

Then, he jumped.

Supreme Lord Mac-N-Cheese had been falling for nearly ten minutes. This was no good. If he fell for much longer, there wouldn't be enough time to make it back to the top. So far, a twenty minute round trip, this only left him with ten minutes of total extra time, but only five more minutes of falling. Then, abruptly, a glint of something caught his eye in the distance. It had to be it. It must be it! What else would glint in a place with no light and supposedly no other objects! It was getting closer.

"Come on! C'mon C'MON!" he shouted, "Fall faster!" Then, the rope ran out. He stopped falling and several macaroon noodles fell out of the top of his head as the rope tightened around his stomach, creasing his cup in some places. But, it was just in reach.

Part 13: Supreme Lord Mac-N-Cheese

Laying on a gray peak, surrounded by the black void, lay Adrienne's scythe. He checked his watch, two extra minutes. This was going to be close.

Little to the supreme lord's knowledge, back at the opening of the void, a giant boulder was cracking. Despite the four meatballs' best efforts, the rope was getting heavier, and they were putting more strain on the rock they stood against. The rope was tugged once. A crack spread down the middle of the rock. The rope was tugged again. The rock completely split and was sent skittering over the edge of the opening, into the void. The four foods leaned backward, desperately trying to slow the pull of the rope as they were slowly dragged into the void. One of the meatballs fell, but managed to grab a hold of a crack in the ground. The last tug came, a forceful one. The other three meatballs were knocked off their feet and they rolled into the void, staying near the opening only by the rope which bound them to the meatball clawing the ground for another handhold.

The crack in which the last meatball gripped onto was widening, and so were the cracks around it. Soon the entire area was trembling and chunks of cliff were falling from above, dismantling the fragile structural integrity of the whole area. Dust began to cloud the air, the smell of ginger and sugar filling the meatballs' noses. Then, a rock came crashing down and landed just right, severing the twizzler rope. Three meatballs, several hundred feet of rope, and about a bajillion rocks all fell into the void.

Part 13: Supreme Lord Mac-N-Cheese

Five minutes passed and still he wasn't being reeled up. Supreme Lord Mac-N-Cheese began to worry that the meatballs had ditched him. That was until the rocks started crashing down. Something had gone awry at the surface. Unfortunately, he started having his own problems. The sounds of the crashing rocks had awoken something. Something that was down in the void with him. The supreme lord reached down and tried to lift the scythe, but it didn't budge.

Of course! The scythe was like a moody teenager with trust issues. It didn't bond itself to just anybody, it only allowed itself to be held by the foods it viewed as inherently good. Supreme Lord Mac-N-Cheese was not, apparently, inherently good. Big shocker.

That's when a loud voice sounded, echoing all around him. "Who... Wakes... Us... From... Our... Slumber..."

He recognized that voice. He had controlled them for a bit of time. Well, himself with the help of the ETM. Even then it had been extremely hard to control such a large entity. The Ayomide Nimat Amani Nour started to buzz all around him.

"It... Is... You...," the Ayomide Nimat Amani Nour started again, "Brainwasher... Killer... Evil... Tyrant..."

"Yes," Supreme Lord Mac-N-Cheese confided, "but I've changed now! I'm trying to help all foods now."

"LIAR!" the Ayomide Nimat Amani Nour shouted, their hissing voices coming closer to him. Supreme Lord Mac-N-Cheese could almost make out the blob of insects moving towards him.

Part 13: Supreme Lord Mac-N-Cheese

"No. I promise I'm not lying! I swear on my grandfather's grave (probably not a great thing to swear on) I'm trying to save food from mass extinction!" Supreme Lord Mac-N-Cheese racked his brain, how had they pacified the insects before!? They were already content when the ETM and Supreme Lord Mac-N-Cheese first interacted with them, but why? The ETM had stated something about Edward and Tiriaq feeding them. The insects were getting closer now, he could almost smell the scent of death on them. How come nothing ever came easy? He wondered for a split second. Then he thought, *Easy. Easy. Easy. What's that expression again? Easy as... Easy as... AHG! It's a dessert I know that. Easy as...*

"PIE!" Supreme Lord Mac-N-Cheese shouted at the top of his lungs. The angry whisperings of the Ayomide Nimat Amani Nour ceased and the hostile energy was replaced by a curious one.

"I give you..." Supreme Lord Mac-N-Cheese proclaimed as he reached one hand and wrapped it around the scythe, "PIE!" It was a total gamble. Sure he could summon things, but only one or two and at times, never the scale as he was trying to do right now. Luckily, the magic of the scythe had decided to aid him. Pies materialized and started falling from the sky. The Ayomide Nimat Amani Nour began jumping into the air catching the pies in midair and devouring them with a ferocity that matched a hangry Chipette on Thanksgiving.

Why he knew what Chipette was like when she was hangry, Supreme Lord Mac-N-Cheese had no clue.

384

Part 13: Supreme Lord Mac-N-Cheese

Within minutes, the Ayomide Nimat Amani Nour seemed to have calmed down.

"Now that I've helped feed your hunger," Supreme Lord Mac-N-Cheese said, "would you very handsome insects consider doing me a favor?" The bugs took a while to answer and the supreme lord was getting impatient. He glanced at his watch, too much time had passed and there was only less than seven minutes to get to the surface.

"...Handsome...?" the Ayomide Nimat Amani Nour seemed almost flattered by the compliment.

"Why yes! Of course, you guys are very handsome creatures! The fairest of them all, by far!"

"What... favor...?" Just at that moment, three meatballs, tied together, fell past the supreme lord and landed softly amongst the black insects.

A lone meatball sat in the middle of a fractured world, hands around his knees, shaking back and forth. Rocks still crashing around him, the cliffs above had already been practically reduced to rubble. Whispers filled the air, softly at first, then louder. Soon it was so unbearably loud that the meatball looked up and saw a giant mass flying out of the void with Supreme Lord Mac-N-Cheese standing at the top, a glowing silver scythe gliding on the black mass beside him. He hadn't resurfaced a second too soon because just at that moment, a giant spaceship blasted into the sky above them.

Part 13: Supreme Lord Mac-N-Cheese

"Grab onto me!" Supreme Lord Mac-N-Cheese shouted to the last meatball guard. He reached out his hand and the meatball ran and grabbed onto it. There was a loud pop, and the group teleported onto the ship. When they rematerialized, the supreme lord stood face to face with a crowd of disgruntled desserts.

"You tricked us!" Sarah Smoothie shouted from the crowd, pointing an accusing finger at the two principals and their peppermint pals. Loud protesting voices began to shout over one another and Supreme Lord Mac-N-Cheese pushed a button, sending the spaceship full throttle back to the Spaghetti Monster. Hopefully that would prevent the desserts from leaving the ship.

Loud whispering voices spoke behind him, "SHUT... UP... STUPID... DESSERTS..."

Supreme Lord Mac-N-Cheese turned around and realized with a shudder that he had accidentally teleported the entirety of the Ayomide Nimat Amani Nour with him. The shouts and jeering from the desserts ceased. Supreme Lord Mac-N-Cheese finally had a good look at who was present on the ship. It appeared that about half the population of Sugarcane had boarded the ship, though about a fourth of the desserts appeared to be affiliated with the SCL. Even Madam Madeleine, the Mayor of Sugarcane was present. He made eye contact with her and nodded appreciatively.

She rolled her eyes. "Umm, so, I am taking you all back to the Spaghetti Monster to help fight the battle against the humans," Supreme Lord Mac-N-Cheese explained, taking full advantage of the silence. "Who brought their blasters?" Still stunned, several cupcakes brought out the cupcake blasters and waved them in the air, the cookies pulled out their cookie blasters, donuts, donut blasters, etcetera.

"How do we know you're not going to enslave us!" a familiar voice shouted. Supreme Lord Mac-N-Cheese looked and saw the cinnamon bun that first heckled him on the Spaghetti Monster.

"What's your name?" He asked the dessert.

"Charlie."

"Well, Charlie. Believe me when I say, I am not behind the disappearances on The Dessert. On The Diner, we've had our fair share of disappearances and I used to think that the desserts were behind it all. But now, the Spaghetti Monster has informed me that the monsters from our fairy tales, humans, exist in real life and are currently eating humans outside of the foodiverse. As for proof you can trust me, I'm fairly sure that if I tried anything," the supreme lord glanced nervously at the black bugs behind him, "the Ayomide Nimat Amani Nour would kill me... or something like that."

"Yes... kill... evil..." the whispers filled the spaceship.

None other than Edward Chip's mother stepped out from the crowd. "How do we know you didn't brainwash that random black mass I've never even heard of before! You've already destroyed my house and almost kidnapped me with a tortilla. I haven't seen my children for days because of you, and oh yeah, MADE ME TAKE OUT A MORTGAGE ON ANOTHER HOUSE!" At this last statement, Mrs. Chip picked up the scythe, which had fallen on the ground after teleportation, and pointed it at the supreme lord's chest.

"The scythe finds you worthy," Supreme Lord Mac-N-Cheese noted, "Keep it. You'll need it."

Mrs. Chip looked at Supreme Lord Mac-N-Cheese skeptically and Mr. and Mrs. Madeira stepped forward and assured him that they would explain to the mother the role of magic in the foodiverse. From then on, the trip was smooth sailing, or flying.

"Well, we at the full patrol from the Popsicle Police support this Macaroni dude." the chief of the disbanded Popsicle Police proclaimed.

"This is why your patrol was dismantled!" The acting chief of the Pie Police sighed.

Tammy Tart jumped up and snapped a picture of the two police chiefs arguing saying,"This is so going on Instagrahamcracker later." The foods started to laugh and it seemed that the supreme lord had gained a small level of trust among the desserts, and just in time, too. He asked Paul and Principal PC to distribute the weapons from the Food Pyramid to the desserts who didn't have weapons. Supreme Lord Mac-N-Cheese tried to give the peppermints weapons, toothpicks at the least, but they insisted they enjoyed throwing their children at enemies much better as it was more accurate, dealt more damage, and most of all was more fun. It wasn't a second after all the foods had been armed that his ship landed once again on the moist, meaty ground of the Spaghetti Monster.

Part 13: Supreme Lord Mac-N-Cheese

Quickly, the entire contents of the spaceship piled out onto the fresh air, which smelled faintly like tomato sauce. They were met by the deviled and extraterrestrial eggs who had brought all the noodle, burrito and churro guards they could find, along with several of their friends; Captain Burrito, Pizza Pirate, Wheese Chiz (The Cheese Wizards twin brother), and something Supreme Lord Mac-N-Cheese never thought he would see again, his old mech. The giant robot had been fully repaired and fashioned with brand new tortilla chip cannons and a jetpack for flying. Eagerly he hopped in the cockpit and admired the buttons.

Then another spaceship landed, this one in the shape of a giant broccoli, the letters VAL painted on the side in fluorescent green paint. Supreme Lord Mac-N-Cheese's heart sank a bit, he was really hoping he wouldn't ever have to fight the The Vegetable Assassin League. Twenty or so roughed up broccoli stepped out along with a plethora of peas and baby corn, too many to count. The supreme lord geared himself up for battle and he heard the desserts behind them cock their various blasters but then heard one of the peas say,

"Yup, this is the address Edward said to go to on the phone!"

"You've got to stop giving our business cards out to random foods! We are not for hire," one of the broccoli grumbled.

"Hey!" a baby corn protested, "those are our friends! And you always say that friends—"

"—have each other's backs. I know," the broccoli said begrudgingly.

Supreme Lord Mac-N-Cheese signaled to the desserts to stand down as the vegetables approached them. "Going to Planet Crumb?" the supreme lord asked the head broccoli.

"Unfortunately, the little ones seem to have insisted on it."

"Glad you're here. We'll need all the help we can get to defeat the humans."

"Gah," the broccoli scoffed, "humans have never been an issue for THE VEGETABLES!" On the word "vegetables," all the broccoli cheered.

"That's just because you all taste bad!" Supreme Lord Mac-N-Cheese retorted.

"You made it," the Spaghetti Monster's voice emanated from below them, interrupting the conversation, "with two minutes to spare. We need to launch immediately Everyone ready?"

A couple broccoli glared at Supreme Lord Mac-N-Cheese one last time. The planet didn't wait for an answer. Spaghetti noodles shot out of the ground and wrapped them around all the foods and somehow every single insect of the Ayomide Nimat Amani Nour.

"Godspeed edibles," the Spaghetti Monster said, then he flung them all into the white void, out of the Free-Idge.

Part 13: Supreme Lord Mac-N-Cheese

The white void faded and Supreme Lord Mac-N-Cheese felt himself being thrown out. He landed, still inside the robot suit, on his feet thankfully, and blinked vigorously. Once the black spots had left his vision he was met with a very frightened Derek Donut.

"Well, don't look so surprised," Supreme Lord Mac-N-Cheese said at the shocked look on Derek's face.

Derek promptly ran out of the room screaming, "WE HAVE ANOTHER PROBLEM! HE'S HERE! HE'S HERE!"

"Wait, no!" Supreme Lord Mac-N-Cheese shouted, but it was too late. Quickly, he looked behind him, no one else had come through the portal yet. He guessed the weight of his robot suit had caused him to travel faster than everyone else. He noted the plastic bags on the ground, seemingly containing melted desserts, and hoped that Wheese Chiz would be able to mend them. He looked around, stepping over a hairy creature with four legs. It seemed to try to protest his existence with a soft, "Mew " but was too tired to care much after that. Then, quickly, he followed Derek outside.

When he emerged outside, he was baffled and frightened at what he saw. Two legged monsters with pale fleshy skin paraded around, attempting to destroy as many foods as possible. These must have been the humans. They looked even more gruesome in person than in the illustrations of fairy tales. And, despite their clumsy appearance, they were still murdering foods with an adept efficiency.

Part 13: Supreme Lord Mac-N-Cheese

There were hundreds of foods and spices, most of which Supreme Lord Mac-N-Cheese had never met before, but they were all armed with makeshift weapons and dressed in shoddy armor. Edward lay passed out on the ground (seriously how many times does this kid faint?) while Adrienne, Chipette and Tiriaq attempted to defend his body with colored javalines labeled "Crayola." Sugar Cookie was zipping around on a black disc that seemed to try and eat everything in its path. But even from where the supreme lord stood, he could see the "low battery" and "full bag please empty" warnings blinking on the screen. Swiss S. Cheese was back to back with several other slices of cheese and crackers that Supreme Lord Mac-N-Cheese had never seen before, throwing his cheese shaped ninja stars at human hands as they tried to pick him up. Cassie Cake was riding a different creature that she called Ronald. The two of them were jumping up to humans and biting slash hitting them in various places, mainly the groin, as it appeared to be the male human's weak spot.

Supreme Lord Mac-N-Cheese reminded himself to get off Cassie's bad side, as soon as possible. Then he noticed the Evil Taco Man, Evil Taquito Lady, and the Cheese Wizard all stacked on top of each other. They appeared to be using the Cheese Wizard to spray fake cheese into the human's eyes. That's when he realized something, The Cheese Wizard wasn't using Vishnu! In fact, none of the foods were using Vishnu! Panicked, he tried to teleport, a thing that wouldn't have taken any thought inside the Free-ldge now just didn't work. Then he spotted Derek, trying to get the food's attention but to no avail. No one was listening to him in all the chaos of battle. It was Chipette who noticed the supreme lord's presence first.

"MR. CHEESE!" she shouted at the top of her lungs when spotting him. Her voice was so loud and shrill that everyone froze and looked in her direction, then in the direction she was pointing. If one had walked into Picnic Palace at that moment, with no context, one might have thought they were playing the most intense game of Freeze Tag.

"That's, what, I've, been, trying, to, tell, you, all," Derek gasped, taking a deep breath in between each word.

"Get out of here!" Adrienne demanded.

"Yeah," Edward rose from the ground, not fully awake yet, "get out of here you... you... you evil, evil food."

"You guys don't understand," Supreme Lord Mac-N-Cheese stated for what felt like the hundredth time today, "I'm trying to help you."

"Well," Cassie said, "*EXCUSE* me if I don't trust the food who has repeatedly tried to kill me and my friends, sent minions to kill me and my friends and is sitting in a fully loaded robot weapon, capable of killing me and my friends in a second." The whispers of the Ayomide Nimat Amani Nour rose behind the supreme lord. The rest of the food must be emerging out of the portal now.

Part 13: Supreme Lord Mac-N-Cheese

"WE ARE SO, LIKE, SCREWED NOW!!" Sugar Cookie screamed, as she snapped a photo of the events on her phone. Derek ran off screaming.

"OH! And *now* you have an army of evil insects backing you!" Cassie said, her voice dripping with sarcasm. At seeing the Ayomide Nimat Amani Nour, a human screamed out,

"Cockroaches! EWWWWWWWWWW!"

"Fine, you know what! I'm here to help! Believe me or don't, I don't care," at this, the supreme lord raised his robotic arms in frustration and accidentally shot a human in the face with a tortilla chip.

Just then, everyone that had been on the Spaghetti Monster had emerged from Free-Idge, Pizza Pirate, eggs, meatballs, his loyal guards, the peppermints, and all the residents of The Dessert.

The human screamed in pain and yelled, "Get them!"

Tiriaq shouted, "We-inforcements! YAY!"

The battle resumed, and this time the foods had a tactical edge. Supreme Lord Mac-N-Cheese exchanged a look with several of the peppermints. The Peppermint parents picked up their children, who were baring their sharp teeth, and nodded back. Then, in a swarm of flying peppermint children, the reinforcements charged into battle.

The first human that ran at him met the business end of a nacho cheese cannon. Behind him, the Ayomide Nimat Amani Nour merged together to create a tidal wave of bugs that chased the humans out of Picnic Palace.

Part 13: Supreme Lord Mac-N-Cheese

Supreme Lord Mac-N-Cheese jumped to where Edward was battling a human and yelled, "Catch!" as he threw down the cookie blaster.

Edward looked up and his eyes widened, "MY BABY! YOU'RE ALIVE!" he squealed and he caught the weapon. He shot out a golden net which entrapped the human he was fighting as well as several others behind him.

The Vegetable Assassin League had gone into formation and were attacking the humans as a group. The broccoli had stacked on top of each other to form a giant vegetable titan while the peas and corn formed a circle around the giant to trip any oncoming humans. Even Mr. and Mrs. Madeira, despite their age, were fighting using karate. They must have seen a strange look on the supreme lord's face because they quickly explained that they had taken karate lessons after being attacked at MilkShakeMart. The Cheese Wizard and Wheese Chiz had met in the middle of the battlefield and were bickering as they dodged the attacks of human appendages.

"Get out of my space! You're in my personal bubble!" Wheeze Chiz whined.

"No! You're in *my* personal bubble!"

"*STOOOP IT!*" The Cheese Wizard smacked the other can of Cheese Wiz and ended the argument. Mrs. Chip ran through the crowd, shoving the humans that got in her way with Adrienne's scythe.

"Edward! How are you!?" she asked while throwing the weapon at a human's nose.

Part 13: Supreme Lord Mac-N-Cheese

"*Mom!* I'm trying to fight off the humans and you're *embarrassing me!*" Edward said as the scythe boomeranged back into Mrs. Chip's hand.

"FINE! I'll just talk to your sisters!" the mom said, marching away while knocking several humans over from a force of Vishnu that emanated from her scythe, but was powered by her anger. Supreme Lord Mac-N-Cheese realized that Vishnu must be working again and he tried to teleport once again. He rematerialized outside of the robot right next to Tiriaq and Chipette, who were manning the homemade cannon with Adrienne.

"VISHNU TO WORKING!" he shouted to Adrienne while giving Chipette and Tiriaq each one of the blue glowing knives.

"Weapons! Cool!" the two children said in unison, and the knives turned into freeze ray guns. Supreme Lord Mac-N-Cheese instructed them to follow Derek (who was nearby) back into The Crumb and reform Ginny and Prince Ice of Cream with the freeze ray guns.

The three of them quickly marched away, Derek knocked any human that approached him back with fireballs to create a safe path. Adrienne yelled a levitation spell and the homemade cannon flew from the ground into a human's face. Supreme Lord Mac-N-Cheese teleported back into his robot and kicked off the humans who were trying to pry open the cockpit. The house in which the Free-Idge lay began to shake violently and the entire front side slid off. The Saibou and a robot named MilkDubBot stood in the rubble, wearing the infamous Plastic Cherry on his head.

"WITH THE POWER OF THE PLASTIC CHERRY AND THE OPENING OF THE Free-ldge . . . VISHU FLOWS OVER THIS REALM!" The Saibou proclaimed.

"And I used my new ability of superstrength to break down the walls! Consider me 100% charged and upgraded!" MilkDudBot exclaimed.

All the foods gasped and cheered while the humans had reactions that varied from, "THEY HAVE A FREAKING DRAGON!" to, "Vishnu? What's that!?"

The ETM laughed evilly and said, "Human amigos, you are the ones that are so screwed now."

"Calm down, honey!" The ETL said, hitting him on the arm.

"Don't tell me to calm down! They are trying to kill us!"

"Fair point." The couple began to teleport from human to human, causing havoc by summoning the ETM's trademarked explosive tacos and hot sauce.

The Cheese Wizard ran over to his beloved contraption/robot/pal and screamed, "MY BABY! YOU'RE ALIVE!"

"Hey! I just said that!" Edward shouted from afar, still firing his cookie blaster at oncoming humans with one hand and shooting fireballs out from his other hand. MilkDudBot seemed to dislike the Cheese Wizard's advances and ran into the heart of the battle, tossing humans out of his way as he ran away crying,

"You can't just abandon me and then expect me to welcome you back into my life with open arms!"

Part 13: Supreme Lord Mac-N-Cheese

"WHAT!" The cheese wizard protested, trying to hug the robot, "I thought we patched everything up between us when we saved Ginny!"

"Well, my newest update allows me to hold grudges! And I do that a lot now, I decided. Say hi to MilkDudBot1.3!" With that, he shoved the Cheese Wizard off of him.

"You made the noob sad!" Chipette hollered at the wizard, "how dare you!"

Supreme Lord Mac-N-Cheese shoved a human over as the battle resumed, again. The Saibou had taken flight and was now knocking the humans over with its large tail. Captain Burrito had put himself in charge of a firing squad composed completely of peppermints, their children's wicked sharp teeth gleaming under the sunlight.

"READY! AIM! FIRE!" he shouted, and swished his cape. The parents simultaneously threw their children at various humans. The peppermint children screamed in delight as they flew through the air.

Other humans, non-hostiles, began to show up at the border of Picnic Palace. They pulled up in large vehicles labeled "City of Littleton Police Department" and "9News" as well as "South Metro Fire Department".

"Yes, Carl Azuz, here we are outside 6979 S Picnic Street where it appears *another* historical event is taking place at the infamous Picnic Palace Park. And this time it's not a radioactive spill that causes rabid mutations in bunny rabbits. That power plant was demolished a *long* time ago. Right now, it appears as if foods have grown sentient and are now fighting back...”

Supreme Lord Mac-N-Cheese was distracted from what the newscaster was saying by he Popsicle Police, who had marched up to the Human Policemen and barked,"YOU'RE UNDER ARREST!”

To which the human policemen responded, “ARE YOU KIDDING ME! *YOU* ARE UNDER ARREST!”

“NO! YOU ARE THE ONES UNDER ARREST!”

“HOW WILL YOUR TINY LITTLE FOOD HANDCUFFS EVEN FIT ON ME!” The human protested.

“BOTH OF YOU ARE UNDER ARREST! FOR DISTURBING THE PEACE!” The Pie Police shouted into a megaphone as they marched up to the scuffle.

The three police departments bickered like this as the supreme lord bounded away, saving several citizens of The Dessert from being crushed by a Human's foot. Suddenly a blue van pulled up, and two humans got out, confused and angry looks on their faces.

“Excuse me!” One of the new arrival humans freaked out and gasped very loudly, “What is happening outside my house!”

“Forking Scary and Jar Jar Binks are back!” the ETM screamed, much to everyone else's confusion. A smaller human scrambled out of the car and took in the scene, breathing heavily.

“Hey Adrienne!” Edward shouted, “remember when you asked when making banana splits from thin air would be helpful? Well, the time is now.” With that, Edward conjured a banana split with a flick of his hand. Adirene understood what she needed to do and thrust her hands at it, palms out. The delectable dessert took off into the sky and smacked the human named Jar Jar Binks in the face, rendering him unconscious.

The human named Forking Scary watched her husband fall to the ground with a look of exasperation on her face. She then wiped the banana split that had splattered on her from her face and shouted to the younger human, "Look at what you have done to your father!!! Isabella Maeve Shuppert, get back in the car, young lady! You are so grounded!"

Instead the young human climbed on top of the car and tried to speak to the crowd. However, her voice couldn't pierce the brick wall that was the commotion of battle. Supreme Lord Mac-N-Cheese jumped out of his robot and snatched the megaphone from the pie police and threw it at the smaller human. The smaller human snatched it from the air and cleared her throat.

Part 14: The Child

   I stood there, megaphone in hand, the scene that lay before me baffled me to my very core. Police men, firefighters, newscasters and paramedics had all gathered at Picnic Palace Park by my house. Several other people I recognized as frequent park visitors were beat up and laying on the ground dazed. Others seemed to be attacking pieces of food. The groups of foods that I had saved from my parents seemed to be in the center of it all.

   My injured leg ruse had been for nothing. My parents had taken me to the hospital and the doctor there, of course, told me there was nothing wrong with my leg. My mom proceeded to ground me indefinitely using plenty of 'young lady's along with my full name. I didn't mind though, as long as it was for a cause I cared about.

   "ATTENTION ALL GROWN-UPS." I shrieked. None of them took me seriously amidst all the fighting. It took bludgeoning a police officer with the heel of my left shoe and throwing my right shoe into the battlefield to get their attention.

   "WHAT ARE YOU ALL DOING?! YOU ARE ALL LIVING BEINGS AND YOU'RE KILLING EACH OTHER?"

   "Nonsense, darling," my father scoffed, rising back up from the ground, banana split bits decorating his hair. "These belong in the pantry, not outside stabbing us with cutlery. Of course they aren't alive."

Part 14: The Child

"How would you feel if you discovered that you lived in a world full of giant creatures who ate you on a daily basis? Huh? How would you feel? How would you feel if you stepped outside for the first time and got shoved into a beast's mouth and crushed up? They have barely begun their lives and you're ending them already? Don't you feel bad?"

"No, why would we? They're snacks! Very delicious ones for that matter."

"They're more than that. See this child?" I picked up a brownie who was in tears on the ground. "You killed his parents!"

"I'll eat him too!" My father yelled joyously. He plucked the child out of my hand and bit him in half.

I screamed."Don't you feel awful? These are living beings! They have feelings!"

"Wanna split it with me? Here's the other half." I was disgusted. As I broke down into tears, I heard trumpets. Was I dead? Was I entering heaven? No, but an ice cream cone wearing the shiniest maraschino cherry marched into the battlefield. I swear I heard a donut in the middle of the battlefield swoon. A mac in cheese cup piloting a robot behind the donut smacked the dessert on the head, telling him to shush.

"Edward, I'm going to need you to do that banana split trick again, but on a much larger scale," the ice cream cone said with a smile.

A rather small, perfectly golden chocolate chip cookie stepped forward and motioned others to join hands with him. Soon there was a circle of foods that had joined hands, a fortune cookie, a taco with a mean mustache, a donut, a cake, and a bowl of instant mac. The ice cream placed the red cherry he wore onto the ground in the middle of the circle. Together they shouted a single word, and a blinding white glow emanated from the cherry.

Suddenly, thunder crackled and whipped cream and chocolate syrup rained from the sky. Pretty soon, the largest banana I had ever seen materialized in mid air along with two scoops of strawberry ice cream. The maraschino cherry sitting regally on top. Then, at first shakily, the cherry rose from the top of the banana split and spun in mid air. All the humans in the park stopped mauling the foods to gawk at the floating projectile. In a blink of an eye, the cherry flew around the park like a boomerang. It landed on the top of each adult's head, but for only a second, before it quickly moved on to its next victim. The adult's eyes began to spin, then rolled up into their heads and they collapsed on the ground.

I completely freaked out and dove for cover inside our minivan, the cherry hitting both of my parents on their heads beside me. I slammed the door closed just in time. Then, the cherry on top of all this (pardon my pun) was that the banana split in the middle of the park completely burst open and showered everyone in sticky melted ice cream as bits of whipped cream floated calmly down from the sky.

The humans were starting to stir again now, and several of the foods looked at each other with uncertainty. The adults groaned, waking from their catatonic state simultaneously and started looking around at each other, confused. They glanced at each other, and then at the foods who were blinking at them. This was followed by confused shrieking and then running. That was the fastest I'd seen my dad move in my whole life.

His beer belly jiggled up and down as he trotted away screaming,"It's not real! It's not real!" Then all was silent, I stepped out of the van and regarded the foods and the foods regarded me.

"VICTORY!!" shrieked a smaller chocolate chip cookie with a bow on its head.

"I can't believe we, like, won!" a sugar cookie squealed, hugging the two chocolate chips cookies present. All the food cheered, waving their toothpicks in the air in celebration. They chased after the police officers as they leapt into their cars and drove away as fast as possible. The younger foods danced around my feet, cheering. Behind the celebrating foods, a grim scene was unfolding.

Crackers lay on the battlefield split clean in half, their crumbs falling off of their bodies. Slices of cheese lay supine across the yard with holes that went clear through their bodies, and these holes weren't the kind that swiss cheese slices had. They howled in agony, spending their last breaths calling out for help. A large carton bled orange juice onto the grass, staining it an ugly dark yellow. Several motionless marshmallows lay impaled together by a large skewer. Lifeless bodies of apples and oranges were scattered across the patio, their juice oozing out of them producing a sweet smell.

Part 14: The Child

Insects swarmed the body of a slain ribeye steak, eating his body away. A potato had been turned to mush due to a stomp from a human, and several cookies were strewn about with bites taken out of their sides.

The scene that lay before me was awful.

Some of the foods rushed to help some of their fatally wounded comrades, while others comforted them as they inevitably died. I did everything I could to help. I tried to perform CPR on a dying egg, but accidentally cracked his shell and killed him instantly. I wrapped dying foods in handkerchiefs to warm them up, but it was no use. The remaining foods covered their dead with napkins and tissues.

After the battle was over, every food rushed inside our house as soon as possible. I helped escort the more damaged foods in addition to taking inventory to make sure everyone was accounted for. A funeral procession was held soon afterwards for the fallen edibles. A rat pulled the dead in a shoebox. The survivors lined up in the kitchen on either side of the makeshift hearse and saluted. Desserts and foods alike were lined up, weeping at the sight of their loved ones being pulled away to the afterlife. The peppermints walked in front of the carriage, spreading petals across the hardwood floor as a sign of respect. The foods wrapped themselves in black napkins to mourn the losses. The procession went out the back door and into the backyard. The foods followed.

The box was gently laid on its side and the foods were lifted out–each placed into a small hole in the ground. I placed a scoop full of soil on each, and the cat rolled rocks over on top of their graves. The foods gathered around the graves of their loved ones and said goodbye to them for one last time. The air was filled with sorrowful weeping and sad final conversations.

As for the injured, I had a plan for them, too. I would single handedly mend each one of them, and simultaneously learn their names. I collected cookies with broken pieces, melted ice cream scoops, and cracked chocolate bars. I used a lighter to melt the chocolate bars back together. I put Prince Ice of Cream in a bin full of ice and cold water to freeze again. He splashed around as his wounds healed. I arranged Edward, Chipette, and Sugar Cookie on a cookie sheet with their broken limbs (Sugar Cookie's hand still gripping onto her phone) next to the rest of their bodies. They came out nice and whole again after lounging about in the 350 degree oven. Immediately after their repairs, the cookie cops labeled "SCL" were already tweeting their whistles at other foods committing even the most minor offenses.

Pretty soon, the police made of popsicles and pie joined in on the fun and arrested two desserts known as Principal Pudding and Principal PC.

"You can't stop our love!" The pudding yelled as it shook free from a popsicle's grasp. His peanut butter cookie girlfriend followed suit and that pair made a dash across my kitchen floor. They spotted the still cracked open fridge and jumped back in where they disappeared in a flash. That was another thing; I'VE HAD A MAGIC FRIDGE THIS WHOLE TIME!?

The pie police started assaulting their popsicle counterparts screaming,"That's it! You guys have let the last prisoner go free! You are hereby disbanded AGAIN. FOR REAL THIS TIME!" The pie police snatched away the popsicle police's badges. The popsicles proceeded to run away crying out fruity flavored teardrops. I was going to have to mop that up later.

I made a new taco shell for a heavily mustached food known as ETM, as his other one had cracked. I tightened the wrapping on some of the burrito guards whose tortillas had been loosened in the heat of the battle. I gently poured piles of ground ginger, cinnamon, nutmeg, allspice and pumpkin spice back into their corresponding shakers while they sang a joyful victory song in perfect harmony. It sounded very rehearsed and they seemed to be some girl band. When the performance was done, I noticed the nutmeg container was almost empty and topped off the container.

"Thank you so much, kind human! I am indebted to you," the nutmeg squealed. The other four spices regarded their friend in shock.

"Your speech is normal again!" the ginger spice said as they embraced the nutmeg. Then she turned to me, "Thank you so much. Might we know your name?"

"Isabella," I laughed, "it was my pleasure!"

Part 14: The Child

I never knew fixing foods was so much work but it was rewarding as well. I had to completely reassemble a banana split who was mortally wounded in the battle. I placed scoop after scoop of ice cream back in the glass dish it started in. Then the banana. The original one was completely smashed by a human's boot, so I had to find a new one at the grocery store. I delicately placed it on top of the ice cream, and then the whipped cream and cherry. The cherry was the only intact part of its original body. It made me happy as it hopped away, gleefully squealing in its new body. I spent the rest of the day mending the wounds of the foods. Some of the sandwiches watched me and started to heal other foods, too. That was the day that some of the sandwiches decidedly became the doctors of the foodiverse. I had no problem with it; it was less work for me.

Just as I was tending to the final brownie in the line for medical help, a group of cookies dressed in vests labeled "SCL" ran up to me. They were carrying a large book above their heads, and a container of cookie dough.

"LOOK! LOOK!" One yelled. "WE CAN MAKE MORE COOKIES!"

I read the cover:

DELICIOUS RECIPES THAT JUMP OFF
THE PLATE
(AND INTO YOUR MOUTH)

They had bookmarked several pages, the first one was titled:

Granny's Chocolate Chip Cookies.

Preheat the oven to 350 degrees. Check. It was a short recipe. It probably assumed you already made dough, which we did. Thanks for nothing, granny. I arranged the dough into circles on the cookie sheet. Blob, after blob, after blob. Eventually I had created an array of little cookie dough lumps. I stuck them in the oven and shut it tight. After 25 minutes of them baking, I took the sheet out. To my surprise, there were small cookie babies crawling around on the wax paper. They wailed and cried. The elder cookies ran and picked them off of the sheet. They rocked them back and forth in their paper napkin swaddles. Foods teamed up to assemble cribs made out of toothpicks for the babies to rest in. They quickly became the center of attention of the foodiverse. I was often sent to the grocery store to buy raw ingredients to make more foods. Soon, all the desserts and entrees were producing more foods. The house quickly grew into a prosperous civilization.

Schools were opened in various cabinets. Foods grow very quickly, apparently. The first batch of babies were already in their teenage years within a week. They were taught the history of the foodiverse from a totally not anti-adult human standpoint. If a food got injured, there were now food-owned hospitals and clinics which had opened up in the living room and the guest bathrooms. They were mostly run by sandwiches, as they had picked up skills in the medical field quickly during the aftermath of the battle. My younger brother, Benji, walked into the wreckage of the house, his mouth agape, when pulled up in an Uber coming from summer camp. Soon he was caught up on the situation and helped the foods open their own businesses.

The vast majority of the foods had decided to return to their respective planets inside the fridge, where most of them lived. Although some chose to live in the cupboard and pantry and help run the city they had created inside our house. One time I opened up the fridge to see what it looked like inside. From what I could tell, it was still a normal fridge, but there was a layer of fog that shrouded the back wall. I reached my hand in, expecting to feel the wall but instead the fridge deepened. I heard the sounds of screaming coming from inside, but I couldn't see where it was coming from. I quickly pulled my hand out and the screaming ceased.

The cinnamon spice had a tearful goodbye with her sisters as she prepared to enter the fridge.

"Do you have to go?" the ginger spice asked.

"This is what I want. I'll be safe; I promise."

"Just wait one more day," the ginger spice bargained. The cinnamon spice agreed and returned to her home underneath the cabinet. The foodiverse was prospering under my and my brother's supervision. We planned to run monthly drills in a scenario where an adult might enter the house with the intent of eating the food. As for me and my brother, we vowed never to eat sentient foods again.

We went completely vegan and ran on salads made of leaves and plants we grew in our backyard. The foods were under our complete protection. It was peaceful.

Everything was going swimmingly until one day there was a knock on the door. Activity across my entire house froze and the eyes of my many foods, now under me and my brother's protection, looked at us expectantly. I walked slowly to the door. Who could this be? I had already made a post on my parents FaceBook account that they had decided to unexpectedly move to Cabo. All their friends should have known not to bother their old house. The person on the other side of the door knocked again. I opened the door a crack...

...and breathed a sigh of relief.

It was only our mailman.

"Your mailbox looks like several burritos knocked it over," he explained, laughing, "what happened there?"

I chuckled uneasily, making a metal note to clean up the front yard. "Foodfight gone wrong."

"Oh! Haha," the mailman pulled out several letters, "give these to your mom and dad for me eh?"

Part 14: The Child

"Will do, sir. Have a nice day!" The mailman walked back through the wreckage of Picnic Palace whistling the tune to The Imperial March. I slammed the door shut and looked at the letters in my hand. They were all covered in red ink that depicted the words "Final Notice" and "Past Due."

"What's that?" Benji asked me, gesturing to the letters in my hand.

"I'm... not sure," I said, "but I do know one thing. These letters mean that other humans know we exist."

"Oh no," Benji gasped, his sweet 10 year old eyes begging me to fix this, "what will happen when more humans come?"

"Don't worry," a voice said behind us, "we've got this." I looked back, and there, on the kitchen counter, stood Edward Chip holding a cookie blaster, an army of battle ready foods behind him.

Acknowledgements

Recipes require lots of ingredients, like, a LOT. All those ingredients come together to make a nice final product for people to enjoy. Sometimes the product is food, other times it's something else like art. Or, art made of food or even a story about a walking, talking cookie who fights a war against the people that inhabit a house. Nonetheless, we couldn't have done it without lots of people who we owe thanks to and boy are there a lot of people to thank. Below are the people who made this possible and helped us to make it happen:

First off, thank you to our families for supporting us through the writing and judging us as little as possible for writing a really long story about a talking cookie. The whole idea of it is so very weird and we understand that at times it might have been very concerning to hear about. Thank you for being there for us the whole way and being understanding. This story has been super important to us. Having families that accept their children for writing stories about living foods is great. Thank you for not writing us off as social rejects. I don't think you did, at least. Not the point.

To all the family and friends that helped edit this story, Junhee Graf, Junah Graf and Erin Traister. What to say? We've known you guys for a long time and appreciate your support bunches. You guys are so fun to be around and having people close to us adding to the story and contributing new ideas was great, especially the one about Simone Sponge Cake and the character of Prince Ice of Cream. Thank you for all of your help as well as your friendship. Thank you especially, Junah. It should've been "ground", not "gro'und". You were right. Also, special shoutout to Erin for helping with the *"About the Author"* photos.

Thank you to Mrs. Russell for helping us edit the story and finalizing some of the details. You and your knowledge of the English language and literary skills have been *enormously* helpful. Thank you for taking our old, fifth grade level writing into something more pleasant to read. We got lots of headaches reading the first few chapters and now we are cured, so thank you for being *biscotti* and pushing through.

To our wonderful editor, Tyler Hauth, your edits and suggestions helped to improve the story beyond our wildest dreams. Thank you for being so prompt and helpful at all times. I genuinely loved reading through your comments and seeing what you thought of the book. You were the third person to read the book all the way through and it means a lot to me that the feedback you had was so positive. I am really glad that we were able to work together on this project and I hope to work with you in the future!

Thank you to Robby Schiebel for creating the cover and designing the inside cover graphics. Your willingness to help on such a short notice really helped us make this dream a reality. Especially since *one of the authors* (hint hint Kaiden) couldn't decide what he wanted and kept asking you to change the cover. Over and over and over and over again. We appreciate your patience with us throughout all this. Even when we've had the most *taco* of days, you've been there to help smile and joke through it.

Nolan Braband, your love of cookies was truly one like no other. In fact, we aren't even sure how to bring up our elementary school friendship without bringing it up. It was really devastating when you had to switch schools after third grade but we are glad to have this as a final product and a reminder of the friendship we once shared. Anyways, from your love of cookies, Edward Chip was born.

Mrs. Ellis, thanks so much for getting us in touch with a place to print the very first edition of this fine masterpiece. Ok, fine, masterpiece might be a strong word. How about a really really really good book? Anyways, it was the final step in making this novel a physical book instead of a google document sitting in the bottom of our google drives. Also, please say hi to Indy for Kaiden. He misses her dearly.

And especially, thank you to Ms. Barrett for helping us get started all the way back in 2016. We appreciate your support and encouraging our creativity. I never thought that our narrative assignment would come this far or that we would continue it past the assignment's due date, but here we are! Thank you so much for assigning us that story in 5th grade. We would not be the critically acclaimed authors we are (unofficially, but just you wait!) without your help in removing over used boring words such as "walked" and replacing them with better words like "sauntered" (see beginning of part 1). You are the reason we have such a strong writing foundation.

Ab🍪ut the Auth🍪rs:

Kaiden Traister, an immigrant from the south, came to Colorado after being a world-renowned cowboy and ranch hand in the fabled Texasland. He was really only ever loved by the one super clingy cow that followed him around, he lived out a miserable existence in Colorado as the senator from the North Pole in the United States government. He worked alongside the elves and Santa Claus himself doing Santa's taxes (yes, presents are tax deductible) until he died at the age of 24 by stapling his finger and bleeding to death as a result. He has no living family, as they all died of disappointment.

In actuality, Kaiden Traister was born and grew up in Colorado. He is part Chinese and exactly 1/128th Mongolian according to his grandfather. He is an outgoing student who participates in several activities, such as search and rescue and yearbook at his high school. He is a great brother to two sisters. He enjoys drawing, painting, playing piano, learning mandarin and all things writing related. He loves his family and close friends dearly. He is an amazing writer with an everlasting supply of creativity and new ideas.

 **Quinn Ellis** was born and raised in Colorado, where he spent the majority of his life on the farm. Everyday he would wake up and feed the chickens who would otherwise find him in his bed and peck at his feet. He was eventually chased out of his home by the chickens unionizing and burning the bed he slept in. He lost his favorite toe to a chicken named Bertha. Loved only by his pet cat, Indy, and his best friend, a soggy piece of toast, he would walk to school uphill both ways 366 days a year. He attended no colleges and died of toilet seat poisoning at the ripe age of 23 while trying to defecate. His hobbies included, trying to get a life and failing numerous times.

In seriousness, Quinn Ellis was raised in Colorado, where he currently attends high school. Being super smart, he participates in TSA in high school but is forever reminded of that one time he wore a beanie to school for half a month and was deemed "emo". He enjoys all things gaming related and spending time with the people close to him. He is a great older brother to his sister (and his dog Ginny) and an even better friend. He has been writing since the fifth grade and is fueled by his outstanding imagination.

Where did these words come from?

Questions?
Comments?
Concerns?
Got a really funny joke?

* still watching "Stranger Cakes" *

Instagram: edwardchipofficial
Email: edwardchipofficial@gmail.com

You should chweck it w-OUT!